CM0092320S

Beyond The
Purple Hills

Beyond The Purple Hills

Heather Graves

PIATKUS

First published in Great Britain in 1996 by
Judy Piatkus (Publishers) Ltd of
5 Windmill Street, London W1

**The moral right of the author
has been asserted**

*A catalogue record for this book is available
from the British Library*

ISBN 0–7499–0333–3

Set in 11/12 pt Times by
Datix International Limited, Bungay, Suffolk
Printed and bound in Great Britain by
Biddles Ltd, Guildford & King's Lynn

For Chris and Nat, for Dot
and for the ladies of Brixham Writers.
My love and thanks to you all.

Prologue

Elizabeth dismounted and looked down to see what was happening in the creek. There were her two boys, one tall and fair as the other was small and dark, wrestling with each other, waist-deep in the water. Entertained by the spectacle, a dozen or so Aboriginal men and women stood watching and cheering them on, shadow-boxing as they encouraged the boys to fight.

'Pax, Hamie. Time to give up. Stop now before you get hurt.' Callum stood away from his younger brother, raising his hands shoulder-high in a plea for peace. He was trying to smile and be reasonable but Elizabeth knew he would be furious with Hamish for showing him up in front of the natives, local Aborigines who had come to do the Mac-Gregors the favour of washing their sheep. Still only twelve years old, Callum liked to maintain his dignity. The sheep, forced into the pens arranged to channel them into the water, were milling around, anxious to avoid a dunking if they could. Bleating their complaints, they were falling over each other and getting stuck in the clay on the bank of the creek. Both the MacGregor boys were soaked to the skin and covered in mud but still Hamish refused to give up.

'I'll show you, Callum MacGregor!' his voice fluted high and ready to break with emotion. 'I can wash sheep just as well as you – I can so!'

'Mother left me in charge here, Hamie, and I'm telling you – no. You almost drowned that ewe and held up the line for ten minutes while I had to swim for it and rescue her.'

'It's not my fault. She kicked me and I had to let her go.'

1

'I know, Hamie.' Callum took a deep breath, doing his best to hold his temper and let his brother down lightly. 'And this time there's no harm done. But you're not strong enough to hold a full-grown ewe – not yet. Maybe next year when you're a bit older. When you're eight.'

'I don't want to wait until I'm eight and all grown up. I want to do it now.'

'Go on home, Hamie. You're wasting everyone's time.' Callum looked up, relieved to see his mother standing on the bank of the creek. 'You tell him, Mother. He won't listen to me.'

'No! No! No!' Hamish cried, splashing water about in his temper. Abdicating responsibility, Callum shrugged and turned his back until Hamish launched himself at him again. Five years the elder and a good deal stronger, Callum held the smaller boy at arm's length while he called out to his mother, asking for support.

'Please, Mother, will you get him out of here? Tell him to stop bothering us and get on home.'

'Come along, Hamie.' Elizabeth spoke kindly, sympathising with the little boy's disappointment. She lifted her skirts and picked her way to the water's edge, holding out her hand, ready to haul him out of the water. 'Shall we go home now and let Callum get on with his work?'

'No!'

'D'you know, Mrs Hallam was baking when I left home and I saw her taking an upside down apple cake out of the oven. If we go quickly, you can be first to taste it.'

'No. I don't care about Mrs Hallam or her mouldy old cake.'

'Now, Hamie, that's quite enough! Come out of the water at once and lets go home.'

'No-oo!' the boy howled, shaking himself like a dog, mud and water flying in all directions. 'It's always the same. Callum can do as he wants and I can't. Why are you always on his side?'

'I'm not on anyone's side. This may be a game for you but for Callum it's hard work. He is the eldest and has to shoulder a lot of responsibility now that your . . .' and she hesitated, furious with the tears that suddenly pricked at the back of her eyes. Even now, after twelve months and more, she found it hard to speak of her husband's death. 'Now that your father can't be here with us any more.'

'And that's *his* fault as well!' Hamish jerked his head at his brother, unwilling to be pacified. 'My daddy would still be alive and with us today if it wasn't for Callum.'

'Now stop that, Hamish! Stop it at once. I won't have you saying such a thing.' The familiar lump of pain was lodged in Elizabeth's throat, making her speak more sharply to the boy than she had intended. 'Wash that mud from your clothes and get out of the water at once. We're going home.'

Insensitive to his mother's distress, Hamish gave in with bad grace. Stubborn and single-minded as only a small boy can be, he made his last bid to stay.

'Can I sit on the bank and watch them, then? I won't move a muscle. I promise I'll be as good as gold.'

'No!' Elizabeth said through gritted teeth.

'It's not fair.' The boy's face crumpled into sullen lines. Scuffling water in front of him, he waded from the creek and allowed his mother to hoist him into her saddle. From the safety of this position, he glared at Callum who was already regrouping the natives, preparing to wash the sheep. 'Just you wait, Callum MacGregor! I'll get even one day. One day when I'm old and grown up like you. I'll take away the person you love most in the world – you see if I don't.'

'Hamish!' Elizabeth stared at him, shocked to see such a look of venom on a childish face. 'You musn't say that, not even in fun. You know you don't mean it.'

'But I do mean it, Mother.' He looked down at her from the saddle, his eyes hard and blue – giving her a glimpse of the ruthless, handsome man he would grow up to be. 'I mean every word of it.'

Chapter One

The storm was over; gone as quickly as it had arisen. Maggi could hear the crew laughing and making jokes again, mocking each other's fear as the winds died down and they unfurled the sails to allow the *Sally Lee* to steady herself and resume her regular forward motion through the waves. A modern three-masted clipper, she was designed to carry passengers from England to the Australian gold fields in record time. But fast as she might be, she was hampered on this journey by severe overcrowding, particularly in steerage. Storms were always worse for the passengers, confined to their quarters and trapped between decks, as water seeped through the hatches and they could only imagine what must be happening above. The winds had been deafening, screaming like the furies as they tore at ropes and sails, while the sea kept pounding the decks and making the ship shudder as she struggled to the top of one mountainous wave only to corkscrew down into the trough of another.

Now it was over, those who prided themselves on being 'good sailors' set about making a late lunch, poking fun at the ones whose faces were still green. But now the hatches had been reopened to let in some light and fresh air, most people were eager to get out; to settle their upset stomachs by taking a turn on the deck.

'Courage, Mam,' Maggi whispered, tucking her mother more securely into the narrow bunk. 'The doctor will be here soon. I sent Tully to fetch him as soon as they opened the hatches. He'll not be long.'

'Sing for me, Maggi,' Shona whispered, her face pale and

4

strained. 'It'll help us to pass the time.'

'Oh, Mam, I don't feel like it. An' what if Da . . .?'

'Never mind your da. If I can't have what I want in my labour, when can I?' The woman was breathless from talking at the same time as dealing with pain. 'Sing for me, Maggi. You have such a lovely voice. So much younger and stronger than mine.'

'Your voice is still beautiful, Mam, and true as it ever was.'

'But I want much more for you, Maggie' Shona's voice was suddenly stronger. 'Much more than bein' poor an' buskin' for pennies. Why else would I go against your father's wishes an' teach you to sing?'

'Please, don't try to talk, Mam. You should be savin' your strength for your labours.'

Shona winced, shaking her head. 'I carry a dream, Maggi. A dream that one day my daughter will be famous. She will be up there on the stage, singin' before the crowned heads of Europe –'

'But that's all it can ever be – only a dream.'

'No. You must believe in yourself, Marigold. Believe in your gift as I do. Only then can you make it happen. Sing to me now – sing me my favourite – *The Black Velvet Band*.'

Maggi began, hesitantly at first in these gloomy surroundings, her voice swelling and becoming more confident as she reached the end of the second verse.

'. . . *And her hair it hung down to her shoulders and tied with a black velvet band . . .*'

One by one people stopped talking and listened, surprised to hear such a strong and melodious voice, coming from a slip of a girl. At the same time, they realised she was singing to comfort her mother so they didn't applaud or otherwise intrude. Maggi sang softly, hoping that wherever her father was up on deck, he wouldn't hear her. It was an old argument and one which had gone on for as long as she could remember.

'No daughter of mine is to sing in public,' he'd say, a stubborn twist to his lips. 'No daughter of mine shall go beggin' for pennies.'

'Then perhaps you'd explain to me, Da,' always she had

the same question ready in return, 'why that should be worse than friskin' a man an' robbin' him of his purse?' She knew the jibe would hit home. Dermot McDiarmit was an accomplished thief.

'Better that than making a spectacle of yourself!' He growled. 'You stick out like a sore thumb as it is wi' that mop o' red hair.'

That too, hit home. He knew his daughter was sensitive about her hair and it was all the more unfair to tease her as it was a legacy from his side of the family. His own curls which once had shone with a similar flame, were now faded to a dull sand, liberally sprinkled with grey.

These family arguments always upset her mother so Maggi made every effort to keep the peace but there were times when Dermot and his petty tyranny were too much to bear. Sparks would fly between them then, making everyone else run for cover as their tempers raged out of control. Maggi was fighting for the chance to make a name for herself; to sing before an audience other than her family and close friends. Dermot, as a horse trader and sometime thief, preferred to go about his business quietly, moving on before his face became too well-known. This went for his family as well. Shona's ambitions for their daughter had long been a bone of contention between them.

Maggi paused in her singing to hug her mother close, supporting her as the ship gave a last sickening lurch. Plates and cooking utensils rattled and people laughed nervously, grabbing them to stop them slipping away.

Shona squeezed her eyes shut, the colour leaving her face as yet another contraction took hold of her, stronger than the earlier ones. She held Maggi's hands for the duration, grunting against the pain and sighing as it subsided, leaving her weak, sweating and gasping for air. Maggi's experience of childbirth was limited but it needed no expert to see that Shona was in for a hard time. Giving birth would be tough for a woman of forty under the best of conditions, let alone on a crowded clipper and crossing the uncertain waters of the Southern Indian Ocean. She felt useless too, not knowing how to help her mother or what to do.

The contractions were coming more frequently now and

Shona's face became a mask of suffering as she struggled for control, refusing to give in and scream against the pain which was like a ball of fire against her spine. Maggi knew that if help didn't come, and soon, the baby might never be born and her mother would die. Already at a low ebb because of seasickness, poor diet and the enervating heat of the tropics, she had no strength left to bring this baby into the world. Fortunately so far there had been no serious outbreaks of disease. All the same, Shona was ill-prepared for the ordeal ahead.

Since leaving Fremantle, where she had docked only long enough to fill her water barrels and take on supplies, the *Sally Lee* had been subjected to the worst weather the Southern Ocean could offer. She had fought her way through a succession of storms and high seas which went on for days. Small children and infants had sickened and died. Only now was there some respite as the ship turned the heel of the most westerly tip of Australia and continued on the last leg of her journey, sailing towards the great Australian Bight.

Below decks on the *Sally Lee*, the quarters were far from comfortable. The ship was carrying more passengers than the owners had planned.Conditions were cramped and unwholesome for anybody, let alone a woman in the last stages of childbirth. There was no privacy and, in the wake of the heavy seas, the air was foul with the stench of vomit and human excrement. The latter could have been avoided were it not for the false modesty of some of the female passengers. Had they been willing to go above and deposit their wastes on the deck as the captain instructed, the problem might not have been so severe. Instead, most women preferred to cower below, relieving themselves in dark corners, allowing urine and excrement to filter into the bilges.

Cleaner and sweeter than most vessels when she set out from Liverpool, the *Sally* now smelled liked an open latrine. She would do well to travel much further without an outbreak of typhoid, cholera or some other fatal disease.

Maggi looked up, hearing someone return from the upper decks, relieved to see it was her brother, Tully, not accompanied by the doctor as she'd hoped but bringing a welcome breath of sea air which clung to his hair and his clothes.

7

'Where is he? The doctor?' Maggi mouthed, frowning at him.

'He won't come,' the boy whispered.

'Why not? Didn't you say it was urgent?' Maggi ran her hands through her matted hair, tugging it in her anxiety. 'Dammit all, Tully. Do I have to do everythin' for meself?'

'Hold on, sis. I'd have gone on my knees and begged the man an' I thought it would do any good. But he's a bastard. He just laughed an' said he had better things to do than bring another tinker's brat into the world.'

'Oh, did he now?' Maggi spoke softly but her eyes were bright with bitterness. 'He was drunk, I suppose?'

'He had been drinking, yes. I smelled it on his breath.'

'And speaking of drink, what's happened to Da? He's another one never here when he's needed.'

'Don't be too hard on him, Mags. He can't help it,' the boy muttered, his gaze flickering towards his mother whose swollen form was scarcely contained by the narrow bunk. 'I think he's scared.'

'Oh? An' you think I'm not?' Maggi hissed through clenched teeth. 'I dunno what I'm doing neither! But trust men to stand up for each other no matter what. God curse the lot of you!'

'Maggi.' Her mother's voice was little more than a croak. 'Maggi, my love, don't curse them so. Have a care for your own soul.'

'Oh, Mama.' Maggi blinked away tears. 'If the good of my soul depends on holdin' me temper, I must be damned a thousand times already. It's just – I can't bear to see you hurtin' this way an no one to help you.'

'Hush, my love. Lean a bit closer, will ye? I've somethin' to tell you, I don't want Tully to hear.'

'Mam, don't –'

'No, listen. It's the baby. I think he's dead.'

'No!' 'Fear clenched Maggi's stomach. 'You can't know that, Mam. Not for sure.'

'But it's been a long time – too long – since I felt him kick.'

'Ah, it's only because you're so tired. The baby is, too. He's jus' sleepin' a bit.'

8

'No.' This time Shona had no time to prepare herself for the contraction which took hold of her body and twisted it in grasp of iron. She gave a low growl of anguish, more animal than human. Horrified, her children could only watch, waiting for it to leave her. At last she fell back on her sweat-soaked pillows, panting and shivering with exhaustion.

'That's it. I've had enough.' Maggi stood up and stretched, stiff from her awkward position crouched beside the bed. 'You stay with her, Tully. I won't be long.'

'Where are you going?' the boy whispered, hardly daring to look at his mother, lying so still on the bed. 'I won't know what to do. What if the baby comes an' you're not here?'

'He won't.' Maggi picked up her old grey shawl and wrapped it around her shoulders. 'This baby's not going to be born – not without a doctor to bring him. Jus' make sure she knows you're here and give her your hands to hold if the pain is bad. I'm going to fetch Doctor Parker. I'll make him come, if I have to drag him down here by his miserable scrap of a beard!'

Doctor Parker wasn't difficult to find. He was exactly where Maggi expected him to be, seated in comfort on one of the upper decks, holding court to his friends. By now a watery-looking sun had emerged from behind the clouds and the swell of the sea had subsided, making it pleasant to be out on deck in the open air although Maggi scarcely took any note of this, having other things on her mind. On the upper deck it was like another world; one very different from the gloom and misery of steerage. Here everyone looked healthy, well-fed and in holiday mood. While most of the ladies were still in their cabins, their children were out in the care of pale-faced nursemaids, shouting and playing as children will. The menfolk were gathered in groups, turning their faces to the breeze or watching the activities of the crew, some high in the rigging, working on ropes and sails, checking the damage caused by the latest storm.

Squaring her shoulders and holding her head high, Maggi slipped past the steward and made her way to that part of the deck reserved for the cabin passengers. The captain, wanting all his passengers to remain healthy and benefit from the fresh air, had decreed that the deck of the ship was

9

for everyone but by unspoken agreement most people kept to that part of the deck nearest their own accommodation. Steerage passengers were to remain in the stern, leaving the rest of the ship to the cabin passengers. Nor were young girls expected to wander about on their own. Maggi received some sharp looks from one or two of the nursemaids.

The doctor and his friends were seated in comfort, their faces turned to the sun, laughing, and passing a bottle of whisky between them. Even as Maggi watched, Parker paused to light an enormous cigar and she knew he wouldn't take kindly to being disturbed. She waited, leaning against the mast to gather her thoughts, wondering how to succeed where Tully had failed. She pulled her shawl more closely about her shoulders, not looking forward to the usual teasing a party of drinking men will offer a lone girl.

'Doctor Parker!' she called.

'Yes?' The man turned immediately at the sound of a woman's voice, his smile fading when he saw it was only Maggi. 'What is it, girl? You can see that I'm busy.'

Very busy getting drunk, she thought, but she knew better than to say so aloud. 'You are the ship's doctor, are you not?'

'Indeed. But I can't be available twenty-four hours in the day.'

'Sir, my mother is sick. She's been in her labour for hours now an' is needin' a doctor's care. Please, if you'd just take a look – jus' show me how best to help her.'

'Great heavens, girl. Aren't there women enough to deal with it? There are midwives and nurses aboard. Where's Mrs Plackett? Ask her.' He turned away, dismissing her with a wave of his hand. 'I'm rushed off my feet as it is without bringing babes into the world – as if, in these crowded conditions, we needed more.' He raised his eyebrows, glancing at his friends to enlist their support. They chuckled obediently. 'And who's going to pay? You look as if you can scarcely afford your passage, let alone my expensive professional services.'

'You have been paid by the ship's owners already, sir. And handsomely enough by the cut of your cloth.' Maggi broke off, biting her lip. She would never get him to help if she

10

angered him. More was to be gained by treating the doctor with respect, much as it went against the grain. So she took a deep breath and started again. 'Please sir, I beg of you, will you come? My mother is desperate sick an' can't birth this child.'

'How's that?' Parker looked at her directly at last, peering at her over his spectacles. 'I thought you gypsy women dropped babies easily as rabbits beneath a hedge? There's no mystery about childbirth. It's meant to be natural as breathing – you women make far too much of it. Go and look for some old dame to attend her. And keep to your own quarters in future. Don't bring the stink of steerage up here on deck.'

Maggi's stomach curdled with rage and she wanted to rake his face with her nails but she knew she must curb her temper and persist for her mother's sake.

'Sir, I'm sorry you feel this way because you leave me no choice. I'll go at once to Captain Carpenter and tell him I found you too drunk to come to our aid.'

'Now, now, Missy, no need for that.' The man's attitude altered at once. Everyone knew Captain Carpenter was one of the old school, fair-minded and just to all the souls in his charge, not only the cabin passengers. Parker rose to his feet, staggering only a little as he pushed himself from his chair. 'Well, if it's urgent, as you say – better take a look.'

As he picked up his bag and swayed past her, Maggi smelled the whisky, sour and heavy on his breath, making her wonder if she was doing the right thing. Was it wise to force a man who had been drinking to attend her mother? But his medical skills were needed and there was nobody else.

'Farewell, good compadres.' The doctor saluted his friends, burping gently. 'I go but I shall return. Don't break out another bottle 'til I do.'

Tully came running to meet his sister as soon as he saw her descending the ladder, followed by Doctor Parker.

'Thank God you're here,' he said. 'The pains are gettin' much worse an' I'm afeared she won't last.'

Parker grunted and would have missed his footing on the last few rungs of the ladder if Maggi hadn't reached out to steady him. He peered into the smoky air and the gloom of

11

steerage and fished in his pocket to pull out a large brown handkerchief which he clapped to his nose. When possible, he avoided coming down into steerage where the acrid smells always took him by surprise.

Following Maggi, he squeezed through the narrow gap between the dining tables to make his way to the cramped dormitory where her mother lay.

The cabin was empty apart from a small group of women huddled together under an oil lamp on the far side of the room. They exchanged meaningful glances, nudging each other as the doctor passed. Maggi could expect no help from these girls. They were entertainers, bound for the bars and dance halls of Melbourne, largely ignored by respectable women aboard the *Sally Lee*. Secretly, Maggi admired them and envied their lifestyle, fascinated by the glitter of their fake jewellery and flamboyant clothes.

Parker didn't speak to Shona or make any attempt to reassure her before flinging back the bedcovers to reveal her lying in a pool of sweat and broken waters. Apart from the swollen hump of her belly, she was painfully and pathetically thin, her face a mask of pain. Muttering to himself, he frowned, prodding her in order to feel the position of the child. Shona gasped and let out a low moan of distress as he examined her more intimately and Maggi glared at him, silently urging him to be more gentle. Over the doctor's shoulder, she caught sight of Tully, white to the lips and ready to faint at the sight of his mother's pain. This was no place for a lad of fifteen.

'Tully,' she snapped, speaking sharply to get his attention, 'Don't stand there lollygaggin' an' gapin' like a fish. Go up on deck an' look for our Da. Tell him he'd better come at once if he wants to see . . . No! Jus' tell him we need him.'

Glad to be given something useful to do, Tully loped away, his bare feet making no sound on the wooden boards of the deck.

Parker leaned forward to speak to Maggi, talking over her mother's head.

'I can't be sure of course but I suspect the infant is dead. No heartbeat. If we crush the head, the corpse will be that much easier to remove.' And without waiting for Maggi's

12

reply, he began delving in his bag to bring out the instruments he needed, muttering about the dangers of having to work in such a poor light.

'Please, sir,' Maggi whispered, 'do you *have* to do this? Sure an' it's a terrible thing to murder an unborn child.'

'But necessary if you want the woman to live.' The doctor was growing impatient with Maggi and her scruples. 'I've told you, I'm almost certain the child is dead. Of course, if you won't take my advice, there's no more to be said. It makes no difference to me.' And he shrugged, turning his back and beginning to repack his instruments.

'Wait. Give me a moment, please' Maggi licked lips that were suddenly dry. 'Mam – Mam, did you hear what the doctor said? He says – he says he must –'

Shona nodded and groaned, too exhausted to protest. Maggi's stomach lurched again when she saw the powerful forceps the doctor would use.

'Please,' she continued to stay his hands 'don't you have some poppy juice? Some potion to dull the pain?'

'Not at this end of the journey – no, I don't.' He shook his head, refusing to meet her gaze. She didn't believe him but there was no point in arguing further as Shona was seized by another powerful contraction.

Mercifully, the struggle was brief. The child was born dead and the afterbirth followed almost immediately. Maggi closed her eyes and breathed a long sigh of relief. The worst was over now and her mother would live. Quickly, while the doctor was packing his bag and Shona lay white-faced and exhausted, her eyes closed, Maggi wrapped the infant in the blood-stained linen from the bed. He was a boy – the baby boy they had looked for and expected – whole and almost perfect. She could have thought him asleep but for the bluish tinge to his skin and the skull caved in at the back like a broken egg.

The doctor snapped his bag shut, impatient to leave. Maggi wanted to ask him how to go on from here, to ensure her mother's full recovery but he would give no her more time.

'There now.' he wagged a finger at Maggi. 'Never let it be said I wouldn't attend.' And with his handkerchief once

13

more protecting his face, he hurried away. Maggi was left to do the best she could with no medical knowledge apart from folklore and a few old wives' tales she'd picked up along the way. To be as clean as possible would make a good start. She fetched a bowl of fresh water, spooning a little through her mother's cracked, dry lips and, ignoring the rule that it was to be used solely for drinking, used the remainder to wash her mother's face and sponge the blood-stains from her body, still tender and bleeding from the doctor's rough treatment. She could only hope that such bleeding was normal and would soon stop. She rolled up the rest of the bed linen, soiled beyond hope of washing, meaning to cast it overboard later, when it was dark. She had no fresh linen to replace it but the sheets from her own bed.

'Maggi,' Shona opened her eyes and struggled to raise herself into a sitting position. 'The baby? Was it a boy?'

She nodded, unable to speak for the lump of misery lodged in her throat.

'Please. Let me see him.'

'No, Mam, don't,' she whispered. 'It'll do you no good. Rest quiet now an I'll make you a dish o' tea to recover your strength.'

'That baby was part of me, Maggi. I have to see him, just for a moment – to say goodbye.' Grim with determination, Shona struggled to her elbows and Maggi saw it would do more harm than good to deny her. Normally peace-loving and uncomplaining, her mother could be just as stubborn if she wanted to be. Carefully, Maggi unwrapped the dead baby and gave him to Shona who received him, folding him into her embrace, crooning and rocking him as if he were a living child. It was only when her eyes closed and she fell into an exhausted slumber that Maggi lifted the child from her arms.

'You're such a good girl, Maggi,' Shona whispered. 'Good and kind. Promise me . . . promise me you'll look after Tully and your – da if – if I don't –'

'Never say it, Mam. Nothing's going to happen to you. I won't let it.'

'Look after Tully. An' don't let your father teach him the

14

thievin'. He's a good boy. I don't want him learnin' bad ways.'

'No, Mam,' Maggi bit her lip, concentrating on tucking the bedclothes more closely around her mother and looking away to hide the expression in her eyes. How could she tell Shona it was herself and not Tully who had inherited her father's knack of picking pockets without getting caught? She who had been his inseparable companion ever since she could walk. There was a time when she had adored the rakish, handsome man who was her father and thought he could do no wrong. It was only now as she grew into womanhood that she fully understood the weaknesses in his character and the flaws in his reasoning.

Not born to privilege but in the shadow of it, Dermot was convinced that the world owed him a living and he should not be obliged to work for it. This was why he was obsessed with the idea of searching for gold, confident that he would be lucky and stumble on a fortune, becoming rich overnight.

Dermot's father was the steward of a great house. The old man lavished as much care and affection on the place as if it were his own. As indeed it might have been, so infrequently did the English milord who owned it choose to visit his lands in Ireland. Dermot could never speak of his father without a sneer, mocking the old man's loyalty to the house and its absent master.

'Misguided old fool,' he would say. 'Devoting his life to a house he can never own.'

In his younger days, Dermot had been employed as a groom on the estate. But he soon discovered a way to supplement the modest income he received, by allowing his lordship's finest Arab stallion to service a local mare. One mistake might have been forgiven but when further enquiries revealed that the Arab had serviced half the mares in the district, Dermot was evicted from the stables and turned from his father's door.

'You've placed me in an impossible situation,' his father said. 'The whole village is laughing at me. You will leave here, Dermot, and you need not return until you have learned to be humble and mend your ways.'

Stubborn to a fault and refusing to bend the knee to

15

anyone, Dermot vowed to prove he was a better man than his father by amassing a fortune before he returned. It was taking a very long time to do so. With only a sketchy education, no trade and no useful knowledge of anything other than horseflesh, he had to scrape an income by living off his wits. He travelled, going from place to place buying promising colts and selling them at a profit. Maggi wasn't sure when or how he met her mother – both parents tended to be secretive about this. She knew only that it had something to do with her mother's musical talents; the only serious disagreements they had were over Shona's music and singing. Liberal in his thinking most of the time, Dermot refused to permit his wife to make money from singing, leading Maggi to wonder if he were jealous of her abilities. Sometimes, grudgingly, he would let her sing before family and close friends. Even then he would sit hunched over his beer, his expression dark with disapproval as he waited for her to finish. And when she sang with Maggi, the similar voices blending in harmony, he could take no pleasure in it.

Even in hard times, when the famine brought hardship and misery to most of rural Ireland, large sums of money changed hands at horse fairs. It was here that Dermot found another way to supplement his income. He became a pick-pocket, engaging his small daughter as his accomplice, pretending at first that it was a new game.

So Maggi learned to keep secrets from both her parents. Her father must never find out that her voice had been trained far beyond the level of singing for pleasure, nor was her mother to know she was a skilful thief, able to pick a man's pockets while smiling into his eyes.

'Be sure of the character of your man before you approach him, girl,' Dermot warned. 'And if he's nervous, patting his pockets, leave him alone. For sure he will have a fat purse but he'll squeal like a stuck pig if you take it. An' another thing – never take from a man unless he looks like he can afford it. The other sort always fetch the constable an' make a fuss.'

Before long, stealing became second nature to Maggi. When she was small she did it to please Dermot and for the praise and treats which would always follow. Later it became

16

commonplace; a way of adding to the family's meagre resources. It didn't seem wrong to lighten the pockets of wealthy men while most of the poor people she knew were dying of starvation. Dermot lost no time in telling her the story of Robin Hood, drawing similarities between the lives of the merry men and their own. She didn't care about the money; that wasn't important. Her father's approval was. So it was Maggi who went to work, stealing enough for the four of them to buy passage from Dublin to Liverpool. There, Dermot would have applied for an assisted passage but he wasn't sure how far the authorities might delve into his background. So he and his daughter went to work on pockets again and soon they had enough to buy the cheapest passage to Australia.

Roused from her thoughts by a sound she thought to be water dripping from above, she looked up to see if it might be seeping on to Shona's bed. But the boards were dry. With a sinking feeling she realised the sounds were coming from the bed itself where her mother lay swooning and half-conscious, barely alive. Gingerly, she pulled back the covers in time to see a fresh flow of blood pulse from her mother's torn body to form a spreading stain on the sheets. Stifling her panic, she looked up, hoping to catch the eye of someone, anyone who might be able to help her. Unfortunately, most of the married women, the ones with families who might have known what to do, were making the most of the fine weather and taking a turn on the deck. Only the dancers remained, crowded around their table at the far end of the room, playing cards for money and chatting amongst themselves.

'Oh, please,' she called out to them. 'Won't somebody help me? My mother's bleeding again and I don't know what to do.'

Most of the girls ignored her, pretending they didn't hear, except the tall girl who was their ringleader. She stood up and elbowed the others out of her way, rolling up her sleeves as she came.

'Bitches,' she said without rancour, grinning at Maggi. 'Still bleedin', is she? Well, don't panic yet. Might not be as bad as you think. Out of the way, pet, an' lets take a look.'

17

Maggi vacated her place at once, relieved that someone else was willing to take charge and warming to the girl whose accent revealed she was Irish, too. By no means beautiful with her well-scrubbed face, she nevertheless moved with the natural grace of a dancer. Maggi liked her immediately.

'The name's Peggy. Peg Riley,' the girl said. 'Can't say I'm much of a nurse but I know what to do when women lose babies. This bleedin' will have to be stopped or your mam's goin' to die.'

Maggi blinked. While she appreciated the girl's frankness, the news still came as a shock. 'The doctor – Doctor Parker:' She glanced vaguely towards the ladder. 'Shall I go up an get him again?'

'Never mind him,' Peggy waved the suggestion aside. 'I'd say he's done quite enough damage already.' All the while she was talking she had been reaching under her skirt and tearing her petticoat into strips. It was a mass of lacy white frills, lovely enough to wear as a dress, Maggi thought, but the girl didn't seem to care. She went on tearing it into strips to make rags. Deftly, she showed Maggi how to roll them into pads and use them to staunch the bleeding. At the same time she took the pillows from under Shona's head and placed them beneath her feet until she was lying flat on the bed, legs raised to discourage the flow of the blood.

For a moment Shona opened her eyes, smiling as her gaze rested on Maggi. 'Don't look so frightened, Maggi I'll be all right in a while. It's just – I'm so tired.'

'Don't worry, Mam. It'll stop soon. You'll be all right.' Biting her lips to hold back the tears, Maggi watched as her mother's face seemed to shrivel and drain of colour, her breathing becoming so shallow it was hard to be sure if her chest was moving or not. 'Oh, please God, let her live,' she whispered. 'I promise I'll never lose me temper again.' She clung to Peggy's hand, relying on the older girl for support.

At last it appeared that the bleeding had stopped. For the moment the crisis seemed to be over. Peg detached herself from Maggi and went to get some of the blankets from her own bunk which she tucked around Shona, saying she was probably in shock and ought to be warm.

'She'll be all right now, won't she?' Maggi insisted. 'She's

18

just worn out, needin' her rest. A good sleep an' she'll wake up feeling so much better –'

'I hope so. But I still think you should be prepared for the worst.'

Both girls looked up, hearing a disturbance at the top of the ladder. Maggi recognised her father's voice, loud with panic and irritation.

'Get out o' me way, then, an' let me get down. Draggin' a man away from his pals. Birthin' is women's work for God's sake, what do you expect me to do?'

Maggi glared at the man who came stamping towards them, making no effort to be quiet. He seemed to fill the room with his bluff presence, untidy hair on end, boots thumping on the bare planks of the deck. *Isn't it just like him*, Maggi thought, *to look so hale, so hearty and untouched, with the rest of us worn to a frazzle an' worried sick?* Tully was following a few steps behind his father, a hang-dog expression on his face.

'See?' Dermot looked over his shoulder, ready to rubbish his son's fears. 'What did I tell you? It's quiet enough now. Fool of a boy. Didn' I say there was no need for alarm?'

'Will you be quiet, Da? Keep your voice down.' Maggi pressed a finger to her lips to silence him. 'Can't you see Mam's exhausted after her labours an needin' her rest?'

'Why send for me then, if I'm to be in the way? An' what eejit invited that tosspot of a doctor to visit me wife?'

As his eyes became accustomed to the gloom he saw his daughter wasn't alone. Another girl was standing beside her, arms folded and with a wry look on her face. 'An' what's that one doin' here? Dammit all, Maggi. How many times must I tell you? I want you to have nothing to do wi' those dance hall girls.'

Peggy shrugged, not in the least put out by Dermot or his rudeness. Placing her hands on her hips, she stretched her back, giving him a direct, assessing look. It was a deliberately provocative gesture and meant to insult him rather than rouse his interest. She held his gaze for a moment and then she relaxed, grinning at Maggi.

'Chin up, kid,' she said before sauntering slowly back to her friends, hips swaying.

19

'Look at that. Brazen harlot!' Dermot snarled, his eyes still on the girl's rear in retreat.

'She is not,' Maggi felt bound to defend her new friend. 'Peg's a dancer, not one of that sort.'

'What would you know? An innocent, wet behind the ears. Dancers! Theatricals! I've no time for such folk.'

'Well, I should have been in trouble enough without her. She's the only one who would help. Ah, how could you, Da? How could you be so rude to her? She's given Mam the blankets from her own bed. It's all very fine for you to come down here creatin' havoc now. Where were you when we needed you?'

'What do you expect me to do? Birthin' is women's work.' Dermot held fast to the only argument he knew.

The girl returned to her companions, responding to their quips and raised eyebrows with a shrug and a smile. Aware that Dermot was still watching her, she poured water into a bowl and stripped off to her corset, leaving her shoulders bare as she prepared to wash.

'Washing in public. Shameless!' said Dermot, glaring at Peggy through narrowed eyes. All the same it was several moments before he returned his attention to his wife and family, rubbing his hands together and smiling. 'How did it all go, then? Where's the new babby?'

'Finally.' Maggi glared at him. 'I was wonderin' when you'd get round to askin'. Too exhausted and emotionally drained to spare him, she pointed to the bloodstained bundle which she had placed beneath the bed. 'There lies your son – what remains of him.'

'Ah, no. God save us all.' Dermot's shoulders slumped and the colour left his face so suddenly, Maggi was afraid he was going to collapse. Immediately, she felt a pang of remorse, wishing she'd taken the time to break the news more gently. 'That murderin' swine of a doctor! He's killed my child.'

'No, he didn't.' Maggi was in no mood for Dermot or his melodrama. 'The baby was dead already. Mam said so herself.'

'And you. You're as much to blame.' Dermot stabbed an accusing finger at her. 'You should've let nature take its course.'

20

'Don't you be tellin' me what I should an' shouldn't have done. An' if you're lookin' for someone to blame – look no further than yourself. You're the one got her pregnant, not me!'

'You've a sharp an' wicked tongue in your head, girl. Button your lip unless you want to feel the flat o' me hand.' Her father's temper was rising to match her own. 'Too cheeky, y'are. Too full of yourself by far.'

'Go on, then. Hit me, why don't you? That's all a coward like you is good for –'

Seeing the argument was about to develop into a full-scale war, Tully tried to break it up by placing himself between them. 'Please, Da. Maggi don't know what she's sayin'. Leave her alone.'

Without taking his eyes from her, Dermot shoved his son roughly out of the way. 'You stay out of this, Tully. This is between her an' me.' And he glared at his favourite child, breathing heavily. 'Since when do you set yourself up in judgement? Who are you to question God's will in sendin' your mother an' me a child?'

'God's will, is it? Cheap whisky more like. Look at him, Da. Take a look at your son. That's your own flesh an' blood lyin' there an' you can't even mourn him. Heartless, that's what y'are. You've not even asked about Mam, sick as she is an near dyin'. . . '

'Ah, no. No!' Only now realising the seriousness of Shona's condition, Dermot started running his fingers through his hair, tugging it in his concern. 'She can't be sick as all that. She never had no trouble birthin' her babies before.'

'You really don't know, do you? Did you never wonder why there were only the two of us, Tully an' me? Mam lost three babies at least that she never told you about. "Your Da has enough to worry him." That's what she said.'

'But why, Maggi? Why did she never tell me?'

'So this baby was precious to her – her last hope. She didn't think to have any more.'

'I know – I know.'

'But you don't know, Da. Mam's goin' to be heartbroken over the loss of this baby. But you don't give a damn, do you? Long as you can get to the bloody gold fields on time.'

21

'Stop it, Maggi. You know I don't like to hear a woman swear –'

'You call that swearing? I've not even started yet.'

'Maggi!' It was Shona, calling from the bed in a voice so weak it was no more than a rasping whisper. This time it was Maggi who pushed Dermot out of the way, leaning close to hear what her mother said. 'Maggi, I'll not have you fight with your father – not over me.'

'But, Mam –'

'No, Maggi. I love you, all of you, an' I can't bear it. Lyin' here listenin' to you tryin' to wound each other, fightin' amongst yourselves.'

'Oh, Mam, I'm sorry. But sometimes he makes me so mad I could scream.'

'An' you know why, don't you? Because you're so much alike.'

'I hope not, Mam. I don't like to think so.'

'Maggi, I want you to make me a promise –'

The girl frowned, biting her lip and hoping the promise wouldn't be too hard to keep. 'Promise me you'll go on with your singing? You're to practise every day without fail – every one of the exercises I taught you. Your voice must fly up an' down the scales, flexible an' true. Because one day I know, I jus' know you'll be up there on the stage, in a real theatre, like I said.'

'Oh, Mam.'

'Yes. Not standin' up on the back of a wagon like I did, singin' for pennies at horse fairs. Promise me, Maggi.'

'Oh, Mam.'

'Promise me.'

'All right. I'll do my best.'

'And never give up?'

'Never give up.' She kissed her mother's forehead, alarmed to discover how cold and clammy it felt beneath her lips.

Dermot seized her by the arm as soon as she turned from her mother's bedside. 'What was it? What did she say?'

'Nothing, Da.' Maggi sighed. 'Jus' women's talk.'

'Tell me what she said.' He was grasping her so tightly she thought he would leave a bruise, his fingers pressing into her flesh.

22

'Let me go.' She spoke softly but through gritted teeth. 'I used to love you, Da. Time was when I thought you were the most wonderful person in the world an' I was the luckiest girl to have you for my da. But not any more. Oh, no, not any more.' And having started on the long list of her resentments, she found herself unable to stop. 'You never – ever – think of anyone but yourself. How many times have you told us your story? How your father turned you out to make your own way in the world. And now you expect the world and everyone in it to pay. It's always what *you* want – what *you* need. Did you ever stop to ask yourself if Mam wants the same? No. All you can see is the gold dust shinin' in your eyes. So we have to pack up and leave. Never mind poor Mam, sick with the mornin' sickness an five months gone with a child.'

'Now you hold it, young lady. You hold it right there.' Dermot's eyes glittered. 'I took desperate measures for desperate times, girl. You saw how it was with the famine. What should I have done? Stayed in Ireland, watching you starve and die on me one by one? Ah, no.' He made a gesture of impatience. 'Why should I explain meself to a child, like you.'

'I'm not a child any more, Da. I'm nearly eighteen years old.'

He ignored the remark. 'Your mam knew of the risks and accepted them. She was more than ready to leave.'

'Oh, it's easy to say that now. Now she's lyin' there half-dead an' can't speak for herself. But that wouldn't matter to you, would it, Da?'

'Shut your mouth, you little bitch!' Dermot raised his hand high, intending to hit her this time. It would be the first time, if he did, but she had never pushed him so far. She felt as if a devil sat on her shoulder, egging her on, as she stared into the once handsome face, the fine eyes now hidden in folds of flesh, the network of veins on his nose; evidence of his fondness for liquor and the good things of life. It was Tully who spoke first, calling their attention to the still figure on the bed.

'Will ye stop it! Stop it, the pair of ye. Can't ye see that she's dead?' Trembling with shock, he stared down at his

23

mother whose face had settled into a bloodless calm, the eyes closed and sunken in their sockets. Quietly, while they had been quarrelling, Shona had breathed her last.

Tully and Maggi stood back, holding on to each other for comfort and support, undone by the rare sight of their father in tears. While Maggi had released some of her own tension by whaling into him, calling him heartless and insensitive, these same faults in him had been her shield against the rest of the world. Dermot McDiarmit, her cheerful, indestructible father. Could this weeping wreck be the same man who outfaced policemen, threw punches over imagined slights and could fight two men at the same time? It was strange, somehow frightening, to see him brought low. Her intention had been to make him face up to his responsibilities, yes. But not to destroy him so utterly, he'd fall apart. Tears sprang to her own eyes as she watched her father fight a battle with his emotions and lose. His face worked and his lips turned down like a child's as the tears streamed from his eyes and rolled down his cheeks, soaking into his grizzled beard. His grief was all the more terrible to watch as he made no sound.

24

Chapter Two

Shona's funeral was conducted the following morning, under grey skies and in haste. The priest did his best to be kind and offer the bereaved family what comfort he could but he had been seasick for most of the journey; his own resources were low. Clutching the ship's rail for support, he was rocked by a blast of wind which snatched away his words as soon as he uttered them and chilled Maggi's tears as they formed in her eyes.

After five minutes of trying to hold on to her composure, Maggi gave up the struggle and wept openly, grieving for her mother and this grim ending to her life. It ought not to be like this. Shona deserved so much more; a respectable burial and a place to lie in the ground. Once Maggi started to weep in earnest she couldn't stop. Huge tears rolled from her eyes which she wiped away with the fringe of her old grey shawl. No one offered her the comfort of a handkerchief. Grim-faced in his determination not to join her, Dermot stood straight-backed, legs astride, with his hands clenched at his sides. Beside him, Tully copied his father's stance. One or two passengers stopped and the men took off their hats as a mark of respect for the funeral but most people found it easier to pass by and ignore it. Maybe they feared that if they paid too much attention, the hand of death might stretch towards one of their own.

The priest mumbled his final benediction and gave the signal for the bodies to be lowered into the water. Without a coffin, in only a winding sheet for protection, they disappeared beneath the surface so quickly that Maggi feared they might have been fed to some voracious creature waiting beneath the surfaces of the waves. Had they been closer to their destination, she would have insisted that the bodies be taken ashore, to be buried in a churchyard in a grave she could tend. She needed time to come to come to terms with her loss. They all did. It seemed so callous, so unfeeling, to cast their loved ones adrift and sail on.

Several ladies swooped on Maggi, to kiss her and murmur condolences, when the service was over.

'So very sorry, my dear.'

'Poor motherless child.'

'And if there's anything, anything I can do . . .'

'If you need any help, my dear, you have only to ask.'

Maggi submitted to their embraces, wanting nothing from these women whose offers of help were as meaningless as their kisses. *Where were you when I needed you?* she wanted to shout. *When you could have done some good? What use is your help to me, now they're both dead?*

At this latter stage of the journey, funerals were commonplace aboard the *Sally Lee*. On an extended sea voyage such as this, only the sturdy would arrive. The old and the very young were always at risk, often unable to survive on the poor fare.

During the long stretch across the Indian Ocean, the preserved meat had turned rotten and the last of the raisins mildewed and had to be thrown away. It was necessary to make do with a spartan diet of dried peas and rice, supplemented by ship's biscuits so hard they could loosen the teeth. Sometimes the seamen captured a seabird or two to supplement this meagre fare and one day there were great celebrations when a dolphin was caught. In spite of her father's ridicule, Maggi went hungry rather than eat any of it. She couldn't forget how it had leaped and played, entertaining the ship's company and trusting the sailors who whistled, encouraging it to come close enough to be caught and killed. She had closed her eyes and covered her ears with her hands, unable to bear those cries which seemed almost human as the creature pleaded for its life to no avail. The sailors leaned into the water to spear it and hauled it aboard to finish it off.

26

Listlessly, Maggi queued for the family's rations and went through the motions of preparing simple meals for her father and Tully, having little appetite herself and taking only enough to keep herself alive. Not even Tully was able to reach her and Dermot didn't try. The truth was that he didn't feel strong enough to face any more of her reproaches and the rift between them grew wider. Avoiding his daughter because of her uncertain temper and his son because he reminded him too much of Shona, Dermot sought comfort in the bottom of a whisky bottle and the comradeship of his peers. Men who would talk at length of the one thing common to all of them: the hope of changing their lives by discovering gold.

While he sympathised with his sister's feelings and understood why she blamed Dermot for their misfortunes, Tully knew it was up to him to heal the breach and bring them together again if he could. There would be enough obstacles, enough dragons to face in this unknown land, without fighting each other as well. He had bad dreams. Some mornings he woke up weeping, haunted by charnel house nightmares and his mother's dead face. The other dreams were much worse. Dreams which allowed him to wake up believing she was still alive. Then he would look across and see his father snoring in his bunk and realise it was an illusion. His mother and her wonderful smile were gone.

Similarly at a loose end without her mother to care for, Maggi spent little time below decks. She discovered a place to hide under one of the lifeboats, becoming so fond of this refuge that she would remain there clinging to the ropes, even when the winds freshened to gale force and the captain ordered the decks to be cleared of all passengers to allow room for the crew to get on with their work. She passed the time fulfilling the promise she'd made to her mother; she exercised her voice by breathing deeply, by sustained humming on one note and also by practising her scales. Sometimes the notes were snatched away, swallowed by the wind before she could hear if they were true or not. And sometimes the seamen would hear her singing, crossing themselves and pretending they didn't, unwilling to admit they were hearing siren songs from the deep.

'One day I'll make you proud of me, Mam. Wait an' see,' Maggi whispered to herself. Sometimes she imagined she heard her mother's laughter in response but when she strained her ears she could hear nothing; only the wind. It was hard to believe that Shona was gone and without even a likeness surviving to comfort those she had left behind. So many precious memories and Maggi wanted to keep them all; memories of the good days in Ireland before the potatoes rotted and famine stalked the land. She remembered warm summers and long balmy evenings of singing with Shona and Tully when Dermot was away. And years before, the first real argument between her parents. Her mother's stubborn refusal when Dermot announced he would teach the infant Maggi to ride.

'Oh, no, Derry, not yet. The child is still too young to sit a horse. You know I give way to you in most things but no – not in this.'

'Ah, Shona, don't you see? It's *your own* fear you're speaking of, not hers. I want her to ride with me now while she's unafraid and still young enough to have faith in herself and the horse.'

'So you admit it – there is something to be afraid of.'

And Shona refused to budge. Maggi's sixth birthday had to come and go before her mother said she was old enough to sit a horse. Soon she was riding bare-backed astride the great hunters which passed through Derry McDiarmit's hands and Shona had to admit her husband was right. The little girl had inherited all of his skills. Maggi and the McDiarmit horses became inseparable and when she was older she was hard pressed to choose between singing and riding, taking equal pleasure in both. This led to sharp words between her parents as they competed for her attention and she was torn apart, trying to please them both.

And now her mother was gone. There was nobody left to encourage her to preserve her voice. If her father had his way, she would never open her mouth to sing another note – certainly not before an audience. But Maggi remembered her promise and was determined to keep it.

Unable to find his sister for several hours, Tully was on the verge of panic and about to raise the alarm. Depressed as

28

his sister was, she might have fallen or cast herself overboard. Fortunately, he looked up and caught sight of her red hair as she ducked down to hide in one of the lifeboats. Grinning, he pulled the tarpaulin aside, preparing to get in beside her.

'This is a good hiding place. But you gave me a scare, sis. I was about to yell man overboard.'

'Go away, Tully,' she snapped. 'If they see you they'll make us get out of here. Jus' leave me alone.'

The boy's face fell. 'What is it, sis?' he said, his voice taut with misery. 'What have I done to make you so angry with me?'

'Oh, Tully, I'm sorry, so sorry.' She burst into tears. 'It's not you I'm angry with, not at all.' And she pushed the tarpaulin aside and came out, falling into her brother's arms. Heedless of the disapproving glances of other people on deck, they stayed like that for some time, crying the healing tears so necessary to both of them. Maggi was first to recover and release herself.

'There now, that's enough,' she said, pulling out a pink silk handkerchief from her pocket and blowing her nose fiercely. 'We'll have no more o' this. Mam wouldn't like it. You know how she hated tears.'

Having no handkerchief of his own, Tully sniffed and rubbed his nose on his sleeve. 'Where'd you get that? Didn' I hear Da say you wasn't to take anythin'? Not on board the ship?'

'I didn't take it – Peg Riley gave it to me.'

'He'll be no better pleased to hear that.'

'Don't tell him, then.' Maggi let out a long sigh as she stared out at the foam in the wake of the ship. 'He's going to be much worse now that she's gone. Without Mam to put the brakes on him.'

'I know.' Tully frowned, considering this. 'She was a natural lady. You'd never think Da was the one who was born in the big house – that he was halfway to bein' a gentleman.'

'No.'

'There he is now.' Tully winced as his father's laughter floated up from somewhere below decks. 'I'd know that laugh anywhere. He'll be makin' the most of it. Soppin' up sympathy along with somebody else's liquor. Sometimes I wonder if he cared about Mam at all?'

'Oh, yes. Yes, he did.' Maggi spoke softly. 'He loved her dearly – well, as much as a selfish man like Da can love anyone. An' I shouldn't have lost me temper an said what I did. But he shouldn't have said what he did, either. Blamin' me for what happened to Mam. An' then Peggy – how could he be so ungrateful to Peg?'

'Well, you have to admit she's a bit –' Tully paused, not knowing how to put it and biting his lip.

'Go on, Tully, spit it out. You've started now so you may as well speak your mind.'

'Peggy an' those other girls. They are a bit much wi' their fake diamonds an' flashy clothes. Bit larger than life, don't ye think?'

'No, I don't!' Maggi's temper flared. 'Because they're dancers – theatricals. An' if you can't see past a bit o' glitter to the good in a person, Tully McDiarmit, you'll make a poor judge of character in the end.'

He grinned at her, not listening to what she was saying, only happy that his sister was herself again, losing her temper and telling him off. He was much more at home with this Maggi, tawny eyes flashing, than Maggi weeping and depressed. Things would begin to get better from now on. He was young enough to be sure of it. Tilting his head back so far he was almost dizzy, he stared up into the rigging, watching the activities of the crew and looking for Jem and Hobley, his particular friends. Seeing him, they shouted greetings and waved before climbing higher.

'Will ye look at that, sis? D'ye see how they do that so neat? How they slip the ropes and let out the sails – and at just the right moment to catch the wind.'

'Tully McDiarmit! Have you been listening to a single word I've said?'

'Ah, you missed it.' He cuffed her gently. 'Want to know what I'm thinking?'

'No.' Brooding and sulky again, she was giving him only half her attention.

'I've talked to Jem and Hobley an' they think it's a great

30

idea. I'm goin' to ask Da if he'll let me sign on as a ship's apprentice. Here, on this same ship. On the *Sally Lee*.'

Maggi's head whipped round. Suddenly, he had all her attention and more. 'Indeed, an' you won't. Have we come all this way jus' to let you go back? It's nonsense, Tully. The silliest thing I ever heard.'

'But sis!'

'But nothing – the answer's no. Haven't you seen enough of the sea to last you a lifetime? I know I have.' And she glanced at the heaving waves.

'It's different for you. But I love it out here on the open sea. It's exciting.'

'Exciting? Downright dangerous, I'd say. They make me giddy climbin' up there.'

'But it's the danger that adds the spice to it, sis. The danger that makes it worth doing.'

'Never you mind the spice, my lad. You can live on plain fare.'

'That's not like you, sis. You're usually the one who's the daredevil, ready for anything.'

'So I was,' Maggi's expression was bleak. 'But that was before we lost Mam. I'm not losin' you, too.'

'Don't be daft,' he said, pulling a face in the hope of making her laugh. She didn't. He wanted to discuss it further, to tell her it wasn't a whim and he was serious about his plans, but he could see she wasn't in the mood.

Dermot McDiarmit, meanwhile, was seated at a table in steerage, drowning his sorrows in hard liquor. His grief was genuine enough – he had loved the gentle girl he had married and it was a bitter blow to lose her. She who had been his life's companion, sharing his joys and sorrows for the past twenty years. But like all men of this era, he accepted death in childbirth as a natural hazard and part of a woman's lot. During much of their life together he had taken his wife for granted. It was a shock to discover how much he missed her now she was gone. At the same time, he allowed himself to be comforted and, if he were honest, the greater part of his sorrow was for himself.

If he'd taken the time and the trouble to patch things up with Maggi, she might have met him halfway. Fearing rejection, he let it drift, too proud and stubborn to make the first move. She prepared his meals and set them before him in silence. In turn he ate them, offering no word of appreciation or thanks. So she took her revenge in the way she knew would irritate him the most. She made friends with Peg Riley: Peg who was young enough to enjoy a giggle yet mature enough for Maggi to hero-worship, unconsciously seeing the older girl as a substitute for her mother.

Peggy had a great sense of humour and was a natural soubrette. Her green eyes would sparkle with merriment as she tossed her dark curls, poking fun at the staid, middle-aged matrons who disapproved of her low necklines and colourful clothes. Maggi would choke with laughter as Peggy imitated their prim, tightly corseted progress across the deck, poking her head back and forth like a chicken as she waddled behind them. She chattered a lot without giving away a great deal about herself, saying only that she had left Ireland for good during the winter of 1848 and her last memories of it were so painful she didn't want to speak of them.

After escaping the famine and getting to England – no mean feat in itself with so little money – she survived by dancing for tips in the dockside taverns of Liverpool. She didn't come right out and say so but Maggi surmised her new friend was paid for dancing without her clothes. Her ambition had always been to appear on the legitimate stage but the dream had never been realised. Tired of life on the docks which would never get any better, Peg and a few other girls scraped up enough money to pay for their passage to Australia. While she was wary of revealing the details of her personal life, she was always happy to talk about life on the stage.

'Now, don't get me wrong,' she said. 'It's not that I didn't like England – it's the very heartland of music hall, after all. But you have to catch the eye of a theatre manager and make a name for yourself while you're young. That or become a darling of the saloons.'

'Saloons?'

'Saloon theatres, I mean. Good lord, girl, where have you been all your life? Sure an' you've heard of the Alhambra?' And she smiled, raising her eyes to heaven, as Maggi shook her head. 'Not a tavern – not a theatre. The stage is this wide and this high.' She demonstrated the size by waving her arms. 'Well, it's huge. Big enough to take a trapeze. And while they're watching the entertainers, people sit down to dine at long tables, like a big dining hall. I tell you, you need a proper voice to catch their attention an' if they don't like you, they'll pelt you with food. There's a Master of Ceremonies who keeps some sort of order – a big man with a voice to match. He shuts the audience up and announces the acts. They have acrobats and jugglers from China. Sometimes fire eaters, too.'

'I saw a fire eater once at a circus,' Maggi nodded. 'He set fire to the tent and everyone had to leave.'

'So he wasn't so good?'

'No. But I used to think what a wonderful life it was to be on the stage.'

Peggy laughed. 'Well, it is. But you have to be better than most to go the distance and they're always on the lookout for somebody new. It wears you down after a while – livin' in cheap boarding houses and movin' on all the time.'

'We're movin' now.'

'But with purpose in mind. We have Melbourne in our sights. D'you know, the place is bursting at the seams with miners so rich they don't know how to spend it? Well, I mean to show them how. Me an' my friends, we'll give them a first-class show. An' with a voice like yours, sweet an' natural as honey drippin' off a comb, you'll be out of your mind if you don't come with us.'

'You think I'm good enough? To be up there with you and the others on stage?'

'I do. Come on, Mags. What do you say? What else are you going to do with your life?'

'Oh, I don't know.' Maggi wrung her hands in an agony of indecision. 'You've seen my da. What he's like. All fired up an' ready to go to the gold fields.'

'So let him go to the gold fields and you stay behind in Melbourne with us. A little coachin' an I can see a fine career for you on the stage.'

'That's what Mam used to say. But I reckon it'll take

33

more'n a bit of coachin' to make a professional out of me. An' I can't dance. Only the Irish jig.'

'Dance the Irish jig then and take it from there. No more excuses. Honest, Maggi, there's more bars an' dance halls in Melbourne than anywhere else in the world. What do you think I'm here for? My health? Not Peg Riley. There's diggers comin' out of the gold fields with money an' I'm goin' to help them spend it. You're not so bad-lookin' yourself. Play your cards right an' you can do yourself proud.'

'Who? Me?'

'Stop saying "who, me?" You sound like an owl. You'll need fixin' up but you'll do. The face of a pixie, the voice of an angel –'

'An' hair from Ole Nick himself,' Maggi laughed.

'Well, you'll certainly stand out in a crowd.' Peggy grasped a handful of Maggi's thick curls, spreading them out to catch the light. 'I think it's beautiful – like a fire. No matter.' She twitched a shoulder. 'If you don't like it, you can always change it.'

'Dye it, you mean?' Maggi clapped her hands to her mouth. 'Da would have a fit.'

'He won't see it, will he? If he's going to the gold fields.'

'Yes, an' I'll have to go, too.' Maggi's smile faded.

Peggy rolled up her eyes and gave a sigh of exasperation. 'Why? I've already said, you can stay with us. Don't you want to?'

'It's not just a question of what I want – it's what I *have* to do. There's Tully, you see. He's only fifteen.'

'Fifteen?' Peggy gave a shriek of laughter. 'My brother got a girl into trouble when he was fifteen. And when her father and brothers came looking for him, he joined up with the crew of a clipper and ran off to sea.'

'Don't let Tully hear that. He's already got some half-baked idea of signin' on with the *Sally Lee*.'

'And why not? Sooner or later he'll have to get on with a life of his own. You can't keep him tied to your apron strings forever. You're not his mother, you know.' As soon as the words were out she gasped, biting her lip as she realised what she'd said. 'Oh, Maggi, I'm sorry – so sorry, I forgot.'

''S all right,' Maggi muttered, pressing her lips together and opening her eyes wide to keep her feelings under control.

Peggy hugged her. 'Maggi, look. I don't say this to hurt you but you must start looking forward – not back over your shoulder at what has been lost.' She turned her face to the breeze, sniffing the air like a dog. 'There! Breathe deeply. Can you smell it?'

'No. Only the stink of this ship.'

'Well, I do. I smell land. It's out there, waiting for us, just beyond the horizon. Australia! All the opportunities you could ever wish for. Don't stay with your father. All he wants is someone to trail after him an' save him the expense of a housekeeper. Sooner or later you'll have to break free and get on with a life of your own.'

'I know, I know.' Maggi refused to meet Peggy's gaze.

'Promise me something before we go our separate ways?'

'If I can,' Maggi said slowly; she was wary of promises.

'If you need me, or if you're just at a loose end, look us up. We're hopin' to get in at Astley's or even the Queen's. Ask for me at either of those.'

'Thank you, Peg. But I wouldn't count on it.'

'Why not? I thought we were friends.'

'We are,' Maggi reassured her with a hug. 'It's jus' that I won't be at a loose end.'

Chapter Three

The first sighting of land was a tonic to both the ship's passengers and crew. Maggi's grief lifted and she was able to forget her sorrows, responding to the air of optimism and general excitement which spread through the ship's company now that the end of the journey was in sight. Petty arguments were set aside and class differences forgotten as people linked arms, crowding the deck to sing hymns of joy, giving thanks to God for their safe arrival. Now they could see the coast of Victoria, they spent long hours staring at it with hungry eyes, fearing that if they looked away it might vanish, leaving nothing but empty seas as before. But as the ship sailed closer and the strip of land lengthened and they could make out the shapes of trees and dwellings on the horizon, people relaxed, confident at last that they were approaching a civilised human settlement, ready and waiting to receive them. The lighthouse at Cape Otway was a further reassurance, a welcoming sight as it winked on and off, warning vessels to keep clear of the coast.

After most people had risen early and breakfasted, the captain made one of his rare speeches to the ship's company, pointing out the sandy hummocks concealing the entrance to Port Phillip Bay. He said the ship would proceed only when a pilot from Queenscliff had been taken aboard; a man with the necessary experience to guide them safely through the treacherous tidal waters at the entrance to Port Phillip Bay. The passengers groaned in unison at this news of delay, everyone impatient to be ashore.

After a long delay, the pilot arrived, greeted by jeers and a sardonic round of applause. He smiled and nodded, accepting the applause at face value. Red-faced and breathing fumes of rum which could be smelled at ten paces, he stumbled a little as he achieved the deck. Seeing this, Tully wrinkled his nose, jabbing his sister in the ribs. But for all that the man was a drunkard, a hazard common to most men of his trade, he knew his business well enough and soon had the ship moving again. One by one the sails were dismantled and furled as the *Sally* reduced speed, sliding across the calmer, more protected waters of the bay.

It was one of those dull mid-winter mornings, when skies are overcast, the sea reflecting the same inhospitable grey. Maggi hugged her skimpy shawl more closely about her shoulders, clenching her teeth to stop them from chattering. One or two people cracked jokes about the weather, saying they'd been deceived. The ship must have made a round trip and was about to deposit them in Liverpool once again. Today the climate was disappointingly similar, a fog on the water, not unlike the English Channel. Had they really arrived at their destination? The land they had travelled so many miles and suffered so many hardships to see? Where was the sun which they had been promised would shine all the time? The days of endless summer they had been led to expect? Fog in August, whatever next? For the moment, they had forgotten they were now on the opposite side of the world. Here Christmas would fall in the middle of summer and the month of January would be humid and hot while July and August would be the most cold.

Soon the early-morning mists gave way to a light drizzle as the passengers hauled their possessions up from the lower decks, preparing to disembark. Sitting hunched over their luggage, they had to wait again, this time for Customs officials to visit the ship.

Hoping to pull rank and be first to disembark, the cabin passengers appeared in their finest clothes. No doubt they hoped to have privileged treatment from the officials by presenting themselves as a cut above the rest. Doctor Parker and the other professionals dressed formally in top hats and frock coats, while the ladies gave off a reek of stale lavender, having unpacked their best satins and silks for going ashore.

Confident that their class and good manners would carry the day, they had forgotten they were entering a largely classless society where a man's status was measured not so much by his pedigree as his purse.

Those who had travelled steerage now huddled together in silent clumps of human misery, their clothes and luggage tainted with the stink that seemed to get into everything below decks: the smell of the ship's bilges. Babies grizzled and children whined, bored and worn out by the long weeks at sea. Everybody longed to be ashore. Melbourne was greeting them with a chill breeze and a mist of rain which collected in fine droplets in their hair and seeped through their clothes.

Nor was the weather the only setback of the day. Instead of guiding the clipper through the rows of ships lying at anchor and depositing them at the quay as they expected, the captain announced that this was as far as the ship could go.

'I'm sorry but we can take you no further aboard the *Sally Lee*. If you look to starboard you will see waves breaking over the ridge of sand which blocks the entrance to Hobson's Bay –'

'So what do we do now, Cap'n?' a man spoke up, voicing the question in everyone's mind. 'Wait for high tide?'

'No. You'll be ferried ashore by boat, a few at a time.' Another groan went through the assembled company as the bad news was relayed. 'I must warn you also that the ferry-men expect to be paid. We have done our best to engage honest men who won't cheat you.'

Tully pulled another face and Maggi sneaked a glance at Da, wondering how he was taking this news. He would be loath to hand the last of their funds to some grasping ferryman. But Dermot appeared unconcerned. It took her no more than a moment to work out why. He was going to steal the money the family needed to get ashore. She could read his mind as accurately as if he'd spoken aloud, although she was far from ready to act as his accomplice. Today everyone was bound to be nervous and careful of their money. She frowned at Dermot, trying to warn him off, but he cleared his throat informing her he meant to do it anyway. Tully was quick to pick up on his sister's tension.

'What's wrong, sis? What is it now?'

'Shut up!' she hissed through clenched teeth, needing all her wits to concentrate on Dermot and the man he had selected as his quarry and whom she recognised as one of the doctor's friends. One of those who had sneered at her when she came seeking help for her mother. A typical remittance man, young and heavy-set, his addiction to the good things of life evidenced by a petulant lower lip and a pair of fishy, red-rimmed blue eyes. He was also uncommonly well-dressed which must have brought him to Dermot's attention. This and the way he drew a wad of money from an inside pocket and riffled it, smirking, when the captain informed everyone that the ferrymen expected to be paid. Gathering up his bags and preparing to leave, he tucked the money into his coat pocket in order to reach it more easily while he was handling his luggage. It never occurred to him that he was making it easy for someone to rob him as well.

Giving Maggi the signal to follow, Dermot wriggled his way through the crowd until he was standing directly behind the young man who ended up in the crush next to one of the nursemaids. She had her hands full, coping with luggage and controlling a spoiled, argumentative child. Dermot chose his moment with care, waiting until the Customs officials had left and people surged to the rail as the first of the ferrymen tied up alongside. He leaned forward, took a handful of the young woman's skirts and squeezed her bottom hard. Having done so, he turned aside, smiling at Maggi, drawing her attention to something on the horizon. The nursemaid whirled, looking for her assailant, her gaze settling on Parker's friend.

'Lecher!' she shouted, whacking him on the shoulder with her umbrella and making him wince. 'I'll teach you to lay hands on a defenceless woman!'

Maggi smothered a giggle as the nursemaid looked far from defenceless. She had muscular arms and was wielding her umbrella like a club. In the midst of the commotion, it was easy for Dermot to pick the man's pocket and pass the money to Maggi.

For a wild moment she hesitated, considering revenge. How like Da, to take it for granted that she would help him.

What if she were to fumble it and drop the money, allowing him to be caught? But the bank notes felt crisp and inviting and old habits die hard. It was easier to slip the money under her shawl and move away. No hue and cry followed her. Nor did Parker's friend think to complain. The last they saw of him he was looking red-faced and abashed, mortified by the woman's accusations. He wouldn't discover his loss until it was too late.

Gratified that it had been so easy to replenish his funds, Dermot elbowed his way to the front of the crowd, ready to strike a bargain with one of the ferrymen to carry himself and his family ashore.

While they were crossing the stretch of water to the beach beyond, Dermot pressed the boatman for local knowledge and in particular the quickest way to the gold fields. Dour and unwilling to talk, the boatman was ready to dismiss them as just another family of 'new chums'. But his tongue soon loosened when Dermot offered money in exchange for information. He warned them to stay away from the Buckland River area where there had been an outbreak of typhoid a few months before and advised them not to go up country to Spring Creek unless they were prepared to undertake a journey of many miles and face the possibility of running into bushrangers on the way. 'Lot of lawless men out there, sir,' he nodded, sucking on a rotten tooth. 'Just as happy to rob ye on the way to the gold fields as comin' back.'

Dermot nodded, only now beginning to realise the enormous distances involved. It was hard to come to terms with the size of the State of Victoria, let alone the whole continent. For the first time, Dermot felt a few pangs of misgiving. But the man went on to tell him that the nearest and most accessible gold fields were those at Ballarat, some seventy miles to the west of the city.

'Yes, you'll be quite at home there, sir,' he nodded, grinning. 'The fields are alive with Irishmen like yourself.'

Cheered by this news, Dermot became his old, ebullient self. The cockiness returned and he winked at Maggi, arousing Tully's suspicions.

'What's with him?' he whispered, nudging her. 'What's he got to be so cheerful about?'

40

'Nothing. Never you mind.' Maggi gave him a sharp jab in the ribs to silence him. It didn't.

'And in case you haven't noticed, I'm not a kid any more,' he said. 'And I wish you an' Da wouldn't treat me like one. Think I'm a fool, don't you? That I don't know what's goin' on? You an' Da – you've been at the thievin' again. What happened to all your promises, Mags? I thought you said you wouldn't do it no more? You were goin' to make a new start – that's what you said.'

'I know what I said, Tully,' she hissed. 'Will ye shut up, ye little gurrier? D'ye want the three of us arrested an' clapped in irons, the moment we set foot ashore?'

'So that's it. Why you an Da was so desperate keen to get off the ship. An' I never had time to see Jem an Hobley – not even to say goodbye.'

'Just as well. Tryin' to get you to sign on as crew.'

'Yes, an' you needn't think I'm through with it. Jus' because you don't think it's a good idea. I can wait. The *Sally* will be in port until Christmas at least.'

'Why?' Maggi frowned. This news made her uneasy.

Tully shrugged. 'If you'd taken the trouble to talk to the crew, you'd know.' And he stuck his nose in the air, pleased to have the advantage over his sister for once.

'Tell me,' she made as if to pinch him. 'Don't play games.'

'Why should I? Why should I tell you anything?'

'Tully!' She went for him again but he twisted away, avoiding her.

'All right then. The *Sally* won't leave 'til the wool clips are in. An' they don't even start to shear 'til the end of October, leavin' plenty of time for the crew to go up to the gold fields. The captain takes half the men while the Mate stays behind with the others to mind the ship. After a month or so they change places and the Mate goes up with the rest. An' after Christmas, when the ship's full and everyone's been to the diggings, the *Sally* will leave. That keeps everyone happy. The boys have a crack at the gold fields and the owners don't lose their crew.'

'I can see holes in that argument already. What if they strike it rich and never come back?'

'I dunno.' Tully shrugged. 'Jem didn't say.'

41

There was no time to discuss this further. By now, the ferryman was wading knee-deep in the water and yelling to some boys on the beach to help him haul his boat up on to the sands. Another boat pulled up alongside, full of ladies who looked at each other in consternation. Where were the trappings of civilisation? A set of steps or at least a ramp leading to a quay? Instead, they were to be set ashore on a beach, a considerable distance from the town itself. The ladies sighed and picked up their skirts, wishing someone had warned them not to wear their best clothes for coming ashore.

The beach was far from deserted. There was a hotel and they could see several drays and also a horse-drawn omnibus waiting to pick up travellers and convey them to the city. It was only three miles but the fees advertised were extortionate, particularly for the transportation of luggage. Women wept bitterly as their menfolk insisted on leaving boxes and precious pieces of furniture behind, some of them family heirlooms. It was hard, after bringing their possessions so far, to be obliged to desert them on an Australian beach. Witnessing these little family dramas, the McDiarmits found themselves at an advantage for once. With little to carry, they could make their way to the city on foot.

Beyond the narrow beach the surrounding countryside looked far from encouraging; a depressing wasteland of mud and swamp with here and there clumps of reeds and stunted trees unable to thrive in the marshy ground. By now the rain had abated and the sun came out, raising Maggi's spirits as it dried her clothes.

They approached the city from Princes Bridge, crossing a narrow, muddy-looking river which meandered on the last stages of its journey to the sea. Shrubs and tall trees crowded the banks which fell away steeply from the river; evergreens with thin, dark green leaves, the trunks of the trees smoother and whiter than silver birch, glistening in the sunlight.

But the outskirts were quickly forgotten as they made their way into the city itself. A place of space and so many contrasts, Maggi's head was spinning as she tried to absorb all the sights and sounds. Melbourne relied on the horse for transport; sturdy beasts with the energy to cover long distances over rough ground. She remembered someone telling her there was one horse to every two men in Victoria and she could well believe it. She saw drays piled high with goods being pulled by fierce-looking, long-horned cattle, yoked together in pairs. But horses dominated the scene. They were everywhere – pulling cabriolets, jingles and omnibuses with slatted seats where people could sit inside or on top – while weaving their way between the slower vehicles, whooping and yelling as if the devil were at their heels, rode wild men on horseback, careless of hazards or of the mud flying up from their horses' heels.

Maggi was bemused until her ears became accustomed to the level of noise. While the language on the streets was mostly English, she heard many different accents and speech in several other tongues, reminding her that the prospect of gold had attracted migrants from all over the world. There was the twang of America as well as the guttural speech of people from Europe which she didn't understand.

There weren't many women abroad on the streets but they seemed grand as princesses to Maggi, gorgeous as butterflies in their clean, brightly coloured clothes. Most carried umbrellas or parasols and wore matching bonnets that framed the face. To present themselves in the height of fashion, no expense had been spared and Maggi stared after them, longing to touch just the fringe of one of those jewel-coloured silk shawls. She looked down at her own shabby, much-mended clothes, stiff with sea-water now and in need of a wash. Dermot saw her, interpreting the look.

'An' ye needn't think you're goin' to get around dressed like that, however much money we make,' he muttered. 'Look at them, flauntin' themselves. No better than they should be, I'll be bound. Probably whores.'

'Shut up, Da. D'ye want them to hear you?'

'What if they do?'

But Maggi refused to let her father's miserly attitude dampen her spirits. Not today. Even the smells of the city seemed alien and exciting; a mixture of sweat, booze and cheap cologne with the occasional whiff of expensive tobacco blown in her face. And, underlying it all, the smell of horse manure, making her feel at home.

The streets were wide and built in straight lines, according to a plan, instead of being allowed to grow up higgledy-piggledy as in the cities of the old world. Two streams of traffic poured constantly in either direction, making it hazardous for pedestrians to cross. The McDiarmits hovered at the side of the road, screwing up the courage to venture into the traffic.

At mid-day the streets were both busy and overcrowded. It was hard to imagine that all this activity was confined to just one square mile and that in comparison with the established cities of Europe, Melbourne was still small. But, in spite of their haste, most people seemed friendly and outgoing, willing to give directions, exchanging a word or two and a smile.

The shopkeepers competed aggressively with their neighbours, some coming on to the streets to bark their wares. It was a city of contrasts and many influences, forced to grow up overnight instead of evolving over the centuries, a street at a time. Behind each great street was a lesser street running behind it – a tradesman's alley for goods and services. The shops were many and varied, most of them barn-like general stores; drapers vying with ironmongers to sell absolutely everything. Others pandered to the whims of those who had come back newly rich from the gold fields, offering expensive jewels set in gold and flamboyant clothes. It was a city of extremes where poverty and extravagance rode side by side. Everything was immediate, to be enjoyed now, with little concern for the future.

Flinders Street housed the ship's chandlers, saddlers and hardware merchants, catering for the more practical day to day needs, offering every piece of equipment for an onslaught on the gold fields. These were the shops that attracted Dermot, while Bourke Street was more interesting to Maggi, boasting the Post Office as well as most of the city's theatres and hotels. She knew Peggy and her friends must be somewhere nearby. Bourke Street was the hub of entertainment in Melbourne and where most people spent their money. She could have stayed there for hours just watching the passing parade.

The McDiarmits had to jump aside as a digger's wedding party clattered past in an open carriage, the groom tricked out in clothes so loud he would have been a figure of fun anywhere else in the world. He sported a checked coat and a waistcoat of brilliant red brocade, topped off with an expensive silk hat. The bride – fat, red-faced and smiling under her orange blossoms – resembled nothing so much as a massive wedding cake herself in a froth of lace flounces. Clearly, no expense had been spared. Beside themselves with laughter, as if the event were a huge joke, the couple scattered flowers and coins from the carriage as they went. Local urchins, used to the custom, rushed out into the thoroughfare, dodging horses and carriages, to seize the coins before they were lost in the mud.

After so many months of experiencing nothing but the sounds of the ship and the sea, the newcomers found the level of noise bewildering. Sometimes they fancied the ground heaved beneath their feet, deceiving them that they were still out on the open ocean aboard the *Sally Lee*.

The Post Office, situated at the busy intersection of Bourke and Elizabeth Streets, was a natural meeting place and clearing house. Sooner or later everyone must go there.

A large number of carriers and horse-drawn cabs were gathered outside it in the street, touting for trade. Among them were a few well-dressed gentlemen advertising for workers, hoping to divert some of the newcomers to more secure employment before they left for the gold fields.

'It's tough out there, fella. You'll be disappointed.'

'People die out there – nothing but flies and disease.'

'Why take a chance on the unknown?'

'Fair wages, good food and work on the land!'

Staying close to her father and Tully for fear of being swept away from them in the crowds, Maggi was distracted by a young man lounging beside his carriage. A country gentleman, obviously well to do, he was staring into the faces of the migrants, assessing them before he made an approach. Clean-shaven, apart from a well-trimmed moustache, his face was tanned and Maggi guessed he spent most of his life out of doors. His hair was dark and curled to his shoulders, fronds of it escaping from beneath a worn, broad-brimmed leather hat. To Maggi, he was everything she had ever dreamed about; the picture of young, healthy manhood. His

45

eyes, more than usually blue in a tanned face, sparkled with amusement as if he were laughing at the world and everyone in it. He had a wide mouth which broke into a slow, heart-stopping smile as his gaze connected with her own. He touched his hat in acknowledgement of her appraisal. Furious with herself for letting him catch her gaping, Maggi tilted her nose in the air and looked away, hoping her father wouldn't have seen the exchange.

'You, sir!' The young man placed himself squarely in their path, addressing himself to Dermot. 'You look like a sensible fellow with both feet on the ground. Surely you don't mean to drag your pretty young wife to the gold fields?'

Dermot's brows shot together as he glared at the man, looking him up and down. 'Wife? Maggi's not me wife – she's me daughter, you fool.'

'Is she now?' The young man stood his ground, continuing to smile into Maggi's eyes. 'That is good news.'

Dermot gave a snort of impatience. 'Good news for who? D'ye mean to stand there oglin' me daughter all day or let a man get about his business? An' if you're hopin' to sell me somethin', you're out of luck. Unless it's a pick or a shovel to take to the gold fields.'

'Oh no, not you, too,' the man groaned. 'I've been waiting for hours and there's no one who wants to come up and work on the property any more. We used to turn swaggies away but they're all gone now – off to the ruddy gold fields. I need one man at least – maybe two. Capable men who know their way around horses, cattle and sheep.'

'Well, I'm not your man.' Dermot continued to scowl. 'If nobody else wants to work for you, why should I?'

'Please, Da. Won't you jus' think about it?' Maggi laid a restraining hand on his arm. 'The more I hear about the gold fields, the less I like the idea. Sure an' wouldn't you rather work in the country again? There's nobody better with horses than you, an' I'd help.'

'Ye'll not flatter me into it, girl, if that's what you're about.' Dermot shook her hand away.

'Jus' listen to the man, why don't you? Hear what he has to say.'

'I tell you, he has nothing to offer me. I didn't come all

46

this way to go workin' meself to death for some other man. No, if I'd a mind to work on a farm, I could've stayed home. We're goin' to the gold fields. An' we'll stay there until I've dug enough gold to buy land o' me own.'

'I'm sorry, sir.' Maggi shrugged, smiling up at the man from under her lashes. 'He isn't to be persuaded. You can see how he is.'

While they were talking, Dermot stumbled forward crashing into the grazier; apparently shoved from behind. As a matter of course, the young man reached out to steady him, saving them both from ending up on the ground.

'Thank ye, sir, you're a gentleman. I'm much obliged,' Dermot grinned and turned to yell at someone over his shoulder. 'An' as for you – learn to look where you're going.' He lifted his cap as a gesture of farewell to the grazier and set off down the street at a brisk trot, taking it for granted that his children would follow.

'Da!' Maggi felt her cheeks burn. She wasn't ready to leave but she had no excuse to stay. Already, Dermot was yards away up the street, being swallowed up in the crowd. Tully seized her by the arm, almost jerking her off her feet.

'Come on, sis. We have to keep up or we'll lose him.'

Maggi looked back over her shoulder but the crowd had already closed in behind them and the young man was lost to view. She took her temper out on Tully, pinching him viciously instead.

'Ow! What's that for?' He stared at her, aggrieved, rubbing his arm.

'I jus' felt like it,' she snapped. Irritated with both her menfolk, she turned her attention to her surroundings instead. Like much of the city Bourke Street was an odd combination of old and new. Many of the newer buildings were built of local stone, solid edifices, three and four storeys high. To Maggi these temples of business were daunting as palaces with their stone pillars of biblical proportions and wide steps. Carriages stood at the kerb outside them, delivering and collecting the men of business, full of self-importance, who rushed in and out.

Alongside, looking more run down than ever in contrast with the glamour of the new, stood the buildings of the

47

pioneer days. Rough shanties, thrown up as a temporary measure and little better than the outbuildings of a farm, now leaning at impossible angles, looking ready to fall down. Again this mixture of wealth and poverty; the makeshift and make-do alongside the most modern of European design.

In the absence of a proper sewage system, the city had to rely on deep gutters to carry its refuse to the sea. Maggi didn't look too closely when she saw they contained dead cats and butchers' garbage in addition to cast off clothes. Mercifully they were moving swiftly after the rains.

But to Maggi even the drawbacks added to the romance of the city; the muddy streets, the makeshift wooden bridges across the flowing gutters. She could have stayed where she was for hours, content to watch the passing parade, but Dermot had other ideas. He was in no mood to let his family rest.

After spending one night in crowded, overpriced conditions, he announced that he had seen enough of the city and they would leave for the gold fields that very day. Already angry with him for rejecting work and security, Maggi seethed when he insisted on selling the last of her mother's good clothes. Even Shona's wedding ring had to go; it seemed he wanted nothing left to remind him of his loss. Tired and in low spirits, his children trailed in his wake as he walked the length of Flinders Street several times, checking and re-checking the prices in all of the hardware stores.

'They all charge the same, Da,' she told him through gritted teeth. 'You'll not get any bargains here.'

Just as she thought he would never buy anything, he discovered a soul mate; a fellow Irishman born and raised within miles of his childhood home. Delighted to come face to face with someone who knew the same places and people as he did, Dermot's defences were down. He trusted the man immediately, taking him at face value. Maggi wasn't impressed. She felt sure the man didn't know that part of Ireland at all; he would change the place of his birth to suit the customer standing before him. Nor did she like his smile which was too eager and too wide, showing a mouth full of sharp teeth. Her misgivings increased when she him draw Dermot to one side. She couldn't hear what they were saying

48

although she could tell, by the way they kept glancing her way, that she was the subject under discussion.

'What are they up to, those two?' she whispered to Tully, straining her ears. 'If I didn't know better, I'd think Da was trying to marry me off.'

'And what would the man want with a skinny rabbit like you?' Tully jabbed her in the ribs.

Dermot slapped the counter, raising his voice to show the private part of their discussion was at an end. 'I thank you, sir, for that last piece of advice an' I'll certainly bear it in mind.'

'You do that, sir.' The man's smile was sly as he glanced at Maggi. 'Take it from me, the gold fields are no place for a . . .' He let the unfinished sentence hang in the air as he realised she was watching him.

'What's he talking about?' Maggi pulled at her father's sleeve.

'Nothing.' Dermot scowled, shaking her hand away.

She watched as her father counted twelve whole pounds into the shopkeeper's waiting hands. Twelve pounds! To Maggi it represented a small fortune. Certainly, money didn't seem to go far on this side of the world. In return for this, the Irishman would supply them with a total 'outfit' for the gold fields, a wheelbarrow, a cradle, a crowbar, a water lifter, two zinc buckets, an axe, a tomahawk and several picks in addition to a bag of nails, tacks and a length of cord. For the business of day to day living, he provided a camp oven, an iron pot, a kettle, tin dishes and – most important of all – a large tent which had cost her father another seven pounds for that alone.

It was a daunting array of camping and mining equipment and represented the prospect of hard, back-breaking work. Maggi thought with longing of the blue-eyed young man and his farm, cursing the demon greed which was driving her father on towards the uncertainties and perils of the gold fields. But there was no point in dwelling on that. The grazier and his offer were long gone. She had seen diggers with money, yes, but by far the richest men she had seen were the shopkeepers; the owners of hardware stores. She was shocked by the amount of money her father had spent, almost without turning a hair. Where did it come from? To be sure, their fortunes had been boosted by the money from Doctor Parker's friend but, after paying the ferryman, there wouldn't be much of that left. And the journey wasn't over yet. There were still many miles of open country to be crossed to get to the gold fields. And now that Dermot had all this equipment he would have to pay for its transportation by bullock dray. And on arrival purchase a claim and a licence to mine. The shopkeeper mentioned this as an after-thought and only when Dermot had paid him and the money was safely put away in his till.

'Thirty bob a month it is now for a licence – an' I'd advise that you pay it, sir. Make sure you keep it up to date.'

'Licence? What do I want with a licence?' Dermot snapped his fingers. 'I don't give a fig for your Government men or their laws.'

'It's no joke, sir, to be sure. You must buy a licence at the same time as you stake your claim. There's troopers all over the gold fields checkin' papers all the time. Oh, yes. Some funny tales get back to us here. Miners locked up an' starved – some even flogged for trying to work a claim without payin' their dues.'

'Ah, so what?' Dermot was determined to be optimistic. 'I'll get me a crock full o' gold an' I won't give a tinker's cuss for their piddlin' licence fees.'

The man laughed, a little too heartily to sound sincere.

'That's the spirit, Mister McDiarmit, sir. Ah, well, no peace for the wicked, eh?' Out of the corner of his eye, he had seen another customer waiting for service. 'I wish you good-day an' may the luck o' the Irish go with you. Oh, an' bear in mind what I said . . . 'bout the girl.'

Outside the shop, Dermot sent Tully to buy them some pies from a nearby pieman while he counted what remained of his money. Maggi stood on tiptoe, trying to see how much he had left.

'Goodness, Da. After layin' out twelve pound for the hardware and another seven for the tent, I'm surprised you have that much left.'

'Don't be so nosy, my girl,' he growled, shoving the

remaining bank notes deep in his pocket. 'None of your business.'

'It is my business when I have to take the same risks.' Maggi paused, clapping her hands to her mouth as a horrible thought occurred to her as she remembered her father stumbling against the grazier and the young man reaching out to steady him, setting him back on his feet. It was the oldest trick in the world and she must have been blind not to have seen it. 'Aw, Jesus wept! Don't be tellin' me you stole it from that man? Ah, no, no.' And she folded her arms and bent double, rocking herself in her misery.

'Get a hold of yourself, girl. People are looking.'

'Oh, I could jus' die – the shame of it! The farmer who offered you work – you took it from him.'

'He'll never know. Besides, it was too good a chance to miss. You makin' cow eyes an' him lappin' it up.'

'I wasn't makin' cow eyes.'

'Could've fooled me,' Dermot grinned, trying to make light of it.

'It's not funny, Da. He'll know. He'll remember how it happened and know it was you.'

'So what? He's long gone, Maggi. You'll never set eyes on that one again.'

Far from being comforted by the thought, she lapsed into broody silence, refusing to be coaxed from it even by Tully who returned with pies so hot they were almost burning his hands.

'What's up? You two fightin' again?' He saw his sister's grim expression. 'What is it this time? What've I missed? Don't you want your pie?'

'No. I couldn't eat a thing.' Maggi wrinkled her nose. 'You can have mine if you like.'

'Thanks.' Tully needed no second invitation.

The McDiarmits were among the last to seek passage to the gold fields that day and while the bullocky waited outside the Post Office, touting for a few more goods to make up his load, Dermot packed his equipment aboard and set Tully to mind it.

Before Maggi had time to gather her wits or ask him where they were going, he seized her elbow and set off with

51

her at a brisk trot down the street. It was only when they arrived at Princes Bridge and she saw he was leaving the city that she broke free, turning to face him.

'Where are we going, Da? I won't go another step 'til you tell me.'

'Never you mind.' Dermot's eyes shifted and he refused to meet her gaze. 'Just you hurry along.'

'I will not. An' you may as well know this, too. I'm not goin' to the gold fields. Not unless you promise me . . .'

'To hell with you and your conditions! You've been a thorn in my side ever since your mother died.'

'Da!' She looked at him, stricken, the undeserved criticism leaving her stunned.

'In any case, I'm not takin' you to the gold fields.'

'What? What did you say?'

'I'm not takin' you to the gold fields. I've made other plans. It would've been different if your mam were alive but I can't be watchin' after you twenty-four hours a day. The gold fields are no place for a girl on her own, with no woman to mind her.'

'But I don't need someone to mind me, Da.'

'Maybe you do. I don't like the way you've been carryin' on of late – hangin' around with those dance hall girls.'

'Are you tryin' to read me a sermon, Da? That's a bit rich, comin from you.' Maggi narrowed her eyes. 'An' you the biggest shyster an' thief in all Ireland.'

'Shut up, will ye – shut the hell up!'

'I will not. I know you. This has nothin' to do with Peg an' the girls. It's about that grazier, isn't it? Are you mad at me 'cos I liked him or 'cos I chipped you for stealin' his purse?'

'Forget about the ruddy grazier.'

'I'd like to, Da, but you're the one keeps remindin' me. You're the one took his purse.'

'I told you to shut up!' Dermot pushed her forward again. 'An' hop it along, will ye? You're making me late.'

'You do realise you've left Tully alone back there in charge of all that stuff?'

'Tully's all right. He isn't the baby you think.'

'How do you know what I think?' She stopped again. 'You never listen to me.'

'Move!'

'No. Not 'til I know where I'm going.'

'Where I won't have to worry about you while I'm at the gold fields. A place where they take in homeless girls.'

'But I'm not homeless, am I? I have Tully an' you.'

'Not any more you don't. The fella at the hardware store was tellin' me how it works. He says folks do it all the time. Leave the girls while they go to the gold fields and pick 'em up on the way back.'

'If they ever get back.' Maggi stood her ground, folding her arms. 'Forget it, Da. I'm not going. I promised Mam I'd look out for Tully.'

'Oh, you'll like it well enough when you get used to it. They'll learn you how to cook an' keep house.'

'I don't want to learn how to cook and keep house. I'm a horsewoman and a sing –' She broke off. Any mention of singing would only strengthen his determination to leave her behind.'I don't want to be a stupid scullion.'

'Be a sensible one, then.'

'Please, Da.' Maggi felt the first stirrings of panic. 'Please don't do this to me. If you didn't want me, why didn't you let me go with Peg and the other girls? Don't leave me to rot in a stinkin' orphanage.'

''Tisn't an orphanage.' Her father's face set into stubborn lines. 'Told you, it's a place where they take homeless girls.'

Before she realised it, they had arrived. Dermot ushered her ahead of him to pass through a pair of tall wrought-iron gates. A drive curved away towards a house in the style of a Georgian mansion, set back in its own grounds and surrounded by tall native trees in addition to newly planted European saplings. Strong iron bars covered all of the downstairs and first-floor windows, ruining the lines of an otherwise handsome dwelling, making it look like an institution. Maggi shivered, wondering what the bars were for. To keep intruders out or the inmates inside?

'I can't leave Tully,' she said at last. 'Not without sayin' goodbye.'

'Tully's all right with me. It's time he took his place in a man's world. And do come on – that bullocky's not goin' to

53

wait forever. Chin up, Mags. One day you'll thank me for this.'

'I doubt it. It'll be a long time before I forgive you for this day's work.'

'Shut up now an' leave the talkin' to me,' he said as they mounted the steps to the front door.

Dermot picked up the brass doorknocker and rapped three times. The sound seemed to echo inside the house. Maggi stared around. She thought of running for it but didn't dare. Not in a strange place. They waited for several minutes and nobody came.

'That's it, then.' Maggi smiled. 'Nobody home.'

'Oh yes there is. There bloody well has to be!' Dermot picked up the doorknocker again, hammering loudly.

This time there was a response. There was a sound of heavy bolts being drawn back and the door opened a few inches to reveal a woman's face. It was small and pasty with a bright pink nose. She didn't look pleased to see them.

'What is it? What do you want?' she sniffed, unimpressed by the untidy pair on her doorstep. 'We give enough to charity already and we're expecting no visitors – not today.' Having delivered her standard speech, she attempted to close the door. Dermot was ready for it and caught it before she did, forcing it open enough to push Maggi inside. 'This here's Marigold McDiarmit – she's expected.' And after this vague introduction, he touched his hat and turned on his heel immediately, preparing to leave.

'Wait a minute, you!' the woman called after him. 'You can't just park a girl on our doorstep with no explanation. It's happened too many times before. There are formalities. Questions to be asked. Have the goodness to wait while I see Mother Bullivant. The girl could be an escaped convict, a Vandemonian for all we know.'

'Well, she isn't,' Dermot muttered, suddenly gruff with emotion.'She's a good girl is Maggi. Goodbye, sweetheart, I must be off.'

'But Da –'

'Don't call me that. I'm not your da and ye know it.'

Leaving Maggi speechless at this last betrayal, he left,

hunching his neck into his collar and almost stumbling down the steps in his haste to get away.

With a snort of disbelief, the woman slammed the door behind him, locked and bolted it. Maggi was trapped inside.

Chapter Four

Tully paced up and down outside the Post Office, looking into the blank, uncaring faces of passers-by. What should he do if his worst fears were realised – if Maggi and his father failed to return? Now that the bullocky had a full load, he was anxious to leave, saying he wanted to cover as much ground as possible before nightfall. He was checking the yokes and chains of the bullocks before setting off. Tully looked at the pile of luggage on the dray, wondering if he could identify his father's outfit from anyone else's and if the bullocky would be angry if he asked him to unpack. While he was plucking up the courage to do so, Dermot came back. The boy's relief lasted only a moment. His heart sank when he realised his father was alone.

'Where's Mags?' he said, seizing Dermot by the threadbare fabric of his lapels. 'What did you say to her this time? What did you do to make her savage enough to leave us?'

'She's safe enough, don't you fret,' Dermot released himself from the boy's grasp. 'Have to get used to it, son. It's you an' me from now on with no womenfolk draggin' us down. I carry no passengers this time – you're old enough to earn your keep. You can jus' buckle down an' do as you're told.'

'I will not. Not 'til I know what's happened to Mags.'

'Shut up? will ye? You're makin' a peep show of us.' Dermot glanced around, beginning to feel uneasy. 'People are lookin' at you.'

'Let them. I've done nothin' to be ashamed of. Which is more than can be said for some people round here.'

'Why you little . . .' Dermot raised his hand, expecting his

56

son to cringe away from it as usual. This time Tully faced him without flinching, standing his ground.

With his fees paid in advance and a full load, the bullocky didn't care if the McDiarmits accompanied him to the gold fields or not. Whooping and cracking his whip, he was shouting at his bullocks, urging them to move.

'Huss! Huss!' he yelled as the whip snaked out and cracked with a sound like a pistol shot over their heads. The leaders strained but nothing happened. Heavily loaded and having stood where it was for so long, the dray was firmly stuck in the mud.

'Come on, put your backs into it,' he jeered at the men who were trying to move it. 'You'll move bigger loads than that when you get to the gold fields.'

'Please, sir, will you wait a moment?' Tully caught the man's arm just as he raised it to give another crack of the whip. Deftly, the bullocky caught up his whip in one hand, swearing softly.

'Bloody hell, boy, that was a close one. Never get in the way of a bullocky's whip – I could've marked you for life. Out o' the way now. I have to get these buggers to move or we won't get away this side o' Christmas.'

'But we can't go yet – not without my sister. She's missing.'

The message was relayed to the other members of the party, most of whom groaned at the prospect of further delay.

'It's a mistake. There's nobody missing, sir.' Dermot didn't care to find himself at the centre of so much attention. 'The boy's raving – don't know what he's talkin' about.' Quickly, he dragged Tully aside where they could talk without being overheard. 'Shut your head, will ye? Showin' me up in front of everyone.'

'Fair go, you two,' the bullocky intruded. 'Make yer bloody minds up. I got to be off. Are you with us or not?'

Tully folded his arms, staring his father down. 'You can go to the gold fields or to hell in a basket, Da. I don't care. But I won't budge. Not 'til I know what's happened to Mags.'

'Ah, be reasonable, son. You saw how she was – takin' up with those dance hall girls, runnin' wild . . .'

'Oh, rubbish. Mags wasn't runnin' wild.'

'Well, she's safe enough for now. I left her at a refuge for homeless girls.'

'You did what?' Tully could hardly believe his ears.

'You heard. She's with a Mrs Amelia Bullivant on St Kilda Road. Very nice house it is, too. Maggi will like it there.'

'An orphanage! You left my sister at an orphanage!' Shocked into silence, Tully absorbed this news. But as he looked at his father again and saw the lines of grief etched heavily into his face, he gained some insight into Dermot's pain. Without his wife, his beloved Shona who had been the anchor and the only constant in his life, Dermot was lost. His eyes were rheumy from lack of sleep and a muscle twitched in his jaw. For the first time the boy could see beyond the jaunty, devil-may-care exterior his father showed the world, to the desperation and sorrow that lay beneath. He had nothing left. Nothing to live for but his quest for gold – his dream of striking it rich.

Tully looked around at the people who would travel with them to the fields. Granite-faced men who had suffered enough of life's disappointments to make them indifferent to the troubles of anyone else. Men who were callous if not cruel and who carried pistols and shotguns as naturally as most people carried picks and shovels. Some were accompanied by downtrodden women. Young girls in their twenties or maybe younger, already haggard and old before their time. Nothing but hard work awaited them at the gold fields. Was this what Tully wanted for Maggi? He couldn't bear to think of his bright-eyed, fun-loving sister, worn down by misery until she looked like one of these girls. Was it possible that Dermot had acted wisely this time? Maggi would be safe as if she were in a convent and he knew where she was. He would know where to look for her when he came back from the fields.

'Huss!' the bullocky yelled again, cracking his whip over the horns of his leading pair. 'Pull! Bluey! Lofty! Put your best feet forward you lazy bloody bastards!' And, without repeating himself, he went into a such a string of colourful oaths than even Tully had to laugh. The bullocks strained and the men grunted, heaving at the dray from behind. With a jolt which landed some of them in the mud, the wheels at last began to turn as the bullocks began to walk up the road.

Inside the house, Maggi ventured a cautious smile. It wasn't returned. Suspicious of newcomers, the housekeeper peered at the girl through a pair of steel-rimmed pince-nez, and sniffed. The woman looked half-starved; certainly she was no advertisement for the cook in this house. Her most arresting feature was her nose which seemed to drip all the time, making her look as if she had a permanent cold. She snuffled delicately, dabbing at the tip of it with a scrap of damp lace.

'Wait here while I go and check with Mother Bullivant,' she said. 'I have to make sure you're expected.'

Left in the hall, Maggi took stock of her surroundings, wondering what was going to happen when they found out she wasn't. Would she have time to catch up with Da if they tossed her out?

The atmosphere of the house was gloomy and oppressive, probably because the windows were surrounded with heavy drapes and the iron bars outside seemed to keep out a lot of light. And the house had a peculiar smell of its own. Later on she found out it was a mixture of eucalypt soap, beeswax, and a strong, tar-based disinfectant.

At the heart of the house was an imposing flight of stairs leading to the upper floors. Several corridors led away to other rooms, doors on either side. Conscious suddenly that she was being watched, Maggi saw faces peeping out from doorways the length of the house. A female voice barked an order, accompanied by a sharp clapping of hands and the faces disappeared as if by magic.

Having spent most of her life out of doors, Maggi felt stifled and out of sorts as the big house and its domestic odours crowded in on her. She had felt the same sense of panic in the early days aboard the *Sally Lee* when storms had raged overhead and the seamen closed all the hatches, trapping the steerage passengers in their quarters below.

Born and raised in a tinker's wagon, 'home' to Maggi revolved around people rather than places and she didn't care to spend too much time indoors. Apart from occasional visits to church, this was the first time she had been inside a house of this size and she was at first overawed by her surroundings. She tilted her head to look up at the high ceiling and marvelled at the etched glass window on the landing halfway up the stairs, depicting a stag at bay. She was still admiring the brass oil lamps with their pretty, cut glass shades when the woman returned, heralding her arrival with a blast of lavender water and a loud sniff.

'Just as I thought,' she said. 'Mother Bullivant knows nothing about you. No wonder that man was so eager to leave you and get away. Who are you to him, then? An unwanted niece? A step-daughter he can't be bothered to keep?'

Take your pick, Maggi thought, unwilling to satisfy the woman's curiosity. She sniffed again, peering at Maggi from behind her pince-nez.

'And a vixen, too, I suppose. With a temper to match that red hair. I told Mother Bullivant you were a lost cause – far too bold to make a good servant – but she'll keep you, anyway. A saint is that woman. Far too generous for her own good. An' taking you in against my advice, you might as well know. Go on.' She jerked her head in the direction of the lower stairs. 'Matron will give you a wash before turning you loose on the other girls. This is a clean house and we'll have no vermin here.'

'I don't have nits if that's what you mean.' Maggi resisted the childish temptation to stick out her tongue.

'Irish, too. I might have guessed.' The woman gave another aggrieved sniff. 'Full of mischief as a cartload of monkeys and always hard to place.'

For Maggi this was the last straw. Disowned by her father and despised by this ugly woman, her temper flared.

'Yes! I am Irish and proud of it. And if I'm not good enough for this place, I'll be only too happy to take my leave.' So saying, she squared her shoulders and marched to the door, expecting the woman to open it. Instead, she gave Maggi a thin smile.

'Not so fast, missie. Here you are and here you'll stay – until you learn how to be a good servant and earn your keep. I am Mother Bullivant's cousin – Miss Prunella to you. Now, get on downstairs. I'll have to look out some new

60

clothes. Those rags of yours won't last a turn in the tub. They'll have to be burned.'

'Indeed an' they won't! Don't you know it's bad luck to burn a travellin' woman's clothes?'

'I don't care about your heathenish gypsy ways. You'll do as you're told. 'Once again the woman took out her scrap of lace to catch another drip which was forming at the end of her nose. Prune by name and prune by nature, Maggi thought as the woman shepherded her towards the bathroom where the Matron awaited her.

Half an hour later, she felt as if she had been pulled through a mangle and back again. The Matron and Miss Prunella had combined forces to scrub her from head to foot. Her hair stood on end, defying gravity and crackling with a life of its own. Her scalp tingled from the matron's attentions with a fine-toothed comb. And she had lost the battle to keep her clothes.

At last, prinked to Miss Prunella's satisfaction and dressed in the same dull uniform as the other girls, she was thought fit to present herself to Mother Bullivant.

After a long and boring wait in a draughty corridor outside the woman's study, Maggi was summoned by the ringing of a small handbell and a crisp order: 'Come in!'

She opened the door and paused on the threshhold, realising at once that she would have to alter her ideas. Indeed, for a moment it crossed her mind that she had knocked on the wrong door. With Miss Prunella for a role model, she was expecting someone much older – a fat widow perhaps or another dried up spinster. But this woman was beautiful, elegant as a duchess in an afternoon gown of the finest grey silk. And she was young, possibly no more than thirty years old. Her thick, honey-coloured hair was gathered into a shining coif at the back of her head and, the only concession to her widowed status, a tiny cap of black lace-perched on top of her head. Fine-boned and even-featured, she had one of those luminous, naturally perfect complexions, her eyes huge and pansy brown in a heart-shaped face. She smiled, enjoying Maggi's expression of stunned amazement. She liked taking people by surprise.

'So.' She stood up and came from behind her desk to walk

around Maggi, inspecting her and speaking in a voice so husky and deep it was like the purr of a contented cat. 'You're the one who's been raising the roof with your cries and ruining the peace of the afternoon. Rarely have I heard such pithy expressions from the mouth of a female. Where did you learn them? On the docks? And was it really necessary to make so much noise?'

Sullenly, Maggi raised her eyebrows and twitched a shoulder. She had fought hard to retain her clothes, unable to make the Matron understand why she wanted to keep them. They were her last link with her past, with the Maggi who used to be. It had taken the combined force of both Miss Prunella and Matron to wrest them from her and while she was floundering in the tub, her clothes had been whisked away and fed to some fire in the bowels of the house. Now she looked like all the others, a slight figure in schoolgirl gingham, a crisp white pinafore covering all but collar and sleeves. Unfortunately, the dress she had been given was too small. The sleeves cut painfully into her armpits and the bodice crushed her breasts. Whether she had done it on purpose or not, Miss Prunella had looked out a dress more suitable for a twelve year old. For now the starched white pinafore concealed its shortcomings and the uniform was completed with a pair of stiff housemaid's cuffs.

Maggi hated the place already. Too angry and upset to pretend a meekness she didn't feel, she returned Mother Bullivant's searching looks with interest as soon as she got over her initial surprise. The woman raised her eyebrows, quick to recognise a rebel; an unwelcome boldness which would have to be crushed. She returned to her position behind her desk, no longer smiling.

'You'll do, I suppose – except for that hair. Far too distinctive and uncontrolled. It will have to come off. Go back to Matron and tell her I want it shorn.'

'No!' In a defensive gesture, Maggi raised her hands, to hide as much as she could of the offending locks.

'And for goodness' sake, learn to show some respect. Nobody likes a servant who stares all the time. Lower your eyes and study the floor when I'm speaking to you.'

'Yes, miss.'

From a drawer on her desk the woman produced a riding crop and thrashed the edge of the desk to emphasise her words. Maggi flinched at every stroke, cursing herself for underestimating Mother Bullivant, assuming a gentle nature because of her beauty and the muted elegance of her clothes. While she had the outward appearance of one, she was no lady at all but a martinet who enjoyed lording it over the unfortunate girls in her charge. Her dark eyes were now snapping with temper and Maggi sensed she was waiting for only the slightest of reasons to beat her or cut off her hair.

But Maggi was a survivor; her instinct for self-preservation was finely honed. So she changed tactics immediately. Her shoulders slumped, her lips trembled and she screwed up her eyes in the hope of squeezing a tear.

'Oh, please, miss – Mother Bullivant – don't let the matron cut off me hair. I'll plait it up real small an' hide it under a cap. You'll not see so much as a wisp, I promise. An' I'll be good – good as gold – I'll do anythin' you want. But please, please, don't cut off me hair.'

'That's good. We understand one another at last. Mother Bullivant gave a small, tight smile. 'Not so difficult, is it? Behave yourself and you may keep your hair. But cause me so much as a moment's disquiet and I'll order Matron to shave your head. You'll serve as an example to other wayward girls.'

Maggi breathed a little easier, realising she'd had a narrow escape. She must learn to guard her tongue and keep her thoughts to herself. This woman was dangerous and probably enjoyed being cruel.

'And don't even think of rebellion because I shall know it!' Once more the woman thrashed the edge of her desk with her riding crop. 'Here at Bullivant House we live by the strictest of rules. Discipline is our watchword – without it no girl can go out into service and survive. I guarantee that my girls will make docile, biddable servants. My clients pay dearly for this assurance and have the right to expect the best.'

'They *pay* you? Are you saying you sell your girls into service?'

'Of course. How else can I keep this charity going?

Maintain this enormous house? Each and every girl has to pay her way. Most of them arrive here as you did – dirty, lousy, and with the reek of steerage in their clothes. I dress them decently, train them, and send them out into the world to earn a living as useful members of the servant class. Isn't it reasonable that I expect to be paid?' She glanced at the clock. 'You can go now,' she said, losing interest and already turning her back. 'Go back to Miss Prunella and tell her I've allotted you a bed in Dormitory Five.'

Hamish didn't remain outside the Post Office for long, once the Irishman and his family had left. A rebuff from such grimy immigrants was a blow to his pride and he lost heart at once, cursing himself for wasting his time. How galling to come all the way to Melbourne only to find out his brother was right. Gold fever seemed to have infected everyone. Nobody wanted to do an honest day's work any more. Not when they could go to the gold fields and make a fortune overnight by ripping it out of the ground.

And he couldn't forget that red-haired girl, the man's daughter. The girl with a face like a flower, in spite of her drab grey shawl and dirty, faded clothes. She seemed to dance through the labyrinths of his memory, mocking him further. So eager and full of life, so different from the dull, perfectly dressed young ladies who were his sister's friends. And Hamish loved red hair, especially hair like hers which refused to be tamed, curling in the light rain which was still in the air; a fiery flame rather than a chestnut or gold.

Why should he feel so drawn to her? Was it just the eagerness of her expression, the naivety that intrigued him? Brief as their meeting had been, he felt she was vital and attractive – unspoiled. She wouldn't take second best or allow the world to crush her because she was poor. He liked her directness, too. The way she appraised him honestly without being coy. Had the choice been left to the girl instead of her oafish father, he would have been travelling up country right now with not one but three good workers to lend a hand at Lachlan's Holt. Instead, he would have to go home alone, admitting defeat. Be damned to her idiot father and his one-eyed pursuit of gold; the wretch had whisked the girl away before Hamish could even ask her name. She was there one moment and gone the next, leaving nothing but a memory of the longing in those warm, honey-coloured eyes.

You're a great fool, Hamish McGregor, he told himself, *mooning over a slip of a girl. You need some light-hearted entertainment and most of all a drink; something to buck you up before setting off home.* Home, where he would have to face up to his brother and say he was right. There was no one willing to labour for wages on a country property, not in these times. His brother would make the most of it, too. He could already see the expression on Callum's face as he said: *'I told you so.'*

Today even the simplest of pleasures eluded him. He went to several bars and left without buying anything, sickened by the 'spit an' sawdust' atmosphere and the sight of too many men, drunk with their success as much as cheap 'nobbler'. The bars were all the same, full of diggers returning from the gold fields, swaggering in and shouting the bar, lighting their pipes with pound notes to prove they had money to burn. Men who perpetuated the myth that the streets of Bendigo and Ballarat must be strewn with nuggets of gold. These were the lucky ones; the ones who inspired the newcomers, making them think it was easy. That gold would be there for the taking, free and for all.

Hamish squinted in the smoky atmosphere, in no mood for such third-rate entertainment; the middle-aged women who danced on the tables in high-heeled boots, flapping their smelly skirts around mottled thighs.

In the end he went to one of his usual haunts – Harry Napier's Silver Star. Here the drinks were expensive but it was worth it. Harry served no 'rot gut' here, none of the cheap 'nobbler' they served in other bars – a rough brandy which couldn't be swallowed unless it was watered and sweetened with sugar. Harry's beer was well-kept, his whisky pure and his dancers on the right side of thirty. An enterprising cockney, Harry had transported himself, his daughter and his talents from London to take advantage of the money to be made by keeping a good hotel while the rush was on.

Hamish leaned at the bar, swallowed two whiskies in quick succession and paid for them with a coin in his trouser pocket. The whisky warmed his stomach but he was still depressed and, disappointingly, sober.

'Well, well, if it isn't Hamie MacGregor himself – I didn' know you was in town!' The greeting came from a tall, dark-haired girl who slung an arm across his shoulder in a sisterly gesture. She dimpled but didn't give him a kiss. This was Harry's daughter, Jinks. She and Hamish were old friends. She peered at him, pulling a face in a parody of his glum expression. 'Wassamatter, luv? Look as if you've lost a shilling an' found a button. Why not buy Auntie Jinks a drink an' you can tell her all about it?'

'I'll buy you a drink, yes.' He smiled, stroking her bare arm, sensual enough to enjoy the silky texture of her skin. He was fond of Jinks and they shared the same birthday, both aged twenty-two. It created a bond between them, although his affection for her had never been other than brotherly; that vital spark which might have led further was missing – perhaps because they were too alike. 'Long as your daddy doesn't give you lolly water and charge me for a glass of champagne.'

She wriggled her shoulders, pursing full red lips into a rosebud. 'Now, Hamish, would my daddy do that?'

'Yes, he would.' He ran a finger down her nose. 'And justify himself by saying he was keeping his daughter from ruining herself with the drink.'

'Oh, I like to keep ruin and drink well apart.' She dimpled again. 'Are you buyin' then, you mean old Scottie, or do I have to go flutter my eyelashes at somebody else?'

'Don't go, Jinks. I need you to cheer me up.'

'Out of sorts, Hamie? That's not like you.'

Hamish sighed. 'I know it sounds petty and stupid but I told my brother that while I was here, I'd pick up a few extra hands. He said I'd get no one and he's right. But I hate the idea of going back home and saying so.'

'Oh, is that all?' Jinks', face fell. 'I thought it would be somethin' juicier than that. You look – oh, I dunno.' She considered him, head on one side. 'Like a bloke who's been given the runaround by a girl.'

'Come on, Jinks. This is Hamish, remember? I'm the one who gives girls the runaround.' And he laughed a little too heartily, haunted by a vision of red hair, twisting itself into a thousand ringlets in the damp air.

'Laugh all you like but I know you – well as I know myself.' Jinks narrowed her eyes at him. 'Underneath all that swash and buckle there's a warm heart, jus' waitin' for the right girl to come an' claim it.'

'Romantic fiddlesticks! Have you had your nose in one those penny dreadfuls again? I should've known it was a waste of time, teaching you to read. Ouch!' he yelped as she picked up a lock of his dark brown hair and tugged it fiercely. 'And in any case, you're wrong. I'm my own man. A free spirit. The girl doesn't exist who can tame the MacGregor.'

'Famous last words. I wouldn't go temptin' fate if I was you – the devil has long ears.' Jinks wagged a finger and dimpled again, giving him her special Mona Lisa smile. Really, she used it to hide a broken tooth. She was self-conscious about the tooth, thinking it marred her good looks, but in fact it softened an otherwise sharp little face, making her human and vulnerable. 'Come on, then. Are you buying or not?'

Hamish smiled and patted his pockets, looking for his wallet. His smile faded as he discovered it wasn't there.

'Would you believe it? I've had my pocket picked.'

'Yes, I would. In the midst of this lot! Lose much?'

'No, thank the good Lord.' He laughed shortly. 'Only some pocket money of my own. I banked the money from the station, soon as I got into town.'

'No harm done then. *C'est la vie*, as they say in France.' Jinks had picked up one or two French expressions from visiting dancers and she used them often, thinking it chic. 'Drinks on the house this time then.'

'That little red-haired devil and her father. . .' Hamish murmured, half to himself. 'Would you believe it? She really took me in.'

'So there was a girl.' Jinks was triumphant. 'I thought as much. I knew there had to be girl in it somewhere.'

Chapter Five

Dormitory Five was an attic built into the roof, originally intended as space for the storage of trunks and other unwanted household items. Ordering Maggi to follow, Miss Prunella hitched up her skirts, revealing a pair of well-worn black boots as she mounted the narrow, twisting staircase to the top of the house. The loft was so cramped that not even a small girl like Maggi could stand erect without bumping her head on a crossbeam. Cold and draughty at this time of year and probably a sweat-box in summer, it had one small window which overlooked the back yard of the house, including the vegetable garden and privy. So high from the ground, this was the only window in the house not protected by iron bars.

'I should come up here more often,' Miss Prunella muttered, frowning at the general disorder of the room; the unmade beds and frowzy smell of sheets which hadn't been changed for several weeks. She flung open the window and the wind caught it immediately, letting in a blast of fresh air. While the woman struggled with the window, trying to close it again, Maggi looked for possible ways of escape. A drainpipe near the window seemed promising until she saw it was unsafe, already detaching itself from the wall. There was a large native eucalypt, growing so close to the house that bunches of its sickle-shaped leaves could tickle the eaves but the upper branches looked too thin and brittle to bear any weight. A fall to the ground from this height would mean certain death.

But, for the next hour or so, Maggi was kept too busy to

think of escape. She had to learn all the rules and regulations of Bullivant House.

Miss Prunella showed her to her sleeping quarters; a narrow iron bed with a lumpy mattress, in the darkest corner of the room. Maggi looked at it with longing, hoping for supper and an early night at the end of such a long day. Miss Prunella had other ideas, announcing that she was to begin her training right away. Together with one of her room mates from Dormitory Five, she was on 'water duty' tonight. Maggi had been looking forward to meeting the other girls in the hope of making some friends but this one looked far from promising and her scowl deepened when she heard she was to work with Maggi and show her what to do.

'Another new girl, Miss Prue?' She wrinkled her nose. 'Why does it always have to be me?'

'You, Ginny? Because you do it so well!' Miss Prunella's mean, boot-button eyes snapped behind her spectacles. With a final sniff, she departed, leaving the girls to get acquainted.

Equally cautious, they eyed one another without saying much as they collected pitchers from the dining room to be filled with drinking water for the table. Maggi was surprised to see the pitchers filled from a store of water in barrels, rather than a well. The other girl rolled her eyes and sighed at Maggi's questions, probably because she had answered them so many times before.

'Water's expensive in Melbourne so we have to be careful with it. A water carrier brings it to the house in barrels.'

'Like ale?'

'I suppose. Local water costs one an' sixpence a barrel and Ma Bullivant grudges every penny she spends on it. Different if it's for herself. She'll spend up to six shillin' a barrel on spring water for herself.'

'Six shillings? For one barrel of water?'

'Spring water. Comes a long way. From the Dandenong Hills.'

'And water for washing? Do they have to buy that as well?'

'Uhuh.' The girl shook her head. 'Rain water. Collects in a tank at the back of the house. That's the next job. We have to cart it through to the kitchens an' bedrooms in covered pails. Come on, better get started – you'll get the hang of it as we go.'

So Maggi spent the next hour or so lifting pails of water up and down corridors and long flights of stairs to fill the water jugs in the bedrooms and dormitories.

'An' this isn't the end of it,' the girl smirked, passing on more bad news. 'We'll have to carry the slops down again in the morning. An' make sure you have the lid tight on the pail and don't spill any on the stairs – I don't want to slip an' break me ruddy neck.'

By the time every jug in the house had been filled, including the elegant set of white porcelain decorated with cornflowers in Mrs Bullivant's room, Maggi's back ached and her legs were trembling, threatening to let her down. She let go a long sigh of relief when the last pail was hung up on the hooks outside the back door.

'That's it, I'm done,' she said, sinking down on the back step. She closed her eyes, resting her aching head against the wall.

The girl folded her arms, shaking her head at Maggi's lack of stamina. 'You'll have to do better than this or you'll never last.'

'I don't care,' Maggi whispered. She could have made excuses, saying she was fresh off the boat and didn't have land legs yet but she didn't want to say too much to this unsympathetic girl. 'Jus' let me sit for a minute. It's so lovely out here – so peaceful and cool.'

'Cool? I'd say it was cold.' The other girl shivered, hugging herself against the chill of late-afternoon. 'An' Cookie won't leave us for long. She'll come out yellin' for us in a minute, wantin' to know where we are.'

'She might think we're still upstairs,' Maggi said, frowning at the back gate. Heavily chained and padlocked, it seemed to be the only exit in a solid, seven-foot wall.

'Not her. Sharp as a needle she is. Counts the minutes it takes for someone to go to the privy. Come on – better go in. If she catches us sittin' down, she'll only find somethin' more for us to do.'

'In a minute.' Maggi was in no hurry to go back inside; to the kitchen, which reeked of boiled winter cabbage, damp wash cloths and the pungent smell of disinfectant, strong enough to bring tears to the eyes. 'I hate it here, it's like being in prison.'

'You'd know, would you?' The girl's smile was wry as she relaxed, sitting down beside Maggi on the back step and hugging her skirts around her knees.

'Cheer up, darlin', you'll soon toughen up. A week or two an' you'll have muscles like mine!' And she adopted the classical boxer's pose, bending her arm and bunching her fist to show Maggi her muscles. 'No rest for the wicked, eh? Laundry duty tomorrow.'

'Laundry duty? What's that?'

'Ooh, you'll love it. Soapsuds up to the elbows and blue all over your hands.'

'Wonderful. I can't wait.' Maggi pulled a face. 'Go on. I may as well know the worst. I wouldn't like to think I was going to be bored.'

'Fat chance.' The girl grinned, studying Maggi through narrowed eyes. 'Irish, aren't you?'

'So?' Maggi nodded, giving her a sharp glance.

'Thought you was. You have that sort of untamed look about the eyes.'

'Oh? An' what would you mean by that?' Maggi drew herself up, unsure if she was being insulted or not.

'I dunno, but I'd change it if I was you. Don't pay to give any sauce around here. Show a bit o' spirit an they'll thrash it out of you. An' stay out of Bullivant's way, as much as you can.'

'I will,' Maggi nodded, the unpleasant interview fresh in her mind.

'What part of Ireland d'you come from? Where's home?'

'Never really had one. We was always on the move.'

'Gyppos! I thought so.' The girl clapped her hands, delighted with this morsel of information. 'No wonder ole Bitchface has it in for you, then. Irish and a gypsy, too.'

'We weren't gypsies.' Maggi ground out the words through clenched teeth.

'No?' The girl sounded disappointed. 'What a shame. I was hopin' you'd tell me fortune.'

'Well, I can't.'

71

'Oh, go on. See if you can anyway.' She shoved a small chapped hand under Maggi's nose.

Maggi pushed it away, refusing to look. 'I can't. We were travellin' folk, I tell you. Not gypsies at all.'

She crossed her fingers in her skirts to make amends for the lie. Her mother's family *were* Romany. She recalled a summer's evening long ago when she was small and her world seemed safe and secure. The air had been filled with the scent of mid-summer blossoms and the musky smell of walnut brown men and women in bright clothes the colour of autumn leaves. Her mother's people. A smiling, happy band of gypsies, delighted to make the acquaintance of Shona's little girl and taking turns to swing her high in the air, making her squeal.

'What then?' the girl interrupted her reverie.

'If you must know, my da used to break and sell horses. You could say he was ...' Maggi hesitated, searching for something that sounded respectable. 'A travellin' veter'nary.'

'You could say that,' the girl smirked. She had noticed the pause. 'More likely he was a horse thief an' a drunk.'

This was so uncannily accurate that Maggi didn't know what to say. Instead, she stared at the wall again, wishing herself anywhere in the world but here. The situation was bad enough without having to endure the teasing and casual malice of this girl whose spiteful nature was clearly reflected in her face. By no means a natural beauty she must have seen far too much of the world at an early age. Deep lines of discontent were scored between her brows and although she was probably only the same age as Maggi, she had early crow's feet around the eyes. Dark, shrewd little eyes like those of a monkey and set close together over her nose. But, surprisingly, this mean little face was attached to a classical female figure which even the uniform of the institution couldn't hide. A fairy with a wicked sense of humour must have been at her christening, to give the girl the body of a Venus and a wizened monkey's face.

She was leaning forward now, assuming from Maggi's silence and bleak expression that she was having an attack of the sulks.

'Aw, come on, don't be like that – don't take the hump.

72

''S nothin' personal. I tease everyone jus' to see what they're made of. The name's Ginny – Ginny Luckett.' And she offered her hand, ready to make amends. 'They used to call me Lucky Luckett but I think my luck ran out when I fetched up here. No hard feelings, eh? Call it quits an' start over?'

Not yet smiling, Maggi accepted the work-roughened hand, small and leathery as a monkey's paw.

''S all right, I won't bite,' Ginny laughed at Maggi's hesitation. 'Come on then. Give us yer name.'

'Marigold – Maggi McDiarmit.'

'Maggi it is, then. Well, Maggi McDiarmit, which of your carin' ever lovin' rellies cast you adrift to end up here?'

Already aware that Ginny was one of those who liked to gather information only to use it against you later, Maggi was hesitant to confide in her. But she needed to unburden herself to someone. So she sketched a brief outline of her life in Ireland, the journey, and touched briefly on her mother's death although she allowed Ginny think it was something that had happened a long time ago. But in the end her tongue ran away with her and she concluded with a tirade against her father which left her breathless and close to tears.

'Jus' wait 'til I catch up with Da. I'll give him a right rollickin' for dumpin' me here.' She tossed back her hair and swallowed hard, determined not to break down and give way to tears in front of someone who would only laugh at them. 'So that's it. Now it's your turn. How do you come to be here?'

'Ooh, there's not much to tell.' Ginny shrugged, far less inclined to talk about herself. 'I've no family – no one who wants to know, anyway. Nobody gives a damn who belongs to who when you live in the city.'

'What city?'

'London, o' course. Is there any other? Ho, they'd like to call Melbourne a city but they're kiddin' themselves. If I'd known it was this small, I wouldn't have come. I was a bounty migrant, you see.'

'A bounty migrant? What's that?'

'Don't know nothin', do yer? An assisted passenger. Some couple agreed to pay me fare. They wanted a maid an' I needed . . . well, jus' say I needed to get out of London in rather a hurry.'

'Why?'

'Never you mind. The ship was delayed an' when it finally got here, the couple never turned up. Left us standin' on the docks, me an two other girls. I didn't care. I never meant to stay with them anyway. But before we had time to get our bearings an' make ourselves scarce, we was rounded up an' bundled off here. In moral danger, that's what they said – too young to be left to fend for ourselves.' Ginny grinned, jabbing her in the ribs. 'I think they was afraid we'd go on the game. Gawd preserve us from nice ole ladies with good intentions.'

Suddenly, this seemed so funny to them that they both bent double, roaring with laughter until Ginny turned red in the face and started to cough. It was a bad cough which seemed to come from the bottom of her lungs, leaving her fighting for breath. When she was done, she wiped her face in her apron, exhausted. The girl was ill, although she was doing her best to conceal it.

'That's a horrible cough. Have you had it for long?' Maggi spoke gently, half-expecting to have her head bitten off.

'You won't tell?' The girl clutched at her wrist, for the first time less than confident. 'Promise me – promise you'll keep it to yourself? I won't get a decent place if they find out I'm sick.'

'Of course I won't tell. But if you're sick, don't you think you should get some help? Ask to see a doctor, maybe?'

'No!' Ginny snapped, pursing her lips.

'We could leave, you know.' Maggi's mind was still running on the idea of escape. 'It can't be all that hard to get away.'

'No? See that wall? A good seven foot an' shards of glass on the top. Cut you to ribbons, if you try.'

'What about the front gate? That isn't locked.'

'No. But the front door is and so are the side doors. Jus' pray there's never a fire – we'd be roasted alive. The back door's the only way out of the house. They have to leave that open to let us get to the privy.'

Maggi heart sank at this news. The house was even more of a fortress than she thought.

Involved in getting acquainted, the girls had lost all track of time. Both started as the back door was wrenched open behind them to reveal the cook glaring down at them, her eyes red-rimmed and sore from working in a stuffy kitchen over a smoking stove.

'Ginny Luckett! I might've known it was you. I suppose you thought you was through for the night? Well, you're not. An' if you an' your friend are so keen on my steps you can scrub them down for me now. I'll look out a pair o' scrubbin' brushes and a cake o' soap.'

Chapter Six

After a day of listening to Dermot's grumbles that he could have piled his goods into a wheelbarrow and run them to the gold fields in half the time it would take with the bullocks and dray, Tully closed his ears and stayed out of the way. He was wretched enough without hearing his father's endless cycle of complaints.

The bullocky had promised that his team could cover the distance of seventy miles in five days if the weather was fair. He neglected to tell them how long it would take if the weather was foul. The skies opened to release a deluge on the unfortunate travellers, many of whom weren't dressed for the rain. And, worse, it was accompanied by a biting wind which seemed to come directly from the Antarctic, penetrating their clothes and chilling them to the bone. Clear of the city, the so-called 'highway' became a rough track through the bush, littered with rocks, dead branches of eucalypt and unseen holes in the ground.

Although the weather reminded Tully of some of their travels across Ireland, the surrounding countryside did not. It was strangely silent, perhaps disapproving of these newcomers who came to wrench the wealth from the soil; a sombre, ancient land which had remained untouched for centuries. The rugged landscape of the hinterland seemed full of hidden menace and Tully was relieved to be travelling with someone who knew where they were going. Alone he was certain that he and his father could have wandered from the track, to be lost forever in the vastness of the Australian bush. His misgivings returned when they travelled for hours without seeing any sign of human habitation as they tramped across mile after mile of rough, unoccupied land. Apart from the beaten track which was littered with broken wagon wheels and other evidence of travellers' misfortunes, the landscape appeared to be undisturbed.

'Where is everybody?' he whispered half to himself as he gazed at the tracts of open land either side of the track, surrounded by squat, sloping hills in the distance, covered with dark green primeval forest and looking still more forbidding in the rain.

They passed through an area which had been scorched by bush fire some months before and was now recovering, the growth more vigorous than in the land that had escaped. Lush new grasses and sturdy saplings were growing up between the blackened remains of old trees and acacias were coming into flower alongside the creek, giving off a powdery sweetness that was almost cloying, making some people sneeze.

It was here that they made their first camp for the night, sheltering from the showers as best they could under the trees. Some people grumbled at the bullocky for calling a halt to the day's travel while it was still light, but he ignored them. He cared more for the comfort of his bullocks than the travellers' complaints, preferring to stop where the water was pure and there was sufficient pasture for the animals to graze.

Amused by the newcomers' futile attempts to build a fire in the rain, the experienced bushmen showed them how it was done. They protected the fire by building it small and in the shelter of a large piece of bark supported on sticks. Tully jumped back, dismayed by the sight of a large brown spider running back and forth, trapped on the bark. One of the men saw him and laughed.

''S only a huntsman, mate. Not gonna hurt yer. It's the littleuns – the redbacks – you gotter look out for.'

Tully smiled but he watched the spider until it shrivelled, overcome by the heat. The fire smoked wickedly at first, giving off the pungent rather antiseptic smell of wet eucalypt, but as the timber dried out and the natural oils allowed it to catch, it provided enough heat to fry bacon and eggs and boil the billy for the hot, sweet tea so beloved of men in the bush. Tantalised by these appetising smells, Tully tried to ignore his growling stomach as he munched on a piece of stale bread and the crust of a pie. Assuming there would be plenty of wayside inns to cater for their needs, Dermot had neglected to buy any food. With the insatiable appetite of a growing boy, Tully went to bed hungry and ill-tempered, wondering where his next square meal would be coming from.

The rain abated at last, allowing the travellers to dry their clothes before settling down for the night. In spite of the lack of comfort, they were exhausted enough to sleep. Tully lay there, breathing in the smells of leaf and damp earth which seemed fragrant and exotic after the stink of steerage which lingered in his blanket and clothes.

Daybreak came suddenly as nightfall and they were roused by peals of raucous, mocking laughter which made the women shriek and the men leap from their makeshift beds and take up their rifles, thinking they were under attack.

Convulsed with laughter at their antics, the bullocky pointed out a bird rather like a large kingfisher, perched high in the eucalypt over their heads.

'It's only a kookaburra – a laughing jackass,' he said, wiping tears of mirth from his eyes. The women didn't believe him. They weren't convinced until they saw the bird tip back its head and give voice to the devilish laughter once again.

Dermot persuaded one of the women to sell him some eggs and with a hot meal inside him, Tully began to feel better. The clouds rolled away and the sun came out to generate a surprising amount of heat for a winter's day, making steam rise from the travellers' clothes. The sun also brought native birds out of hiding. Pied crows fought over the corpses of small, furry animals and other scraps at the roadside, flapping their wings and uttering their musical, warbling cries. Rosellas flew overhead, shrill and sweet, a momentary flash of red and blue before they vanished into the shelter of the trees. Tully liked the big, sulphur-crested cockatoos that frequented more open ground. Common as seagulls and just as raucous, they flew overhead, screaming at these travellers invading their territory and settling to watch them from the safety of the bare branches of a dead eucalypt which had been struck by lightning. From a distance the tree looked as if it were blooming again as the big white birds fluffed their feathers and screeched, raising their bright yellow polls.

After nearly a week, Tully had made no friends among his companions of the road. The men looked like desperadoes, their women sharp-featured and nervous, huddling together for comfort and speaking in whispers, daunted by the numbing silence of the bush. One or two of them carried infants who whimpered constantly, exhausted from crying and being ignored. The older children were like little wild animals, clothes and faces covered in mud. There were no boys his own age.

Hoping his father's temper would have improved along with the weather, Tully ran to catch him up. Dermot had found a friend – an old hand who knew his way around the gold fields.

'Gold, Mister McDiarmit, gold for the takin'.' The old man winked, his rheumy eyes almost disappearing in the folds of a face seamed and brown as a well-worn saddle. 'Like an Aladdin's cave it was in the early days – gold everywhere, jus' lying around on the ground. I came across an' ole girl once on the river bank – old enough to be me mother she was – filling her apron wi' mushrooms. Or so I thought. "What have you there, Mother?" I says to her, civil like. "Can I give you a hand?" An' d'you know, th'ole bitch turns on me, growlin' like a she bear. "You get on your way, young man!" she says. "I don't want no other folks 'ere." She were in such a pother, I decided to take a look. You'll never guess what I saw.'

'Surprise me,' Dermot said, knowing what the answer would be but still hanging on every word.

'It weren't mushrooms at all – she were fillin' her apron wi' lumps o' gold.'

'An' what did you do?'

'Whaddya think?' The old man grinned unpleasantly, showing tobacco-stained teeth. 'Had to teach 'er a lesson, didn' I? Selfish ole cow!'

Dermot laughed politely but Tully looked away, sickened,

no longer interested in the old man's tales. He was missin' Jem and Hobley, his friends from the *Sally Lee*. They had been so generous with their praise, telling him he was a natural sailor, born to go to sea. It was true, too. He had never suffered a qualm, not even when the ship had been tossed on mountainous waves and the most seasoned travellers had given up, taking to their bunks. Hungry for approval, their words of encouragement had gone to his head. Da never praised him, never saw him as a person in his own right, with dreams and hopes of his own. He saw only an unpaid servant; an extra body to lend a hand when he needed it. Growing pink in the sunlight under his old cap which wasn't large enough to shade his face, Dermot was still engrossed in what the miner was saying.

'You betcha,' the old man nodded. 'I learned better'n to come up this road on me own.'

'Why?' Dermot glanced around at the undulating, rather featureless countryside. 'Afraid o' gettin' lost?'

'Lost? Ha! I never get lost,' the old man snorted. 'No. Bushrangers, I mean. It's jus' askin' for trouble to travel alone. I've 'ad mates bailed up an' robbed, left wi' nowt but their breeches an' boots. An' sometimes not even those! Vandemonians. Hard cases, they are. If they can't dig up a fortune quick enough, they take to the road an' go bushrangin' instead. Or join the police force. More villains in uniform than out of it, these days.'

'How's that?'

'Ticket o' leave men. Do their time, then they cross to the mainland to join the police. Make a bleedin' fortune some o' them do.'

'Talking of fortunes – what was the biggest nugget you ever saw?' Naturally averse to policemen, Dermot preferred to talk about gold.

'The biggest? S'easy. The Canadian. Proper sight for sore eyes. I wouldn't be here now if that had been mine.'

Tully stared at his father and the old miner, seeing two faces alive with the same greed. Gold fever, they called it, and Da seemed to have it bad. He and his father had little in common before. Now they would have even less.

Music was Tully's first and greatest love. Like Maggi, he

had inherited his mother's perfect pitch. His voice, before it broke, would have earned him a place in any choir but it was an untrustworthy instrument these days, quavering out of control. So instead of singing, he played. Any musical instrument he could get his hands on. Flute or guitar, it didn't matter; his fingers would itch to play it. The last time his father caught him playing a borrowed fiddle, he snatched it from him and broke it across his knee.

'What have I raised here? A pansy? A little gilliflower? You're a boy, for Chrissake, Tully! A boy! Why the hell don't you act like one?'

'I do!' Tully was rash enough to answer back. 'I have to thrash kids who tease me, callin' you a horse thief an' a drunken bum.'

'Out! Get out o' my sight afore I land you one!' Dermot raised his hand in a threatening gesture.

'Yeah, go on. Hit me, Da. That's your answer to everything, isn't it? Why won't you let me play? I could make money for you if I had a fiddle or a squeeze box o' me own. Didn't me Uncle Declan travel the length and breadth of all Ireland, singin' an' playin' in a band?'

'Your Uncle Declan was a no hoper – a wastrel from way back. An' from your mother's side of the family, not mine. I'll see no son o' mine goin' beggin' outside a pub with his cap on the ground – travellin' around the countryside with a third-rate band.'

'Oh? An' is that better than bein' a third-rate horse trader an' a thief?'

Dermot hit him then. So hard that he loosened a tooth. After that the subject was closed, never to come up again. And Dermot became more intolerant than ever. Any mention of his wife's family or their musical talents was sufficient to send him into a rage.

United in the face of this tyranny, Shona and her children hid their talents, making music only when Dermot wasn't at home. Shona's most prized possession was a small harp, a family heirloom. She kept it out of Dermot's sight until he turned it out of the cart when they were leaving Ireland for the last time.

'It won't take up much room,' she said softly, hoping he

wasn't going to make an issue of it. 'An' I'd like to keep it, Derry, for old times' sake.'

'Whatever for? What do we possibly want with an old-fashioned harp?' And he kicked it, making the strings jangle. Shona winced as if he had kicked her instead. 'Got to be worth a few bob to someone. Silly to keep a harp when nobody plays.'

And Shona had to stand by and watch him sell it for a matter of pence, knowing better than to complain. Only her children saw how it wounded her, the loss of her lovely old harp. Tully had promised himself he'd buy her another when they reached the new land. No point in remembering that promise now.

The land between Melbourne and the diggings wasn't entirely unoccupied but settlements by the roadside were few and far between. One they stopped at was no more than a general store, a coaching house and a rough weatherboard shack, calling itself an inn. Such establishments offered little in the way of home comforts, kept by unscrupulous landlords with an eye to a quick profit.

But as night was about to fall, the weather deteriorated yet again. Faced with the alternative of renting a louse-ridden mattress or spending another night out in the rain, the McDiarmits and their companions decided it was better to pay up and smile.

'An' I'll see your money in advance,' the landlord added, unimpressed by the bedraggled company seeking refuge at his door. 'I've had too many take off at daybreak, skippin' the bill. For a pound you can have a good square meal an' a dry mattress for the night.'

'A pound, is it?' Dermot hooted. 'I'll expect to see roast turkey an' pheasant for that.'

'Stewed mutton or boiled beef,' the landlord said, failing to appreciate Dermot's attempt at wit. 'Take it or leave it. 'S'all the same to me. A pound a head and a pound to stable a horse.'

'Come on, Da.' Tully plucked at his father's sleeve, looking with longing at the open fire which he could see burning on two sides of the chimney in the centre of the room. 'Pay the man. We'll get pneumony if we have to spend another night out in the rain.'

The fire was the only comfort offered by this inn and that only because the patrons had picked up the timber and built it for themselves. There was no home-brewed beer or wine on offer to quench the travellers' thirst. Only stewed tea or a dubious concoction which went by the name of 'coffin varnish'. The old miner whispered to Dermot, advising him to leave it alone.

'Filthy stuff,' he said. 'Rots yer brains.'

'What is it?' Tully sniffed, wrinkling his nose.

'Don't ask. A rough rum cut with oil of vitriol, I suppose. Stick to the tea. T'isn't the best but at least yer know it won't kill yer.'

The meal lived up to the worst of their expectations. The beef was old and tough, the boiled mutton greasy and seasoned with too much salt, probably to encourage the customers to drink.

Remembering with regret the well-kept alehouses they had left behind, the English were the first to complain.

'Scandalous!'

'For a pound I expect clean sheets and a room of my own.'

The landlord received their complaints with a twitch of the shoulder, unmoved by their words. His house was the only shelter for miles around and he knew his rooms would always be full. There was simply nowhere else for people to go.

Tully woke up early, itching and tormented by fleas. Later a Scot rose from an unsatisfactory breakfast of burned porridge, voicing the thoughts of them all. 'Call that porridge?' He too had spent a wretched night on a mattress infested with bed bugs and fleas. 'Yon shifty-eyed thief! You might as well bail us up and take the rest of our money now. Highway robbery, that's what it is.'

When the travellers resumed their journey, they were joined by a party of Americans also making their way to the fields. Big men who were generous with advice as well as supplies, having had the foresight to stock up on rum, brandy and sides of bacon before leaving town. When Dermot discovered they were also experienced miners, fresh from the gold fields of California, he deserted his erstwhile companion, joining their throng of followers.

Avoiding the old man who wanted to bend his ear, complaining of Dermot's ingratitude, Tully excused himself, jumped down from his perch at the back of the dray and ran through the crowd to catch up with the bullocky who was striding ahead, whistling and flicking his whip over the horns of his team to keep them moving. The leaders were a matched pair of handsome brown and white bullocks, who moved with a brisk yet measured tread, forcing the rest of the team to keep pace. The man greeted Tully with a cheeky, gap-toothed grin. Strong, well-built and probably not more than thirty, his weatherbeaten complexion and full beard gave him the appearance of a man of forty-five. 'G'day, nipper,' he said. 'Wondered when you was goin' to get tired of hangin' around with those old blokes. Ye'll get a numb bum, parked on yer' arse all day.' His accent was fascinating to Tully – the emerging accent of Australia which seemed to lie somewhere between the nasal speech of the cockney and the lilt of the Irish. Frequently, he cursed at his team, making Tully smile.

'I have to swear at the silly buggers or they think I don't mean it,' he said.

'Mind if I walk with you for a while?'

'Nah. Glad o' the company, son. You gotta have a bit more to say for yerself than these dumb bastards,' he said affectionately, nodding at his bullocks and flicking his whip across their horns once more for good measure.

'My name's Tully – Tully McDiarmit.'

'Tully McDiarmit, eh? Sure an' begorrah! Ye can't get more Oirish than that,' the man said, delighted with his painful imitation of an Irish accent. 'Matthew Bradley.' He gave himself a slap on the chest by way of an introduction. 'But mos' folks call me Cabbage Tree.'

'Cabbage Tree? What sort of a name is that?'

'For the cabbage tree hat.' He pointed to the shapeless, sweat-stained object squashed on to his head until it looked as if it was growing there. 'Never without it, you see.'

Tully had found a friend. The man had a simple, straightforward outlook on life rather similar to his own. Cabbage Tree had no interest in chancing his luck on the gold fields, preferring the more modest but certain income from his bullocks and dray.

'But couldn't you go prospecting jus' for a little while?' Tully insisted. 'You wouldn't have to give up the bullocks and dray. Sure an' everyone says the gold is there for the takin' – jus' lyin' there on the ground.'

'Mebbe it is. Mebbe not. Shouldn't believe all you hear, mate. An' I'd take the American legend with a pinch o' salt.' He winked, jerking his head at the Americans and their admirers who were hanging on every word. 'Look at the silly buggers. You could spin them any ole yarn an' they'd swallow it, hook, line an' sinker. Oh, I grant you, there's one or two mines so rich they call 'em the jeweller's shops but diggin' for gold is a risky business an' bloody hard work as well. I seen folks starvin' out there for the want of a penny to buy a crust, never mind thirty bob a month for the flamin' licence fee.'

'Well, if it's as bad as all that, why do you keep takin' them there? Why don't you warn them off as you're warnin' me?'

'Think they'd listen?' Cabbage Tree gave a bark of laughter. 'Nah. If I don't take 'em, some other bugger will. An' I've a livin' to make – a wife an' two nippers dependin' on me back home.' The bullocky wagged his head, no longer smiling. 'But this last six months, I've seen some changes an' none o' them for the better. We thought we'd see some improvement with a new Guv'nor an' all, but there's not. Bleedin' desperate wouldn't be statin' the case too hard. The miners have to spend more money an' dig deeper to get to the gold. Mining equipment doesn't come cheap.'

'I know. Da spent twelve whole pound . . .'

'That's nothin'. Jus' the bare bones of it. An' the mines are so close together it's gettin' to be like a giant rabbit warren out there. Sometimes the whole bloody lot collapses, burying men alive. But still they keep comin' in droves. White people, Chiny people – diggin' up the land like there's no tomorrow.'

'So what are you saying? That we're too late? An' the gold is all gone?'

'Lor bless ye, no! There's more land out there than you can poke a stick at – an' always some new rush on the go. But it isn't as easy as some people think. You have to build a shaft and dig the wash-dirt out of the ground –'

85

'Wash-dirt? What's that?'

'The clay that carries the gold. You have to pan and cradle the wash-dirt to flush out the gold – hours and hours of back-breakin' work.'

Cabbage Tree went on to tell more hair-raising tales of the bushrangers who hid in the forests, finding it easier to rob other miners than pay their dues and dig for themselves. As if to support his tale, the track was now littered with fallen trees, broken axles, the fly-blown remains of dead horses and bullocks, and sometimes a coach, left smashed where it stood or hopelessly bogged in the ground.

In the midst of exchanging confidences with his new friend, it wasn't long before Tully brought the conversation round to the sea. Happy to talk about his friends and life aboard the *Sally Lee* he avoided the subject of his mother – the pain of her loss was too new. But he did speak of his sister and how angry he was with Dermot for leaving her behind.

Cabbage Tree didn't react as he expected. 'Sounds like a sensible move to me. Best thing he could do for the lass. Miserable life for a woman out there on the fields.'

The more he heard about the gold fields, the less Tully looked forward to what lay ahead. He marched along beside the bullocky in silence, coming to terms with what he'd been told. A party of Chinamen jogged past, overtaking them, distinctive in their coolie hats and with pigtails of shiny black hair hanging down their backs. Barefoot and lightly clothed, they balanced their possessions, even their mining equipment, on long bamboo poles, moving more quickly and easily than the Europeans who had to trudge alongside the dray, hampered by their thick boots and heavy clothes. Some of the men called out to the Asians, jeering at them as they passed. Their behaviour made Tully uneasy. Life on the gold fields was going to be hard enough without the added pressure of disputes between men of different colour and creed.

Chapter Seven

At Bullivant House, Maggi soon learned not to draw too much attention to herself. It was better to bite her tongue rather than answer back; to be on time for everything, blending into the background and fitting in with the routines of the household. Perhaps because they were both outcasts, sharing the cramped quarters in the attic, she found herself working with Ginny more often than not. The other girls avoided the Londoner because of her cruel wit and her liking for practical jokes. One night she terrorised her room-mates with an enormous huntsman spider which had come in out of the rain, tormenting it until it crouched, raising its fangs ready to bite. She didn't tell them it was harmless until she tired of the game and dropped the unfortunate creature out of the window.

The routine of Bullivant House was always the same. Miss Prunella roused everyone at six, sounding a brass dinner gong on the landing of each floor. The older girls had only ten minutes to wash, dress, plait up their hair and assemble downstairs to begin the daily chores. Maggi trained herself to fall out of bed at the first chime, otherwise Ginny would wake her by throwing a wet face cloth at her head.

The younger girls were allowed to remain in bed until seven. Maggi's heart went out to these little ones who were the real orphans of Bullivant House; children whose parents had died or deserted them, leaving them stranded, alone in a strange land. If she wanted to keep the good opinion of the city fathers, who believed the home existed for the benefit of the girls, Mrs Bullivant was obliged to take them in. Only those on the receiving end of her charity knew how she really felt; how she resented these youngsters who would have to be fed and clothed for years before they could repay her.

Afraid of the future and far from home, many of these children wet their beds. Maggi, passing the junior dormitory one morning with a pail of slops, stopped to listen, disturbed by the sound of Miss Prunella's voice raised in anger.

'You filthy little animal, you've done it again! This is the fourth time this week, Kitty Smith. What do you have to say for yourself?'

The child's reply was no more than a frightened whimper. 'I'm sorry, miss.'

'Not as sorry as you're going to be. Strip that bed and take the sheets to the laundry at once. Matron will give you some soap and show you what to do.'

Maggi knew Kitty. Undernourished and small for a child of seven, she would scarcely be able to carry the sheets to the laundry, let alone wash them. Swiftly, she ran down the stairs and disposed of the bucket of slops, returning to meet the little girl who was struggling, a step at a time, trying not to trip over the sheets. When she saw Maggi, she burst into tears.

'O, Kitty, don't cry, it's not worth it.' Maggi hugged her. 'Give me the sheets and let me help you.'

'N – no,' the child tried to speak between sobs. 'You'll get into t – trouble, too.'

'Trouble's nothing to me,' Maggi said bravely, taking the sheets from Kitty's arms and leading the way to the laundry outside. The Matron was already there, standing beside a tub of water and waiting for the child. When she saw Maggi she narrowed her eyes; small, mean eyes, lost in the puffy flesh of her face.

'What are you doing here? No work of your own? We'll soon remedy that –'

'It's all right, Matron. It won't take a moment. I'll jus' help Kitty to wash up her sheets an' I'll go.'

'Kitty's here because she needs to be taught a lesson. How can she learn to be clean if you pamper her?'

'It was only an accident,' Maggi said easily, smiling at the little girl who was staring at the Matron, lips trembling and tears standing in her eyes. 'You didn't do it on purpose, did you, Kitty?'

The child shook her head, unable to speak.

'Lazy, she is.' The Matron fixed her with a venomous look. 'Too lazy to wake herself up and go to the privy.'

'I wish I could,' Kitty whispered. 'But I dream that I'm at the privy and by the time I wake up it's too late.'

'That'll do, Margaret, you can go now,' the Matron shoved Kitty towards the laundry tubs, placing her bulk between them. 'I'll see to this now.'

'My name isn't Margaret, it's Maggi. An' I don't think she's –'

'I didn't ask you to think – I asked you to go.'

Slowly, Maggi opened the door and went out but she didn't go back to the house. Instead, she waited outside, certain the Matron was going to bully or punish the little girl. She could hear the woman's voice, low and threatening, and Kitty's responses, pleading at first and then fearful. She was about to return anyway when she heard Kitty scream. Inside the room which was already murky with steam, she could see them standing at one of the tubs. The Matron was holding Kitty by the arms, forcing her hands into the near boiling water to scrub the sheets.

'Let her go at once, you bitch!' Maggi was so angry, she could hardly get the words out. Releasing the child, the Matron turned to face her, breathing heavily, her eyes glittering with malice, like a cat cheated of its prey.

'What did I tell you? Lazy! Won't even wash her own dirty sheets.'

By now Kitty had sunk to the floor, doubled up, whimpering and nursing her bright red hands in her skirt. Maggi picked her up as if she weighed nothing and ran with her across the yard to the kitchen where she knew there would be butter or dripping at least which would soothe the child's burning hands. The Matron came to the laundry door, calling after her.

'I'll teach you to interfere. You haven't heard the last of this, Maggi McDiarmit! You'll be reported for this!'

'Stupid. Heroic, yes, but very stupid,' was Ginny's verdict

89

when Maggi recounted the incident later. 'You've made yourself an enemy there.'

Maggi shrugged but for the present she had no time to concern herself with the Matron's revenge and what form it would take. Slops had to be emptied, beds made and the tables set for breakfast, all before they assembled for morning prayers at eight o'clock. Only after Miss Prunella had snuffled her way through several pages of the prayer book, were the girls permitted to sit down to a breakfast of lumpy porridge, followed by chunks of the cook's tough, home-made bread – a test for anyone's teeth. There was no sugar to go on the porridge or jam for the bread.

After breakfast, the rest of the morning was devoted to polishing and cleaning the house. Vital training, Mother Bullivant insisted, for girls who were to be household serv-ants. Maggi lived in an agony of suspense all morning, waiting for something to happen; for a summons to Mother Bullivant's office. It never came. Perhaps the Matron thought better of it, realising that if she reported Maggi, she would have to tell of her own part in the affair.

Maggi detested all household chores. Her only pleasure lay in caring for the infants. After the scene with Matron, even that was in jeopardy now. When the others begged off, worn out after a day on their feet, it was always Maggi who offered to see the little ones off to bed and sing them to sleep.

It wasn't until mid-day that she managed to excuse herself from Miss Prunella's sewing lesson to visit Kitty who had been sent to bed. The child had received a lecture for scalding her hands.

'I wanted to tell Miss Prunella but she wouldn't listen,' Kitty whispered, still shocked and close to tears. 'I don't like it here, Maggi. Do you think my mummy will come for me soon?'

'I don't know, pet.' Maggi stroked the child's hair, damp with tears, away from her face.

'You'll take me with you, if you go? You won't leave me here?'

'Oh, Kitty,' Maggi sighed, not knowing what to say. It would have been easy to comfort the child with a lie but

Maggi didn't believe in making promises she couldn't keep. It wasn't fair to let Kitty depend on her when she didn't know what the future held for herself.

A day or so later, Kitty disappeared. Maggi asked but nobody could say where she'd gone and nobody seemed to care. Two other girls had gone from the attic bedroom, leaving Maggi and Ginny to share it alone. They pushed their beds closer so that they could whisper after lights out without being heard.

'I wonder what happened to Kitty?' Maggi whispered. 'There's something not right, I jus' feel it.'

'Oh, I dunno,' Ginny shrugged. 'Wherever the kid's gone, she'll be a damned sight better off than she was here.'

'I suppose,' Maggi sighed. 'What do you want to do, Ginny? When you get away from here?'

Ginny sat up and grinned, always happy to talk about herself. 'Me? I'm waitin' for Mister Filthy Rich an Jus' Right, that's who. Catch me workin' meself to a frazzle for one of those jumped up old trouts who call themselves ladies. Bullivant herself, fr' instance. Think she started out with a silver spoon in her mouth? Nah. She married a rich old man twice her age an' he left her the lot. Half her luck! I wish I could marry a rich old man who'd leave me a house.'

'Maybe you will. We have a sayin' at home – if you wish for somethin' hard enough when you're twenty, by the time you're forty, you have it.'

'Forty! But that's old! I don't want to wait 'til I'm forty.'

'No. Nor do I.' The colour rushed to Maggi's face and her heart lurched as she remembered a lazy smile and a pair of piercing blue eyes, mocking her from beneath a wide-awake hat. ''S only a saying, anyway.'

'I'm not waiting for luck to catch up with me. I'm going to make me own.'

'I don't suppose I'll be here for long.' Maggi was thinking aloud as much as talking to Ginny. 'My, da will be comin' back soon. Soon as he has enough gold to make a fresh start.'

'Hah! You mus' be greener than the Emerald Isle itself, if you believe that.'

'He will be back!' Maggi insisted, trying to read the girl's expression in the semi-darkness. Ginny was voicing her own worst fears. What if Dermot had really abandoned her? What if he and Tully never came back? 'You're jus' trying to scare me. You know nothin' about us – me or my da.'

'No. But I know about men, ducks. Show me the man who ever had *enough* gold. You'll be long gone from here by the time he remembers he has a daughter – if he ever does. You'll be sold off into service and the record closed. Hey!' she broke off, seeing Maggi had thrown back the bedclothes and was getting out of bed. 'Where are you off to?'

'To see Mother Bullivant, of course. Now. Tonight. I'll not get a wink of sleep if I don't.'

'Don't be silly, Mags. She'll have you on water duty a week if you bother her now.'

'I have to tell her there's no need to find me a post. My da will pay for me when he comes back.'

'Are you out of your mind? You're supposed to be an orphan, you idiot. She finds out you're not, she'll have you sold off quick smart – to the first dirty ole man who comes here lookin' for someone to warm his bed.'

'Why? Why should she do that?'

''Cos she don't like to be made a fool of, see? Too many done it across her before.'

'Oh? An' how come you know so much? An' how come – as you've been here so much longer than some of the others – that you're still here?'

'That'd be telling.' Ginny's smile was mean. Satisfied she had thoroughly upset Maggi, she was bored with the game. She yawned daintily, stretched and turned over, composing herself for sleep. 'G'night, Mags.'

'Oh no you don't! You started this an' you'll finish it. I'm nobody's fool. I've been to mop fairs an' I know an agreement has to be made between master and servant alike. Even a tweeny maid has the right to choose.'

'Not here.' Ginny giggled until her laughter turned into the familiar, rasping cough. Maggi turned her back, pulling the threadbare blanket over her head to shut out the sound.

'Maa – gi!' Ginny taunted, tweaking the blanket and leaning across to whisper. 'Maa – gi! Don't you want me to tell you? Why the Sunday visitors never choose me?'

'Go away. Jus' go away an leave me alone.' Maggi pulled the covers more tightly around her head.

'Sulk then, you silly bitch. I should care.'

Seconds later it was her turn to give a small shriek as Maggi sprang at her. A child of the streets again, she was dangerous as a spitting cat as she seized a handful of Ginny's hair and pulled it viciously.

'Tell me!'

'All right. No need to get rough.' Ginny prised Maggi's fingers from her hair and winced as she saw there were more than a few strands left behind. 'And don't make such a racket. D'you want to bring Miss Prunella up here?'

'Jus' tell me!' Maggi gave her another shake.

'It's like this, you see. Nothin' to it at all . . . '

If Dermot and his companions had been hoping for a warm welcome and country hospitality from the settlers whose property they crossed on the way to the gold fields, there was none to be had. Disillusioned by the carelessness of the prospectors who came swarming across their lands without permission, chopping down trees, lighting fires, stealing sheep and disregarding the simplest of country courtesies, those who could afford it erected fences to keep them out. It wasn't always so, Cabbage Tree said, but the carelessness of a few people had spoiled it for everyone else. The property owners, once renowned for their generosity towards wayfarers, now hardened their hearts against them. Sometimes the farm dogs were released and set on them, to encourage them not to stay.

But, with the gold fields less than a day's march away, those on horseback decided to speed up and ride on ahead. The heavy rain had turned the track into a quagmire and the womenfolk, who had been lucky enough to ride for most of the journey, now had to walk in order to lighten the load. One or two carried infants as they struggled along, the mud soaking into their long skirts and dragging them down. Suspicious of everyone, even those who offered to help them, they hugged their children and possessions close.

Cabbage Tree let fly with a mouthful of curses as the dray ground to a halt, tilting at an alarming angle in the mud at the side of a creek. Weary now, the bullocks were no longer at their best. Their feet were becoming sore and they hadn't the strength to move the dray on their own. Every able-bodied man had to lend a hand, wading into the water, pulling and pushing the wagon across the creek.

After the trials of the journey, it was with a sense of relief that Tully saw the township of Ballarat unfolding before him. It had taken them ten days to cover the distance of seventy miles. While retaining much of the 'rough and ready' atmosphere of a frontier town, Ballarat was striving to copy the wide streets of Melbourne and was already emerging as a prosperous and attractive town.

Having reached their destination, the travellers said their farewells and began to disperse. By the time the bullocky called his animals to a halt outside the Post Office, only those with cargo remained with the dray. Dermot sprang up at once and began untying their load while Tully paused to say goodbye to Cabbage Tree.

'Watch yerself, nipper,' the bullocky grinned, pushing his hat to the back of his head. 'Keep yer powder dry.'

'I will.' Tully clasped the man's hand, sad to be parting from yet another new friend.

'Ah, dammit.' Cabbage Tree hesitated, taking off his hat to scratch at his balding head. 'I mind me own business as a rule an' leave other folks to mind theirs – but if that bloody ole man o' yours drives you nuts an' you need a lift back to town, leave a message for me with Bill at the Post Office on Eureka. You can hitch a ride with me any time. 'Catch up with that flamin' ship o' yours, if you want.'

'Thanks, Cabbage Tree. 'I'll bear it in mind.' Tully frowned, chewing his lip.

'An' there's no need to look like that, yer silly galah. I don' wanna be paid. You can earn yer keep as me sidekick on the way back.'

'Thanks!' Tully grinned, his spirits lifting for the first time.

'Awright, don't get carried away.' The man backed off, half afraid the boy might embrace him. Dermot looked up in time to see them slapping each other on the shoulder and shaking hands.

'Get over here and give us some help, you lazy little tyke! He's had our money, hasn't he? Doesn't need thankin' as well.'

Cabbage Tree pulled a face at Dermot's back. 'Chin up, son,' he muttered, winking at Tully. 'Jus' see you stand up to the old bugger an' give 'im as good as you get.'

'Tully!' Dermot's tone was now threatening but the boy didn't care. It would take more than a bit of bullying to crush his spirits today.

Acting on information he'd gleaned from the Americans Dermot steered clear of the older mining areas where the claims would be too expensive. Leaving the township behind he turned left through the fields towards Black Hill and the New Eureka; there he was hoping to find a piece of unoccupied land and stake a claim. Like many a man who adds to his income by thieving, Dermot lived in fear of being robbed or cheated himself. Thus he preferred to break new ground rather than take up a claim which was no longer wanted by somebody else.

Tully's euphoric mood didn't last for long. He was unable to share his father's excitement at the sight of the camps and diggings which seemed to spread in all directions, as far as the eye could see. The scene was one of complete devastation: good farming land gone to ruin, torn apart and laid waste. People were swarming over the fields like so many ants. At first glance it looked like a fairground but there the similarity ended. There was no music; no fun. Jealous of his own tiny portion of the gold fields, each man wanted to camp alongside his claim. But since the claims were no more than a few feet apart, this wasn't always practical. Many diggers had to work back to back in close quarters as they attempted to follow the twists and turns of the river of gold underground. In their haste to wrench the last ounce of gold dust from the soil, the miners had created an eyesore; piles of dross and an ugly rabbit warren of holes. *It's like a huge cemetery*, Tully thought, *every man digging his own grave*. He found out later he wasn't so far from the truth. Weaknesses developed in the network of shafts and it wasn't uncommon for the sides of a deep mine to cave in, burying the occupant alive.

Dermot paused on the outskirts of the field, trying to

95

decide which direction to take. Between the holes, the up-turned soil lay in mounds and ridges. Here and there the flyblown carcass of a horse or a cow had been left for the scavengers. There were no trees left standing and the wind howled across the plain with nothing to stop it. This was a draughty place. Timber was always needed for tent poles, firewood or to shore up the sides of a mine. All of the sizeable trees had been felled and the upper branches lay where they'd fallen, green gum leaves and the pale yellow fuzz of wattle left to shrivel in the watery winter sunshine.

No one had taken responsibility for the removal of garbage or other unpleasant duties like digging latrines and filling in old ones. The place was a breeding ground for all sorts of flies. Tully couldn't decide which he hated the most: the fat lazy blow flies, feasting on carrion, or the small bush flies which tried to settle on his mouth and around his eyes. The fields stank like a gigantic midden and he could only hope to get used to it after a while.

More flies congregated around the butchers' shambles, which had started life as tents though now the sides were filled in to give better protection against the weather and make them more permanent. Seeing the carcasses of several sheep and a side of bacon hanging outside, Tully thought he was hungry until the smell of stale offal drifted towards him, making him gag. He closed his eyes, trying not to breathe as he waited for the nausea to pass. The stink was coming from the open cesspit alongside the shops where the butchers were throwing the offal from slaughtered beasts. Half-starved dogs were feasting on it, growling and stirring up a cloud of flies.

Dermot was unaffected by these horrors, blind to every-thing but his purpose: to find a vacant place as soon as possible and stake his claim.

'Watch that cradle,' he said to his son whose muscles were already straining under the load. 'Put it down for a bit while we decide where to go.'

Gratefully, Tully did so, shaking his hands which were getting numb.

'Don't stop here, Da.' He was looking at a man whose face and clothes were encrusted with filth and who stood there, waving a bottle and laughing like a madman. 'Some of these men look half-daft.'

'It's not madness, it's gold fever, me boy. Won't be long before you catch it yourself.'

Behind his father's back, Tully shook his head.

'Hey, you!' A man raised his head from a hole in the ground, calling out to them. 'Get out of it! We don't want any new chums here!' And he fired a rifle into the air to show that he meant it.

It was the same throughout the whole of the Black Hill and Eureka districts. More stores, more tents, more rubbish and still more holes in the ground. Nobody raised a hand in greeting. Nobody wanted them to stay. Some people had dogs guarding their holes but most of the animals they saw were neglected and left to starve. Dermot put down his load to offer a crust to a horse but it staggered on, too weak to respond. There was no pasture to feed any animal, only diggings from here to the horizon.

Tully closed his eyes for a moment, hoping that when he opened them again it might not be so bad as he feared. He hated it here and he wanted to leave. Now. Today. Dermot poked him in the ribs, bringing him back to reality.

'No time to be dozin' off now, me boy. This'll have to do. It's the best I can find today. Give us a hand an' we'll put up the tent. Soon have it looking like home.'

Dermot had chosen to break new ground near the creek. Fortunately, it was a fair distance from the butchers' shops and away from the stink.

'Right.' His father clapped him on the shoulder when the tent was erected to his satisfaction. 'You stay here an' look out for the tent and equipment while I go up to the Government Camp to buy a licence and register the claim. Lord only knows how long that's going to take. An' keep your eyes open for thieves. I don't want to come back and find everythin' gone.'

'You *are* goin' to get a licence, then?' Tully squinted at him. It wasn't like Da to concern himself with keeping to the letter of the law.

'Jus' for a month or so.' Dermot grinned. 'I'll find out how to fiddle it before we need to buy another one.'

Another one? For the first time Tully realised his father was here for the long haul; he didn't care if they stayed here indefinitely. And if they did, what would happen to Mags? He drew a deep breath, wondering how to mention this without sending Dermot into a rage.

'Da. We can't leave Mags in Melbourne forever. She'll be waitin' –'

'Your sister's in good hands. It's a nice place.'

'Like a school. Maggi will hate it.'

'An' ye think she'd like it any better here?'

Tully sighed, still thinking the family ought to have stayed together but knowing it was useless to say so.

'Be different when the weather warms up an' we start comin' up with gold.' Dermot grinned, rubbing his hands in anticipation. 'We're stayin' 'til we've made us a fortune, me boy. Work hard an' the next few months will see us set up for life.'

Tully turned up his collar against a fresh shower of rain, watching his father stride off in the direction of the Government Camp, just visible at the top of the rise. It had been positioned where it could overlook the vast panorama of the gold fields. In front of the Gold Commissioner's tent was a Union Jack, limp and flapping in the rain.

He didn't begin to take heed of his surroundings until his father had gone, becoming aware that he himself was the subject of another man's scrutiny. He had come out of his mine and was standing on the pile of mullock at the entrance to his claim, legs straddled in a king of the castle attitude, his expression far from encouraging. He carried an axe, weighing it in his hands. To Tully he looked like an evil gnome – squat, pot-bellied and dressed in the clothes which had become the uniform of the gold fields; a red flannel shirt tucked into a pair of dirty moleskins and held together by a broad leather belt. He wore heavy boots and a thick waistcoat designed to keep him warm while leaving his arms free to wield a pick or an axe.

'Orright, sonny, what you lookin' at?' he muttered, head poked forward aggressively, spoiling for a fight.

'Me? N-nothing, sir.'

'And that's no place to put your tent. Pack up at once an' get out of here'

'I'm sorry, sir. I'd like to oblige you but I can't. This claim isn't mine, you see. It belongs to my da. He's at the Commissioner's tent right now, buyin' a licence an stakin' his claim.'

'He should have asked me first.' The man waved his arm to encompass a general area. 'This section as far as the creek is all mine.'

'Is it?' Tully glanced around, wondering if his father might have made a mistake. 'But I don't see any markers or pegs to show that it's yours.'

'Jus' you take it from me – this land is all mine. Your camp is right next to my claim.'

'Next to it, yes.'

'On top of it. An' I don't take kindly to neighbours. People workin' too close, makes me nervous. I put two men in the cemetery already for tryin' to jump me claim.'

Tully's heart began to beat faster. He was no weakling but he was light and only a boy. If it came to a fight he was sure to lose. All the same, he faced up to the man, standing his ground. 'I'm sorry, sir. If it were up to me, I'd do as you ask, but I can't.'

Making a harsh, animal sound the man lunged at Tully, swinging the axe high above his head. The boy stood still with his eyes closed, hoping that death, when it came, would be clean and quick. Any moment he expected to feel the blade of that axe as it sliced into his skull. But the axe fell and he felt no pain. Cautiously, he opened his eyes to see their neighbour hacking at the ropes of their newly erected tent, satisfied to see the canvas deflating, settling into the mud.

'That'll teach you to have some respect for your elders.' The man nodded. 'Now, then, you can heave the rest of that hardware over to my place and get out.'

'Indeed an' I won't!' Slow to lose his temper, Tully was coming to a slow boil. Having come through the first test unscathed, he was ready to call the man's bluff. 'Those things belong to my da an' I'm here to mind them.'

'More fool him then. Leavin' good tools with a pipsqueak like you. I can just do with a new pick an' shovel. A nice new cradle, too . . .'

By now Tully realised the man was teasing, playing cat

99

and mouse. And while he was wondering whether to take up a shovel and start making threats himself, he heard someone come up behind him and give a deep rumble of laughter.

'Well, I'll be damned. If it isn't young Tully McDiarmit. In trouble already if I don't miss my guess.'

Tully whipped around to see who it was. He had never been so pleased to see a friendly face. 'Jem! Oh, Jem, is it really you?'

It was indeed Jem Burden and Hobley, his friends from the *Sally Lee*. Sizing up the situation immediately, Jem was pulling a wry face at the expanse of canvas lying on the ground. 'What's happened here, lad? No one ever show you the right way to put up a tent?'

Tully glanced around, ready to involve their disagreeable neighbour. But the man wasn't there. While he was happy to throw his weight about and threaten a boy, he wasn't prepared to tackle two burly seamen. Quietly, while Tully was greeting his friends, he'd retreated into his own mine.

'So where are you staying?' he asked the seamen. 'Have you set up camp yet? Staked a claim?'

'One thing at a time, lad,' Jem laughed. 'Cap'n Carpenter and the rest are over to Black Hill, but Hobley an' I liked the look of it here, near the creek.' He glanced at his friend who nodded vigorously. Hobley was a man of few words and it was his habit to agree with everything Jem said. 'Mebbe we'll peg out a claim next to yours if your da doesn't mind. From the looks of old chummy next-door, you could do with some beef on your side.'

'You saw him, then?' Tully's smile faded. 'The man in the red shirt.'

'They're all men in red shirts,' Jem grinned, rolling back his sleeves and pushing his seaman's cap to the back of his head. 'Now then. Let's see what's to do about this tent.'

Chapter Eight

Like most people who long for something and look forward
to it for a long time, Dermot found out that life at the gold
fields wasn't at all as he'd pictured it. Used to having his
own way – to having other people fall in with his plans – he
was less than pleased to return and find that his camp site
had been reorganised and practically taken over by his son's
friends. And this in the time it had taken to buy a licence and
lodge a claim.

Hobley was smiling and biddable as always but Jem was
older and more set in his ways. Never totally at home away
from the ocean, he kept reminding them that this was only a
vacation so far as the seamen were concerned. In a few weeks
they must return to Melbourne and the *Sally Lee*. His talk
was always of seafaring and adventure on the high seas,
adding fuel to Tully's ambitions and keeping them alive. He
was taking it for granted that the boy would go with them
when they returned.

In the hope of straddling as much land as he could and
making a fortune as soon as possible, Dermot had staked
two claims, one in his son's name as well as one in his own.
He resented the seamen for crowding him as he put it, and
taking up the option on the other side. From the outset it
was clear that the seamen knew what they were about,
having money enough to invest in the right equipment. They
had a windlass while Dermot and Tully had to make do with
picks and shovels, sometimes their bare hands. No matter
how many times Tully put forward the argument
someone else would have come to take up the vacant space

if Jem and Hobley weren't there, Dermot continued to resent them.

'If I'd known you was goin' to spend every wakin' moment wi' those two, I wouldn't have bought you a claim of your own,' he growled.

'You didn't buy it for me – you bought it for yourself, Da. They wouldn't have let you take out two claims in one name.'

'All in the family, isn't it? You should be over here, diggin' with me. What if you find a nugget on their piece o' ground? What happens then? You don't think they'd let you keep it?'

'I wouldn't expect it, Da. I didn't have any idea how to go about minin' before they showed me, an if you're honest about it, neither did you.'

'No, I didn't. An' I thought it was goin' to be a helluva lot easier than it is.'

'So you should be grateful to Jem an' Hobley for teachin' me.'

'Teachin' you, is it? Sometimes I think you're silly as those pink parrots you love so much. Teachin' you! Usin' you up, more like. Can't you see you're no more to them than an extra pair of hands?'

Tully ignored the jibe. 'Jem doesn't know any more'n we do but Hobley's from Cornwall – used to work in a Cornish tin mine. Who was it showed you the safe way to go about sinkin' a shaft? Who showed you how to make a calico tunnel to stop it gettin' airless down in the mine? You wouldn't have thought that one up on your own.'

'Mebbe I wouldn't. But I'm still sayin' they've got you fooled.'

A working day in the mine started soon after daybreak and went on until nightfall. Tension would mount and tempers fray as the gold continued to elude them although the work of digging and sifting seemed easier now that the weather was mild. But with the advent of warmer weather came still more flies, filling the air with noise near the butchers' shops and bringing new epidemics of dysentery and eye disease. Tully walked through the children's cemetery one day and saw a row of new headstones, a tragic reminder of the hardships of living at the gold fields.

Also he learned to be less particular about his food. Today

he was boiling a neck of mutton, seasoning it with plenty of spices and trying to forget the slime and the unpleasant grey-green hue of the meat before contact with hot water. The choice was simple. He could eat the mutton or starve and he was far too active and growing too quickly to starve. In a matter of weeks he had turned from a gangling boy whose feet and hands were too big for him into a strapping, well-muscled young man. Cabbage Tree was the first to remark on these changes when they met outside one of the stores.

'Land sakes! What are they feedin' you, nipper? Shot up like a bloody weed since I saw you last – had to look twice to make sure it was you. Keep growin' like this an' you'll end up taller'n me. How the bloody hell are ye, then?' He clouted Tully on the shoulder, almost knocking him off his feet. 'How's that bloody ole man o' yours?' Cabbage Tree always spoke of Dermot as if he were ancient although he was probably only ten years older than the bullocky himself. 'Thought you'd be ready to sell up by now – come swankin' it over us poor bastards in Melbourne.'

'Not yet.' Tully wrinkled his nose. 'Oh, most days we see a bit o' colour in the pan. Da's turned up the odd nugget or two – enough to keep goin' – but I wouldn't call it a living. Not for the back-breakin' work we have to put into it.'

'Told you so.' Cabbage Tree nodded. 'You can always come an work for me. Run ragged I am. More work than I can poke a flamin' stick at. The missus is fed up. Turned on the waterworks an' howled the place down only the other day. Says she'll forget who she's married to, if I don't stop home for a while.'

'Tully! Where the hell are you?' Dermot had come out of the ground and was bawling across the fields. 'How long does it take to buy a hammer an' a bag o' nails? I gotta shore up the mine or the whole bloody lot'll fall in.' It hadn't taken him long to pick up the language of the gold fields.

'Put a sock in it, Da. I'll be there in a minute.'

'The hell ye will, ye cheeky young devil!'

'Top o' the morning to ye, Mister McDiarmit,' Cabbage Tree greeted him, mocking his Irish accent. Dermot snorted, retreating into the mine.

'Ha! I see the ole bugger's temper hasn't improved.' Cabbage Tree's smile faded and he pushed his hat to the back of his head. 'I've news for you – not all of it good. About the place your sister's stayin' in Saint Kilda Road . . .'

Sunday evening and the routine of Bullivant House was returning to normal after the afternoon visitors had come, chosen the girls they wanted as servants, and gone. The seed cakes were back in their tins, jam and sugar back in their pots, before the girls tried to sample them. Amelia Bullivant was happy. She counted her money and put it away in her cash box, pleased with the profits of the afternoon. Several girls been placed but, as usual, those two from the attic had been ignored. As always, her brow creased when she reminded herself of those girls. What was it about those two? Why did nobody take them? Luckett should have been placed weeks ago. And as for that Irish girl – the sooner she left, the better.

At the same time, Maggi and Ginny were shaking hands, congratulating themselves on yet another lucky escape. The ruse was simple but effective. When Mother Bullivant wasn't looking, they let their mouths hang open as if they were simpletons, certain nobody would pay good money to employ a fool. Not when there were so many sensible girls.

Pleased with their continued success, Maggi and Ginny bounded up to the stairs to the sanctuary of their attic which they still shared alone. Mindful of expense, Miss Prunella had taken away the oil lamp, leaving them only a single, foul-smelling candle which cast a dim yellow light, throwing goblin-shadows across the walls. To Maggi it was an unpleasant reminder of their quarters in steerage aboard the *Sally Lee*.

'Saved yet again,' Ginny crowed, peeling off her clothes and stepping out of them, leaving them in an untidy heap on the floor. 'Sunday afternoon gone and we live to fight another day.' She pulled on her nightgown and without taking the trouble to comb out her hair, flung herself full-length on her bed, making the springs rattle. 'Did you see that parson and that long-nosed wife of his? Worse than Prunella! Poor twins, having to work for her. That woman's going to be a slave driver, I can tell. I've met her sort before. Never mind. Here's hopin' for a better class of customer next week.'

Maggi took off her outer garments and washed herself quickly before changing into the prickly, calico nightshirt which was the standard issue at Bullivant House. Sighing with pleasure, she released her hair from the cruel plaits which restrained it during the day and shook it out, massaging her scalp before she took up a comb to wrestle with the tangles – never an easy task with such unruly hair.

'Quite a colour, isn't it?' Ginny grinned. 'Bet you could light up the sky on a dark night.'

Maggi smiled vaguely, not wanting to be drawn into a discussion about red hair.

'You've been here such a long time, Ginny. Why don't you want to leave?'

'Want to get rid of me, do you?' Ginny lifted her chin, always ready to start an argument. 'I'll leave when I'm good an ready an' not before. Why don't *you* leave?'

'You know very well. I have to wait for my family.'

'Wake up to yourself! Nobody's family ever comes back here.'

'Kitty's did.'

'Orright. If that's what you like to think.'

Maggi looked at her sharply. 'What do you mean?'

Ginny shrugged.

'Come on, Ginny. It isn't exactly home from home here.'

'Why do you stay?'

''Cos I'm waitin' for someone special. I'm not goin' to be dumped on some psalm-singin' parson an' his long-nosed, penny-pinchin' wife. No, I'm waitin' for a man on his own. Not too young, not too old, an' I shan't care if he's ugly as sin, long as he's rich. He'll tell Mrs B he's lookin' for a housekeeper but I'll get to be his wife.' She paused, breathless after the long speech.

'I don't know.' Maggi frowned. 'A rich man can find him a housekeeper any time – why would he come here?'

'Women are scarce in the colony.'

'Are they? There seemed as many as men aboard the *Sally Lee*.'

'Yeah. Wives, mothers and the usual bunch of draggle-

105

tails – they don't count. I'm talkin' about ordinary single girls like you an' me.' She saw Maggi was still looking doubtful. 'Oh, I know what you're thinkin'. Why would a rich man give a second glance to pie-faced little mutt like me?'

Maggi coloured up because she had been thinking just that. 'No, I wasn't,' she murmured.

'Don't worry. I'm the first to admit I've a face like a barbary ape. But I've got somethin' else to make up for it, too.' With a throaty giggle, she pulled up her nightgown to show the upper part of her body. Startled by her room mate's brazen display of nakedness, Maggi averted her eyes, but not before she'd seen a slender torso and a pair of rose-tipped breasts against a background of flawless, milk white skin. 'Well, what do you think? Pretty enough to please any man?'

'Cover yourself, you'll catch cold. You don't want to start that cough up again.'

Ginny frowned. She didn't like anyone to mention her cough.

'Ginny.' Maggi was suddenly thoughtful, 'Ginny, you haven't ever – you haven't done it, have you?'

'Done what?'

'You know. Lain with a man.'

' 'Course not,' the girl snapped, answering too quickly to be telling the truth. 'Do you take me for a fool? A maiden-head is a prize – too valuable to be thrown away on the first joker who pinches your bottom and asks for it.' Her face split into its monkey grin, eyes glittering in the candlelight. 'But that don't mean I haven't a trick or two up me sleeve. There's more than one way to pleasure yourself an stay intact, as they say. Come over here an' I'll show you.'

'No!' Maggi curled forward, hugging her nightshirt around her knees. 'Thanks all the same but no thanks.'

'Why not? Come on, Mags, don't be such a spoilsport. You're the last person I'd have taken for a prude. We should make the most of it while we've got the place to ourselves.'

'No!'

Ginny cackled wickedly, her fingers stretching into goblin

106

shapes on the wall behind her as she pretended to reach for Maggi.

'Come to me arms, me darlin' Irish girl.'

'I said no and I mean it, Ginny. Lay a hand on me an' I'll pluck every hair out of your head.'

'You would too, wouldn't you, little hell cat?' All the same she made no further move, daunted by the fury glinting in Maggi's amber-coloured eyes. 'Come on, Mags. You know I won't hurt you.'

'No. Because I won't give you the chance! Listen to me, Ginny, an' listen good so you have this loud an' clear. I keep meself to meself. I don't want to experiment in – in bedroom matters – with other girls.'

'Bedroom matters?' Ginny gave a shriek of laughter. 'Oh, Mags, that's so funny. You'll be the death of me yet. Why ever not? What's the difference? Why is it all right for a man to touch you that way an' not me?'

'I don't want anyone to touch me – anyone at all.'

'No? Not even your lovely man at the Post Office? He of the beautiful, ice blue eyes and the coal black hair?' Ginny mocked. 'You'd like him to touch you, all right. Oh, yes, and a whole lot more. You dream about him, don't you? How he'll lift up your skirts and put his fingers in your –'

'Ginny, shut up! You make everything dirty and cheap. I wish I'd never told you about him now.'

'But you did tell me. Everything. His firm lips and strong, capable hands. An' I say you're a fool, Maggi McDiarmit, to be savin' yourself for the likes of him. You wouldn't stand a chance. A man with lady-killin' looks and a lump of land to go with 'em!' And she fell back, giving another snort of laughter.

'I know. I know all of that.' Maggi's voice was small. 'You don't have to rub it in.'

'So what do you expect? For him to ride up to Bullivant House on a snow white charger and whisk you away? Carry you off into the sunset to live happily ever after?'

'No, Ginny. I'm not that stupid.'

'I hope not. Because it won't happen. A man like that is a challenge all right but he's not for you. Oh, he'll look you over in passing and raise your skirts if you'll let him – they

107

all do. But when it comes to marriage he'll choose someone of his own class, someone his family will approve and who comes with a nice lump of money to add to his own.'

'I know,' Maggi said through gritted teeth. 'You don't have to spell it all out.'

'Forget him, Mags. He won't be wasting any time thinkin' of you.'

'Ah, that's where you're wrong.' Maggi looked up and grinned, full of her old mischief. 'He'll be rememberin' me very well. My da took his purse.'

For some reason this struck them both as outrageously funny and they fell about, giggling like children, until Miss Prunella heard them and shouted up the stairs.

'Be quiet up there, you pair of laughing jackasses. Pipe down or I'll have you on water duty for a month.'

This sobered them at once and they smiled, allowing the awkward moment between them to be forgotten and passed off as a joke. But Maggi didn't forget. Never at ease with Ginny because of her spiteful ways, she was doubly cautious now and made it her habit to dress quickly while her room mate was downstairs in the privy. Forced into each other's company, they had never been close friends. They were more like enemies now.

Everything might have been different if it had been Dermot who made the first substantial discovery of gold. But it was Tully who found a sizeable nugget and on his own claim; a gold nugget about the size of a baby's fist. Not a fortune but it was a 'nice find'.

Jem and Hobley's deeper mining had also paid off, showing them a handsome dividend for their time at the gold fields, if not sufficient to make them consider deserting the *Sally Lee*. One or two other seamen did. They called by to invite Jem and Hobley to join them, saying they were on their way to some new diggings, opening up to the north-west at Fiery Creek.

Hobley looked thoughtful and might have been tempted but Jem overruled him, determined to go back to sea. He said he was longing for the sight of a tall-masted clipper, the tang of salt in the air and the special cobalt blue of a tropical sea. Taking it for granted that Tully would also follow his lead, Jem was taken aback when he heard the boy was staying behind.

'But in God's name, why?' Jem shook his head, finding it hard to believe the boy could turn his back on his dreams so easily. 'Is it the gold? Just because you've found one little nugget, it doesn't mean there'll be more. If you told me once, you must've told me a hundred times, how you hate living here.'

'I know, Jem. I know what I said. An' one day I'll do it – I'll go to sea. But will ye look at the ole fool – how can I leave him now?' He jerked his head at Dermot who was standing beside the creek, working his cradle as if his life depended on it, his clothes and hair thick with the dust of weeks. 'He won't even eat unless I remind him. He's lost it he's – no good on his own any more. Somebody has to look out for him.'

'Yes, but why does it have to be you?' Jem pursed his lips, resenting Dermot for his place in the boy's affections. 'I know he's your da an' I shouldn't interfere, but I wouldn't speak to a dog the way he speaks to you.'

'Ah, Jem, he don't mean nothin' by it – it's just his way.' Tully wanted to get out of the argument which was progressing along all too familiar lines. 'An' there's me sister to think of as well. I'll need more'n one nugget of gold if I'm to spring her from the orphanage. Cabbage Tree told me, it's not much better than a prison.'

'Cabbage Tree! Don't listen to him. He tells you the worst of it like all these Australians. They'd have us believe there's spiders big as dinner plates and snakes under every stone. You can't believe a word the man says.'

'I like Cabbage Tree. He's all right.' Tully tried to be loyal to all his friends.

'So he is. If you don't mind a foul-mouthed bullocky.'

'Well, I don't. I'm sorry, Jem, but I have to stay. At least until I see me sister all right.'

'Of course she's all right. Women are always all right,' Jem growled. It was well known that he had no time for the fairer sex. 'Women are like cats – always land on their feet. Sounds like one lame excuse after another to me. All right, be a land-lubber if that's what you want.'

109

'It's not what I want, Jem, but what I have to do. Mam would expect me to look out for Mags as she's always looked out for me. I can't turn my back on her.'

'There's far too many people dependin' on you, son.'

'Only two.' Tully smiled.

'An' that's two too many. But each to his own, lad.' The seaman shrugged, finding it hard to hide his disappointment. 'If it makes you happy, grubbin' around after gold, who am I to tell you otherwise?' Conveniently, he chose to forget that for the past two months he, too, had been grubbing around after gold.

'Come off it, Jem, that's unfair. You know I'd give my eye teeth to be going to sea. An' some day I will. I'm jus' sayin' it can't be now.'

'There's still time if you change your mind. The *Sally* won't sail before Christmas, not 'til she has her full cargo of wool. Jus' get a message to us by New Year. An' if things cut up ugly here, get away before –'

'Why? What do you think will happen here?'

'I dunno. But something's gotta give, I can feel it in me bones. I seen men desperate like this before, when some bullyboy of a captain pushes 'em too far. An' I'm tellin' you, these men are at the end of their tether – fed up o' starvin' their families to pay unfair licence fees. All because some new Governor in Melbourne says they can afford it. If he lived here for a while instead of jus' visitin, he'd see that they can't. And there's more. That Scotsman murdered. A hotel burned to the ground. The wrong men arrested and the right ones allowed to go free. You mark my words, this place is gettin' to be a right powder keg. All it needs is one good match to set it off. You could end up with a full-scale pitched battle here. The diggers on one side, law an' order so-called on the other.'

Tully whistled. 'Da will be in the thick of it, if there is. Nothin' he likes more than a good punch up.'

'This won't be a punch-up, son, it'll be a bloody massacre. The traps are jus' waitin' for an excuse to have a go and they've got more weapons and ammo than you have.' Jem spat in the direction of the Government camp. 'Commissioner Rede's in trouble enough as it is. Got to show the Governor

110

what he's made of – prove he has the situation in hand. He's not going to stand for all these meetings an' talk of revolution.'

'Talk, Jem. That's all it ever is. Booze an' talk. Never comes to anything.'

'This time it will. The men are coming to a slow boil and when they reach it – look out! All the bad hats'll show up like crows on a corpse, stirrin' up trouble an making the most of it.' A thought seemed to strike him and he frowned. 'What did you do with that nugget of yours? Sold it, I hope?'

'No. But I have it safe – tied up in a corner of me shirt.' And Tully began to pull out his shirt to show it until Jem stopped him, glancing around.

'Keep the thing out of sight. An' if I was you, I'd sell it to one of the shopkeepers.'

'Why? You didn't sell yours.'

'Ssh!'

'You know they'll give me half what it's really worth if I sell it here. I'll get a much better price if I keep it an' sell it when I get back to town.' He grinned as Jem continued to frown. 'You worry too much. It's safe enough. Besides if I sell it and Da knows I've got money, he'll only weasel it out of me, a little bit at a time.'

While they had been talking, they had been walking slowly from the diggings back to town. Outside the main Post Office there was much back-slapping and teasing as Jem and Hobley joined up with their shipmates before climbing on to the coach which would take them all back to the coast and the *Sally Lee*.

'Take care of yourself, son,' were Jem's last words to Tully. 'An' if you're sailing with us, make sure to be back by New Year.'

'I will,' Tully said, although he knew it was a forlorn hope. Dismayed by the surge of emotion which unmanned him now the moment had come to say farewell to his friends, he gave a loud whoop and grinned widely, pulling off his cap and capering to amuse them as the coach started to move away. It was top heavy with the seamen and their bags. They preferred to ride on top where they could smoke their foul-smelling tobacco without giving offence.

111

Tully watched it until it was out of sight, a coach built along American lines, slung on wide leather straps instead of the usual springs to cope with the rough bush tracks which were similar to the pioneer trails of the American West. Freeman Cobb knew his business and guaranteed speed rather than comfort; his coaches were famed for rolling like ships on the open sea – no problem to Jem and the other seamen. It was a magnificent sight, taking a team of eight horses to move it; horses which would be changed every ten miles to ensure that the coach would be able to keep up its speed. Cobb had worked hard to corner the market on good horses and now offered the fastest, most reliable transport to and from the gold fields.

Taking only a seaman's bag each, Jem and Hobley were travelling light. They'd sold their claim which showed them a handsome profit for the time they'd spent at the fields. The men who bought it were two middle-aged Englishmen new to the fields. Used to clerical work indoors they were enthusiastic enough but had no idea how to go about working a mine. Like a pair of bad housewives, they asked stupid questions and were always borrowing pieces of equipment which they were slow to return. Tully had little patience with them. Unfairly, perhaps, he resented them for taking the place of his friends.

Troubles never come singly. In the absence of the seamen, Dermot began to take his son for granted again, expecting him to do the lion's share of the work in the mine. And about this time he made some new friends – hard-drinking Irishmen who had started a gambling school. While drink on the fields was now legal and respectable, gambling was not. Innocent card games were tolerated but the serious gamblers still met in secret and at night. Dermot spent most of his evenings in the Irishmen's tent, gambling away the few grains of gold he found during the day. And, more often than not, what Tully had found as well.

'What about Mags?' He tried to put the brakes on his father's new interest. 'We'll never save enough to pay for her, if you keep gambling it away.'

'Shut your head,' Dermot growled. 'When my luck turns, I'll have enough to pay for her twice over.'

But he always lost. Exhausted after nights of drinking and gambling, he would sleep late the next day, leaving Tully to work alone. The boy's resentment grew and he learned to hide most of what he found, including the nugget tied in the tail of his shirt. And still he dreamed about going to sea. He could send a message to Cabbage Tree and leave the gold fields tomorrow but loyalty to his father impelled him to stay.

By now it was early-November and, although the weather was variable, there were strong indications that summer was on the way. Strange to think that soon the weather would be hot and Christmas would come in less than two months. Everything was upside down on this side of the world where even the trees were odd, retaining their foliage all the year round and growing hard gum nuts which could withstand the fires which sometimes raged out of control across the land. And instead of shedding their leaves, they shed bark instead, leaving the trunk beneath shiny and new. Red-haired and fair-skinned like his sister, Tully was inclined to burn in the strong spring sunshine. He gave up his cap for a wide-brimmed hat and learned to keep his arms covered up with a long-sleeved Crimea shirt.

With growing apprehension he listened to the talk of anarchy which spread through the fields. Dermot argued with the Englishmen who had taken over the seamen's claim and who sided with law and order.

'Governor Hotham's a Navy man,' one of them sniffed. 'A stickler for discipline. Fees have been set and they ought to be paid. At least until the law itself is changed.'

'Then we'll bloody change it for him!' Dermot roared.

'It's people like you who make it hard for everyone else,' the Englishman persisted, pursing his lips and not realising how close he was coming to a punch on the nose. 'It's because of people like you who defy the law that they've stepped up the licence hunts. Three times last week the troopers fetched me out of the ground to show it. They were rude about it, too.'

'Ew!' Dermot raised a little finger in a parody of the man's English accent. 'Ay'm so sorry they were rude!'

Dermot was making a joke of it but the troopers were diligent in the search for miners evading their licence fees.

113

Down at the creek one morning, Tully was operating the cradle, sifting wash-dirt while his father slept. Lost in his thoughts, he didn't hear the trooper approaching until the man spoke up behind him, saying: 'Licence, please!' This in itself was a surprise. 'Show us your bloody papers!' was the request most miners received.

The trooper was a young Aboriginal policeman, smartly dressed, proud of his uniform, and looking as if he was prepared to be civil, to begin with at least. He had dismounted and was leading his horse.

Tully was in a tight corner. Caught without a licence and unable to pay the penalty, he might find himself chained to a log or even sent away to build roads in the company of hardened criminals, if his fine remained unpaid. He knew both their licences were out of date, Dermot had paid nothing since that first day at the fields. He grinned at the policeman, pretending to go through his pockets.

'Licence . . .' he said. 'I have it here somewhere.' His hand closed on a tattered one pound note which he had managed to prise out of Dermot to buy food. He withdrew it and smoothed it with muddy fingers before offering it for inspection. Unable to read himself, he gambled on the fact that the Aborigine would have no more knowledge of the written word than he did. He held his breath as the policeman examined it carefully, turning it over in his hands.

'Thank you.' He smiled as he gave it back, his teeth very white in the dark face. Relieved but at the same time shamefaced at his deception, Tully watched him move along to speak to the next group of men. When they heard what he wanted, they shouted and spat at him, upsetting his horse and making it rear in fright. Tully squared his shoulders, preparing to join in and catch the horse if it came to a fight. Fortunately, there was no need. Grim-faced, the Aboriginal officer swung himself into the saddle and rode away, most likely in search of reinforcements. He had learned a hard lesson today. Next time he would know better than to approach the miners alone or make the mistake of treating them with respect.

Chapter Nine

'Margaret McDiarmit and Virginia Luckett!' Mrs Bullivant's voice rang out, echoing along the hall and causing both girls to halt in mid-step on their way to the kitchens. It was Sunday, breakfast was over and they were both staggering under the load of heavy white ironstone soup dishes which doubled as porridge bowls in the morning.

What does the old witch want with us now?' Maggi whispered, raising her eyes to heaven before turning to speak. 'If you please, Mother Bullivant,' she managed to bob a curtsy, making the dishes wobble perilously as she did so, 'me name isn't Margaret, it's –'

'Speak when you're spoken to and not before.'

'But you did speak to me, Mother Bullivant.'

'Enough. Have you learned nothing at all since you came here?'

'Oh, yes, Ma'am.' Maggi smiled, looking innocent. I know Cook gets hoppin' mad if we don't get the dishes in quick when she's wantin' them washed an' out of the way. So if you'll excuse us?'

'Not yet.' Mrs Bullivant snapped. She inspected them, looking for faults and unable to find any. Both girls were clean and neat without even a wisp of hair escaping from their mob caps. Disappointed, she sniffed, sounding uncommonly like her cousin Prunella. 'I've a bone to pick with you two. I've looked at my books and you, Virginia, have been with us for all of five months while Margaret . . .'

'Marigold, ma'am,' Maggi corrected again and smiled.

'Marigold! You two have been living high on the hog and

115

eating me out of house and home for too long. It's time I had a return for your keep. I want to know how it is that no one has seen fit to employ you? Why you are both still here?'

'Sure an' I wouldn't know, ma'am.' Maggi's smile was becoming fixed. 'Please, can I go now? If I have to stand here much longer I'm afeared I'll drop these plates at your feet.'

'I wouldn't, if I were you. I'll make you sorry, if you do.'

'You see, ma'am, there's no accountin' for people's taste.' Ginny thought it was time to intervene. 'Too many girls here – maybe the clients are spoiled for choice. An' maybe they're looking for prettier girls than us.'

'You wouldn't look quite so plain if you made yourself more agreeable, Ginny, and smiled.' Mrs Bullivant took a step backwards as Ginny bared her teeth at her and simpered. 'Oh dear, no, I didn't mean that.'

'Sorry, ma'am.' Ginny shrugged, closing her mouth like a trap. 'I can't help it if I'm without personal charm.'

'No.' Mrs Bullivant sighed. 'And I suppose Margaret – I mean Marigold there – looks too puny to cope with heavy domestic work. All the same, I have a feeling there's more to all this. I've disposed of far less promising girls and fail to understand why you two remain.'

'Jus' unfortunate.' Ginny sniffed. That's what we are.'

'Well, I can promise you this much. You'll certainly learn the meaning of the word *unfortunate* if I have to keep you much longer.'

'Please, ma'am. Can we take these dishes to the kitchen an' come back?' Maggi felt as if her arms were being pulled from their sockets and the pile of dishes wobbled again.

'Stop that, or you'll do an extra water duty for every plate that you break,' Mrs Bullivant glared at them. 'Go on, then. Get out of my sight. But while you're washing those dishes, think on this. I have three new clients coming to afternoon tea today which means there will be three new vacancies to be filled. Two of them are to be filled by you.'

'Why?' Ginny's voice rose in a wail of protest.

'Because I'm sick and tired of seeing you passed over for others when you should have gone long ago. So you make yourselves agreeable and try a little harder today. If not and if either one of you is left at the end of it, you can forget the home comforts you have received until today. It'll be bread and water from now on. And you'll clean the privies and empty the slops for a month!'

Maggi was scarcely aware of these threats as she was biting her lips and straining every nerve to hold on to the plates. She couldn't win either way. She must become a servant to people who might take her away where her father and brother could never trace her, or remain to become an Aunt Sally – a target for the taunts of the other girls as she cleaned the privies and carried out other demeaning tasks at Bullivant House.

At three o'clock that same afternoon, four girls were lined up in the bay window of Mrs Bullivant's private sitting room, Maggi and Ginny among them, faces scrubbed until they glowed and wearing aprons so heavily starched they crackled whenever they moved. All four smelled of home-made eucalyptus soap. Ginny had pinched her cheeks so severely to colour them that she looked like a badly painted doll. By three-thirty, two of the visitors had made their choices and left. Both had been pleasant women, kind and sympathetic to the plight of the orphans. The girls who left with them had been delighted to be chosen. The third visitor, said to be a doctor in search of a housekeeper, had not yet arrived. Only Ginny and Maggi remained, Mother Bullivant regarding them with a steely look in her eye.

'Privy duty for a month!' Ginny whispered out of the corner of her mouth as the clock chimed the three-quarter hour and still the expected visitor hadn't arrived. Mrs Bullivant sent to the kitchens for a fresh pot of tea and the silence in the room grew oppressive. Both girls watched the grandfather clock as the hands crept towards the hour, its ponderous ticking the only sound in the room. At four, the clock paused and wheezed, preparing to strike, and everyone, including Mrs Bullivant, started as there was a loud knocking at the front door. A man's voice was heard booming in the hall, apologising for being late.

Maggi's heart set up a slow and painful rhythm as the sound of that voice brought a scene now buried in her memory – a scene she would rather forget. Her mother's struggles to give birth in the cramped, suffocating quarters aboard the *Sally Lee*. It was the voice of Doctor Parker, she was sure of it. She closed her eyes, hoping against hope that she was mistaken and it would turn out to be somebody else; maybe all doctors spoke with authority and in that tone of voice. Hope vanished as the door swung open and Miss Prunella gave her customary sniff as she ushered him in.

'Doctor James Parker,' she announced.

As Maggi feared, it was the same man who had been the ship's surgeon aboard the *Sally Lee* and the sight of him brought all the worst of her memories flooding back. She remembered his callousness, his indifference to her mother's plight. Such a man wasn't likely to treat a servant well.

She felt rather than saw Ginny tense beside her and tried to see him as he must appear to the other girl. He was tall and even-featured if thin-lipped, and even his lines of dissipation might be appealing to someone like Ginny. Having shaved off his beard and discarded the salt-stained jacket he had worn aboard ship, James Parker looked like a fashionable man about town.

'Just stay clear of this one, Maggi.' Once more, Ginny spoke out of the corner of her mouth. 'This is the man I've been waiting for – this one is mine!'

'Oh, Ginny –' Maggi began.

'I mean it, Mags.' While no one was looking, Ginny pinched the soft flesh of Maggi's upper arm; it was a vicious pinch and certain to leave a bruise. 'Just stay out of it,' she hissed. Stepping forward, she appeared to bloom, changing from a gawk who slumped, hanging her head, to a graceful woman with the natural boldness of an experienced courtesan. Then she smiled – an expression having nothing in common with her usual monkey's grin. A slow smile that made her eyes crinkle into seductive slants. She giggled softly, parting her lips so that they no longer looked thin but full of promise.

And just as she intended, James Parker was entranced. If he recognised Maggi, he gave no sign and she was grateful for it; she didn't want to be pointed out as the ragged tinker's lass from the *Sally Lee*.

Parker's nostrils flared like those of a big cat scenting prey, and he looked Ginny up and down with interest and

118

greed, his gaze coming to rest on the aggressive lines of her bosom, straining against the crisp whiteness of her pinafore. Mrs Bullivant coughed gently, reminding him there was still an agreement to be reached, and rather pointedly offered him tea. Thereafter she engaged him in conversation, turning her back on the girls.

'Ginny, listen.' Maggi's whisper was urgent. 'For your own sake, I beg of you, don't go with this man.'

'For my sake or for yours?' Ginny pinched her again, making her wince. 'What sort of a fool do you take me for? D'you think I'm going to stand back and leave a doctor for you?'

'That's not what I meant, you don't understand . . .'

'Oh yes I do. It means you've taken a shine to him yourself.'

'No. Ginny, I know this man. He was our ship's surgeon aboard the *Sally Lee* – he spent most of the journey half-drunk and he's a womaniser, too.'

'So are most single men when they get to his age.' Ginny wasn't to be put off. 'Nothing the right woman won't be able to cure.'

'That's what you think. I know this man – he's callous and cruel. He cut my mother's baby from her body and left her to die.'

'He's a doctor, Maggi. He can't cry over every patient he loses!'

'Girls!' Amazed that they would forget themselves enough to squabble before company, Mrs Bullivant clapped her hands to bring them to order. 'Our visitor will think we teach you no manners here!'

Maggi sighed, realising it was too late to persuade Ginny otherwise. She had set her sights on Doctor James Parker and now nothing and no one was going to make her change her mind.

Not long after the seamen left, Tully was reminded of Dermot's prejudice against music. It happened when he was given a mandolin.

Saturday night and, as usual, Dermot was out playing rounce: a game introduced to the fields by the Americans and guaranteed to part a digger from his money in record time. Alone and having nothing better to do, Tully worked until nightfall then after a supper of cold mutton, wandered off through the camp, vaguely in search of someone to talk to – someone to raise his spirits and take his mind off things. Drawn towards the sounds of music and laughter coming from a large hut in the Italian quarter of the camp, he made his way towards it, hoping he would be welcome there. A party was in progress and someone was playing a piano accordion, to the accompaniment of singing and stamping feet. Self-conscious all of a sudden, he hesitated in the doorway, unwilling to join the party without being invited.

'*Buona sera* – welcome.' A small, chunky Italian caught sight of him and beckoned him in. After introductions all round, the Italians made him so welcome that the boy forgot his shyness, stamping and clapping with the rest of them in time to the catchy Neapolitan tunes. He could make little sense of the words but he knew some of the songs were suggestive as there was a lot of laughter and thigh-slapping at some of the lyrics.

At last it was the turn of their host to entertain them. Brown as a walnut and wearing a red-spotted scarf, he put Tully in mind of figures remembered only vaguely from his past; his mother's brother and other older relatives. People Shona used to meet in secret, warning her children that Dermot must never be told.

Waiting for everyone to settle down and be quiet, the Italian took his time, tuning and plucking the strings of his instrument and striking some chords. Tully had never seen one like it before. Similar to a guitar, it had eight strings and the sound box was richly decorated and inlaid with gold and mother of pearl. It had a haunting, romantic quality when it was played. An experienced singer, the man seemed to be out of practice and his voice cracked on one or two of the higher notes. It made Tully wonder if Maggi had time to practise these days, keeping her high notes effortless and her voice true and supple as it had been before. Shona had insisted on that. He was unable to understand the words of the plaintive Italian love song, but it had to be of a lost or unrequited nature and seemed painfully familiar to the Italians. Hands

120

prematurely aged and cracked from working the fields wiped away tears of sentiment and one or two noses trumpeted into handkerchiefs as the last few notes of the love song died away.

'Mandolina.' The little man patted his instrument in answer to Tully's raised eyebrows and struck a few chords, demonstrating the way the eight strings had to be tuned in pairs.

'Please?' Tully looked at it, longing to find out if he could coax a tune from it. Smiling, the Italian nodded, placing it in his hands. It was an expensive instrument, the wood seasoned and faintly scented like that of a well-worn fiddle. Tully experimented, testing one or two chords. With a little encouragement and tuition, he could play adequately, although its plaintive, romantic quality wasn't entirely in keeping with the rollicking cheerfulness of his own Irish folk songs.

'You boy – natural – very good,' the little man nodded. 'You like – you keep. You take care my mandolina.'

'Oh, but I couldn't.' Tully felt a surge of colour pass over his face and leave it again. 'I couldn't possibly . . .' Much as he longed to own the instrument he knew enough about the effects of drink to realise the Italian would regret his generous impulse in the morning. He thrust it back into the man's hands before the temptation to keep it became too strong.

'Nah! Nah, you don' understand – look!' The old man held up his hands to the lamplight, showing fingers cramped and twisted with rheumatics. He shrugged. 'You see? Soon no play at all. *Bene, bene* – good boy. I know you love my mandolina – you take good care of her.' So saying, he waved Tully away.

Choked with gratitude, he could hardly stammer his thanks as he accepted the loveliest thing he'd been given in all of his life. He held it close as he made his way back to his own camp, nursing it as if it were a precious child, taking extra care as he picked his way over the rough ground, afraid of falling with it in the darkness. Unfortunately, Dermot was home before him and in the blackest of moods; perhaps because he had lost his money and had to leave the game early.

'Where have you been, you little jackanapes, 'til this hour

o' the night? I was thinkin' you'd run off to those bloody sailor fellas, after all.'

'No, Da.' Tully's shoulders slumped with weariness.

'And what's that you have there?' Dermot squinted, peering at him in the darkness.

'Nothing!' The boy reacted as if a bucket of water had been thrown over him, remembering too late his father's hatred of musical instruments.

''S no use trying to hide it – I can see. Who gave you that bloody guitar?'

''Tisn't a guitar, it's a –'

'Bloody plinky-plonk. Give it here to me now. Like a bloody disease with you, isn't it? You and your mam before you.'

'I don't see why you're so down on it. What's wrong with making a bit o' music, Da? It makes people happy.'

'That's all you know. Give it here, you little mongrel. I wanna take a look at it.'

'No.' Tully didn't want to place the mandolin into his father's rough and unsympathetic hands. With a cold feeling of apprehension, he put it out of sight behind his back, guarding it with his body. He knew it was hopeless; he would have little chance of protecting it if his father was determined to be rough. 'It means nothing to you, Da. You can't even play.'

'And you're sayin' you can? Give it here, I say!'

'No!' Tully tried to remain calm but he was remembering the incident of the fiddle, when Dermot had snatched it from him and broken it across his knee. 'The mandolin – it's not mine, ye see. I jus' borrowed it. It belongs to Rocco over at the Italians' camp.'

'Then you give it back to Rocco first thing in the morning. An' if I hear you tryin' to coax so much as a note out of it tonight, I'll smash the bloody thing over your stupid head, d'ye hear?'

'I hear you. G'night, Da.' Anxious to avoid any further argument, Tully took off his boots and threadbare moleskins ready to get into his hammock, slung between two sticks for comfort. To keep the mandolin safe, he hid it under the covers, cradling it in his arms, reassured by the wonderful smell of antiquated wood. It wasn't a comfortable way to spend the night and he slept only fitfully but he wasn't going to run the risk of leaving it on the floor. Dermot might get up and step on it – accidentally on purpose – in the middle of the night.

In the morning, he hid it in the mine. Dermot was happy to leave most of the work of digging to his son, these days, and was unlikely to find it. Certainly not if Tully pushed it to the back of the bottom shelf, wrapped in his old overcoat. Fortunately, as the weather was getting warmer, moisture would be less of a problem these days and the mandolin would be safe in its hiding place underground. It was a gift from a friend and he intended to keep it, even if he could never play it when Dermot was around.

During the following week there was another incident to test his affection for his father. He had to sell his one and only sizeable nugget to spring Dermot from the local lock-up, and for a fraction of what it was really worth. This time he wept tears of anger and frustration over losing the only thing he had managed to keep from his weeks of back-breaking work on the fields.

Scornful of those in authority, Dermot had been less than civil to the troopers who'd inspected his licence, finding it months out of date. Had he spoken to them reasonably, he might have talked his way out of trouble but, reinforced by the order from Governor Hotham, the troopers decided it was time to make an example of someone and this Irishman would do; he and six miners who couldn't or wouldn't pay. Chained to a log, the men were left to fry in the sun for the whole of one day. Seeing his father likely to die for his stubbornness, Tully had no choice but to pay the fine. Apart from his mandolin which had been given to him in good faith, he had only his nugget to sell and the shopkeeper who bought it cheated him, aware of his need.

He didn't expect any thanks from his father but was shocked when Dermot turned and shouted at him as they made their way back to camp.

'An' how long have you been holdin' out on me, you dirty little miser? How long have you been keepin' that nugget to yourself? You told me we was skinned out, we had nothin' left.'

'An' so I did.' Tully glared back at him, exasperated by the old man's lack of gratitude. 'You'd still be chained like a bear to a log if I hadn't. Well, next time I'll let you stay there 'til you rot. You can pay your own way out of trouble.'

'There isn't goin' to be a next time.' Dermot's eyes lit up with fanatical zeal. 'Not now we have a good man like Peter Lalor to fight for our cause. You should've come with me to that meetin' the other night. It's official. We're a force to be reckoned with now. Members of the Ballarat Reform League.'

'I wish you'd have nothin' to do with it, Da. The troopers have you marked as a troublemaker already. Do you want to bring them down on our heads?'

'Damn me if I haven't raised a sook! You've spent far too much time around womenfolk, boy. If everyone was content to cower in their holes as you do, nothing would ever get done. You'll see some changes this time. They can't ignore us any more. Not now we have an educated man like Peter Lalor to speak for our cause. We're sworn to pay no more taxes, not 'til there's a fairer voting system and every man jack on these fields gets a vote.'

'Oh, Da,' Tully groaned. Until now he hadn't realised how deeply his father was involved in the politics of the gold fields. Dermot seemed to be revelling in the thought of this new dragon to fight.

'You'll see. We'll show Governor Hotham he can't ride roughshod over the likes of us. An' we're ready to fight for our cause if need be. We'll have the Gold Commission disbanded and the licence fee abolished at one and the same time.'

'It's a pipe dream, Da. It won't happen. Jem says if there's any more trouble, they'll jus' send for the soldiers to back up the police. They're jus waiting for the miners to make a wrong move, to give them an excuse to . . .'

'Jem sez this, Jem sez that,' Dermot mimicked, his lips curling with scorn. 'Forget about Jem. He's not here any more. Why must you always put the opinion of that damned sailor before mine?'

'Because he talks sense.'

'An' I don't? Is that what you mean?'

'That's not what I said, Da.'

'What are you saying, then? That ten thousand miners are wrong? Because that's how many was at our meetin' at Bakery Hill.'

'Of course. People go to meetings because they like to know what's going on. You'll be lucky to see more'n a hundred or so, if it comes to a fight.'

'They'll fight all right. It's only by takin' a stand that we can bring about change. I swore my allegiance along with the others under the flag of the Southern Cross.'

'A flag? I wish you'd be more careful, Da. The military won't like a flag. They'll see it as the first step towards revolution.'

'Who's been filling your head with all this? You're only a boy. You wouldn't have dreamed up these arguments all on your own.'

'Well, Jem was sayin' . . .'

'Jem again. I might've known. What is it, then? Are ye scared? Too lily-livered to take up arms for a worthy cause? Have I spawned me a coward here?'

'Now that's not fair, Da. I'm no coward and you know it. Take that back.'

'Say you're with us then. Say that you'll stand up beside me an' fight.'

'Of course I'll fight, if I have to. But we'll be throwin' our lives away. Trained fightin' men won't be scared of a handful of diggers wavin' pikes.'

'That's all you know.' Dermot's smile was sly. 'We've been layin' plans for days.'

A few nights later Tully was woken by screams and shouts. A glance at his father's hammock showed Dermot was not at home. Moments later there was the sound of running feet and Dermot burst in, breathless and bright-eyed.

'Quick! Help me hide these,' he said to his son. Automatically, Tully did as he was told, surprised by the weight of the box which he pushed out of sight under his hammock, drawing the covers down to conceal it.

125

'What is it this time, Da? You've not been at the thievin' again?'

'Only from the bloody redcoats! Relievin' them of a little ammunition.'

'You stole from the soldiers?'

'Not just me, you fool. All of us. Stupid redcoat captain, ridin' ahead of his men packed in carts. Must've lost his way.'

'You didn't hurt them, Da?'

'This is war, me boy. Can't make breakfast without scramblin' a few eggs.' Dermot took a brand new rifle off his shoulder and gave it to Tully.

'I can't, Da. I don't know how to use this.'

'Tomorrow I'll teach you.'

But there was no time the next day. Retaliation was swift. Dermot was lucky not to be rounded up with the scores of miners from the Gravel Pits, hunted down by the mounted police. He insisted that Tully attend the meeting to be held at Bakery Hill the next day. The boy joined him only reluctantly, unable to understand his father's zeal for the miners' cause. But the speeches convinced him, made by reasonable men and not by fanatics as he expected. Reasonable men who wanted only to improve the lot of the miners and gain them the right to vote. If that meant they must take a stand against the rule of an oppressive British Government, so be it. The miners would show they were a force to be reckoned with; they must take a stand. At the end of the day, Tully knelt with the rest of them, swearing allegiance to the flag of the Southern Cross which fluttered bravely in the sunlight – a silver cross standing out against a background of bright blue.

Alongside Dermot, he helped to build the stockade behind which the miners would make their stand and took part in the Prussian-style drilling which went on inside.

With the stockade built, there was nothing to do but wait. They waited and waited. Nothing happened. On Saturday afternoon, one man spoke up, becoming restless.

'Sunday tomorrow. Nobody's going to attack us on Sunday, are they? The missus always makes a nice hot-pot on a Saturday night.'

126

The man's remarks put other people in mind of their stomachs. No one was in charge of food for the makeshift army inside the stockade and they had no supplies.

'Go on home, son.' Dermot clapped him on the shoulder. 'Put a light under that bit o' mutton stew. I'll be there by an' by.'

Tully looked sideways at his father, hoping it wouldn't be an empty promise. Dermot was all too likely to be lured into a card game on a Saturday night and he wasn't surprised when his father didn't come home.

It was only when he awoke from a bad dream in the early hours of the morning that he realised it wasn't the dream which had woken him but the sound of gunfire, followed by shouts and screams. He looked across and saw that his father's hammock was empty and swore under his breath, certain Dermot would be at the centre of whatever disturbance was going on.

He pulled on his boots and went outside, blinking in the pale blue light of early morning. He looked up in time to see a series of explosions after which the sky became bright as day, lit up by a wall of flame. The stockade! Gunfire and shouts went on for some minutes, accompanied by the terrified whinnying of horses to be followed by a further series of explosions and more screams.

'Oh, Holy Mother!' Tully murmured to himself, breaking into a run as he made his way towards the flames. He was stopped by a large hand which reached out to grab him by the belt, almost pulling him off his feet.

'I wouldn't go up there, sonny. Not yet,' a man growled in his ear. 'No point in throwin' your life away. The soldiers an traps are mad for revenge, an' they're killin' anythin' that moves inside that stockade.'

'But my da! I think he's up there!' Tully began to struggle in the man's grasp.

'Nothing you can do about it, if he is. Wait a little longer, then you may be able to help.'

Gradually the gunfire ceased until there was only the odd volley of shots, although more fires seemed to be breaking out all the time. The troopers must be setting fire to the tents and huts inside the stockade. Tully at last pulled free of the

127

hands which restrained him and, although the man shouted after him, ran on up the hill towards the scene of disaster.

He almost bumped into a party of grim-faced soldiers coming down, pushing a party of prisoners before them. He raised his hands shoulder-high as one of them paused, threatening him with an exposed bayonet. Another soldier came to his rescue, turning the bayonet away.

'Leave him, Bill. He's only a kid. We've enough on our hands as it is.'

'Leave him? What for?' The first soldier continued to menace Tully, pressing the point of the bayonet against his chest. 'Did these buggers show any mercy to our lad?' He was referring to a drummer boy who had been injured the night the miners raided the soldiers' carts.

'No need to sink to their level, Bill.'

The soldier spat on the ground in front of Tully but shouldered his weapon and moved on. Tully looked into the faces of the prisoners but Dermot wasn't among them.

On reaching the site of the battle, he could see little remaining of the stockade. Tents and buildings were burning out of control, including the stores. Others had reached the scene before him and were working frantically to douse the flames but the air was still thick with smoke and the smell of spent ammunition. He pulled his scarf up over his face but his eyes continued to water, making it hard for him to see.

'Oh, Jesus,' he whispered as he almost tripped over the body of a man who had been shot first and then bayonetted to finish him off. Nauseated by the smell as much as the sight of so much blood, Tully fell to his knees and vomited last night's supper on the ground. Shivering with nausea and the horror of the scene before him, no less than the aftermath of a battle, he had no way of knowing what had happened to Da, whether he had been slaughtered, captured or burned to death. This was armed reprisal, a reaction out of all proportion to the minor incidents which had gone before. A massacre and which ought not to have happened at all.

Some men lay crippled and wounded, crying for help and for water. Anxious as he was to discover what had happened to Dermot, Tully felt bound to attend their needs. He dribbled water between parched lips, fighting down nausea as he reassured them, saying their terrible wounds were slight and that help was on its way. He had no way of knowing if he was speaking the truth or not. Here and there he gleaned fragments of information which allowed him to build up a picture of what had happened here. He gained most information from a man with an injured leg.

'Must've been less than two hundred of us even before the Californian Rangers took off for the day. Not a trained soldier among us, anyway.' The man broke off to wince as Tully tried to move his leg into a more comfortable position. 'We weren't ready for battle – nobody was. It was Saturday night, for God's sake. We didn't think they'd make a move until Monday. Dawn on Sunday an' I'll never forget it . . . that's when they came in. Took us all by surprise.'

'I'm looking for Dermot McDiarmit,' Tully began, but the man wasn't listening, his mind filled with the horrors of the night before.

'Redcoats and police, all armed to the teeth with Minie rifles. We didn't stand a chance. They had weapons that can blow a man's head off at two hundred yards.'

Tully swallowed, his imagination working overtime.

'They blew up the stockade as if it was made of matchsticks. Fifteen minutes an' it was all over. I saw Peter Lalor fall, God only knows what's happened to him.' He turned to look at Tully, seeing him properly for the first time.

'Why are you here, son? Who are you looking for?'

'My da,' Tully said, staring around at the scene of devastation, thinking that if Dermot had been inside the stockade it was unlikely he had survived.

'God help him too, then,' the man sighed.

Chapter Ten

Tully stumbled on through the battleground, appalled that the stockade could be reduced to smoking rubble in such a short time. From behind the brick-built chimney which was all that was left of one of the huts, he watched a trooper haul down the flag of the Southern Cross to the cheers of the redcoats who were whooping like savages, tearing it with their boots as they stamped on it, trampling it into the dust. The brave symbol of freedom was gone, crushed by the soldiers and troopers, just as they'd crushed the miners for trying to improve their lot; for making a stand against a government which favoured the land grabbers with more than enough already, oppressing those less fortunate with unfair laws.

Half an hour later, and having found nothing to prove that his father was dead, Tully allowed himself to hope. Perhaps Dermot had left the stockade last night shortly after himself, to meet his friends as usual and play cards.

He was about to give up and return to the creek to see if Dermot was home or if their neighbours had any other news, when he caught sight of a hat lying on the ground. It could have been anyone's wide-awake hat but for the shrivelled bunch of heather which had been tucked into the band – Dermot's memento of the mountains of Ireland and the symbol of his promise one day to return, wealthy and successful.

A quick search revealed his father, lying ominously still and trapped under a thick slab of wood which had once formed part of the outer barriers of the stockade. He must have been in the front line of the diggers' defence. When Tully heaved at the slab, struggling to lift it from his father's inert body, the man groaned. He was still alive. The piece of wood lying across him was charred and still hot enough to burn the boy's hands, yet at the same time it must have acted as a shield, saving Dermot from being captured or slaughtered by the soldiers. But when Tully succeeded in removing it, his father fell back with his eyes closed, his face drained of all colour. His eyelids fluttered at the sound of his son's voice but he made no attempt to move.

'Da! Oh, Da!' Tully fell to his knees beside him, not knowing what to do. There was an unpleasant smell of overdone meat and, with horror, he realised it was coming from his father's left leg, so badly burned the flesh was as one with the fabric of his trousers. The other leg was twisted beneath him at an unnatural angle, obviously broken. If Dermot survived, he would face life as a cripple, but that wasn't the worst of it. He had been bayonetted as well. Blood seeped through his shirt from a wound just under his ribs. Obviously, the blade had not pierced the heart but it must have damaged the lungs. His breathing was shallow and it was several seconds before he could open his eyes, recognising his son who was trying to pour a little water between his parched, blood-encrusted lips.

'Bastards,' he whispered, holding the wound in his side. 'Stealin' up on us like Arabs in the middle of the night. Not brave enough to fight – like men – in the daylight.' He broke off, the effort of trying to speak making him cough. Finding it painful he winced, fighting to suppress it. 'Can't let them win. Not now. You must find Peter Lalor – fight on –'

'Lalor's fallen, Da. A man told me.'

'Dead?'

'I don't know.'

Dermot fell back, dismayed at this news. Tully peered around, hoping to see someone who might help. 'We must find you a doctor, get you patched up.'

'Too late for me, son, I'm finished,' Dermot managed to gasp.

'Don't say that Da. Jus' hold on. Ye can't give up.'

'No. 'S all over for me, lad. I had a life an' I wasted it.

131

Came here to do so much – never meant to end my days like this – lying like a dog in the dust.'

'You're not goin' to die. I won't let you, Da.' Tully took hold of the man and shook him to emphasise his words, making him cry out in pain. 'There! If it hurts, it means you're alive. Lie there an' gather your strength while I go an' get help.'

'No!' Dermot clutched at his son's arm, a surprising amount of strength left in his grip. 'Don't leave me, son. If you do, I'll be dead by the time you get back.'

'Don't say that. You're frightenin' me, Da.'

'Frightened? A great lummox, like you? Nah!' Once again Dermot started to laugh and stopped, giving a grimace of pain. Blood trickled from the corner of his mouth and he spat it out, wiping his mouth on his sleeve. 'Filthy, coppery taste.'

'Now will you let me go for the doctor, Da?'

'No. He'll have enough on his hands.' Dermot settled his grip more firmly on his son's wrist and held on to it. 'You're to leave the fields, d'ye hear me? Soon as I'm gone – now, today.'

'I thought you wanted me to fight on?'

'Too late. I want you away from here. We made our stand and it failed. But the troopers won't rest 'til they have all our names. McDiarmit's sure to be high on the list an' I don't want them to get you, too. Don't let them run you to earth here.'

'But, Da, what about our claims?' Tully was beginning to think his father was raving. 'We can't jus' run out an leave them. Not after all that hard work. Please, let me go for the doctor now. He must be able to help you.'

'Not unless he's willin' to send me to oblivion, a little before me time. Stay with me, son. There's somethin' I need to tell you before I go.' And he lay back, panting gently, his eyes wild with anxiety.

'Not now, Da. You should be savin' your strength.'

'What for? I'm done for. It's you I'm thinking of now. Had plenty of time to think, lyin' here in the dust. I've been a rotten father to you, haven't I, son?'

'No, I wouldn't say that, Da.'

132

'I know ye wouldn't because you're a good boy. But don't bother to lie to me now – I haven't the time. Rotten an' selfish, that's what I've been. Crushin' your ambitions an' talent. Makin' you dance to my tune.'

'I didn't think you liked me to dance to anyone's tune, Da.' Somehow, and in spite of everything, they could laugh at the stupid joke although Dermot stopped as soon as he started, groaning in pain.

'Why, Da?' Tully asked him gently, fearing the question might provoke his father's anger, as usual. 'Why are you so against music? I've never been able to understand it.'

Dermot sighed and turned aside, haunted by painful memories. 'It was your mother,' he muttered. 'Your mother and the way that we met.'

'I dunno.' Tully shook his head. 'You make it sound as if there was some shame in it, Da.'

'Oh, shame there was an' plenty, but never on her side. My poor love. The shame was all mine. Winnin' a woman the way I did. Winnin' your mother from the gypsies on the turn of a card.'

'You won our mam in a card game? Like a prize?'

'Yes.'

'I don't understand.'

'Wait. You see, while Shona was *with* the Romanies, she wasn't *of* the Romany – not Romany born. I dunno. Maybe they stole her from the pram when she was small. She said she sometimes had dreams of luxury, a huge nursery and being dressed by gentle hands. But she had no real memory of such a time.'

Suddenly, Tully was apprehensive. He wasn't sure he was ready to hear these long-buried secrets; these deathbed confessions of his father. Having just turned sixteen, he didn't feel old or confident enough to absolve his father or shoulder the burden of his guilt, whatever it was.

'Maybe I shouldn't be hearin' this. Will I fetch the priest to you, Da?'

'Indeed an' you won't.' Dermot opened his eyes wide, showing a little of his old fire. 'I won't have none of those cantin' hypocrites, waggin' their fingers an' chastisin' me on me deathbed!' He attempted to spit and failed. 'What's the

133

use? How can I look to God for forgiveness when I'll never be able to forgive meself?'

'But –'

'Will ye be still an' listen or not?'

'All right, Da.' Tully licked dry lips.

'Where was I? What was I saying?'

'How you – how you won our mam on the turn of a card.'

'Yes . . . oh yes. I'll never forget the first time I set eyes on her – beautiful an' unspoiled as an angel, an' a voice to match. To hear her sing was to become her slave – to desire her more than anythin' else in the world. And, God help me, desire her I did – I wanted her more than I'd wanted any woman in the whole of my life. Somethin' special it was, to do with her singin'.' All men felt the same about her when she sang – I could see it an' I hated it, the greed and the lust in their eyes. The gypsy owed me money for a pair of horses an' he wouldn't pay. I'd been drinkin' an' I was angry but that's still no excuse for what I did. He was an old man an' I threatened to horsewhip him if he couldn't pay.'

'Oh, Da.'

'I know. I'm not proud of meself but it's the truth. There it is. The old man could see how I felt about Shona – she was all he had left – so he made me a special deal. The chance to win the girl in a game of cards. If I won, I was to take the her an' forget the money. If I lost, the debt was to be written off. In hindsight, I don't think it was the first time he'd made such an offer and he didn't expect to lose, particularly as I was drunk. But that night the cards fell my way and I played like a man inspired. The gypsy was whey-faced when he lost; he looked as if the devil had stolen his soul. The girl was like a daughter to him, you see.'

'But –' Tully could hardly speak; he felt as if there were a tight band constricting his chest. 'But you didn't have to take her from him, did you? Surely, you could have come to some other arrangement?'

'And waived the debt? Ah, but I didn't want to, son. It was the singin', you see. This singin' that was my undoing, luring, spurrin' me on to do wrong. It was only later when the madness left me that I realised what a jewel of a woman I

134

had. But I treated her so cruel on that first night – so mad to get her, I never thought. I didn't see that she was an innocent. She'd never lain with a man before.'

'But Mam loved you, Da, she was always sayin' so.'

'I know she did, though I never deserved it. I took her to wife and a poor time of it I gave her. My only joy in life was that she forgave an' came to love me, in spite of everythin'. But I could never forget it was the singin' and the music that drove me to madness. I needed somethin' else to blame because I couldn't bear to admit the fault was all mine. Her singin' reminded me, you see. Of the beast in myself an' what I did.'

'She forgave you, Da, I'm sure of it, a long time ago.'

'Yes. An' if only it had finished there. But I nearly throttled her when I came upon her teachin' our Maggi to sing. Two voices, so perfect together they blended as one. But to my jealous and benighted mind they were like sirens, those two, calling men on to the rocks of their own desires. I had to protect you, all of you – my wife, my son and my daughter from this damnable gift of music, this two-edged sword within yourselves.'

'It's over, Da. You don't have to torture yourself no more. Our mam never blamed you for anythin' – she loved you, sure. You've tormented yourself for nothin' all these years. It was all in your mind.'

Dermot hiccoughed and a stream of fresh blood spurted from his mouth. Tully wiped it away.

'I do wish you'd let me get help, Da.'

'No. They've work enough to do with the ones they can save. Silly, isn't it? We think we have all our lives ahead of us and there's really – no time at all.' Dermot's eyes glazed and Tully bit his knuckles, suppressing a cry as his father's body went into a last convulsion and was still. There had been many times over the years when he had hated Dermot, even wishing him out of his life. But now it had happened; now that his father lay dead on the ground beside him, his sightless eyes staring up at the brilliant blue of a cloudless Australian sky, he was able to mourn. So he wept, allowing the huge hot tears to spill unchecked from his eyes, to mingle with the blood from the wound in his father's chest. There he stayed until rough but kindly hands took him by the shoulders and one of their English neighbours – a man he had once despised for his mildness – raised him to his feet and led him away.

In less than a week, Ginny Luckett was back at Bullivant House. This in itself was an event. Such a thing had never happened before. Within moments of her arrival, news spread through the house like wildfire. The morning's housework had been interrupted by such a hammering at the door that Maggi and the other girls thought the troopers had arrived to arrest someone. They paused in their labours to peer down the stairwell and see James Parker admitted into the hall, waving his arms and saying he was displeased with the bargain he'd made. Ginny had fallen short of his expectations. Hovering behind him, her face concealed by a brown silk bonnet, she was barely recognisable in her new dark brown skirt and neatly buttoned jacket; typical housekeeper's clothes. Miss Prunella fluttered around them, wringing her hands.

'This is most irregular, Doctor,' she said. 'I don't know what to say – only that you're setting a precedent. This has never happened before.'

'Well, it's happening now! And I demand satisfaction. What do you propose?'

The sound of raised voices was sufficient to bring Mrs Bullivant from her office and she stood at the top of the stairs, assessing the situation, cool and unruffled in her lavender silk which rustled as she descended towards him. But even Mrs Bullivant at her most tactful was unable to pacify Parker and he continued to rave. All over the house the girls paused in their work to listen, enjoying the woman's discomfiture. It wasn't often they had the luxury of seeing Mother Bullivant caught at a disadvantage and at a loss for words.

'I am a doctor, for heaven's sake! And trying to build up a practice in this town. I need to impress people – to gain their confidence – and you fob me off with a girl who's going to cough in their faces as she answers the door! What sort of advertisement would she be? An asthmatic with a chronic

136

bronchial condition. Probably in the early stages of consumption, for all I know.'

'Oh, surely not? Ginny was always one of our most energetic workers.' The girls, listening, smirked at the blatant lie. 'Really, Doctor, won't you take some tea and discuss this calmly and amicably? I can assure you . . .'

'I no longer have any faith in your assurances, madam, and I'll give you no chance to cozen me over a cup of tea. Either you take her back and replace her with a healthy girl who can give me a good day's work, or you give me no option but to hound you through the Courts. Soon the whole of Melbourne shall know of the shabby trick you played on me.'

'Through the Courts, you say?' Mrs Bullivant's voice was glacial. 'And on what charge? I should be very careful, Doctor, if I were you. I have influential friends in this town and you are but a newcomer here.'

'Are you threatening me, madam?'

'Oh, not at all. But as a respected businesswoman, I must take every precaution to protect myself and my good name. I am above such shabby tricks as you're pleased to call them.' Suddenly, her mood changed and her face broke into her most charming smile as she offered him both her hands. He would have been a churl indeed not to have taken them. 'No, no, we can't let it come to that, sir. Surely we can reach a conclusion satisfactory to both of us? But this isn't a game of musical chairs – we must consider the feelings of poor Virginia here.'

Hearing this, Maggi exchanged a glance with one of the other girls. Everyone knew that Mother Bullivant was sensitive to nobody's feelings but her own.

'After all,' the lady went on, gently squeezing the doctor's hands, fully aware of the effect this warm, physical contact would have on a man, 'the girl has spent six nights alone with you under your roof. If you cast her adrift without a character, people will talk. You can't expect to pick a girl up and discard her like a piece of fruit on a barrow.' Clearly, she hoped to appeal to his better nature. In the case of Doctor Parker, Maggi knew she was wasting her time.

'How very apt.' He smiled, withdrawing his hands. 'I

couldn't have found a better simile myself. So will you take back your rotten apple, madam, and give me what I have paid for – a good apple which is both ripe and sweet?'

Mrs Bullivant frowned at these words which produced a sob from Ginny who, until now, had been standing back, rigid with tension and with her head bowed, her face concealed by the brim of her bonnet. Once more the girls exchanged glances, concerned on their own behalf this time. No one wanted to be chosen by the doctor for fear of being similarly rejected. Instinctively, Maggi took a step backwards, hoping to hide behind one of the taller girls. She knew Mother Bullivant was more than anxious to be rid of her and was afraid of being offered in Ginny's place. But this time she was in luck. Mrs Bullivant wanted to resolve the matter quickly rather than use the circumstances to settle old scores.

In haste, half a dozen of the older girls were called down into the hall and Doctor Parker inspected them in much the same manner, Maggi thought, as her father might choose a horse. In the end he picked a sultry, dark-haired girl who was a recent arrival. But not before he had humiliated her before everyone by carrying out a medical examination in public and opening her mouth to examine her teeth. Careless of her feelings, he embarrassed her further by tapping her chest and listening to it, to make certain her lungs were sound. Mrs Bullivant nodded but her smile was cool as he agreed to the exchange. He wasn't to know that the dark-haired girl had been smuggled into the house in dubious circumstances, arriving wet and bedraggled in the middle of the night. The girls knew better than to discuss it among themselves but it was more than likely she was an escapee from Van Diemen's Land.

Maggi had no opportunity to speak to Ginny in private until they retired to their attic dormitory later that day.

'Just don't say it!' Ginny turned on her, eyes blazing. 'Don't you dare say "I told you so".' And she flung herself face down on her bed, sobbing bitterly. At last she felt free to shed the tears she had been bottling up all day, refusing to break down before the taunts of the other girls. Remembering her past unkindness, they wouldn't be slow to take their

138

revenge, delighted to see an old enemy humiliated and brought low.

'I wasn't going to say anything.' Maggi sat on the edge of the bed, waiting for Ginny to stop crying and not knowing how to comfort the girl who appeared to be choking on her tears, sobbing wretchedly and coughing at the same time. 'Can you tell me what happened?'

'What do you think? He was all you said he would be, and worse.' Ginny sat up, hugging her brown dress around her knees and rocking herself in her misery. She spoke with her face buried in her lap and Maggi had trouble making out what she was saying between the sobs. 'He's bought a big house on Lonsdale Street. I think somebody left it to go to the gold fields – layers of dust and dirt and a filthy, old-fashioned stove that must have come out of the ark. I was to be his cook-housekeeper and though he didn't come out with it and say so, he made it clear that I was expected to serve him in bed. I thought I could handle him – keep him at arm's length and hold out for marriage like I said . . .' Here Ginny began weeping afresh. 'Oh, Maggi I called you a green fool but there was never a bigger fool than myself. He just laughed and told me not to be silly. I thought as he was a doctor, he'd act like a gentleman. That if I locked myself in my room, he'd accept it and wouldn't do anything. He was so angry, he broke down the door. He tore off my nightgown and took me – right there on the floor.'

'Oh, Ginny, I'm so sorry. Ginny, you poor –'

Amazingly, she grinned through her tears. 'Good job I wasn't a virgin – it might've hurt.'

'Not a virgin? But didn't you tell me . . .'

'I lied. Ginny waved away Maggi's queries. 'But you can't fool a doctor, can you? I was hopin' to get him to the altar before he found out. Oh, well.' She shrugged. 'There goes another good idea up the spout. What are you lookin' at me like that for? You'd have done the same in my place. Anyone would.'

'I don't think I want to hear any more of this.'

'Oh, don't be such a prude. You're a pick-pocket, an' I'm a – well, never mind what I am. I don't mind a man gettin' carried away and showin' a bit of passion but Parker's

139

difficult to handle. Can't seem to get any pleasure without being rough. So, after five nights of gettin' bruised an' slobbered over, I decided not to take any more. I thought he might let me alone if he heard me cough but that only made him madder than ever.'

'So that's why he brought you back? After hearing you cough?'

'Oh, no, that was just his excuse. I do have a weak chest but it isn't consumption an' he knows it. No. He wanted rid of me because I can't cook. Can't fry an egg without it gettin' brown on the bottom an' jelly on top. Can't even toast a piece of bread without burnin' it to a crisp.'

'Oh, Ginny.' This ridiculously simple explanation on the heels of tragedy was too much for Maggi. She covered her mouth to stop the giggles but they kept welling up, refusing to be suppressed. At last, on the verge of choking, she laughed aloud, unable to stop. 'Oh, Ginny, I'm so sorry. I know it's not funny at all but I can't help myself ...' Fortunately, the laughter was infectious and after a half-hearted attempt to cuff her about the ears, Ginny saw the funny side of it too and laughed as well.

'Thank God for you, Maggi McDiarmit. You an' your stupid cackle. I feel better already.'

'Good. And you can't say you had nothing out of it. At least he gave you a decent dress. You won't have to wear this beastly gingham any more.'

This sent them both into more gales of laughter until Ginny sobered, pushing her hair back out of her eyes and rubbing her nose on the back of her hand. 'There's still Bitchface. She won't let me forget this little jaunt in a hurry. She'll have it in for me, now. Have me up at dawn chasin' spiders in the outside privies for a month.'

'Yes, an' I'll be right there with you.' Maggi also stopped laughing, remembering Mother Bullivant's long memory and her capacity to bear a grudge.

Daisy Bradley wasn't pleased. It showed in the frown which puckered her clear white forehead and in the pursing of her full red lips.

'It's no good, Matthew, I can't be doin' with the boy. You

140

can't expect me to take him in here.' Daisy was the only person to call her husband by his given name. She detested the nickname of Cabbage Tree which she thought undignified. Matthew, in turn, was irritated by his wife's delusions of grandeur which she fondly imagined he knew nothing about. Mrs Bradley dreamed of a time when she would no longer be a mere bullocky's wife, occupying a draughty weatherboard cottage on The Flat at Swan Street, but the mistress of one of the grand new mansions she saw going up on nearby Richmond Hill.

These daydreams were a comfort to her while she wrestled with the primitive outdoor washing facilities and the privy from which she was always chasing ugly if harmless 'triantelope' spiders before her children would go in. One day soon she was going to have dishes like ornaments and wear beautiful clothes, taking her place in polite society with her husband at her side. He would no longer be a bullocky, a carrier taking luggage from place to place, nor would she be obliged to take in washing to make ends meet.

These daydreams sustained her as she slaved over her laundry and she couldn't or wouldn't believe they would never come true. Because even if, by some miracle, everything else fell into place, her good-natured but foul-mouthed husband would never be accepted in the drawing rooms of Melbourne and her snivelling, unattractive offspring had no place in her schemes, let alone this orphaned Irish boy her husband had befriended on the gold fields and who now stood shuffling and looking uncomfortable, cluttering her tidy room.

As a rule, Cabbage Tree left Daisy alone with her foibles but this time he was angry with her. Tully didn't deserve such a paltry welcome.

'Bloody hell, Daise, have a heart. 'T'isn't as if we can't afford it – we're not hurtin' any these days and we're not pushed for room.' He spread his arms to indicate the living room and the yard beyond.

'That's right. Raise your voice to me and frighten the children.' Daisy's lips trembled and she was able to squeeze out two tears which rolled down her plump cheeks. 'Not

141

home five minutes an' you're ef'in' an' blindin' at me – worse than your father, you are.'

'Bloody hell, woman!' The bullocky pounded his fist against the doorpost, making the house shake. 'The boy's lost his parents. He's alone in the world.'

'Forget it, Cabbage Tree.' Tully was casting anxious glances at Daisy, whose face was crumpling again. He had no wish to be caught in the middle of a domestic argument. 'Your wife doesn't want me an' that's fair enough. It was a dumb idea anyway. I'll be on me way.'

'No, you won't, nipper. You bloody well stay where you are! This is my flamin' house an' I pay the flamin' bills an' I'm damned if I'll be ordered about by a piece o' skirt, wife or no!'

'Call this a house, do you?' Daisy flared her nostrils, glancing around the sparsely decorated room. 'My poor mother would turn in her grave if she knew I'd come down to this.'

'That does it. Don't you mention your flamin' mother to me.' Warming to the argument, Cabbage Tree was losing his temper in earnest. 'A bloody Vandemonian, that's all your mother was. A bloody light-fingered lucy who came out with the first fleet . . .'

Daisy's mouth worked. This was the first time her husband had trampled on her illusions and made her face up to the truth. After a moment, she opened her mouth and emitted a wail of distress. Taking it as their cue, her children joined in, howling in unison as they clung to their mother's skirts.

'Don't worry, Cabbage Tree I'll be all right.' Tully mouthed the words so that his friend would understand him over the screams of the younger Bradleys which threatened to raise the roof. 'Don't want to be no trouble. Best if I go.'

'I'm sorry, mate.' Cabbage Tree shrugged. Following Tully to the door, he closed it behind them, shutting the noise inside. 'Dunno what's got into Daise – she don't often turn ugly like that.'

'It doesn't matter, really. You've done more than enough already.'

'Who'd want to come and stay in that flamin' madhouse, anyway?' Cabbage Tree looked glum. 'Is it any wonder I'd rather be out on the road? Oh, I know I shouldn'a said what I did – touchy about her mother, she is. But the silly cow gets me so mad, if I don't shout, I'm likely to knock her block off one o' these days.'

'Don't do that. She has enough on her hands with her laundry an' those kids. She's probably tired out. You can't blame her for not being keen to take on any more.' Having kept house for himself and Dermot at the gold fields, Tully had a little more insight into a woman's lot than many young men of his time.

'I don't care. She could've made you a damned sight more welcome than she did.'

'Honest, Cabbage Tree, I don't mind.' And as he said it, Tully realised it was true. If Daisy Bradley had opened her heart to him and made him welcome, it would have been difficult to turn his back on his friend and leave. Forced to grow up more quickly than most, Tully had plans of his own. First he had to find Maggi and see her safe. Only then would he feel free to follow his own inclinations and go to sea. He had never given up his dream of joining the crew of the *Sally Lee*. So he grinned at his friend and gave him an affectionate punch on the shoulder. 'Cheer up,' he said. 'I'm not goin' to lose you – not now I know where you live.'

'Bloody well see that you don't. I know this town. It can be a dangerous place for a boy on his own.'

Chapter Eleven

Tully had seen great houses in Ireland but only from a distance and when he had been left to hold the horses in a lane at the back while his father went to make the acquaintance of those in charge of the stables. His heart sank when he saw Bullivant House for the first time, the big gates and high walls. Everything about it was forbidding; it was obvious that uninvited visitors were unwelcome here. The hairs on the back of his neck prickled, warning him to take care. People narrowed their eyes and gave him considering looks when he asked for directions to Bullivant House and the question was always the same: 'Bullivant House? What business can a boy like you have at Bullivant House?'

Never you mind! he wanted to say. But he stifled the words, knowing he would gain much more by being polite. 'An orphanage, isn't it?' he prompted. 'A refuge for homeless girls?'

'That's what they say,' said the last man he asked, indicating the house. It was a handsome house, no doubt custom built for some gentleman and his family. A house which should have been well maintained to show a welcoming face to the world. The bars on the windows and the neglect of the formal gardens were evidence of the institution it had become. After making sure no one was in the garden to see him, Tully approached the front gate and peered through the strong, wrought-iron bars, topped with arrow-heads which made them look like spears, more and more worried about his sister and her fate. Even if she wasn't a prisoner she'd feel like one, surrounded by all these hedges and iron bars. The front gate didn't appear to be locked but some instinct told him not to go up to the door. Servants were usually talkative and he'd find out much more if he went to the tradesmen's entrance at the back of the house.

But, if anything, the approach to the back of Bullivant House was still more daunting than the front, the back yard surrounded by a solid brick wall with wicked-looking shards of glass set into the mortar on top. The back gate was chained and padlocked but there was a brass bell beside it and a notice which Tully took to be a request to ring for attention. He seized the rope and rang the bell, enjoying the noisy clangour which broke the silence, dispelling the oppressive atmosphere surrounding the house.

He watched and waited, looking at the back door. Nothing happened so he rang again, more vigorously this time. The back door opened and two girls' heads poked out. They might have been twins, both faces flushed from working in the heat of the kitchen and both wearing identical mob caps.

'On your way, boy,' one of them shouted. 'Cookie's in a foul temper today. She'll have your guts for garters if she catches you playin' "knock up ginger" round here.'

'Please, I'm not here to cause any trouble,' Tully called through the iron bars of the gate. 'I'm askin' after Maggi McDiarmit. I think she's a – a student here.'

'A student?' The girls collapsed into gales of laughter until one of them recovered enough to speak.

'Oh, yes, darlin, we're all good scholars here! What sort of a place do you think this is?'

'A prison, if this wall is anythin' to go by. Please, is there a Maggi McDiarmit here?'

'*A* Maggi McDiarmit? You mean there's more than one? God forbid.' The girl giggled and then her smile became sly. 'What's in it for me? For a start you'll have to ask me a whole lot nicer than that.'

Tully ground his teeth. 'Please, miss. I don't have time to play games. Is she here or not?'

'That'd be tellin', wouldn' it, Nance?' The girl nudged her companion and gave Tully a sidelong glance. 'We don't speak to the rats that run in the attic, or carry messages for scullery maids.'

145

'Cookie's comin' – look out!' The other girl jabbed the speaker in the ribs and the two faces vanished, to be replaced by the broad figure of the cook. She stood in the doorway, legs straddled and her head poked forward aggressively, her cook's hat hanging like a limp sock over one eye.

'Who's there?' she demanded. 'I can see you, boy – no use hidin' behind the hedge. Can't you read?' And she pointed to the notice hanging over the bell. 'It says *No hawkers or pedlars* – by the order of Mother Bullivant herself.'

'I'm not selling anything.' Tully decided his best hope was to charm her. 'An' I'm sorry if I disturbed you by ringin' the bell. I was wonderin' if I could have a word with me sister? I think she's stayin' here.'

'Sister, is it?' the cook snorted. 'As if I haven't heard that one before! Be off with you now. Followers aren't allowed here.'

'But I'm not a follower. Maggi McDiarmit's me sister an' I know she's here.' Tully had been through far too much at the gold fields to be intimidated by a fat cook.

'Be off with you at once, or I'll let loose the dogs.'

'Dogs? I didn't hear them bark when I rang the bell.'

'Too smart for your own good, that's what you are. Should be ashamed of yourself. Comin' here danglin' after girls an' you scarcely old enough to grow a beard. On your way, before I send for the troopers an' have you arrested.'

'On what charge?'

The cook didn't answer him. Instead she bounced back into the house, slamming the door. He could hear her clattering pots and shouting to someone inside. No one had confirmed or denied it but he was certain his sister was there.

He followed the line of the wall and walked all round the outside of the property, looking for another way in. There wasn't one. He realised his best chance of gaining entry without being seen was by scaling the wall and that would have to be at night. He made up his mind to return when the house was asleep.

The rest of the day seemed to drag as he waited for nightfall. After parting company with Cabbage Tree he'd had nothing to eat but he wasn't yet hungry enough to beg on the streets like some others he saw. At a pinch he could

146

always take up his mandolin and sing for his supper. On the gold fields, although he and his father had lived hand to mouth, they had always managed to scrape together a few grains of gold which could be traded for something to eat. Here, in the city, he didn't know his way around. Prices varied alarmingly, the traders taking advantage of the newly rich who indulged themselves with shameful recklessness and a total disregard for those less fortunate than themselves. There wasn't even a workhouse – no provision or place for the poor whose only recourse was to steal or beg.

He had gone through the last few weeks in a trance, still shocked over his father's death. His first thought had been to follow Dermot's last orders and get away from Eureka and all that it represented. He hadn't the heart to try to sell anything so walked away without marking his claim. It was usual to leave a pick in the ground as a sign of intention to return. It wouldn't have mattered if he had. He knew their disagreeable neighbour would steal it the moment his back was turned. Numbed by his father's death, it never occurred to him that he should have sold the claims which would have given him money enough to survive on. All he took was his mandolin hanging by a cord made out of some bootlaces and slung across his shoulder.

Together with other people similarly bereaved, he had returned to the field of Eureka one last time to bury the dead. By tacit agreement, they joined forces to dig a communal grave as the ground was too hard at this time of year to bury each man individually and leave a mark. So Dermot was laid to rest with his companions. Fearing reprisals, many people buried their relatives under false names. Tully did the same. Then he went to see Bill at the Post Office, asking him to send a message to Cabbage Tree. Not realising at first that he was being insensitive, Bill wanted to talk.

'Shocking business. Told them so all along. I said it was crazy, setting themselves against the military. No good will ever come out o' that, I said. An' I was right.'

'A lot of good it'll do us, you being right!' Tully found he was shaking, unable to stop. 'My da's out there! Dead an' buried because he was prepared to fight for what he believed in. Prepared to stand up an' be counted – which is more than

147

some others I know.' Even in his fury, he was gratified to see Bill look away, shamefaced.

'Sorry, lad. Didn't know of your loss.'

'You didn't see it as I did. Men blown to pieces by those ugly weapons of war. The soldiers set fire to the tents where the wounded were lying – men with broken limbs an with their insides fallin' out. What chance did they have? Screamin' as they burned alive, unable to get away from the flames!'

'Ah, no, no,' Bill whispered, turning whey-faced. 'Don't tell me any more.'

'So don't let me hear you tryin' to be wise after the event. Don't come crowin' to me about bein' right.'

'No.' The postal officer looked thoughtful, addressing the boy with a new respect. 'So what can I do for you, son? There's no letters in or out, what with the curfew . . .'

'I don't want to send a letter. I need you to get a message to Cabbage Tree.'

Only now, a week or so later, could Tully fully appreciate the support and generosity of the bullocky during those first grim days and sleepless nights. Immersed in grief, he took Cabbage Tree's friendship for granted, travelling with him free of charge and sharing his simple meals. At this moment he hadn't the price of a pie in his pocket and his stomach gurgled and growled, reproaching him for his neglect.

Drawn to the smell of cooked chickens and ham coming from the row of pie stalls set up outside the Eastern Market, Tully inhaled the delicious savory smells, feasting his eyes on one stall in particular where a man had just set out his pies to cool. The pieman watched him just as carefully, having lost pies to beggars before. He thought this boy looked hungry enough to snatch one and run.

While Tully hovered there, unable to bring himself to ask for charity or leave, a nursemaid came up to buy a pie for the little girl in her charge. A spoiled little girl dressed in royal blue damask and with matching silk ribbons in her hair. The child was jumping up and down, demanding the food with shrill cries.

'I can't let you have it – not yet.' The nursemaid discovered the pie was so hot, she could scarcely hold it in her gloved hands.

148

'Now! Now! I want it now!' the child roared.

'Be careful, then. Blow on it first and make sure it has cooled before you take a bite. It's come from a hot spot.'

Ignoring the nurse's warning, the child snatched the pie and took a big bite, only to scream and stamp her foot as she burned her mouth. Flinging the pie to the ground, she burst into tears of disappointment and pain. While the nursemaid was leading her away, cossetting and scolding, Tully swooped on the pie, narrowly missing the jaws of a big dog which had caught sight of it at the same time. But instead of snarling or trying to bite, the dog sat down on his haunches, gazing with longing at the pie in Tully's hands, exerting emotional pressure with his eyes. He drooled long loops of saliva as Tully flicked the dirt from the crust of the pie, preparing to eat it. But he couldn't ignore the plea in the dog's eyes.

'Oh, all right. Jus' don't be lookin' at me like that, I can't stand it.' And he broke the pie in half, sharing with the dog who snatched his portion and gulped it down, raising his ears in the hope of more.

'No, you don't, Pieface. I'm hungry, too.' Tully grinned, happy to have someone to talk to. 'Go. Go on home, now.' But it was no use. Now that the dog had been fed and given a name, he was convinced he had found his new master and continued to follow Tully, ignoring all his efforts to send him away. Tully liked the dog as it reminded him of one they had once in Ireland when he was small. This one was the same; something between a gypsy's long dog and an Irish wolfhound, with soulful brown eyes and covered in wiry, reddish hair. It was a big dog and would have been handsome once but now it was painfully thin, the ribs sticking out even under the fur. 'Come on then, Pieface. I guess we're in this together. But you're not to bark or make the smallest sound while I get over that wall or I'll disown you.'

The dog seemed to understand, laughing at Tully, tongue lolling.

After nightfall, Bullivant House looked more brooding and sinister than ever, the bars outside the windows accentuated by the lamplight inside.

Crouched in the bushes behind the back wall, Tully was glad of the comforting presence of the dog who seemed happy enough to respond to the name of Pieface and understood perfectly about being quiet.

'You poacher's dog, you,' Tully said affectionately, ruffling the tough curls on the dog's head. Together they watched and waited as the lamps in the house were extinguished, one by one.

To aid him in his unlawful entry, Tully had stolen a length of rope from the landing stage by the river. His conscience plagued him as he was a reluctant thief. Stealing had never come naturally to him as it did to his father and Maggi.

Tossing the rope in the way Jem had shown him, during many long hours abroad the *Sally Lee*, he hitched it to the gatepost, testing its strength before taking off his boots and his mandolin and hauling himself barefooted up the outer side of the wall. Pieface whined softly, not wanting to be left behind.

'Stay! Good dog! Look after my things!' Tully whispered, thinking of the glass on the top of the wall and hoping the dog wouldn't try to follow and injure his feet. But with a sigh, Pieface settled down to wait, his head on his front paws.

On the other side of the wall, Tully waited, listening, wondering if the yard was protected by a dog. Fortunately, there was no sound of a heavy body plunging through the undergrowth to bring him crashing to the ground. Not at all comfortable as a trespasser, he unfastened the rope and brought it with him as he stared up at the house, now in darkness, wondering where his sister was likely to be. Silly to make a mistake after coming so far. If he should be caught in the grounds, lamps would be lit, women would scream and he would be accused of being a potential rapist – at the very least, a peeping tom. Then he remembered the words of the girl at the back door: *We don't speak to the rats that run in the attic*. The clue was vague but it was the only one he had. Was Maggi asleep up there? Behind the only window in the house without bars – an attic window cut into the roof?

Chapter Twelve

There had been little joy in Maggi's life in the week Ginny was away and there was even less when she came back. The two girls were seldom away from the kitchen sink or the tubs in the laundry unless they were chopping wood, or carrying heavy pails of water up long flights of stairs. Cook and Matron competed to keep them on their feet all day, fetching and carrying, scrubbing and scouring, until their hands were chapped and sore, their legs aching with weariness. Matron rewarded any tardiness with a cuff on the ear. Ginny's new skirt was now as ragged as Maggi's old dress and no one suggested they should be replaced. Mrs Bullivant could see no value in providing her scullions with new clothes. And not once since Ginny's return had either of them been asked to assemble before the visitors who came looking for servants on a Sunday afternoon.

Grimy as a pair of sweeps, they were no longer allowed to eat with the others in the dining room. Like poor relations in a household where supplies of food were watched and counted, their main meals consisted of scraps returned by the other girls. They survived on what they could steal when the cook wasn't looking.

Ignored before, they were now treated with contempt by the other girls. It wasn't surprising. Nobody dared to offer a kind word for fear of being sent to join them. By nightfall both Maggi and Ginny were too exhausted to do anything but fall into their attic beds and revel in the simple luxury of sleep. They paid scant attention to personal hygiene and never combed their hair. There just wasn't the time. Maggi knew she looked awful but she was too tired to care. The days passed into weeks and it was hard to believe it would soon be Christmas, particularly as the weather was getting so warm.

Ginny sank into a depression; life was no longer a joke or a challenge. Maggi waited, expecting her to rally and show some of her old spirit but she didn't. Much as Maggi dreaded her practical jokes, even those would have been preferable to the sounds of muffled weeping which came from Ginny's pillow night after night. Sounds which ate into Maggi's own reserves of good humour and hope. At last she sat up, able to bear it no longer.

'Will you stop that, Ginny? This weepin' of yours is no good to either of us. I know you're disappointed but I tried to warn you about Parker – I told you what he was like. Really, you've had a lucky escape.'

'Lucky?' Ginny uncovered her head to glare at Maggi, eyes swimming with resentful tears. 'I don't call it lucky to be kept as a prisoner, forced to scrub floors every day.'

'It won't be forever.'

'No? I used to know what I wanted. I had a plan.' Her voice rose in complaint, grating on Maggi's nerves. 'But it all went wrong and I don't know what to do any more. We're never going to get away from here – never! We'll be here until we rot!'

'We will not,' Maggi snapped, although Ginny was voicing her own worst fears. 'We won't starve, anyway – not so long as my hand can move faster than the cook's eye. Hard work never hurt anyone, Ginny. It'll make you strong.'

'I wish you'd stop being so beastly cheerful.'

'Yes, I am cheerful, an' I won't let you drag me down. Can't you see, you won't get better until you stop feeling so sorry for yourself?'

'You don't know the half of it. Maggi, I'm scared, so scared of what Bitchface will do to me when she finds out.'

'Finds out what?' Maggi rolled her eyes heavenwards, thinking Ginny was being melodramatic as usual. She stretched her legs down the bed, too tired to give more than half her attention as her overworked body began to relax.

'You won't tell? Promise me? Cross your heart an' hope to die?'

'Hope to die,' Maggi whispered, closing her eyes, already drifting towards sleep.

'I think – I think Doctor Parker's made a baby in me. I'm having a child.'

Maggi's eyes snapped open. Suddenly, she was wide awake. She sat up in bed to stare at Ginny who was staring back at her, white-faced.

'You can't be sure of that, Ginny. It's too soon.'

'Oh, yes I am. You've seen me sick in the morning.'

'Who wouldn't be sick? Living on bits of gristle and stale left-overs as we do? We never get any real food.'

'My teats itch. And – and I've missed my flux by more than two weeks.'

'Why didn't you tell me all this before?'

'I'm tellin' you now, aren't I? An' I'm scared. Scared of what Bitchface will do. She'll make me get rid of it.'

'How?'

'Don't know nothin', do you? A girl turned up here pregnant once before. She wasn't found out until she started to show. Bullivant sent her to Matron – it was awful, we heard her screamin' all night. Next day she was dead – bled to death.'

'How – how do you know?'

'Because we was sent in to clear up the mess. There was blood all over the bed an' the floor.'

Maggi shivered. She had seen the look of unholy glee on the Matron's face as she stood over Kitty, forcing the little girl's hands into near-boiling water. The woman would enjoy being cruel, Ginny was right.

'So what can I do?' Ginny punched herself in the stomach, making Maggi wince. 'I wish I could fall down the stairs an' lose it before Mother Bullivant finds me out.'

'Don't say that, Ginny. There must be another way.'

As if in answer to her question a shower of pebbles struck the window which was half-open behind them.

'Hailstones?' Maggi frowned. 'I didn't hear any thunder, did you?'

'It's not hailstones, you idiot, there's somebody down

there – trying to get our attention.' Her troubles for the moment forgotten, Ginny leaped out of bed as if she hadn't a care in the world. Going to the window, she peered into the bushes in the garden below. There was nothing to see. Only the long purple shadows cast by the trees in the light of a full summer moon. 'Anyone there? Who is it? And what do you want?'

'Please – don't be afraid,' somebody whispered, scarcely loud enough to be heard. 'An' please don't shout or raise the alarm. I only want to know if me sister's there?'

'It's my brother! It's Tully!' Maggi skipped out of bed and elbowed Ginny aside to appear at the window herself.

'Thank the good Lord I've found you, sis.' He smiled in relief. 'My lucky stars must be shinin' tonight.'

'How did you get here?'

'Never mind.'

'Where's Da? Is he here, too?'

'Later, Mags. First, I have to get you out of there. Provided, of course, you're ready to go?'

'Ready and willing. But how?'

'Stop that talking up there!' The sharp, nasal tones of Miss Prunella made them all jump. 'If you're not tired enough to sleep, then you've not enough work to do. That can be rectified in the morning!'

Maggi stuck out her tongue although she knew Miss Prunella couldn't see it and held her breath until she heard the woman's slippered feet hurrying away across the polished floors. Nerves made Ginny giggle and she went into a paroxysm of coughing.

'Tully?' Maggi whispered, peering into the darkness, concerned that he might have taken fright and disappeared.

'I'm still here.'

'How am I to get out?'

'You tell me. Can't you leave by the back door?'

'No. It's locked overnight and the cook has the key. I think she sleeps with it under her pillow.'

'Have to do the rope trick, then. Catch hold of this an' tie it firmly to somethin' that won't give.'

After several attempts, Tully succeeded in throwing the rope for Maggi to catch. Ginny helped her to secure it to one of the heavy iron beds which they jammed against the window frame.

'Right. I'm goin' first,' Ginny said, making Maggi stare at her in surprise. 'Well? You didn't think I'd let you go without me, did you? I'll cry rape and scream the house down, if you do.'

'Ginny, you wouldn't?'

'Try me.'

Maggi hesitated. It was no bluff. Ginny was desperate enough to do as she said. Maggi thought quickly. They had never been close friends but could she live with her conscience if she left, knowing of Ginny's plight, and leaving her at the mercy of Mother Bullivant and the Matron?

'I suppose so – all right, you can come.' She gave in with bad grace. 'But I'll have a solemn promise out of you, before you do.'

'Anythin', dearest Mags.' Ginny kissed the air towards her, almost her old self again.

'No, Ginny, I'm serious. I want you to keep your sticky paws off my Tully. I'll not have you makin' a fool of him to give Parker's baby a name.'

'Lawks, Maggi, what do you take me for?'

'D'you really want me to say?'

'Jesus, you're like an old mother hen with him. I've not even seen the lad up close an' you're warnin' me off.'

'Because I know you. And I'll have your solemn oath or we're not goin', neither of us.'

'All right, I promise.'

'Mags!' This was an urgent whisper from Tully outside. 'You comin' or not? The sky's gettin' lighter, it'll be daylight soon.'

It wasn't easy to get Ginny to trust herself to the rope and the tree. She had no head for heights and had never done such a thing before. She got out of the window and froze, and it took all the persuasive powers of both Tully and Maggi to coax her to transfer to the tree. Her boots slipped, she succumbed to panic and stopped again. Tully had to climb up and help her get down.

'My, how strong you are!' Ginny looked up at him through her eyelashes. 'I had no idea.'

155

'Ginny!' This came as a growl from Maggi above them.

'Only looking,' the girl said. 'I won't touch.' All the same she continued to smile at the boy, devouring him with her slant-eyed gaze.

Maggi slid down the rope with ease, without needing the support of the tree, and Tully caught her, setting her on the ground.

'Good grief,' he said, feeling how thin and fragile she'd become. 'You're nothin' but skin an' bone. Turn sideways an you'll disappear.'

'An' we'll have less of your lip, young man.' She hugged him. 'Is it that I've shrunk or you've grown? You're a mile taller than I am now. You went away a boy an' you've come back a young man.'

'I know,' he said, his expression bleak. 'You grow up quick out there on the gold fields.'

With her brother's assistance, Maggi didn't find it too hard to climb over the back wall, avoiding the shards of glass. Ginny wasn't so lucky. She fell in a heap on the ground on the other side, whimpering and nursing her foot.

'It's broken, for sure,' she said, and shrieked as Pieface, having given Tully an ecstatic welcome, now turned his attention to her, seated on the ground. 'I don't like dogs! Get him off!'

'Here, boy!' Maggi held out her hand to the dog who came to her eagerly, more than happy to transfer his affections to someone else. She ruffled the wiry curls on his head as he looked up at her with adoring eyes. 'You're an old charmer, aren't you? What a rogue. Where did you get him, Tully?'

'Never mind the dog, let's get away from here.' Ginny aimed a half-hearted kick at Pieface who avoided it. 'Filthy animal, full of fleas and lice. His breath stinks as well.'

'So would yours if you were as hungry as he is,' Tully defended his dog. By now Pieface had drawn back his lips, growling at Ginny. 'Stop that.' He slapped the dog on the muzzle. 'I know you're bad-tempered because you're hungry – we all are.' And his stomach gurgled as if on cue.

'Are you saying you have no money either?' Ginny asked, glancing at Maggi as the boy shook his head. Harsh as life had been at Bullivant House they had never gone hungry. Now they would have to live off their wits.

Taking Tully's advice, they stayed away from the wide thoroughfare which was Saint Kilda Road, following the path which led past the boatsheds on the bank of the River Yarra instead. They returned to the main road only to walk in the shade of a market gardener's cart going into town, filled with fresh vegetables and cut flowers. Hoping to slip through the toll gate unobserved, they remained out of sight behind the load as the driver paid the keeper and continued across the bridge. Seeing it as a chance to cross the bridge unobserved, the three young people and the dog remained close by the market gardener's cart, trying to look as if they belonged.

The streets of Melbourne were far from deserted even at this early hour. To celebrate the coming of Christmas the shops and alleys were decorated with garlands and greenery, making them look like leafy lanes rather than the streets of a city. At Bullivant House every day except Sunday had been the same. Mother Bullivant didn't believe in holidays. Maggi felt the excitement welling inside her as she realised she wouldn't have to worry about that woman's moods any more. She was free. Free and with nothing to do for the first time in weeks. She glanced at Tully and smiled warmly. He responded with a twitch of the lips but his expression remained bleak.

'What is it?' she whispered. 'Something's wrong, isn't it?'

'Not now, sis,' he murmured, glancing at Ginny.

Maggi walked on in silence. Her brother had changed and not only physically. They had been living apart for only four months but he seemed like a stranger, grim and hollow-eyed from experiences he wasn't yet ready to discuss. And why didn't he mention Da? She would get to the bottom of it later. For now, she could only suppose that they'd quarrelled and fallen out. That would explain Tully's bleak expression as well as his lack of funds.

With her mind running on these matters, she scarcely noticed when the market gardener turned right into Bourke Street and started up the hill. He shook the reins and clicked his tongue at his horse, encouraging it to pull the cart those

157

last few yards which would bring them to the Eastern Market at the top. But the load was heavy today and the horse failed, allowing the cart to slip. The gardener shouted but to no avail. The horse was old and he had covered more than a few miles that day. Maggi and Tully came to the rescue, shoving the cart from behind. It was second nature to them, having done the same thing for their father so many times before. All the same it was hard work on a day which was already uncomfortably hot. There wasn't a breath of wind and it had that oppressive, airless feel to it, promising a heat wave later on. Ginny stalked ahead, refusing to get involved.

'The Eastern Market is as good a place as any if you're poor an' down on your luck,' Tully whispered to his sister. 'Easy to disappear and blend with the crowd.'

'You've been here before, then?'

'It's an eye opener, sis. So much food I can't think who's going to eat it all. An' everyone dressed from the rag bag. Nobody's going to notice two more grimy scullions amongst that lot.'

'Speak for yourself!' She took her hand off the cart to punch him on the shoulder. 'Have you looked in the mirror lately? You should. Not so much of the elegant, man about town yourself in those filthy moleskins an' brokendown boots. And who gave you that?' She was looking at his mandolin. 'It's a wonder Da let you keep it. And even more of a wonder he let you come back to Melbourne on your own.'

'Not now, sis.' His throat was taut with misery. 'I really don't want to talk about it now.'

'So you fell out with him? I can guess that much at least. What about?'

'Not now!' he said through gritted teeth.

'If it's *her* you're worried about, then don't.' Maggi glanced at Ginny. 'She never listens to anythin' unless it's about herself. Come on, Tully. I know you an' Da have never seen eye to eye but it can't be *that* bad . . .'

'Well, it is.' And he pursed his lips, willing to say no more. Maggi didn't press him. She'd seen that look before. She knew her brother was battling with strong emotions and was

158

afraid of giving way to them in front of Ginny. She would
have to contain her patience and wait.

Business was brisk at the Eastern Market. Even before
they reached it they could hear the buzz of excited conversation and the cries of the stallholders, trying to shout one
another down as they barked their wares.

'New season's canteloupe. Ripe and bursting with juice!
Try before you buy!'

'Onions! Shillin' a dozen!'

'New baby carrots, shillin' a bunch!'

'Cabbages – two for a shillin' an' big as yer 'ead!'

The market occupied a large open space at the top of
Bourke Street. Market gardeners and other traders had set
up their stalls, some under rough awnings, protecting themselves from what promised to be a scorching day. While they
gave some protection from the sun, the tent-like structures
contributed to the general airlessness and the noise was
deafening to the newcomers, disoriented after a sleepless
night. The dog pressed close against Tully's legs, determined
not to lose him. Domestic fowl, trapped in wicker cages,
added their frightened voices to the hubbub.

Maggi looked around, loving all of it and savouring the
freedom of a life without gongs or impatient voices ordering
her about. Finding it easier to let the market gardener cut a
path for them through the crowd, they continued in his
wake. Maggi sniffed, enjoying the wonderful earthy smells of
root vegetables – parsnips, turnips and potatoes freshly torn
from the ground, combined with the more pungent, exotic
aroma of others unknown to her; warty-looking foreign
vegetables which she'd never seen before and had no idea
what they tasted like. Then there was the acrid smell of
frightened animals mingled with human sweat, suddenly overtaken by a blast of sweetness from fresh flowers. Maggi
breathed deeply, enjoying the market atmosphere as well as
the laughter and friendliness between the stallholders and
those who had come to buy.

The season of Christmas was much in evidence here.
Saplings were laced to the support posts throughout the
market and the stalls were all decorated in festive spirit.
Children darted through the crowds, waving huge fronds of

fern – the local substitute for holly and fir – and singing Christmas songs which were just an excuse for their begging.

'Christmas is coming! The goose is getting fat! Please to put a penny in the ole man's hat!'

Adding to the volume of noise were buskers and hawkers carrying trays of cheap trinkets and novelty toys, all pushing their way through the crowded aisles and crying their wares as they went.

'Ribbons and laces! Newest colours – fresh off the ship from France!'

'Buy a monkey on a stick! Two for the price of one!'

The sun was high and the sky outside already a cobalt blue by the time the gardener reached his destination at the far end of the market, yelling a greeting to those awaiting him.

'Blimey, Tom! Can't you get out of bed of a mornin'?'

'Aft'noon, Tom. We was about to give you up for dead!'

Having made her escape from Bullivant House in haste and in the middle of the night, Maggi had given no thought to protecting herself against the sun. Now, she wished she had her mob cap. That would have afforded some protection against the sun which was burning into her bare head, giving her a headache. Grateful as she was for the shade inside the market, the crush of bodies prevented it from being cool.

The market gardener couldn't help but see that the young people who had helped him were in desperate straits. On parting company, he thanked them again for their efforts, rewarding them with a sixpenny piece which he handed to Maggi. She looked, amazed at such generosity – in Ireland this payment would have been far too much for such a small service. Soon she discovered it wasn't so generous, after all.

'Do they sell nothin' in here for less than a shillin'?' she frowned.

'That's nothing,' Tully smiled, shaking his head. 'You should see what they charge for vegetables at the gold fields.'

'Bleedin' daylight robbery,' Ginny grumbled.

'Yes,' said Maggi, grinning. 'Thanks, Ginny. You've given me an idea.'

'Now then, Mags,' Tully warned, recognising a certain look in his sister's eye. But half an hour later he found himself hungry enough to eat her booty as they sat behind a

160

mass of ferns to munch on a loaf of bread which had fallen off the bakery stall and a lump of cheese which she'd filched from somebody else.

'That's more like it.' She burped gently. 'What shall we have for afters? Fancy a peach?'

'Peaches cost money. Don't you go stealin' them.' Once more Tully tried to warn her. 'Nobody's goin' to complain of a bit o' bread an' some cheese, if we're starvin', but peaches, Mags . . .'

'Nothing but the best today,' she grinned. 'We're celebrating our freedom.' Deftly, she slipped a few apricots into her pocket and moved to the front of the stall where the best peaches were on display. This time she wasn't so lucky.

'Stop her! Stop, thief!' the shopkeeper yelled, pointing at Maggi. With a peach in each hand, she ran, weaving her way in and out of the crowd until the stalls had been left far behind and they were out in the sunshine again at the other end of the market. Pieface caught up with her first, tail wagging and tongue lolling, enjoying the chase. Ginny and Tully arrived as she was laughing breathlessly, holding a stitch in her side.

'You'll be the death o' me, Mags,' Tully began.

'Oh, shut up an' get your face round a peach,' she grinned, offering one as she held up the other, closing her eyes in ecstasy as the juice ran down her chin. 'Mmm. It's true, you know – what they say about forbidden fruit.'

'But it won't do, Mags. Not here. They take a poor view of thieving. You'll get into serious trouble one o' these days.'

Rudely, she blew a raspberry. 'Don't be such an old kill-joy. We've had plenty to eat and still have our sixpence, too.' She spun the coin up in the air and caught it again. 'Look at all that food. Half of it's going to waste. An' it's Christmas, isn't it? They'll have done more than enough trade to stand the loss.'

'I don't like it, sis. I've never liked it. Stealing is stealing, whatever you say.'

She wrinkled her nose at him, pulling a face.

'Eat,' she said. 'Eat and shut up.'

He continued to resist although his mouth was watering as he watched his sister bite into the soft-furred skin of the

161

peach, the juices running down her chin. Finally, he accepted the fruit although he ate it slowly, a brooding expression on his face.

'Right then,' said Ginny. 'What now?'

'I think we ought to split up,' Tully said, not troubling to conceal his dislike of the Londoner. 'If Mrs Bullivant's looking for two missing girls . . .'

'Not her.' Ginny shrugged. 'She won't trouble herself to look for us. Glad to see the back of us, I'd say. Besides,' she linked arms companionably with Maggie, 'your sister and I are friends. And friends ought to stick together.'

'Peggy! Peg Riley!' Maggi said suddenly, making the others stare at her in surprise.

'Peg Riley, my friend on the ship. She told me if I was ever at a loose end in Melbourne, I was to look her up.'

'Then what are we waiting for?' Ginny laughed. 'I could do with a nice cuppa tea an' the chance to take the weight of me feet.'

Tully sighed, raising his eyebrows at Maggi. Ginny was going to stick like a limpet, whether they wanted her or not.

By late-afternoon, weary and footsore after tramping the streets of Melbourne during the hottest part of the day, they were no nearer to finding Peggy. They paused under a tree in Collins Street for a few moments' rest. If anything the noise was even more deafening than it had been at the market, dozens of horse-drawn vehicles trundling up and down all the time. Maggi appraised the local horses with a practised and critical eye. They were sturdy, yes. They needed to be. But she saw none so fine and well-bred as the hunters Dermot had been raising in Ireland.

Shouting to be heard over the general hubbub, Ginny poked Maggi in the ribs. 'All right, dolly daydream, what now?' Tired, she was at her most caustic. 'If you was to ask me, I'd say you made it all up. You don't know any theatricals an' dancers at all. It's jus' more of your romancin', that's what it is.'

Maggi didn't know what to say. Visits to the theatres on Spring Street, Queens, and then progressively lesser theatres and dance halls had thrown up no news of her friend. At the Royal, the stage door keeper had been openly rude.

162

'Tatterdemalions! Be off with you!' he shouted, waving his arms to drive them away. 'An' don't come back 'til you've had a wash. We can do without grubby urchins hangin' round our doors, lowerin' the tone of our Shakespeare.'

'What did he mean by that?' Tully asked as they were leaving. 'What's *our Shakespeare*?'

'Don't know nothin', do you?' Ginny said. Smarting already because she sensed the boy didn't like her, she lost no opportunity to be spiteful. 'I don't suppose you can read or write.'

'Can you?' he said, quick to respond to the challenge.

'That's enough, you two,' Maggi sighed, weary of Ginny's bickering. 'We're in trouble enough without fightin' amongst ourselves.'

'I don't think you know anybody called Peg Riley, at all,' Ginny grumbled as they set off again down the hill. 'An' even if you do, she's not here. Bloody hell, Mags! She could've gone to the gold fields. She could be anywhere between here an' Sydney an' you'd never know.'

'So she could, but she isn't.' Somebody spoke up right behind them.

'Peg!' Maggi turned, unable to believe her ears. 'Oh, Peg!' And she hurled herself into her friend's arms.

'Holy Mary, but you stink!' Peg stood Maggi away to look at her. 'An where on earth did you get those frightful clothes?'

163

Chapter Thirteen

Peg lived in a clean if sparsely decorated boarding house. It was favoured by dancers and other entertainers not only for its homely atmosphere and because it was cheap but because it was also within walking distance of Bourke Street, home to most of the city's theatres, dance halls and drinking houses – a long, narrow, weatherboard home which seemed, at first glance, to be much smaller than it really was. The front door opened to reveal a long corridor with rooms on either side, leading through to a communal kitchen and dining room with washing facilities at the back. The house smelled of beeswax disinfectant and soap.

Peggy explained that most of these buildings had been erected in haste to replace 'Canvas Town' which the city fathers had seen fit to close down. The city of tents had been a breeding ground for diseases of overcrowding such as typhoid and cholera, and also a nursery for crime. While most of the permanent residents of the city had heaved a sigh of relief when the tents disappeared, it meant that permanent accommodation was at a premium and hard to find. With newcomers arriving from all parts of the world en route to the gold fields and others, disillusioned, returning to the city empty-handed and looking for work, there was never an empty bed in the town.

Peg's landlady acknowledged her cheerful, 'Good day to you, Mrs Hennessy!' with a curt nod. She wasn't at all pleased to see Peggy arriving home early and with three ragamuffins in her wake and couldn't wait to pick on Tully about his dog.

'Out with it,' she said. 'I want no mangy curs brought into my house, stinkin' out the place and bringin' in fleas.'

There was no defence against this argument. Pieface was very smelly. Grinning at the woman, tongue lolling, he sat down to scratch himself vigorously, dislodging several fleas. Before she could draw breath again to ask them to leave, Tully grabbed the dog by the scruff and led him around to the back yard where he drew off a bucket of water from the rain barrel, meaning to give his dog a drink and wash the pair of them at the same time. Mrs Hennessy followed, liking this no better.

'Are you goin or stayin', young man? 'Cos if you're stayin' you'll have to pay. An' go easy on that water. That's for my lodgers. I can't afford to have it wasted on a dog. Water's scarce enough at this time of year.'

Tully gave her what he hoped was a winning smile. He didn't want to commit himself. Nor did he think it wise to mention that he had no money at all.

While Tully was outside in the back yard washing the dog, Peg was showing the girls the big room at the back of the house which she shared with two other dancers. The beds had been hastily made and there was brightly coloured clothing, odd stockings and shoes scattered about the room. A typical dancers' dressing room.

'Sorry about the mess.' Peg gave a small frown. 'D'you want me to ask Mother Hennessy if you can stay? It'll be crowded, I know, but I'm sure we could squeeze in two more.'

'Please don't trouble yourself on my account,' Ginny said airily. 'I wouldn't be comfortable. Not if I had to share.'

Maggi stared at her, too astonished to say anything.

'Good,' said Peggy. 'That's settled then. You'll make your own arrangements while Maggi stays here with me.'

'She will? Oh, I see.' Ginny's face fell as she realised she had painted herself into a corner, overplaying her hand in her efforts to impress. Jealous of the way the two Irish girls had picked up their friendship where they'd left off and of the memories which they shared, excluding her, Ginny ignored Peggy's hints that it was time for her to leave. She insisted on sharing the water when Maggi washed the worst of the grime from her face and borrowed a dress from Peggy. Rather pointedly, Peg didn't offer Ginny a change of clothes. But still the Londoner followed when Peg took her friends to the bar where she was working at present – Harry Napier's Silver Star.

The Silver Star was in the town centre in the busiest part of Bourke Street. Shabby yet comfortable, it was a place where all classes could meet. The liquor was good, the entertainment free and most people felt relaxed and at home there. Nowhere in the old world, except perhaps on a race-course, would you see so much excitement and raw energy. The room seemed to pulse with the laughter and high spirits which infected Maggi as soon as she walked through the door. Even the smell was attractive – a mixture of ale, tobacco and greasepaint, with the occasional whiff of horse and harness as well. She loved it already, the shabby, glittering world which was Harry Napier's Silver Star. Ginny, squinting in the pall of tobacco smoke, was trying not to cough.

'Come in then, if you're coming.' Peg took hold of Ginny's arm and hauled her none too gently into the room. 'Don't stand in the doorway – you'll stop the paying customers coming in.'

'I thought you said your friend was on the stage?' Ginny poked Maggi in the ribs, shouting so as to be heard over the general noise. 'I thought you said she was a dancer, not a hoochi-coochi girl.'

'Shut up, Ginny.' Maggi frowned, glancing at Peg to see if she'd overheard. Ginny smiled wickedly. Having discovered a new way to tease Maggi, she wasn't about to be subdued.

'Call that a stage?' She nodded at the makeshift platform on stilts which occupied the far corner of the room. A flickering candelabra swung above it, spotlighting the singer who was hovering at the back of the stage, half-afraid of her audience, but doing her best to entertain.

Two mirror-backed bars ran the length of the room on either side, making the room appear twice its size. Men crowded against them, ten deep in the press to be served. Ginny nudged Maggi again. 'I thought you said she was a professional dancer. So what's she doin' in a third-rate bar?'

'Never mind what I said – jus' shut up!' Maggi whispered through clenched teeth, her patience exhausted.

The Silver Star catered mainly for men, successful diggers back from the fields, who returned to the capital with money to burn. Men who wanted to brag and show off their good fortune and get roaring drunk at the same time. No one was making any effort to hold down the noise and no one was paying any attention to the girl on the stage. Only Maggi was watching her, sympathising with her difficulties before such an unappreciative audience. But at the same time she wished the girl would show a little spirit; throw back her shoulders, step up the volume and take command. Instead, she was shaking with stage fright as she strained her voice to be heard.

'Early one morning, just as the sun was rising . . .'

'Take a bit more'n you to get a rise out o' me, luv!' a man quipped, raising his glass to her as his friends slapped him on the back, roaring with laughter and congratulating him on his wit. Hearing him, the girl faltered, close to tears as she struggled to keep pace with the pianist who was thumping the piano, doing his best to help her and murdering her song at the same time. Maggi and Peg exchanged glances, suffering with her. Ginny showed no such concern.

'She should sing somethin' to make em sit up an' listen. No good hangin' around at the back of the stage bein' scared of 'em.'

'It's not her fault.' Peggy rounded on Ginny, angered by her criticism and snide remarks. 'And before you open your mouth to say any more, you should know she's a friend of mine. Jilly's a dancer, not a singer, and that's not her song. The girl who used to sing it took off for the gold fields.'

'She's a silly Jilly then, isn't she? She should stick to what she knows an' leave the singin' to somebody else.'

'Oh? And who would you suggest?' Peg spoke softly but her eyes were very bright as she glared at Ginny. 'Yourself, maybe?'

'Matter of fact, I *can* sing.' Ginny's eyes grew suddenly wide. 'An' I bet I can make 'em sit up an listen better 'n your friend Jilly there.'

'Oh, do you?' Peg's gaze hardened. 'I might just take you

167

up on that. Wait here an' I'll have a quick word with Fred.'
And she nodded towards the Master of Ceremonies who was
mopping his brow and casting anxious glances at the crowd,
now becoming restive. He was standing by the curtain, fidget-
ing, in two minds whether to ring it down or not, motioning
to the girl and telling her to get off.

'Oh,' said Ginny puffing her cheeks, 'I'm not really dressed
for it, am I? Maybe some other time . . .'

'Cold feet?' Peg asked sweetly.

'Not at all.' Ginny shrugged. 'It's that fumble-fingered
pianist of yours. How do I know he can play in my key?'

'Wilfred? He's a professional – he could accompany a
barnyard fowl,' Peggy said smoothly, raising her hand and
waving to the Master of Ceremonies who was looking more
and more discomfited as Jilly faced a growing murmur of
disapproval from the crowd. 'Fred!' She waved more vigorously. 'Hey, Fred! There's a lass here who says she can sing.'

And in less than five minutes Ginny Luckett was standing
under the lights on centre stage, to be greeted with hoots and
catcalls from an already unsympathetic crowd.

'Where'd you get this one, Fred? Fresh off the boat?'

'Looks like a bit o' rough to me, Fred.'

'Scrapin' the bottom of the barrel this time!'

'D'ye know *The Coal Heaver's Daughter*, luv?'

Ignoring the taunts, and after a brief head to head with the
pianist, Ginny gave them her most mischievous monkey grin
before launching into her song. Expecting the worst, Maggi
cringed behind Peggy and groaned, scarcely daring to look.
Peggy stood there, arms folded and with glittering eyes,
confident they were about to see Ginny howled off the stage.

But Ginny wasn't intimidated. She rose to the challenge,
realising she must make the most of this opportunity. Hands
on hips, she swaggered to the front of the stage to begin a
saucy parody of a London costermonger's song.

The men roared with laughter as she leaned forward shaking her breasts and leaving them in no doubt as to the
double meaning of her words. Making full use of the tiny
stage, she whirled, using her figure to best advantage until
the men began pressing forward, hanging on every word.
Though breathless at times, she showed no sign of nerves

and it was clear that she was no stranger to the stage. Her voice was loud enough to command attention and she was a born comedienne. The men loved her. Soon they were laughing with her rather than at her, enjoying her mischief. By the time she reached the second chorus of the song, the whole room had joined her, singing along.

'Well, if that don't beat all.' Maggi nudged Peg. 'Ginny never told me she could sing.'

'She can't,' Peg said, not without bitterness. 'That isn't singing, it's sex. Look at the daft buggers.' She nodded at the men, now fighting for positions at the front of the stage. 'She's got them exactly where she wants them. Eatin' out of her hand an' beggin' for more.'

'She's full of surprises,' Maggi agreed. 'I had no idea she'd be so – so professional.'

'I'd say she's capable of anything.' Peg frowned, cursing under her breath as she watched the Master of Ceremonies, mopping his brow with relief this time as he hurried from the room. She knew he had gone to fetch Harry Napier. He wanted the owner of the tavern to see the new girl and the effect she was having on his crowd.

Roused from his afternoon slumbers, Harry took his time. Past middle age, he had the figure of a much younger man, remaining trim and dapper in a pair of tight-fitting black trousers, a crisp white shirt and a fancy waistcoat trimmed with gold braid. Pale and tired, he came in frowning, shaking the weariness from his shoulders and the sleep from his eyes. He came to life immediately when he saw Ginny and her talent for working an audience. Stamping their feet and cheering, the men were captivated now, beginning to throw coins on to the stage. Even a small gold nugget came rolling towards Ginny's feet. She stepped forward at once, hiding it under her skirts. Much as she was longing to pick it up, she wouldn't show the extent of her need by gathering up her tips before she reached the end of her song.

She concluded to a roar of applause and loud cries of 'More! More!' Refusing an encore, she ran from the stage and only Maggi realised it was because she was severely out of breath. She returned to them, eyes sparkling, flushed with her success. But her chest was heaving painfully and Maggi knew the effort it was costing her to suppress her cough.

'How was I?' she croaked, soon as she could trust herself to speak. 'Surprised you, didn' I?' She jabbed Peggy hard in the ribs, making her wince. 'Didn' think I could do it, did you? Thought I'd make a fool of myself.'

'Stop crowing, Ginny.' Maggi glared at her. 'You don't have to rub it in.'

Fred was pushing his way through the crowd, anxious to talk to her.

'Don't you run away now, will you, miss? Mister Napier says he'd like to have a word an' it don't do to keep him waiting.'

As Fred took her by the elbow to lead her away, Ginny turned and grinned at the other girls, her face alive with malice as she stuck out her tongue.

'Damn her,' Peggy muttered as she watched them weave their way through the crowd. 'I fell nicely into that one, didn't I? Me an' my big mouth. I'm sorry, Mags. I was all set to ask Harry to make a spot for you an' Tully – she knew it, too, the little bitch. Now he'll make an offer to her instead – an' no one to blame for it but meself. I shouldn't have needled her. Oh, I know she's a friend of yours, Mags, but I've met too many like her before. Greedy, graspin' an' never givin' a tinker's cuss for anyone else.'

'She can't help it, Peg. She's never had any luck in her life.'

'Oh, and we have?' Peggy remained unconvinced. 'She'll hang around jus' so long as she needs you. An' if ever you find the boot's on the other foot an' you need any help from her, she'll be long gone.'

'Oh, Ginny isn't so bad when you get to know her, is she, Tully?' Maggi turned to her brother, looking for his support. He rolled his eyes to heaven which Peg found eloquent enough.

'Your brother's the soul of tact but I see he's on my side,' she laughed. 'Come on. Let's go see Harry ourselves before that little bitch does you out of your job.'

They were too late. By the time they reached Harry's Office, Ginny had been engaged to cover the Christmas and

New Year period at least and been directed to wardrobe to choose some clothes. Peg and the McDiarmits stood looking at Harry, unable to hide their disappointment. In other circumstances, Maggi would have been fascinated by the walls of the tiny office, covered with signed cartoons and sketches of entertainers, some famous now, who had once been Harry Napier's friends, happy to appear on the tiny stage at the Silver Star. Unused to finding himself on the wrong side of Peggy, Harry looked sheepish and uncomfortable, rubbing the back of his neck.

'I'm sorry, Peg, but, how was I to know? Not often we get a talent like that – a girl who can make the boys laugh.'

'It's easy, Harry. Everyone laughs at a bawd who can shake her tits and tell dirty jokes.'

'That's a bit rough, Peggy, even from you,' Harry looked at her under his eyebrows. 'Come on, luv, we don't have to fall out over this. You know I try to give everyone a fair go.'

'You won't give my friend a fair go.'

'I can't, Peg. You're too late. I've already agreed to take on the other girl an' I'm not going back on my word. It's no use tryin' to browbeat me now.' His gaze flickered briefly over Maggi and her brother. He didn't say anything but he made it clear that he wasn't impressed. Standing before him were a pair of vagrants who looked as if they could do with a good scrub. Fastidious almost to a fault, Harry's nose twitched as he detected more than a hint of stale sweat, oppressive in the small room. 'Jilly goes back to the chorus and Vanity's place will be taken by Ginny Luckett. And that's that. I can't see my way clear to take on anyone else.'

'Why not?' Peggy placed her hands on the desk and leaned forward, thrusting her face into his. 'Why must you pin all your hopes on that little monkey-faced tart?'

'You really don't like her, do you?' Harry smiled.

'Easy come, easy go, Harry. That's how it is with the Ginny Lucketts of this world. All it needs is some stage door johnnie to dangle a bracelet under her nose an she'll be off. You won't see her for dust. Else she'll marry a digger, one afternoon.'

'No skin off my nose if she does,' Harry shrugged. 'I tell you, she knows how to work an audience – not many girls have the knack. Six days or six weeks, I don't care. I'll make the money out of her while I can.'

'Forget it, Peg,' Maggi sighed, weary of it all. 'Come on, Tully, we should be off.'

'You stay where you are.' Peggy's mouth set in a determined line. 'Dammit all, Harry Napier, you owe me. Who was it went down to the docks last week, looking for new girls? Who risked her neck goin' round all the clubs to recruit more dancers when you needed 'em?'

'I know that, Peg.'

'And I'm the soubrette here, aren't I? Or are you plannin' on replacin' me?'

'I'm not planning anything. I never saw the girl 'til today. Your place is safe here for as long as you want it – you know that, Peg. But that girl will inject new life into the place and business is business after all,' Harry said, wriggling uncomfortably in his seat.

'Business is business, indeed! Don't you talk down to me, Harry Napier, you know how wild it makes me.' Peggy wasn't about to let him off the hook. 'All I want is a chance for my friends – an' I don't think that's too much to ask. Tell me, how many Irishmen do you have in the Star today?'

'I dunno. You tell me. I haven't the time to count heads.'

'I will tell you. We outnumber the others, three to one.'

'Make your point.'

'Don't you know how sentimental we are about our homeland? It's not that we want to go back an' live there – those days are gone. But Maggi sings Irish folk songs. The songs of the old days; the songs that bring back memories, a breath of home. Go on, Mags, show him. Sing that song you used to sing on the ship.'

'You want me to sing for him now?' She glanced uncertainly at the man who was now hunkered down in his chair, looking far from receptive. 'Oh, I don't think so, Peggy.'

'Now!' she ordered through clenched teeth, sneakily pinching Maggi's arm and making her gasp. 'Sing a few lines for him now.'

Hesitant at first, and then gaining in confidence as she worked her way into the song, Maggi launched into the one tune she could always sing to order – her mother's favourite,

The Black Velvet Band. Tully picked out a few notes, accompanying her on the mandolin, bringing pathos to a song which was already haunting and sentimental.

Maggi's well-trained voice echoed off the walls, too strong and vibrant for such a small room, and when she was done, Harry was left in no doubt that she could sing. As the last notes died away, there was silence in the room, apart from a burst of laughter from the saloon beyond, muffled by the curtain of green baize on the door.

'I have to say I'm surprised,' he said, stroking his chin and speaking to Peggy, dealing over Maggi's head as if she weren't there. 'Your friend has a fine voice but I'm still not convinced that she's right for us here. She'll have the lads crying into their beer. They'll light out of the place to cheer themselves up next-door. Ginny's obvious, I know, but that's what they like. She'll tease the money out of their pockets an' make 'em laugh.'

'Do they need an excuse to laugh?' Peg wasn't ready to give up the fight. 'Enough drink in them an' they'll laugh at anything, including themselves.'

'All right. I'll do this much for you, Maggi. Anything, to get a bit 'o peace.' Harry held up a hand for silence as Peg drew breath to argue again. 'An' this is my last word, so think carefully before you turn it down. You can borrow a costume from wardrobe but I can't afford to pay you a regular wage.'

'Oh, Harry!' Peggy said, shocked at his meanness.

He silenced her with a look. 'You can appear as an extra attraction, an amateur act. I know it's a hard way to make a beginning but you'll make a fist of it if you're as talented as Peggy thinks. Most of the girls earn more than I pay them in tips.'

'I've never heard anything so mean and unfair.' Peg was pink with anger now. 'Nobody else who works here relies on tips.'

'Take it or leave it,' he shrugged.

'We'll take it an' thank you, sir!' Maggi grabbed his hand, shaking it quickly to seal the bargain before he could change his mind.

*

Back at the boarding house, Mrs Hennessy was no better pleased to see them and would relax none of her rules concerning the dog. For a few pence extra per night, she was willing to let Maggi squeeze in with Peg and the other girls while Tully had to make do with an alcove no bigger than a cubby hole, adjoining the kitchen. There was no room to put up a bed but he didn't care; a roof over his head was a luxury after so many nights of sleeping rough.

Pieface found it hard to understand why he wasn't allowed indoors but this was where Mrs Hennessy drew the line.

'Thievin' gypsy's cur!' She glared at the dog who wagged his tail and cocked his ears, trying to charm her. 'Look at them greedy eyes. Not a morsel of food would be safe in this house – he'd be off with the Sunday joint as soon as my back was turned.'

Knowing Pieface as he did, Tully had to admit this was true and went out to settle the dog under a lean-to in the yard, meaning to stay with him until he was comfortable and understood this was to be his new home. With a sigh, Pieface lay down with his head on his paws, although his eyes remained open, watching Tully's every move. Now he had a master, he wouldn't lose him. They stayed there until the brief twilight was gone and Tully began to swing on the back gate, gazing up at the stars and trying to pick out the Southern Cross. It was here that his sister found him.

'What are you doing out here?' she said. 'You'll be bitten to death by mosquitoes now it's gone dark.'

'You wouldn't trouble about a few mosquitoes if you'd been to the gold fields. There's flies big enough to wear boots an' they bite as they land.'

'Never mind that,' she said gently. 'Tully, isn't it time you told me what's happened between you and Da?'

Tully's face twisted as if he had a bad smell under his nose. 'He's dead, Maggi. Killed by the soldiers.' He blurted it out, still too emotional about it himself to soften the blow.

'I see.' She nodded, suddenly very still. 'I think I must have sensed it, even before you spoke.'

Tully bit his lips, bracing himself for a storm of tears. They didn't come. And somehow he found her quiet acceptance much more disturbing than if she had wept.

174

'How did it happen?' she said. 'I need to know.'

Haltingly, he went on to tell her all he knew of the events of Eureka and their father's involvement in the miners' revolt. She listened, grim-faced, nodding from time to time.

'We should be justly proud of him, Mags. For all his faults, Da was a hero – certainly in most people's eyes.'

'But not in mine. Ah, the great fool . . .' She was expressing her grief in anger rather than tears. 'Da was never a soldier. Whatever possessed him to think he was? Why did he have to make the stand? Nobody asked it of him – nobody forced him into it, did they?'

'No. No, but – it's hard for me to explain how it was. To make you see it as we did. There was a flag, too. We saw it as the symbol of freedom.'

'A flag?' She found it hard to keep the scorn from her voice.

'It's no good. I'll never be able to make you understand because you can't. Not unless you were there.'

'And I should have been there. This would never have happened if I had been there. I'd have made him see sense. Oh, but it's so like him, isn't it? Selfish to the end.'

'Selfish?' Tully was looking at her, astounded.

'Yes. Selfish to the core with never a thought for the future or what his actions might mean to anyone else. Going off to play soldiers, leaving you to fend for yourself.'

'We weren't playin', Mags we were in desperate earnest – fighting for justice, for a place in this community, for the right to vote. And, in the end, for our very lives.'

'Words! Cant from the lips of rabble rousers busy stirrin' up trouble.'

'What's the use? Women always see things differently. How can I make you understand?'

'Oh, I understand, all right. You were a pack of fools, thinking to stand against the military an' the police. An' Da was the biggest fool of all for draggin' you into it.'

He knew that expression. That certain set of her lips. No point in trying to change her opinions now. Later, when she was over her anger, he would try to make her understand. Later, when she was ready to grieve.

Chapter Fourteen

Christmas came and went although it seemed strange to the McDiarmits to celebrate the season by eating roast fowl and a steaming plum pudding in the middle of a heat wave. The traditional carols, telling of holly and snow, seemed oddly out of time and place while the sun scorched the ground to dust and the skies were often lowering with the dark blue clouds which came before thunder storms.

While Maggi seemed almost content, honing her skills as a performer and settling into the routine of a life spent between the narrow boundaries of Mrs Hennessy's boarding house and the Silver Star, Tully found himself growing more and more restless. After the danger and excitement of life on the gold fields, when each day held the possibility of making a fortune, the life he was leading in Melbourne seemed orderly and tame, almost dull. And much as he loved his sister, he resented her for taking him so much for granted. Rather like their father, she saw him not as a person in his own right but as a prop, a support for her own success. He was always the younger brother, the accompanist, standing off to one side in the shadows, playing his mandolin; a child with no mind of his own. Conveniently, she'd forgotten that but for his efforts, she would still be at Bullivant House.

Whenever he tried to talk to her about their father and the part he had played in shaping the events of Eureka, she listened with only half her attention, a sullen look on her face. She refused to see it as more than a skirmish in the camp: 'Jus' the usual fallin' out of the menfolk,' she would say, dismissing it with a shrug. She couldn't see that the miners' stand could have far-reaching results. Because of what happened at Eureka, the Governor was obliged to take them seriously. No longer were they to be considered transients without any human rights. Now they were a force to be reckoned with; men who should be allowed to vote and have a say in who ruled their lives.

For all his size – he was sixteen now and towered above his sister – she couldn't accept that Tully's responsibilities and experiences at the fields had matured him, making him old before his time. Scenes of that dreadful Sunday morning still haunted his dreams and many a day he woke up sweating and coughing in the stifling cubby where he slept, believing he was back at Eureka, caught in the smoke and the gunfire. Still he could hear the soldiers' mocking laughter as they dismantled the miners' flag, trampling it in the dust. The same blue flag with the stars and the silver cross which had been the brave symbol of their cause.

One morning he made the journey to Sandridge to look for the *Sally Lee* but the heat haze made it impossible for him to pick out one among the scores of vessels lying at anchor or abandoned in the bay. And by now it was probably too late. Christmas had come and gone. Jem and Hobley would no longer expect him. For all he knew, the ship could have sailed already.

He made some friends at the Silver Star and began a half-hearted flirtation with Harry's daughter. The rest of his spare time he spent with his dog, going for walks along the river bank and sometimes going to see Cabbage Tree although he never called at the house unless the dray was outside and he knew his friend was at home. Pieface at last succeeded in engaging the affections of Mrs Hennessy. He was becoming a handsome dog, growing even larger than Tully had expected.

Comforting himself with the thought that his sea-going ambitions were shelved rather than cancelled, Tully was almost happy. Until he found out Maggi was stealing again.

Harry Napier kept his part of the bargain. While he refused to take the McDiarmits on to his payroll, he did allow them to perform on his stage and also under the covered verandah outside his premises, attracting customers inside.

Maggi sang effortlessly and moved with a natural grace, in spite of the motley, sometimes alarming collection of clothes she chose from the wardrobe of the Silver Star. She loved bright colours: voluminous dresses of scarlet or purple which had to be hauled in at the waist with a scarf to make them fit. On her head she would wear a tarnished silver headband with a broken feather or else a brightly coloured bandana which clashed with her hair. The effect was rakish and she looked like a gypsy girl. Before long she had her own staunch admirers and a wider following than some of Harry's paid entertainers, who were jealous that she should succeed in the face of such odds. Ginny was patronising and distant, thinking herself a cut above Maggi these days.

And Harry remained stubborn in his refusal to pay her a wage. His daughter tackled him about it one afternoon when they were alone in his office.

'Why can't you pay the McDiarmits, Pa? Haven't they proved their worth by now? Don't be so mean. 'T'isn't as if you can't afford it.'

'Exactly. I have money because I'm careful with it. An' it's not your place to tell me what I can afford. If I pay the girl, I must pay the brother as well – an' I can't. Not now I've taken on Ginny Luckett.'

'You an' your precious Ginny Luckett!' Jinks' nostrils flared in disapproval. 'Oh, yes. You're happy enough to pay that monkey-faced slut!'

'Don't, Jinks.' Harry spoke quietly but his complexion had gone a dull red. 'Just don't call her that.'

'Why not? Because that's what she is. But maybe you're not payin' her to entertain the customers, Pa. There's a whisper goin' round that you pay her to entertain yourself.'

'Jealousy and gossip. You shouldn't listen to it, daughter.' His face went a deeper red. Until now he'd imagined his infatuation was a well-kept secret. 'You have a dirty little mind.'

'*I* have a dirty little mind? God, that's rich. Everyone's seen you, Pa, and I hate it. I hate to hear them sneering, laughing at you behind your back.'

'I think you've said quite enough!' Harry banged the desk with his fist, making her jump back. 'This is my affair an' I don't have to answer to you – my own child!'

With tears in her eyes, Jinks fled from his office, knowing it was useless to say any more.

So, while their tips continued to be generous, the McDiarmits weren't making enough to live on. Too proud to ask Peggy or anyone else for help, Maggi preferred to make up the difference herself. Things came to a head when Tully discovered her counting a wad of notes in the dressing room backstage.

'What's that, sis?'

'Nothing!' She smiled brightly, putting her hands behind her back. 'Nothing at all. Tully, what do you want? This is the girls' dressin' room after all, an' you shouldn't –'

Stronger than she was, he soon overpowered her, twisting the money from her hands. 'This? All this money? Too much for tips. Ah, no.' He caught sight of her hang-dog expression. 'Don't tell me you've started the thievin' again?'

'All right, I won't. I won't tell you anything.'

'Oh, sis.'

'I don't take much. Only enough to pay Peggy the rent and to buy something new for once; something that's not second hand, worn to a thread by somebody else. You could do with a pair of new trousers yourself.' She frowned at his shabby breeches, shredded to rags below the knees.

'I want nothin' that hasn't been paid for with honest money,' he growled.

'That *is* honest money. I worked very hard to get it.'

'I'm serious, Mags. You have to stop doin' this.'

'An' so I will,' she said airily. 'Smile, Tully. It's still Christmas, for heaven's sake. Cheer up, an' I'll buy you a present.'

'Not with stolen money, you won't. For the love of God, Mags, have a care. You're not at some country fair in the depths of Ireland where you can pick a few pockets an' get out before you get caught. We're entertainers, on show all the time, an' our faces are well-known. They take a poor view of the thievin' here. You could end up in gaol, Mags, branded a thief.'

179

'Oh, it won't come to that,' she laughed. 'I'll soon smile me way out of it, if it does. They jus' love me here.' She nodded towards the saloon. 'Maggi McDiarmit – the waif in the borrowed clothes.'

'They won't love you for long when they find out you're takin' them down. I've seen men fight to the death over sixpence, treadin' on each other's hands. They'd kill you.'

'Puh! They don't care about money – look how they fling it around.'

'It's one thing to fling it around and another to lose it. I know them better than you do. I've seen what they suffer to get to the gold. They spend months, years, waitin' to strike it rich. Mining's a desperate business, sis.'

'So what do you want me to do? Give it back?'

'How can you, without causing a riot?' He knew she was mocking him. 'Jus' promise that this is the last of it. You won't do it no more.'

'Why should I?' she snapped, eyes sparkling with defiance. 'Jus' because you helped me get free of the girls' home, I don't owe you me life, Tully. You're a right little misery – spyin' on me, and fussin' over me all the time.' Breathing heavily, she was working herself into a temper.

'And do you know why?' He stared at her, shaking his head. 'Because you don't have the guts – the courage – to strike out alone. Go on. Cut yourself free of my apron strings, why don't you? Get a life of your own.'

'Do you mean it, sis?' Tully stared at her, feeling as if the weight of the world had suddenly been lifted from his shoulders. 'Really mean what you said?'

Too late, she realised she had let her temper run away with her and he was about to take her at her word.

'Oh, no, Tully! Of course not. You know how I am – how my stupid tongue runs away with me.' She was crying now, great gulping sobs. 'Oh, Tully, forgive me. How could I say that to you, when you're all the family I have left in the world?'

And she flung her arms around him, almost knocking the breath from his body as she pressed her face into his shoulder. He could feel the urgency of her tears, hot and scalding through the thin fabric of his shirt. As a matter of course, he

180

opened his arms to receive her, mending the quarrel as he had done so often in the past. But this time it was different. This time he didn't break down, adding his tears to hers, remaining thoughtful and dry-eyed instead. He knew she didn't mean it; didn't mean to wound him. She was angry only because she knew she was in the wrong. But in harsh words there is often a kernel of truth. Maybe this was the time for the parting of the ways. Time to take up the threads of his own life. And now the idea had taken root, he was unwilling to let it go.

He held her for a long time as she cried herself out, his mind already racing ahead, making plans. Tomorrow he would go back to the wharf. This time he wouldn't leave until he had found out if the *Sally* was still in port and if there was a place for him. If there was, neither his sister nor any other power on earth should stop him from sailing with her when she left.

Never entirely at ease with Ginny whose outlook on life was so different from her own, Maggi had had no choice but to make the best of it when they were forced into each other's company at Bullivant House. Here at the Silver Star where Ginny was employed as a soubrette and Maggi only a busker, the rift in the friendship could only grow wider. They had little in common these days nor did they return to the same household at night. Maggi was happy to stay in Mrs Hennessy's traditional Irish household, sometimes attending church on Sundays in order to please the old lady. She didn't trouble herself to wonder where Ginny Luckett was spending her nights although some people whispered about her, saying she didn't bother to rent a room; that she slept on a couch in the dressing room of the Silver Star.

So, when Ginny sailed past with her nose in the air, Maggi was amused instead of offended that she should be snubbed by her old room mate. She knew far too many of Ginny's secrets for the girl to ignore her for long, including the pregnancy which must now be in its third month and which Ginny had failed to mention for some time. Unlike Maggi, who preferred to face up to problems squarely, Ginny fooled herself, hoping for the unwanted pregnancy to terminate

181

naturally or, by some miracle, cease to be. If not, she would need to find a protector – better still a husband – and quickly, if the man was to be convinced that the expected baby was his.

Maggi raised the subject one afternoon when they were alone in the dressing room, Peg and the troupe of dancers on stage. A rhythmic pounding informed them that the dancers were well into their routine. Ginny leaned forward to gaze at herself in the mirror, stretching her mouth to apply a poppy red salve, working her lips and pouting at her reflection. She wriggled, pushing her breasts a little further out of her bodice, pleased with their firmness. Still the only real evidence of her condition, they swelled from her bodice more magnificently than ever, delighting her male audience.

'You're not showing yet,' Maggi said, watching Ginny smooth her hands over a flat, impeccably corseted stomach. 'My mother used to get huge after only a month or so. Ginny, have you thought about it? Made up your mind what to do?'

'Will you shut up!' she growled through clenched teeth. 'Walls do have ears, you know. Shout it from the rooftops, why don't you? Why not tell everyone?'

'They'll have to know sooner or later, won't they? You can't keep a baby a secret forever.'

'No, but I'll keep it a secret as long as I can,' Ginny hissed. 'And if you drop so much as a hint to anyone, I'll throttle you with my bare hands.'

'All right.' Maggi shrugged, holding up her hands in a gesture of surrender. 'All I'm saying is you'll be needin' your friends about you when the baby comes.'

'I won't need you, if that's what you mean. I can take care of myself – or I'll find someone with money who can.'

'Please be careful, Ginny. Promise me you won't go in for one of those digger's weddings? Tully was saying he heard a man boastin' he'd married four women in less than a week.'

'Don't bother your head over me, Mags. I'm after a bigger fish than one of your come-day, go-day miners. Matter of fact, he's here now.' And she nudged Maggi, giving a lewd wink as there came a soft knocking at the door.

'But who –?' Maggi started to ask, falling silent as she recognised the voice of Harry Napier. Not the Harry Napier she knew, bellowing at his barmen, telling them to 'Look lively, there! This isn't a funeral, y'know!' This was a man in love; the pleading tone of a middle-aged man with a young girl.

'Ginny? Ginny, my sweet? Are you alone in there?'

'Sweet?' Maggi echoed, mouthing the word.

'Yes,' she called out, frantically waving at Maggi to leave by the other door. 'Yes, Harry luv, I'm here. Give us half a mo'.'

Maggi refused to do as she was told. Instead, she spoke to Ginny in hushed tones. 'Sure an' you're not settin' your cap at poor ole Harry? Think about it, Ginny, afore you get in too deep. Not seein' yourself as the next Mrs Napier, are you? And what about Jinks? She won't wear it, you know. She's not goin' to like it at all.'

'So what?' Ginny's whisper was viperish. 'I can handle Miss Jinks. You jus' stay out of it, Mags. Mind your own business an' leave me alone.'

'The Napiers *are* my business. They've been pretty good to Tully an' me. To you, too, for that matter. They don't deserve –'

'Will you get out, Maggi? Go!'

'So I will. But this isn't the end of it, Ginny. I want to see you outside in half an hour from now.'

'I can't,' Ginny pouted, sullenly. 'I have to go on.'

'All right then, when you come off. But no later than five. An' don't let me down or I promise I'll cook your goose for good an' all. Jinks would be very interested indeed to hear about Doctor Parker, and the baby.'

'You wouldn't!'

'Ginny, my love,' Harry's voice intruded, urgent against the keyhole. 'I can't stand outside here forever – open the door.'

'I mean it, Ginny. Be there,' Maggi whispered before she hurried to the other exit which led to the kitchens.

An hour later, Ginny stepped out of the back entrance, joining Maggi in the street. Warm as it was, she was completely covered in a black, fringed shawl, wrapped around her head and shoulders and hiding half of her face. Seeing it, Maggi laughed.

'Aha! Eet ees Virginia, ze beautiful spy!'

Ginny glared at her. 'I haven't time for your nonsense. I'm here, aren't I? So make it quick. I have to get back before Harry misses me.'

'We're going for a little walk, you an' I.' Maggi linked her arm with Ginny's in a way that was more forceful than friendly. 'You do know you can't do this, Ginny? Not to Harry. Not to any man.'

'And why not?' Ginny protested, pulling free to look at her. He'll be thrilled. A man of sixty, like Harry. He'll have cigars and champagne all round – pleased as punch to have fathered a child.'

'Except that he hasn't.'

'That's a detail. An unimportant detail. If you can't care about me, think of the kid. Spoiled rotten, he'll be. He'll have everything.'

'I doubt if Harry would call it an unimportant detail. Jinks wouldn't. Don't you forget about Jinks.'

'I haven't forgotten anything.' Ginny narrowed her eyes, looking more like a spiteful monkey than ever. 'An' I'm not the only one with somethin' to hide. What about that petticoat of yours? Stuffed like a mattress with so much stolen cash you can't hardly walk.'

Maggi stopped but she was no longer listening. Someone had caught her attention. Someone she thought she knew. A little girl, thin and fair-haired, her hand tightly enclosed in that of a well-dressed middle-aged man.

'Kitty?' she murmured, taking a step forward and placing herself directly in their path. 'It is Kitty, isn't it?' Suddenly, she wasn't sure. The child seemed to be Kitty but she had been carefully and expensively dressed in a gown of navy and royal blue silk; a gown which would have been more suitable on a grown woman, low-cut and accentuating the waist. The gown had been scaled down, 'specially tailored to a fit a child. Completing the outfit she wore a fashionable bonnet, trimmed with silk roses, and Maggi was surprised to see she was wearing red salve on her lips. She looked like a lady of fashion but in miniature; a tiny adult.

'Maggi, leave it. It isn't your business . . .' Ginny muttered, grabbing her by the arm to pull her away. Maggi shook herself free, trying to speak to the child again.

'Kitty? Kitty, my love, I'm so pleased to see you. I've been so worried, wondering what happened to you.'

The child licked her lips and shot her a nervous glance but gave no sign of recognition. She looked up at the man and then straight ahead, blinking rapidly.

'Kitty, it's me. Maggi. Surely you know me?' Maggi persisted. 'Don't you remember?'

'I'm afraid you're mistaken, miss.' The man gave her a thin smile. 'This girl is my niece and her name isn't Kitty. You're confusing her with somebody else.'

'I'm sorry, sir.' Ginny took Maggi by the arm, taking charge. 'My sister's a bit simple, you know. Always going up to strangers in the street.'

Briefly the man raised his hat, and seizing the little girl, hurried off. But not before they heard him questioning her.

'Who was that, Kitty? Tell me quickly and don't lie!'

'There!' Maggi stared after them. 'He called her Kitty – I heard him. That *was* my Kitty, I'm sure of it.'

'Of course it was,' said Ginny. 'But do you want to ruin everything for her?'

'What do you mean, ruin everything? You must have seen it. She's terrified of that man.'

'Not as terrified as she is of being sent back to Bullivant House. And that isn't funny, I can assure you. Look at her now – good food, lovely clothes. I'd say it's a small price to pay for growin' up a bit ahead of her time.'

'What are you saying?'

'Christ, Mags, do I have to spell it out for you? He didn't take Kitty into his home because he wanted a niece.'

'Oh.' Maggi shivered. 'You don't mean –?'

'Finally.' Ginny nodded, raising her eyes to heaven.

'But that's wicked,' Maggi whispered. 'And Mother Bullivant? Do you think she – knowingly –'

'I expect so. Don't look so stricken, Mags. These things happen an' worse. After a while you learn not to lose any sleep over them.'

'How can you say that? Poor Kitty.'

185

'One thing she isn't is poor. Spoiled rotten, I'd say. She'll be safe enough, too, long as you stay out of it an' leave her alone.'

'She's not safe at all – with that man.'

'She's alive. And she won't be, not for long, if he thinks someone's goin' to come looking for her. I tried to warn you.'

'You mean me? *I've* put Kitty in danger?'

'Maybe not.' Ginny sighed. 'Nothin' you can do about it now if you have.' She jumped as several clocks chimed the half hour. 'Come on. You brought me out here to haul me over the coals, so get on with it. Are you telling Harry about me or not?'

'I ought to. But I won't, if you tell him yourself.'

'How can I, Mags? Harry loves me. It'll break his heart.'

'And you? Do you love him, Ginny?'

'Come on.' She laughed shortly. 'He isn't exactly Prince Charmin', is he? A skinny ole man with bad breath an' losin' his hair. But I do care about him, yes. An' I'll do me best to be a good wife. I won't cheat him again, not never, if I can jus' get away with this.'

'It's Harry you should be promising, not me.'

'I know. But I'm scared, Mags. I won't last a month if I get chucked out on the streets – pregnant and with a chest like this.' She gave a barking cough as if to illustrate her point. 'Please don't spoil it for me, Mags. It could be my last chance.'

'If Harry loves you, surely you can trust him with the truth? He'll understand.'

'Oh, yeah? Don't know so much about men, do you, darlin'?' Ginny's smile was wry. 'All right. I'll tell him. But in me own way an me own time – unnerstand?'

Maggi felt sure she was being fobbed off but she had more on her mind than the welfare of Harry Napier who was old enough to look out for himself. It was Kitty she was concerned about – Kitty with that awful blank expression in spite of her beautiful clothes.

Exactly a week later Maggi's heart lurched when she heard the girls whispering about a child's body found in the river. A little girl had been found washed up on the banks of the

186

Yarra, dressed in what had once been an expensive blue silk gown. She had been in the water for several days. Maggi tried very hard to convince herself it couldn't be Kitty.

Chapter Fifteen

Callum MacGregor hated coming to Melbourne. Not that he had anything against it in particular, he would have felt the same about any city. But Melbourne, celebrating its newfound riches as well as the coming of 1855, seemed to his country-bred tastes particularly noisy and offensive this time.

Everywhere he went, there seemed to be men in loud suits and their painted women; women who shrieked with laughter as they rode in open carriages which thundered up and down the streets, stirring up a miasma of dust in the already stifling air. Quiet conversation was impossible; everyone had to shout, adding to the already unbearable volume of noise. Longing for the peace and quiet of the bush, Callum resolved to complete his business as soon as possible and get out of town. Home. Never had the leisurely pace of the small town of Beechworth and its surrounding countryside seemed more appealing although, during the past few years, the search for gold had brought miners to the Ovens River and other parts of Victoria, as well. Callum tried not to think about them, preferring to think of his flocks of well-kept MacGregor sheep, grazing a countryside of rolling green slopes with here and there an outcrop of granite. A countryside not unlike parts of his native Scotland – or so his mother always said. Only the sluggish, meandering creeks, tall eucalypts and the strange animals with their mild, expressive faces and sharp claws, were there to remind him that he was living in a very different land. His own memories of Scotland were fragmented; he had been too small to recall much more than a comfortable house in Edinburgh and the kindly faces of his grandparents.

And he could never think of home without thinking also of Elizabeth, his mother. The two were inextricably combined.

'It's time you were married, Callum,' she had been saying of late, and at twenty-seven years of age, he had to agree she was probably right. Yet among the daughters of his mother's friends – which weren't many in this remote part of Victoria – there had been no one with whom he wanted to spend more than five minutes, let alone the rest of his days. Elizabeth would be the last to admit it, but she was probably relieved, in no hurry to take second place to a new mistress of Lachlan's Holt. She was aware that it was time for her sons to marry but she was in no hurry to relinquish her hold on the sheep station she had inherited when her husband died.

Alone and with children to support, the neighbours expected her to give up and return to her parents in Scotland and had been surprised when the young widow elected to stay. With only hired help and her two small boys to assist her, Elizabeth had succeeded where many others had failed; she developed the property into a successful, going concern. At the same time, while Lachlan's Holt was at the centre of a vast tract of land, it managed to remain a simple, working homestead with housekeeping routines conducted along thrifty, Scottish lines. While their neighbours engaged architects and builders, competing to build mansions resembling small castles with towers of the local granite, the MacGregor homestead never changed. Over the years it had been extended to build a dairy, a separate kitchen and quarters for the cook-housekeeper and her scullery maid, but essentially it remained the same. Instead, Elizabeth chose to enlarge the stables to accommodate the MacGregor horses. Callum had been thinking of building a larger home and even engaged an architect to throw up some ideas but both his mother and Hamish were against the idea.

Hamish! He could never think of his brother without his brow creasing in a frown. Hamish, his younger brother – always the sour note, the fly in the ointment. No matter how many times they shook hands for their mother's sake and

189

tried to be friends, they knew the truces they made wouldn't last.

But Hamish wasn't to blame for his present misery. This time he had brought it on himself. Only now, experiencing the ripe smells coming from drains blocked after weeks of hot, sunny weather, the dust clogging his throat and the sheer volume of noise that went with a crowded city, he cursed himself for his stubbornness in refusing to let Hamish come to town in his place. A refusal which had exasperated his mother. She tackled him at the breakfast table which was where they always met to make plans and go over the business of the previous day.

'I don't understand you, Callum.' She spoke with the crisp accent of the Scottish Highlands which she had never lost. She plucked at the tablecloth, absentmindedly finding a loose thread in the handmade lace. 'Why make a rod for your back when there's no need? Hamish is quite as capable as yourself of seeing the wool to the wharf. Why not let him go in your place?'

'Trust Hamish with my clip?' Callum's nostrils flared. 'I don't think so, Mother. It was against my better judgement that you let him go to Melbourne the last time. Look what happened then – he went missing for weeks and turned up with empty pockets and no new hands. Oh, no, it'll be a long time before I send Hamish to Melbourne again.'

'I'm still saying it wasn't his fault – you're being unfair.' As usual Elizabeth found herself defending her younger son. 'We can't all be as perfect as you are, Callum. You're much too ready to judge and criticise. Good men are hard to find. I doubt if you'd have done any better yourself.'

'At least I should have tried. Hamish never took it seriously. It was a chance for him to have a holiday – to kick up his heels and play man about town.'

'Yes, and it's a pity you don't kick up your own heels once in a while. You're getting dull, Callum – sour and pinch-mouthed as a spinster, these days.'

'A spinster, Mother?' He raised a quizzical eyebrow.

'An old bachelor, then. Where's your sense of humour? You used to have one when you were small. You've become far too solemn and serious of late.'

190

'I'd rather be solemn and serious than irresponsible like he is. Where was Hamish last night? Gully raking again, I suppose?'

'He was not!' Elizabeth rose to her feet, too angry to remain where she was. 'If you must know, he was rounding up wild cattle. He has to – since you grudge him every penny he takes from the property. Rounding up wild cattle to sell to the butchers' shops on the new gold fields.'

'Wild cattle?' Callum's mouth twisted into a wry smile. 'If you say so, Mother.'

'Stop it, Callum. I'm not a fool and I won't be treated as one. How is the boy to learn if you never put any trust in him?'

'But he's not a boy any more, is he? He's twenty-two years old.'

'Then give him some responsibility, some useful work becoming to his age. You can't expect him to take any interest in the property if you hang your nose over him, criticising his every move. He'll rise to the challenge, I assure you. He'll surprise you yet.'

'That's what I'm afraid of.'

'There you go again. This suspicion, this scepticism . . . I have to say it, Callum, I've had enough. Your attitude to your brother is wearing me down. Sometimes I could even believe you're jealous of him.'

'Jealous? Of Hamish? Really, Mother, now I've heard everything.'

'All right, prove it. Let Hamish ride shotgun with the clip this time and see it safe aboard the *Sally Lee*.'

'Ah, and that's another thing. I wanted to talk to you about the *Sally Lee*. I'm not sure we should send the clip with Carpenter this time.'

'Whyever not? He's been a friend of this family for years. Your father trusted him and I won't have him upset. Why, we've been sending our wool with Captain Carpenter for as long as I can remember.'

'Exactly. Which leads me to believe it's time for a change. He's not so young as he was and nor is the *Sally Lee*. Talked to Athelstane Gurney the other day – he's sending his wool with the *Bonaventure* instead. Built for speed, he says, and should make the journey in half the time.'

'Athelstane Gurney?' Elizabeth repeated the name as if it brought a sour taste to her mouth. 'A new chum. A remittance man who's been here all of five minutes. Yet you're ready to take his advice? These new ships are all very well, and I know they're fast, but they also take risks. I'd much rather our cargo arrived safely than –'

'Not at all.' He finished the sentence for her. 'All right, Mother. I take your point.'

'And I wish you wouldn't talk to me with that pained expression on your face. I'm not in my dotage yet, you know.'

The reproof brought a rush of colour to Callum's tanned cheeks. He loved his mother dearly and, except on the subject of Hamish, they rarely exchanged harsh words. Too late he realised he had overstepped the mark.

'So what do you say?' Seeing his hesitation, Elizabeth pressed home her advantage. 'You'll let Hamish go this time?'

'No. Oh, I know you think I'm hard on him, Mother, but Hamish always reminds me of a wild horse. If somebody doesn't keep a firm hand on the reins he'll run amok. And as for that story of being robbed outside the Post Office – I don't believe a word of it. I think he lost all his money gambling and was too ashamed to say.'

'And what if he did?' Elizabeth was dangerously mild. 'The money he lost was his own.'

'All right, I'll make you a compromise. I'll be going to Melbourne myself, that's already arranged. But for this year at least we'll stay with Carpenter and the *Sally Lee*.'

'Good,' Elizabeth smiled, knowing better than to argue with Callum once he'd made up his mind. He returned her smile, happy to have made his peace with her. He knew she loved him most dearly of all of her children. Not just because he was her firstborn but because, in appearance at least, he was most like his father, the similarities increasing as he grew more mature. Hamish and Lilias, their sister, had inherited the patrician, dark good looks of their mother. But Elizabeth kept a miniature of Lachlan MacGregor on her bedside table; a picture which was often mistaken for Callum. Here were the same piercing, cornflower blue eyes, the same shock

192

of unruly blonde curls which might have been girlish, were they not balanced by a strong masculine jawline and cleft chin. Hamish was so different that some people wondered if they were truly related. Hamish was dark as Callum was fair. Only the blue eyes were the same, although Hamish's eyes burned with a passion for life that was missing from his brother's calm azure gaze. All Hamish had of his father was the same strong build; the strong jaw and cleft chin. These, combined with a mobile, sensitive mouth and lazy smile he used to devastating effect in attracting women. The daughters of their neighbours were particularly susceptible; girls who lived on remote homesteads and saw few eligible men. Girls who surrendered their hearts and sometimes their bodies in the full knowledge that Hamish belonged to no one and was certain to stray.

Callum was no less handsome, yet he lacked his brother's talent for seduction. So far his mother was the only woman with whom he felt completely at ease. Could she be right, after all? Was he jealous of Hamish? If only for his charm, his knack of breaking down barriers quickly and winning friends. Callum knew he would never be close to his brother; they would never subdue the old animosities long enough to be friends. The feud which had blossomed in childhood was now a habit, the rivalry ingrained. Too late now to change the pattern of a lifetime although they knew the bitterness between them was tearing their mother apart.

These gloomy thoughts remained with Callum for the rest of the day. Not even a visit to Kirk's Bazaar to treat himself to a new hunter lightened his mood. The big black stallion was an extravagance, yes, but it wasn't often that he indulged himself. His frugal Scottish nature prevented him from buying anything that wasn't a bargain. But there was another buyer after the same horse and, spurred on by the competitor breathing down his neck, waiting to take up the offer if he refused, Callum paid up and smiled. Before buyer's remorse could set in, he comforted himself with the thought that the stallion was a prize, sure to repay him a thousandfold at the country races.

As a matter of form he celebrated his purchase by allowing the vendors to buy him a drink at the Lamb Inn but after a while he made his excuses and left. Bored, he sauntered through town, wondering where to go next. It was a pity his business with Captain Carpenter could not be concluded today. Then he could go home. But the last of the ship's cargo, including the MacGregor bales, was to be stowed in a higher part of the ship where there was less chance of contamination from water in the bilges. The bales were due to be taken aboard the following day. Having spent more money on the stallion than he intended, he saw little point in looking at any more horses and the time began to hang heavy on his hands. Sated with the conversation of other country gentlemen which was always of sheep and the price of wool, he didn't feel like showing his face at their ususal haunts. So he wandered down Bourke Street to acquaint himself with some of the new establishments which had grown up since he was last in town. Attracted by the sound of music, it wasn't long before he found himself standing on the threshold of Harry Napier's Silver Star.

If anything the atmosphere in the bar was hotter than the street outside, already sweltering in the heat of the afternoon sun. He peered through a fog of smoke which began to sting his nose and eyes. The laughter was strident and the music which had first attracted him seemed too loud. But the heat had given him a thirst so he went inside.

There were diggers, still in their red flannel shirts and moleskins fresh from the fields, and others who had taken the time to visit a gentleman's outfitter to spend a fortune and come out looking anything but gentlemen in their striped suits, fantastically embroidered waistcoats and expensive top hats.

They were the colourful ones yet it was Callum who looked out of place in his restrained, well-pressed trousers and elegant grey frock coat. He could sense them nudging each other and saying, 'Who's the toff?' as they sneered at the quality of his waistcoat, high-collared shirt and bow tie. He held his breath and tried not to recoil as a man with a week's growth of stubble on his face leaned forward to speak to him. He had been drinking whisky which was stale and heavy on his breath.

'Wot you lookin' at, sport? Not good enough for yer, eh?'

194

The man had been drinking all day and was looking for a fight. 'Wot you come in 'ere for, lookin' like there's a bad smell under yer nose? Bet I could buy an' sell you twice over – you an' yer fancy clothes. You should come on up to the fields an' get some dirt under your nails.'

Before Callum had time to say he wasn't a city boy either, someone dragged the man away. 'Come on, Tom, leave the poor blighter alone. 'Ave another drink an' shut up.'

Callum would have left but his throat was still parched so he pushed his way through the crowd to get to the bar. He intended to buy one drink and stay only long enough to get it down. The ale was cool and surprisingly good, better kept than at some of the fashionable clubs. He swallowed it in one draught and called for another, feeling better as the alcohol hit his stomach and spread through his system, mellowing him. With his second glass in his hand, he looked up at the stage where the master of ceremonies stood sweating and blotting his face with a large red handkerchief. He too appeared to be suffering from the heat in a suit several sizes too small for him and was blinking in the harsh lights at the foot of the stage.

'And now, ladies and gentlemen! At great trouble and very little expense, I give you the shamrock of the Silver Star, your own Marigold McDiarmit!'

A ripple of laughter went through the crowd and Callum laughed with them, entertained by the introduction as much as the young lady herself who sprang to the stage ahead of her introduction and almost before her predecessor – a monkey-faced girl with an incredible bosom – had finished curtsying and receiving her own applause. They exchanged venomous glances before the other girl pushed past her and stamped down the steps at the rear. Callum looked at the audience of drunken miners and wondered how this slip of a girl was going to hold their attention. Presently, they seemed more interested in where the next drink was coming from than in the entertainment taking place on the stage.

The girl was young but she had plenty of confidence, evidenced by her gypsyish, outlandish clothes – a faded pink dress several sizes too large for her, hauled in at the waist with a bright yellow sash. Like a magpie she'd been collecting brooches and, unable to decide which one to wear, she was wearing them all. A broken purple feather drooped from a band on her head. The pink dress had slipped from one shoulder, making her look more vulnerable than seductive, and she scattered spangles as she went. She made Callum think of his sister, Lilias, when she was small, dressing up in their mother's clothes and making everyone laugh as she paraded around the house, small feet shuffling along in the oversized shoes. This girl didn't wear any shoes at all and probably never did. Her feet were calloused, covered in grime and the toes splayed like those of a native, unused to being confined.

But the girl's most startling feature was her hair; a riot of flame-coloured curls, thick as a hedge. He thought it possibly the most violent shade of red he had ever seen. It made her face look unnaturally pale and her eyes more golden than brown. He had been on the point of leaving but waited to see how the girl would deal with this less than promising audience. Callum bought another beer and drank it more slowly, leaning against a pillar to watch her performance.

He was relieved when, instead of going into the parody of seduction the dress suggested, she launched into a rousing, toe-tapping Irish folk song, accompanied by a young man playing a tiny, whittled flute. The boy was sufficiently like her to be a close relative, probably a brother; a lad not yet comfortable with the hulking man's body he had grown into.

The girl was a skilled performer and well received, especially by the Irish who crowded to the front of the stage, applauding with tears in their eyes. Homesick, far from their native land and sufficiently drunk to be maudlin, they were stamping their feet, encouraging her to sing on. Heartened by her success, the girl dropped into a deep curtsy, smiling down at them. It was such a brilliant, heartwarming smile, it made Callum gasp, catching him unawares. Soon he too was under her spell. She had star quality all right; the ability to light up the room and make each man feel she was singing only for him. Callum too felt as if the sun had come out from behind a cloud. He forgot the ludicrous costume; that didn't matter. Everyone loved her because she could sing. And sing she did, her voice soaring as she progressed from

196

simple Irish folk songs to romantic arias, accompanied this time by her brother's softly thrumming mandolin. The rowdy element seemed to melt from the room and those who remained called for silence. Soon she had the attention of everyone, enthralled as if they were watching a theatrical performance rather than free entertainment in a bar.

With a small thrill of surprise Callum realised he was enjoying himself, really enjoying himself for the first time since he came to town.

His troubles receded, for the moment forgotten. His concern that the *Sally Lee* wasn't fast enough to reach England in time for the last of the wool sales. His ongoing feud with Hamish which so upset his mother. The wanton extravagance of his sister, Lilias. His mother's hints that it was time he was wed.

The girl finished her song to a storm of applause and left the stage to mingle with her audience. Within moments the room was pulsing with noise as before. Following the singer, two plump young women began to pound the stage as they presented a ragged, badly rehearsed version of the French can-can. Flushed now and elated with her success, the Irish girl was still smiling and nodding as she paused at various tables, weaving her way through the crowd. Callum watched, following the progress of that impossible hair. He couldn't hear what she was saying over the general noise but she left people smiling and laughing wherever she went.

Moments later, he realised what she was doing and swore softly to himself. She picked the pockets of three men in quick succession and hid the booty in pouches under her skirts. The boy followed, glaring at her and shaking his head. Laughing at his agonised expression, she poked out her tongue and, with particular daring, stole a gold watch and chain from a man's vest and tucked it into somebody else's pocket. Clearly, she was a mischief maker as well as a thief.

Callum worked his way through the crowd until he was directly in her path, leaving his wallet in his coat pocket within easy reach. He waited for her to make her move and slapped his hand on her own, catching it just as she was sliding it into his pocket. He smiled grimly as she gasped, and held on to her wrist, twisting her round to face him.

197

'Are you out of your mind, girl, or just stupid?' He gave her a shake to emphasise his words. 'D'you expect these men to play the gentleman and let you go? No. I don't think so. Look at them, girl. These men are wild. Some of them will have killed to get what they have an' they won't think twice about killing again to get it back.'

'They'll have to catch me first.' She dimpled at him, flashing her eyes, yellow and cat-like against the flame of her hair. Her speaking voice surprised him; low and pleasing with its soft Irish brogue. 'Faith, an' it came easy enough to them, didn't it? Why not to me, too?'

'Not so easily they won't complain if they lose it. Oh, shit!' Uncharacteristically, he swore as somebody punched him in the ribs, surprising him into letting her go. Not unexpectedly, it was the boy.

'Let my sister alone, you. Or there's more where that came from.' The boy spoke quietly enough but there was no mistaking the menace. Callum massaged his bruised rib cage, watching them leave, surprised at how quickly those two could weave their way through a crowd. They disappeared into the street and not a moment too soon as several men began to complain, discovering they had been robbed.

'Dang it all, Harry! What sort of house are you runnin' these days?'

'Who has my gold watch?'

Callum also decided it was time to leave. It wouldn't be long before the gold watch was discovered, men would start blaming each other and the situation could deteriorate into a brawl. He edged his way to the door and stood there for a moment blinking in the afternoon sunshine which made his eyes ache as they adjusted after the gloom of the Silver Star. He glanced up and down Bourke Street but there was no sign of the Irish girl or her brother. He wasn't surprised; he didn't expect to set eyes on either of them again.

Chapter Sixteen

Maggi spent hardly any of the money she picked from the miners' pockets, but squirrelled it away, sewing it into the deep pockets of her petticoat until it resembled a quilt, padded with banknotes instead of cotton. Though Tully protested that by now she must have more than enough to protect them against any emergency, she continued to steal. He tackled her about it one afternoon when the sultry weather in the city had driven them to take the omnibus to Sandridge and seek relief by turning their faces into the sea breezes as they walked along the wharf. Pieface, tongue lolling, strolled at their heels.

'I take the money, Tully, because we need it,' she insisted, stubborn in the face of his criticism.

'But we don't need it – you're hoarding it. Jus' because Da showed you how to pick pockets for him when you were small, you don't have to fall back on the habit now.'

'Da knew more of the hard facts of life than you do,' Maggi tossed her hair. Ginny had still not fulfilled her promise to tell Harry about the baby, she felt terrible about Kitty and her brother's criticism made her feel as if she were under attack from all sides. 'Too lily-livered even to try, that's what he used to say about you.'

'Don't give me that old flannel. An' don't you dare say I'm lily-livered 'cos I'm not. I don't like the thievin' that's all.'

'It's our safety net. Bit of insurance against the uncertainties of the future.'

'That's not true. There's nothin' uncertain about the future now. You're makin' a name for yourself – Harry has to recognise it before long. He'll have to pay you a proper wage or lose you to somebody else. You should be on the stage, singin' professionally. That's the dream Mam always carried for you an' it's only a question of time until it comes true. You'll have so much to do, you won't even notice I'm gone.'

'Gone?' Her head whipped around and she glared at him. 'And where d'you think you're going?'

'To sea. C'mon, Mags. You said yourself that I ought to cut the apron strings and get a life o' me own.'

'I lost my temper. I didn't mean it, you know I didn't.'

'Perhaps not. But it made me think all the same.'

'Think all you like but you're not going. An' that's my last word.'

'Your last word, is it? I have no say in the matter?'

'No.'

'All right, sis. I'll make a bargain with you. You put a stop to thievin' an' you won't hear another word from me about goin' to sea.'

'But –'

'Because you can't, can you?'

'I –'

'You're not savin' against the future, sis, you're putting it all at risk. How long will it be before Harry figures it out? That you're the one who's robbin' his customers blind – emptyin' their pockets afore they can spend all their money on whisky and beer?'

Maggi pouted and shrugged. 'Harry has other things on his mind. Ginny Luckett for one. You should hear what Jinks had to say.'

'Jinks?' Tully's eyes softened immediately as Maggi spoke of the object of his affections, a tremor coming into his voice. Jinks Napier, the girl he idolised from afar, hoping nobody guessed. 'She's the one with the sharp eyes. She'll wake up to it even if Harry's blind.'

'Bit sweet on Jinks aren't you Tully?' Maggi cocked her head to one side, mocking him gently.

'Oh, God, don't. Don't say it shows.'

'Only to me. What's the matter? 'Fraid she won't like you if she finds out your sister's a thief?'

'She doesn't like me now. Why should she?' he murmured, staring moodily at his feet. He found it hard to discuss this painful first love with anyone, even Maggi. 'It's hopeless. A girl with prospects like Jinks isn't goin' to look at a clod-hopper like me. She'll want somebody rich who can shower her with presents and jewels.'

'I think Jinks has more sense than that. She's seen more than enough eejits with money; diggers fresh from the gold fields, blessed with more nuggets than brains.'

'She still says I'm too young for her, anyways.'

'Aha, so you did ask!' Maggi grinned, pleased to have caught him out. 'Too young for her now, maybe. There's a world of difference between sixteen an' twenty-two.'

'Don't tease me about this, sis.'

'I'm not. I'm saying there's no need to be so cast down. Six years might seem a lot to you now but she'll be happy enough to forget them when she's pushing twenty-eight an' you're twenty-two.'

'So what shall I do?'

'Don't rush the girl. Stand back and give her some air. Great heavens, you've only known her a matter of weeks.'

'That doesn't matter,' he said softly. 'How long does it take to fall in love?'

'*No time at all,*' Maggi answered the question in her mind, her heart beating a little faster as she remembered a shock of dark hair and a pair of piercing blue eyes, sparkling at her from beneath a wide-brimmed hat.

'It's all very fine for you to tell me to wait. I feel as if live coals are burning up my insides every time I see her smiling – even talking to somebody else.'

'She has to, silly. That's her job.'

'And another good reason for me to go. If she falls in love with some other man, I won't have to be here to see it. Let me go, Mags. It'll work out, you'll see.'

'Oh, will it?' She stopped and placed herself in front of him, legs straddled and hands on her hips. Pieface whined and barked at them, reacting to the tension which fairly crackled between them. 'What kind of fool d'ye take me for, Tully McDiarmit? This has nothing to do with Jinks Napier, has it? It's another sneaky way of tryin' to get around me to let you go off to sea.'

'No, Mags, I'm serious. It's not puppy love, calf love or whatever else you call it.' Tully was biting his lip, desperate to make her understand. The last thing he wanted was to quarrel with her and leave under a cloud. 'But what can I offer her now? Nothing. I could chance it and go back to the gold fields but even if I found the golden hand, I'd still be nothing in her eyes; just another digger who struck it lucky and ended up rich. But if I do the time as a ship's apprentice an' work me way up, one day I'll be somebody. A first officer maybe, captain of me own ship . . .'

She gave a brittle laugh. 'Oh come on, Tully. That's a pipe dream and you know it. Nobody needs seamen, let alone ship's officers these days. Look at them.' She indicated the forest of masts, already crowding Hobson's Bay. 'They've stood there for months already, deserted by captain and crew. Many won't sail again – ever. They'll stay in port 'til they rot.'

'No they won't. Not all of them. Not the *Sally Lee*.'

'Ah, so we're back to that, are we? The good ship *Sally Lee*. That's why we find ourselves down at the wharf all the time; nothing to do with getting the afternoon breezes or filling our lungs with fresh air. You're like a damned terrier worryin' a bone. Won't let it go, will you? Still bindin' on about joinin' the *Sally Lee*. Forget it, Tully, because I won't let you. What d'ye think I'm saving this money for? A dowry for meself? I don't think so. It's for your education – to give you a start in life. I want to send you to school.'

'Hold it right there, sis. You can save your money because I don't want it.' He spoke softly, shaking his head. 'Can't you see, it's too late? I'd be shamed to go to school for the first time now – learnin' to read and write with the little ones. Havin' them laugh at me 'cos I'm slow.'

'You're not slow, you haven't had the right chances, that's all.'

'I can't, sis. I don't want to go to school now, any more'n you want to go back to Bullivant House.' He sighed and shook his head as she remained unconvinced. 'What is it with womenfolk they set so much store by book-learnin'? All a seaman needs is to know how to read a ship's compass an' tie a few knots.'

'Quite right, lad,' a deep voice spoke up behind them, making them both start. 'So he does!'

Maggi turned, not entirely pleased to see Tully's friends, Jem and Hobley, from the *Sally Lee*; the last people she could expect to support her own argument.

'Got your bags packed, have you, son? Last of the wool's been stowed an' the tide won't wait. Up anchor within the hour.' He smiled, tipping his cap to Maggi. 'Squared it with your sister, I see. Nice of her to come down to see you off.'

'I haven't come to see anyone off,' Maggi's cheeks flamed as her temper rose. 'My brother stays here with me.'

'Oho, does he now?' Jem pulled a face, amused rather than put out by her show of temper. 'That's not what he said when he came down to sign on with the Cap'n yesterday. Ask him. It's official. Your brother has joined the crew. He's a ship's apprentice an' with papers to prove it.'

'Papers? What papers are those?' She jabbed the burly seaman in the stomach, viciously enough to make him wince. 'He wouldn't know what he's doing, he can't even write his own name. Show me your wretched papers an' I'll show you what I'll do with them. Tear them up and throw them in the sea! You can't hold him to this promise, he's only a boy. I'm his guardian – his only surviving relative – an' he can't go anywhere, not without my say so.'

'I'm sorry, sis, but that just isn't true.' Tully spoke quietly, stating his case. 'I've turned sixteen an I'm old enough to take charge of my own life.'

'Tully, shut up,' she said through gritted teeth. 'You got yourself into this mess an' now I'll have to get you out of it.'

'Please, sis, don't interfere. I don't want you to.'

'Then what about Pieface?' Maggi would stoop to any emotional blackmail in order to keep him. 'If you can't care about me, what about him? He adores you. He'll pine an' die if you go off an' leave him.'

'He will not.' Tully frowned, uncomfortable at the thought of parting from his dog. 'He loves you as much as he ever loved me.' And, as if to prove it, Pieface made a figure of eight around Maggi's legs, tongue lolling in a doggy smile.

'Your mandolin!' She was clutching at straws. 'Sure an' you won't be goin' without your precious mandolin?'

203

Tully looked embarrassed. 'I asked Peggy to keep it safe. To look after it for me.'

'So Peggy knows all about this, does she? You trusted Peg when you wouldn't trust me?'

'Because I knew this would happen; I knew what you'd say.' Tully turned to Jem for support, mute appeal in his eyes.

'Now be reasonable, miss.' Jem spoke firmly although he wasn't unkind. 'The lad's sixteen and old enough to do as he wants. There's some rotten captains but Carpenter's one of the best. This is a grand opportunity for the boy. As his sister you should applaud him an' accept his decision with good grace.'

'Don't you be tellin' me what to do.' Maggi felt far from gracious.

'Look, he'll go anyway if he's made up his mind to it – an' thinkin' the worse of you for holdin' him back. We need him, miss. Good boys like your Tully are hard to find, light enough to go up in the riggin' an' old enough to have some sense in their heads.'

'No wonder sacrificial lambs are so hard to find!' Maggi's control finally snapped. By now she was shouting at Jem, past caring that she was attracting a crowd. On the fringes of it, Tully recognised the blond man, the man who had so nearly been the cause of their downfall the day before. 'Tell me, how many boys do you drown? How many fall out of the rigging or get swept overboard into the sea?'

'Mags,' Tully whispered, plucking at her sleeve. The toff was squinting at them already, remembering where he'd seen them before. Also approaching were a couple of troopers, attracted by the disturbance and waiting to see if they would be needed to break up a fight on the wharf.

'Come on, miss, be fair.' Jem gave it his last shot. 'We're two days overdue an' Cap'n Carpenter's waiting. He's already sent up a signal he wants us aboard. Don't try to stop the lad now. Look at him, he's fair itchin' to go.'

'All right! All right!' Maggi raised her hands in sign of surrender. 'I give up. He can go. But only if I can go, too. If he can do it, so can I. I bet I can shin up the riggin' fast as a boy.'

'Oh, sis, don't!' Tully chewed his lips in an agony of indecision, not knowing how to tell her he didn't need such a sacrifice; he didn't want her to go.

Jem came to the rescue again. 'You're a game one, miss, I'll give you that. But the answer has to be no. No females, not on this trip. The Cap'n would have my hide an' nail it to the mast.'

'Because it's too dangerous, is that it?' Maggi stared into the crowd, looking for someone – anyone – who might lend her some support. 'You, sir,' she said, too agitated to realise she had picked on Callum. 'You look like the sort of man to stand for fair play. Will you take my part in this?'

'Maggi, for God's sake, not him!' Tully hissed, once more plucking at her sleeve. 'Will ye leave him alone?'

But she was in no mood to listen. Freeing herself from Tully's grasp, her sense of drama took over as she began to play to the crowd. 'Oh, please, sir. Don't let them take my brother from me. My only livin,' sole relative in this distant land.' She fell to her knees mimicking to perfection a picture she'd once seen of the Maid of Orleans, Joan of Arc, arms thrown wide in an attitude of appeal. There was a mild ripple of applause from the crowd. 'He's far too young to be goin' to sea.'

And Callum looked, seeing a broad-shouldered, strapping lad who looked older than his supposed sixteen years. The boy was staring back at him, mute appeal in his eyes. Callum raised Maggi to her feet, at the same time denying her his support.

'Let the boy go. I know Carpenter and he's a good skipper. I don't think your brother will come to much harm. My own cargo of wool travels with the *Sally*, bound for the English wool sales. I'm risking a year's income myself on the safe arrival of this ship.'

'I see.' Maggi removed her hands from his, wiping them on her skirts as if to clean them. 'Picked the wrong man, didn't I? Perish the thought that your cargo be delayed for the want of a crew.'

'It'll do him the power of good. He'll prosper and in a year or so, he'll come swaggering back.'

205

'A year or so?' Maggi's voice rose in hysteria. 'Did you say a year?'

'Yes. The ship will make a round trip, travelling to the Americas before she returns to the Southern seas. It'll be the making of the lad. He'll see the world and learn a new trade at the same time.'

'Yes,' Maggi sneered. 'As a grubby jack tar, stinking of oil and fish.'

'Better that than end up hanged as a common thief.' He spoke softly, so that only she would hear. Maggi stared at him, recognising him at last.

'Oh, sir, you're not – you won't –'

'Give you up to the troopers? No. Not if you smile like a good girl and tell the boy he can go. With your blessing.'

'Oh.' Maggi's shoulders slumped but still she hesitated, unwilling to admit defeat. Finally, she looked at Tully who was watching her, scarcely daring to breathe. 'All right, you can go. If you're so certain it's what you want.'

'It is. Oh, sis!' Tully swept her into his arms in a bear hug, nearly choking the breath from her. 'I'll make you proud of me, you'll see. An' give my . . . – that is – my regards to Jinks an' tell her I'll be back.' Maggi nodded, taking little note of what he was saying, she was trying so hard to hold back her tears. 'You'll be all right, I know, with Peg an' the other girls.'

Maggi nodded again, not trusting herself to speak as she watched Jem and Hobley clap him on the shoulder and lead him to the small rowing boat which would take them out to the *Sally Lee*. Even that short journey looked perilous to Maggi; a small coracle on the murky waters of the inner wharf. Pieface jumped aboard after Tully, rocking the boat.

'Pieface!' Maggi screamed at him, her voice cracking with hysteria. 'Come back here, you naughty dog!'

'Let him go, miss.' It was Jem who laughed, ruffling the wiry hair on the dog's head. 'We can eat the skinny rascal if we get a bit short.'

Flattered by the dog's loyalty, Tully looked both sheepish and pleased that he didn't have to leave Pieface behind. 'Look out for yourself, sis,' he called out. 'Now I'm gone, perhaps Harry will pay you a proper wage. An' stay clear of that Ginny Luckett. She's bad news. An' . . . oh, jus' try to stay out of trouble until I get back.'

'Tully! Tully, wait! I can't do this – I can't let you go!' Even at this late stage, she would have run after him, except Callum caught her about the waist, lifting her off her feet to prevent it. She fought him, struggling to free herself from his grasp.

'Stop it! Stop that right now!' He spoke with such authority that she gasped, looking up at him, eyes wide. 'D'you want him to carry a memory of his sister distraught and in tears? D'you want him to blame himself and feel guilty for every moment he's gone?'

'You know nothing – nothing about us!' Roughly, she tore herself free, hating the man for his lack of understanding. 'You know nothing of how much we've lost – what we've been through.'

'No. But this way the boy has a fighting chance, to make something of himself and rise through the ranks at sea. What sort of life did he have with you? A thief, always running from trouble, trying to keep a few steps ahead of the law. A life all too likely to end with the jerk of a hangman's rope.'

She blinked at his callousness but made a quick recovery. 'And what would you know of hardship, Mister Gentleman Squatter? You with your wealth and your wool? I bet you never had to worry about where your next meal was coming from? You wouldn't last five minutes if you had to live off your wits as we do.'

'You have no parents living? No one to care for you?'

'A little late, isn't it, to concern yourself about that? It's no business of yours, anyway.'

'I think you made it my business when you asked for my help.' Callum was firm but gentle, realising the girl was shivering, probably in shock. 'And I don't know your name – although we seem well acquainted enough to fight.'

'I'm not sure I want to give you me name,' she muttered, sulky and not yet willing to make friends. 'Me gran was a romany. She said it gave strangers the power over you to tell them your name.'

'Then I'll give you the power over me first. Callum

MacGregor of Lachlan's Holt.' He held out his hand, waiting to see if she'd take it. 'My friends call me Callum or Cal.'

She looked at his hand for a moment before accepting it. 'Marigold McDiarmit. Most people call me Maggi.'

'Maggi it is.' He glanced around looking for transport. 'Where to now, Maggi? Can I offer you a lift back to town?'

'In a cab?' She brightened until she recalled some advice from Peggy: *Never accept a ride from a stranger, particularly if he's a gentleman.*

'No. Better not. Thanks all the same.'

'But you can't stay here on the wharf, all alone.'

'Then I'll walk back to town. I'm not that hard up, you know, I have friends of me own. No need to bother your head about me.'

'As a matter of fact,' he said before he realised how it would sound, 'I was thinking of taking you home.'

'Indeed an' you won't!' She leaped away from him as if she'd been stung. 'What do you take me for? A threepenny whore? I don't do that sort of thing. Not for you or any other man. My body is still me own an I mean to keep it that way.'

'Very creditable, I'm sure.' Callum's eyebrows almost disappeared into his hair. 'Don't flatter yourself. I'm not so desperate for female company that I need to take advantage of a grubby, foul-smelling urchin like you. I was offering to take you back to the station, that's all. My mother will find you some work.'

'Work?' Maggi wrinkled her nose. 'What sort of work?'

'I don't know. Whatever girls do. Keel the pots in the kitchen, turn the sheets . . .'

'That sounds like a thrill a minute, to be sure. I don't know as I'm cut out for housework. I've a career to think of, you know.'

'As a pickpocket? Or do you mean busking in the street outside Napier's Silver Star?'

Maggi ignored him, the whole of her attention now taken up by the movements aboard the *Sally Lee*. The ship had weighed anchor and some of her lesser sails were being unfurled. Whistles shrilled and sailors could be seen running

208

about the deck, each bent on his own task of preparing the clipper for the first stage of her journey to the open sea.

As the *Sally* began to glide away, Maggi screamed and picked up her skirts to run down the wharf, following the ship's progress and waving her arms to attract attention. Callum lengthened his stride to keep up with her, hoping she wouldn't do anything stupid. But instead of hurling herself into the water as a last dramatic gesture, she stood cupping her hands to her mouth, shouting last-minute instructions to Tully who was leaning out from the prow, grinning and waving his new seaman's cap. He couldn't hear what his sister was saying but smiled and nodded, pretending he did.

As the ship began to roll, moving towards the open sea, more sails were unfurled to catch the freshening breeze. Maggi watched as the clipper negotiated a path through the deserted vessels, gathering speed as she did so, like a great bird preparing to take wing. The girl stood quietly as if she were made of stone, her arms stiff at her sides, seeming scarcely to breathe as she fought to prevent the tears which stood in her eyes from escaping and rolling down her cheeks. Touched by her fortitude much more than if she had broken down, Callum continued to watch her, straight and still as a statue, a living testimony to the thousands of women over the centuries who had watched their menfolk set out to sea, wondering if or when they would ever see them again. Her gaze never wavered until there was no more to see than the highest sail of the ship. Moments later that too became no more than a speck on the horizon when it dipped out of sight and was lost to view.

With the ship gone, the crowd began to disperse. The troopers cantered away, disappointed that there had been no excitement, no arrests to be made. Callum said nothing but offered Maggi his own clean white handkerchief. She wiped her eyes and blew her nose noisily before giving it back.

'Better keep it,' he said, taking a gold watch out of his waistcoat pocket and glancing at the time. 'It's late and I must be going.' He tipped his hat to her and began glancing around, hoping to see a vacant cab. 'If I can be of no further assistance?'

'Thank you. I'll be jus' fine.' There was a lump rising

painfully in her throat. All she wanted now was for him to leave so that she could give way to her emotions, indulging herself in a good cry.

But at that moment their attention was diverted by what seemed at first to be a runaway horse bolting with a cab. The driver was crouched forward, clutching the reins, while the two wheels of his jingle bounced dangerously on the uneven boards of the wharf, threatening to overturn it. Men scattered, shaking their fists at the driver and one or two women shrieked, holding on to their hats and cowering away from the flying vehicle. In response to the cries of his passenger, the driver hauled on the reins, pulling up alongside them. The door flew open and Peg Riley hurled herself out. She was so anxious to speak to Maggi that she caught her foot in her skirts as she did so and almost fell.

'Maggi! Oh, thank the good Lord I found you! I was afraid you wouldn't be here –'

Blaming her friend for her part in aiding and abetting her brother's departure, Maggi was cool.

'I've nothing to say to you. I wonder you've the hide to show your face to me at all, Peg Riley. Not after what you've done.'

'What did I do?' Peg looked astounded. 'That's a fine greetin', Maggi McDiarmit. An' after I come all this way, payin' a cab to ride hell for leather to find you!'

'You knew what Tully was plannin' an' never said nothin' to me. For all I know, you told him it was a good idea.'

'Later, Mags.' Peggy was almost vibrating with anxiety. 'We don't have time for this now.'

'We have all the time in the world.' Maggi's nostrils flared. 'Because he's gone. Sailed out not ten minutes since with the *Sally Lee*.'

'Thank the good Lord for that, too. He'll be well out of it.'

'What are you talking about?'

'Trouble. Deep trouble. Maggi, you mustn't come back to the Silver Star.'

'An' why not?' Maggi's voice was small because she thought she knew.

Callum, too, waited and listened, realising the newcomer was the bearer of more bad news for Maggi. Had he moved

210

off more quickly, he might have taken Peggy's cab but a group of seamen were already climbing aboard, instructing the driver to carry them back to town.

'Ginny Luckett. She's at the bottom of it, of course,' Peggy said. 'Did you know Harry asked her to marry him?'

'I'm not surprised. She's been setting her cap at him ever since we arrived.'

'Well, it worked. No fool like an old fool, eh? I had a morning of it meself, I can tell you. Jinks fit to be tied, crashin' about the place breakin' glasses an' weepin' with rage. Harry, the fool, didn't think she'd oppose it. Clutchin' that tart by the hand as if his life depended on it.'

Maggi nodded, raising her eyes to heaven.

'Then it all seemed to blow over for a while. I should've known it was only the calm before the storm. Bar got busy as usual around lunchtime. Jinks dried her tears and went back to work. But I was keepin' an eye on Ginny. You know how she is. Grinnin' that monkey grin of hers; smirking like the cat that's been at the cream. Smilin', smilin' an' makin' changes, throwin' her weight about as if she was married to him already. I tell you, Mags, there won't be a show girl willing to work the place if Harry goes through with it.'

'Yes, but what happened? What brings you here?'

'I'll get to it. Around four o'clock it gets quiet. Lunchtime crowd's peeled off and we're all sat around havin' a nice cuppa tea. – "I been thinkin' Harry", she says in that voice of hers – the one she uses when she wants to sound stuck up. "Ain't it funny no one's missin' a wallet all day? Not a single complaint. Not a one." 'Course, Harry shrugs it off. Got other things on his mind. Where's he goin' to get the energy, for one thing, to keep up with a young bride? But will she let it drop? No. Not Miss Ginny. "Well, I think it's odd. Reely I do", she says in that prissy cockney of hers. "Nobody misses no money when those McDiarmits ain't here." Oh, you should've seen Harry – she had his attention then. Didn' take him long to put two an' two together an' make six. "By God, you're right, gel," he says. "I'll have the bloody law on those kids. Red-haired witch an' that brother of hers. After all I did for them, too!" I tried to tell him, Mags. Tried to tell him he was makin' a bad mistake.'

211

Maggi sighed and stared at the ground, unable to meet her friend's gaze.

'It *is* a mistake, isn't it, Mags?'

'Oh, Peg, it's not how it seems. I did it at first to pay the rent and get food. It didn't seem right we had nothin', Tully an me, while men wasted good money, lighting their pipes with their five pound notes.'

'Maggi, why? Why didn't you tell me you were so short? I'd have helped out.'

'I know, Peg. But I didn' feel it was wrong. It was as if I was savin' the money, not stealin' it. Savin' the money to put to a better use.'

'The law won't give a damn about that. The girl has betrayed you; fingered you for a thief. Why, Maggi? I thought she was your friend?'

'We've been thrown together, that's all. Never real friends. And I know too much about her. She's scared, Peg. She wants to make a new life with Harry and she can't afford to have me around.'

'So what are you going to do? You can't come back to the Silver Star if Harry's reported you. They'll be watching Ma Hennessy's too.'

Maggi sighed. Tully was gone and her life was in ruins.

'I don't know, Peggy,' she whispered. 'I really don't.'

Chapter Seventeen

It was only later when the city had been left behind and the long shadows of afternoon lengthened towards nightfall, that Maggi calmed down enough to realise she was travelling to an unknown destination with a man she didn't know. It had seemed so sensible, so reasonable, when Peggy arranged it. Peggy, so cautious as a rule, so suspicious of strangers that Maggi never questioned it. But so far as Peg was concerned, the man wasn't a stranger; she was acquainted with his brother who was a friend of Jinks and a regular visitor to the Silver Star.

Under other circumstances, Maggi might have raised more objections to being posted off like a parcel but in the space of an afternoon her world had been turned upside down. Stunned by the loss of Tully and the speed with which Ginny had cut the ground from under her, she was in a daze, almost like a sleepwalker, allowing Peg and Callum to arrange the immediate future on her behalf. She had no choice. As the matter stood, she might be hunted down and arrested as a criminal. At the very least she could be sent back to Bullivant House. Either way, she would be a prisoner, no longer in charge of her life. And Callum was her only means of keeping in touch with her brother. With a year's income riding aboard the *Sally Lee*, he would remain in close contact with the captain and his ship.

After embracing Peggy and saying a farewell in too much haste to be tearful, her mind still reeling from the events of the past hour, she followed Callum to the mews where his animals were being stabled. There, she brightenened immediately. This was familiar ground. She inhaled deeply, relishing the pleasant, musky odour of well-kept horses and clean straw. Expecting Callum to saddle up and ride, she was surprised when he led her to the other end of the stables and laid claim to six bullocks and a dray, half-loaded with iron-mongery, sacks of flour and other tins and boxes of groceries needed by the housekeeper at the station. With an eye to the difficulties he must face in controlling so many animals she wondered how he would have coped on his own. Falling back on old habits, she assisted without being asked. His two horses were eyeing each other uneasily, snorting and skittish after so many days without exercise, the mare in particular, rolling her eyes, uneasy in the presence of Callum's new stallion.

'Come now, me beauty, no need to be scared. I'll not let him hurt you,' Maggi reassured her. The mare relaxed under her hands and she turned, smiling at Callum who was check-ing the yokes and chains of the bullocks before setting off. 'I don't know what you'd have done without me to help you.' It was good to feel harness and leather under her hands again; horses had been absent from her life for too long. 'Fancy you, drivin' bullocks, Mister Gentleman Squatter,' she mocked him gently. 'I thought you'd have a man to take charge of the bullocks and dray?'

'Until a week ago, I did.' Callum's smile was wry. 'But he met up with some friends who persuaded him he'd make a fortune more quickly digging for gold. I suppose I should be grateful he left me the team and the dray!'

But Maggi was no longer listening, gazing with admiration instead at his latest acquisition: the fine black stallion now stamping and lashing his tail, fighting the harness which secured him to the back of the dray.

'Oh, you lovely, lovely fellow,' she breathed, taking hold of his bridle to calm him and running her hand down his nose.

'Be careful,' Callum warned, jealous of her rapport with the horse who responded immediately to her touch. 'He's new to me and I don't know his foibles yet. But in my experience stallions don't take kindly to women – they need a much firmer hand.'

214

Giving the lie to his words the big horse began nuzzling Maggi, almost knocking her off her feet as he nibbled her hair, making her giggle.

'What do you call him?'

'Bothwell.'

'That's a funny name for a horse. What does it mean?'

'Bothwell was the ambitious husband of a Scottish queen,' Callum said. 'Brave and a little bit crazy, like this horse.'

'I don't think he's crazy at all, he's just bored. An' you can't expect him to walk behind a dray. It's not dignified.' Hitching her skirts as she'd done ever since she was a child, she was preparing to mount. 'I'm good with horses. I'll ride him for you, if you like?'

'No, I don't like.' Callum frowned. 'If it's riding you want, you can get up on the mare.'

Maggi glared back at him, annoyed that he doubted her capabilities and, sulking, declined to ride the docile mare. To her dismay also, she realised he was leading his team over Princes Bridge, leaving town by way of the wide avenue that was Saint Kilda Road. Before setting off up country, he said, they must collect the last of his bags from his lodgings. Still more disquieting, his lodgings were almost next-door to Bullivant House. Maggi's heart swooped unpleasantly as they approached. Nothing had changed. It was still the same gloomy place where she'd been a slave to housework for so many weeks. Looking up at the windows again, still heavily barred, she shivered as the worst of her memories came flooding back.

Callum was gone for less than ten minutes but to Maggi it seemed like an hour as she imagined every woman who passed to be either the Matron or Miss Prunella in her cracked boots and her dusty, black bonnet. Miss Prunella who would point at her, giving a shout of recognition. *'Maggi McDiarmit, is that you? Where have you been all this time, you wicked girl?'* But this happened only in her imagination and she felt almost weak with relief when Callum reappeared, having changed his smart city suit for his country clothes.

So it was only now, when it was late-afternoon and the

215

city and suburbs had been left behind, that Maggi thought to enquire exactly where he was taking her.

'Up country,' he said. 'A little town called Beechworth is the nearest centre to our home.'

'And how many hours will it take us to get there? Will we get there before nightfall?'

'Before nightfall? Bless you, no.' Callum gave her an odd look and then he laughed. 'You really don't know, do you? You have no idea how vast this country really is. We measure the journey in days rather than hours. On horseback and alone, I can do it in maybe three or four days. But the bullocks are slow and won't cover more than ten, maybe twelve miles a day. And we'll have to stop to allow them to rest and graze. If the rivers are up, I'd say it'll take us the best part of two weeks.'

'Two weeks?' Maggi's senses reeled as she tried to make sense of what he was saying. 'And rivers? There are rivers to cross?'

'Some aren't much more than creeks. Nothing to worry about.' He shrugged. 'The weather's been dry for months.'

Maggi chewed her lip, stunned by this latest news.

'You'll be quite safe with me. I never get lost,' Callum said, mistaking the reason for her agitation. 'All we have to do is follow the compass and keep bearing north east and we could be there in ten days or so.'

Maggi didn't know what to say. Foolishly, she had assumed the MacGregor homestead to be on the outskirts of Melbourne. Only now as she looked around her, seeing nothing but empty countryside on either side of the track, miles and miles of grasses burnt brown by the sun and the tall gum trees, standing still as sentinels in the heat, did it come home to her that she must travel for days in this uncharted wilderness. And with someone she didn't know. Covertly, she watched him, searching for signs of menace she could have missed before.

Happy to be going home at last, Callum seemed to have no inkling of her misgivings and nothing on his mind but the journey ahead. He pointed out colourful parrots that she might have missed, surprisingly disguised by the muted, grey-green leaves. And the bellbirds, still more difficult to see,

216

whose sharp cries almost hurt her ears, ringing like a spoon striking glass.

Relaxed and whistling softly through his teeth, Callum flicked his whip over the horns of the bullocks from time to time to keep them from slowing down. A true son of the country, his spirits rose as soon as the city had been left behind. He looked much more at home in his riding jacket, leather waistcoat, moleskins and battered sheep farmer's hat than in the formal clothes he had to wear in the city.

She left her appraisal of his clothes to study the man himself, unable to make up her mind if she thought him good-looking or not. The mass of golden curls which still escaped from under his hat could have been womanish on a less craggy and weatherbeaten face. His eyes were his finest feature, a dark cornflower blue, but he spent so much time squinting into the sun that they were surrounded by early crow's feet and when he smiled they almost disappeared. And there was a stubborn curve to his mouth that she hadn't noticed before. Here was a man used to giving orders and expecting them to be obeyed. And the first order he had given her was to wear one of his spare hats. It was too big for her but it afforded the necessary shade.

Perched up on the seat of the dray, after tiring of the mare, she was aware of the lithe strength of his body and of the muscular calves encased in riding boots, stretched out before him. Her own skinny legs had to dangle as she struggled to keep her balance, bracing herself with her hands. After less than two hours of this travel, she was tired and aching in every limb – how was she going to feel after more than a week on the road?

She sneaked a sidelong glance at Callum and saw that he too was preoccupied with his thoughts. For all he cared she might as well not have been there. What was she to him? Less than nothing. A pest. An additional female servant for his mother's house. A grubby urchin who held no charms. But would that still be true during the days and nights of the journey that lay ahead? Soon it was going to be dark and they'd have to stop and make camp for the night. Unfamiliar as she was with these empty tracts of land which thrummed with the singing of unseen insects during the day, they would be more scary at night when owls and other strange creatures of the bush would leave their holes and burrows to search for food. Nobody had troubled to tell her there were no lions and tigers in Australia – indeed she had never thought to ask. Night time and they'd be alone. Was that when Callum would make his move? Pouncing as they sat at the camp fire? And what would he do to her if she refused him? Turn her loose to be lost in the bush?

Maggi's over-active imagination took flight as she saw herself as a persecuted heroine, hunted down and devoured by wild dogs or other unspeakable beasts of the night. The more she thought about it, the more real her fears became. Better to take her chances in the city where her enemies were at least human and known to her, rather than face a violent death out here in the bush. Callum glanced at her and smiled but to Maggi, unable to see the expression as his face was shaded by his hat, his smile seemed more wolfish than reassuring.

'Sir! Sir, I have to ... Can we stop a moment if you please?' she quavered, furious with herself for the tremour in her voice.

'To relieve yourself – yes, of course.' And he jumped down, waving his whip over the heads of the leading bullocks, yelling at them to stop. 'We're making good time time and we can afford a rest. I'll fill the canteens and water the bullocks while you're gone.' So saying, he jerked his head in the direction of a nearby creek. 'Take no more time than you need. We're still close to Melbourne and there may be bushrangers about.'

'Bushrangers?' Maggi craned her head in all directions, able to see no more than the eucalypts, fast becoming silhouettes against the flame-coloured sunset. 'But I haven't seen any.'

'Don't worry, you won't.' His smile was grim. 'Not until it's too late.' He took a step forward, meaning to place his hands on her waist to lift her down, but she slid down the side of the wheel, avoiding him. He smiled and shook his head, acknowledging her independence, and shouted after her as she ran for the shelter of a stand of wattle growing up by the creek.

'Don't walk through the long grasses and keep your eyes peeled for snakes and red backs.'

'Red backs?'

'Poisonous spiders.'

'Ugh!' She cringed, no longer anxious to crouch and relieve herself. Really, she hardly wanted to at all; it was just an excuse to get away. Already her mind was racing ahead as she wondered how to make the best use of what little time she had. How long would he leave before coming to look for her? How far had they travelled already? How many hours would it take her to find her way back to the city on foot? Yes, there was danger there, too, but at least a danger she knew and understood.

She dropped down to the creek where the water was surprisingly cold, running sluggishly over the stones. Tucking her skirts up into her drawers, she started downstream. Surely the stream must join up with a river, which in turn would flow into the Yarra and take her back to town? Using the foliage on the bank as a shelter, she began to move as fast as she could.

'So there you are! I was wondering where you'd got to.' Callum startled her by reappearing a few yards ahead of her on the bank. He watched, hands on hips, as she scrambled out of the water, losing her footing more than once on the slime-covered stones at the bed of the creek. 'What are you doing? Tickling a fish for our supper or running away?'

Furious at being outwitted, Maggi decided the best form of defence was attack.

'Do you make a habit of springing out at folk when they wish to be private? It's a good job I don't have a weak heart. You scared me half to death, jumpin' out like that. Can't I have so much as a moment to meself?'

'A moment, yes. But you've been gone for over half an hour. What is it, Maggi? What made you decide not to trust me? Was it something I said?'

'No.' She stared at her sodden feet, beginning to shiver. The water felt freezing now and she folded her arms against the cold. Callum held out a hand to pull her the last few feet up the bank and away from the creek. His hand felt warm

219

and sure and his touch gave Maggi a jolt of pleasure which surprised her.

'What is it, then? Can't you tell me? What can I say to make it all right?'

'I don't know.' She hung her head, feeling foolish and miserable. 'Why didn't you tell me you lived so many miles from the city?'

'It never occurred to me. What difference does it make?'

'What difference?' She glared at him. 'What if I don't like being miles from anywhere? What if I change my mind?'

'Well –'

'And another thing. If you have no – no desire for me as a woman –'

'None at all,' he said quickly. 'I thought we established that?'

'Then why bother with me at all? Why offer work to someone you know is a thief?'

'Why indeed?' He gave a wry smile. 'Which question do you want me to answer first?'

'Don't tease me jus' now, I'm not up to it.'

'What do you expect me to say? I'm not entirely heartless, you know. How could I leave you standing there on the wharf, alone and with nowhere to go?'

'Oh, you're such a saint.' She rolled her eyes to heaven. 'Come on. You'll have to do better than that.'

'I don't know.' He shrugged. 'I felt responsible for you, I suppose.'

'Why?'

'Why! Why! Why!' At last his patience was exhausted. 'I don't know why. I don't always weigh up the pros and cons before I take action, do you? I was sorry for you, if you want to know. Are you satisfied now?'

'You're – you're shouting at me.' Suddenly and without warning, her eyes filled with tears and her face crumpled as she gave way to the emotions she previously had been able to hold at bay. Everyone she held dear – mother, father, brother, and even Peggy, her friend – was lost to her. Callum could only stare at her, helpless in the face of her sorrow. Maggi's genuine and uninhibited grief left him speechless; he had no idea how to comfort her. Awkwardly, he put a hand on her shoulder.

'I'm sorry I yelled,' he said. 'I didn't mean to scare you.'

'Well, you did.' Maggi paused in her weeping to glare at him.

'Cheer up. I'm sure things aren't nearly as bad as they seem.'

'No?' She scrubbed her face on her sleeve. 'My brother gone – probably to be lost at sea. And what do I have to look forward to? Nothing. Nothing but endless days of drudgery in your mother's kitchen.'

But instead of sympathising as she expected, he laughed. 'I wouldn't worry too much about your brother – he can look out for himself. He's a sensible lad and he won't be taking too many risks. And as for my mother, if you're expecting her to be a gorgon, you're out of luck. She has the kindest heart of any woman I know. Now then,' he glanced over his shoulder to where the bullocks were attempting to graze dry grasses as they waited with the dray, 'we ought to get back before those beasts discover there's no one to mind them and take off for home on their own.'

Back at the dray he took a big rug from beneath the seat and wrapped it firmly around Maggi's shoulders. By now she was really shivering and had to clench her teeth to stop them from chattering. This time she let Callum lift her up on to the seat and tuck her in, making sure she was comfortable before he cracked his whip at the bullocks, yelling and whooping at them to get them moving again. Maggi flinched at the crack of the whip which sounded very loud in contrast to the silence of the bush all around them, broken only by the occasional thrumming of a cricket or a cicada seeking a mate. The horses, tethered to the back of the dray, also whinnied their complaints. The bullocks snorted their protest, having hoped their travels might have been over for the night, but they obeyed the whip, lumbering onward with their swaying, measured tread. Callum could crack the whip as much as he liked but nothing was going to make them move any faster.

From her position above, Maggi was free to watch him without being observed and once more she wondered why he should put himself out for a lost cause like herself – a thief likely to be more trouble than she was worth. He made it clear there was no spark of desire, no sexual motive so far as he was concerned. Certainly, there was none on her side. She wasn't the sort of girl who spent every waking moment sighing for lovers. If she hankered for any man it wouldn't be someone sober and solemn like Callum with his lantern-jawed looks, but the dark-haired man outside the Post Office. A man not so far from her own age and with the wickedness and mischief shining from his eyes. He who still haunted her wilder dreams.

Unfortunately, Ginny was right. A man like that could have any girl he wanted. Why should he remember herself at all? And if he did, he wouldn't think well of her – not when he knew he had been robbed. Yet she recalled every detail of his appearance as if it were yesterday, building the dream and imagining virtues he probably didn't have. He was her hero – her ideal – it didn't matter that she would never see him again. In Melbourne there was always that possibility. He might walk into the Silver Star and remain to be charmed by her singing. But as the wheels of the dray rumbled and bumped along the dusty track, taking her further and further away from the city, she knew she would have to let the dream die. The young man was gone from her life before he ever came into it. She must forget him.

Seeing her bleak expression, Callum misinterpreted it. To take her mind off her misgivings he began to talk of his plans for the night.

'We have two choices, Maggi. We can stop now while it's light enough to find wood and build a fire in the shelter of one of these trees, or we can press on to Donaldson's which is a mile or two more up the track.'

'Donaldson's?'

'A wayside inn – so-called. Really it's more like a flop house, selling liquor on the side.' He wrinkled his nose and Maggi did likewise, mimicking his expression. 'The food isn't up to much and the comforts are few. As a rule I don't put up there, not unless it's raining.'

Maggi was quick to read between the lines of what he was saying. Ill-assorted travelling companions such as themselves

222

would attract more than their fair share of gossip and speculation. Having made up her mind to trust him, she agreed it was best to spend the night out of doors, sleeping before their own fire. As soon as they found a sheltered spot with some trees where the animals could be hobbled and allowed to graze, they searched in the gathering darkness for sufficient bark and wood to build a small fire protected in the base of a tree.

The dried bark of the eucalypt caught quickly, giving a clean yet pungent odour which made Maggi's eyes water when the smoke blew in her face. When the flames had died down and the fire was hottest, Callum suspended a billy full of water over the embers, saying she was about to have the best cup of tea she'd ever tasted. As she watched, he added a gum leaf to the pot.

'Are ye tryin' to poison me now?' she teased.

'If you're worried, I'll drink it first,' he offered. 'I promise there's nothing quite like it – billy tea, made out of doors under the stars.' She tilted her head back to look up at the bowl of the heavens, higher than she had ever seen before, the colour of dark blue velvet and studded with so many stars it was making her giddy. Somehow it had happened without her noticing; the brief twilight had given way to nightfall. There wasn't a cloud in the sky and the stillness which was almost eerie, promised another hot day on the morrow.

Maggi sipped the tea which was both refreshing and delicious. Rugged up in Callum's horse blanket more for comfort than warmth, she held the mug in her hands and blew on the surface to cool it as she stared into the fire. While the late-afternoon had been hot enough to make her miserable, her face pink and sweaty, damp patches forming under her armpits and bush flies feasting upon another damp patch on her back, there was relief at night which would allow them to sleep. She was hungry now and clenched her stomach to stop it growling as she waited to see what Callum had brought for them to eat.

Supper turned out to be a simple meal of salt beef, bread and a handful or two of dried fruit, a parting gift from his landlady in Melbourne. Conversation lapsed as they both

223

did justice to the food and when they had finished it, not even Maggi could think of anything to say. Her normal flow of chatter had dried up as she sat hugging the blanket around her and staring into the fire. Immediately, her thoughts strayed to Tully. She missed him dreadfully. Now even more than when she had been at Bullivant House. She wondered if he was happy now he had achieved his long-held ambition to go to sea. Was he staring out at the open ocean tonight, even as she herself was staring out at the bush, finding the emptiness of the landscape equally daunting?

Lounging before the fire, Callum pushed his hat to the back of his head and chewed a straw as he lay back, regarding her, once again misinterpreting her bleak expression.

'You don't have to do this, Maggi. It's still not too late to turn back. You don't have to come to the homestead if it's really not what you ...' He didn't voice the rest of his thoughts as she was turning to glare at him, her eyes snapping with temper.

'I haven't much choice, have I?' She sprang to her feet and began to pace to and fro before the fire. 'I suppose you've thought better of it? You'd like to be rid of me now? Not good enough, am I? Not even good enough to be a kitchen maid in your mother's house.'

'Whoa! You've got the wrong end of the stick again. That's not what I meant. I just want you to realise that life on the land here is different; it isn't to everyone's taste. I don't want to take you so far away from the city if you're going to be miserable there. Please, will you sit down and talk it over calmly, without getting upset?'

She did as she was told but shivered although it wasn't cold, peering into the bush as if she expected wild animals or demons to come prancing out of the darkness at any minute. The fire which he had rebuilt caused leaping shadows and to her overwrought imagination the long, curved leaves of the eucalypt resembled fingers stretching out for her, forming weird and menacing shapes in the firelight. She imagined strange tall figures hovering just out of her line of vision, perhaps the spirits of this ancient land, watching and waiting for them to become sleepy and inattentive when they would strike.

'I don't know.' She sighed. 'It's jus' so different. Not like Ireland at all where everythin's soft an' green, an' smellin' of ferns an' moss.'

'Oh, we have places like that here, too,' he said. 'In the hills where the ice cold waters spring from the rocks and everything's green and lush. There are ferns as big as umbrellas, big as trees.'

'Sure an' it can't be the same at all, then.' She was determined not to be comforted. 'There's nowhere in Ireland where there's ferns as big as trees. It's jus' so . . . so huge out here an' so empty; so deathly quiet all the time.'

'Well, it's not going to be quiet at home, if that's what you think. The place is a hive – people coming and going all the time.'

'You have visitors?'

'Of course. We country people work hard but not all of the time. D'ye think we live in splendid isolation, my mother and me? Lord, no! There's my sister, Lilias – she can't be much older than you – and my brother, Hamish. Then there's the housekeeper, Mrs Hallam, and Cassie, her maid. Our overseer, Paddy Hegarty, and his family . . .'

'They're Irish?'

'Yes. Not that it's any recommendation.'

She looked at him sharply until she saw he was teasing and smiled, waiting for him to go on.

'And at the last muster we had about three thousand sheep and five hundred head of cattle. Sometimes Hegarty has up to half a dozen rouseabouts and the local Aboriginals and their womenfolk who help out when we need them.'

'Blackfellers! Aren't you afraid they'll come by at night when you're sleepin' an' murder you in your beds?'

'No. Renegade white men – bushrangers – are a far greater risk. And don't call them "blackfellers" – not in my mother's hearing, anyway. She's very fond of our local tribesmen and says she would never have managed without them in the early days. While most early settlers went to war against the natives, she and my father preferred to make peace and live in harmony with the native people. They've worked with us on and off over the years ever since. It doesn't pay to rely on them – sometimes they get the call of the wild, step out of their clothes and disappear in the night. But they come back when they're ready. All up, they're a lot more reliable than some of the white men our neighbours employed. Men who packed their traps and took off for the diggings the moment they heard there was gold at Spring Creek.'

'Just like my father,' Maggi muttered, unable to keep the bitterness from her voice. 'He couldn't wait to rush off to the gold fields, the moment we got off the ship at Hobson's Bay.'

'You have a father here?' Callum sat up, startled by this piece of news. 'I thought you said you and Tully were orphans – alone in the world?'

'So we are – now.' To Maggi's dismay she felt tears threatening again. 'Mam was having a baby – she died on the ship comin' out. My da was killed at Eureka.'

'I'm sorry to hear it.' Callum stared into the flames. 'Bad business that. But the diggers should have known better than to go burning their licences, flouting the law. There must be easier ways to get justice than that.'

'What else could they do?' Previously, Maggi had been inclined to pour scorn on the miners' rebellion, calling it futile, but in the face of this casual criticism, she found herself supporting the opposite view. 'Men without votes, without rights. Of course they had to take a stand.'

'Maybe. But it was ill judged. They couldn't expect Governor Hotham to sit back and let them defy him. He had to make a show of force; send in the military to restore law and order.'

'Restore law and order? By killing defenceless men?'

'Not that defenceless. By building a stockade and raising a rebel flag, the diggers knew they would provoke an attack. They wanted to bring everything to a head.'

'And why not? They had right on their side. Tully said so.'

'A boy of sixteen? He'd know all about it, of course.'

'At least he was *there*. You weren't.'

'And neither were you.' Callum placed a finger on her lips to silence her. 'We must agree to differ until we can find out the truth of it.'

'Ah, now, is it the truth you want?' Impatiently, she brushed his finger away. 'That's easy. I'll give you the truth of it.'

226

'Peace, I say. No point in getting heated – it's over and done. You weren't there and neither was I. There was poor judgement on both sides – at least we agree on that – but you can't look at it from an unbiased viewpoint, not when you're so emotionally involved.'

Maggi opened her mouth to say more but Callum silenced her with a look. Certainly, he seemed to be a stickler for truth and self-discipline. She had to respect him for that. He threw more sticks on the fire to make a satisfying blaze before changing the subject yet again.

'So tell me, Maggi. How long have you been a thief?'

She glanced at him quickly, trying to see if there was an edge to the question, any mockery, but his expression was only calm, interested. 'What drove you into a life of crime?'

She spoke hesitantly, not sure how much to tell. 'It started a long time ago when we were in Ireland. Sometimes we had to steal if we wanted to eat. Other times Da liked to do it for the sheer hell of it an' because he could.'

'And why do you do it now? For the sheer hell of it? And because you can?'

She glared at him. His calm questioning was starting to get on her nerves. 'That's all you know, Mister Gentleman Squatter. Everything comes so easy to you. I promised our mam I'd look after Tully; to help him make a new life for himself so he'd have a fair chance in the world.'

'How? Teaching him to profit from a life of crime?'

'D'you know, sometimes you give me a pain! You're so smug and so sure of what's wrong and what's right. You judge and you think you know all about us. But you don't. It's not like that – not at all. I never meant to do it for long. Only 'til I had enough money for . . .' She broke off, unwilling to give him any more ammunition to toss back at her and sat, hugging her knees, staring moodily into the fire.

'Go on. Enough money for what?' he prompted.

'It doesn't matter. Not any more,' she muttered, making him all the more certain it did. She flashed him a small, bright smile in the hope of changing the mood. 'Please, I'd rather not talk about Tully jus' now. You were tellin' me about your family – where you live? A big place is it? Bit more 'n a squatter's hut?'

'Is that what you thought?' Callum grinned. 'No. Although the first home we built was made of timber slabs and had a traditional ironbark roof. Today the original cottage is a bit rundown and sad – nobody lives there any more – but it serves to remind us where we came from. How we started at Lachlan's Holt. It stands alongside the family cemetery – my father's grave.'

'Oh? An' how did –' Maggi whispered. She was about to ask how the older MacGregor had died until she saw Callum's expression didn't invite it. She fell silent, waiting for him to tell her only as much as he wished.

'We came from Scotland by way of Van Diemen's Land – that's where my father bought the sheep and cattle he needed. We came to the mainland with other squatters but while most of them wanted to take up runs in the Western District and the Mallee, my father chose to go north, to be nearer the border of New South Wales.'

'Why? Wouldn't it have been easier to go with the others? Where you'd have friends?'

'Maybe. But before my mother would agree to leave Scotland she made him promise that her children would receive as good an education as they would have received at home. And when we came to this country some twenty years ago, the only college for boys was in New South Wales.'

'But sure'n you had all the education you needed? You could read an' write?'

'Well, yes.' Callum smiled at her simple idea of schooling and what it meant. 'But my mother thinks learning of any kind is never a waste. She was determined we shouldn't grow up as farm boys with no knowledge of anything else. I think she hoped one of us might take after her own father and study law but we're not cut out for it. Hamish hates to be cooped up indoors and so do I. It's the only thing we can agree on – my brother and I.' Callum paused, his face sombre with old memories, staring into the flames and seeing more than the fire.

'The neighbours thought my mother would throw it all up when my father died. They didn't know her. She said Lachlan didn't bring her thousands of miles to have her turn tail at the first setback; she would finish building the house and

228

raise his children here, in the place he had chosen for us, just as he had planned. She made a good job of it, too. Taught herself how to breed sheep sturdy enough to stand up to the heat and supervised the completion of the homestead herself. Then she named it Lachlan's Holt, for my father.'

'Did you love your father very much, Callum?'

'Yes,' he whispered, concentrating on the embers of the fire. 'Yes, I did.'

'I did, too. I loved my da. But sometimes he made me so mad, I could scream. An' sometimes I almost hated him. I just wish he'd been a different father, that's all. More like other people's.'

'Maybe he didn't get the same opportunities.'

'Oh yes he did. He had a good start in life. He jus' made a mess of everythin' – too greedy for gold. An' I'll never forgive him for bein' the death of our mam.'

'You can't blame him for that, Maggi.' He spoke gently, once more prodding the embers to stir up the fire, and concentrating on the task so that he didn't have to look her in the eye. 'A lot of women die in childbirth. It's sad, I know, but it happens.'

'How like a man to say so – to take it for granted! It was Da's fault. He should have waited 'til the baby was born before takin' ship.'

'Perhaps he had no choice?'

'Why do you take his part?' She glared at him. 'You didn't even know the man.'

'Maggi, your mother's dead now and he is, too. If you keep on blaming him, the only person you'll hurt is yourself.'

'Well, I do blame him.' Shoulders hunched, she stared into the fire. 'I always will.'

Suddenly, Callum sat up straight, becoming tense with anticipation as he held up a hand for her to remain quiet while he listened.

'What is it?' she whispered, straining her ears to hear what it was.

'Horses – more than one – coming this way. Damn! Has to be bushmen – they've spotted the fire. Stay wrapped up in that blanket and don't say a word, no matter what. Leave the talking to me.'

229

'But why?'

'Just do it. Do as I say.'

There was no time for him to explain further as three men rode out of the darkness, bringing their horses to stand in a semi-circle around them, faces sombre in the firelight. One man dropped lightly to the ground and flung the reins of his horse to one of the others. All three were armed with rifles and carried an extra weight of ammunition in the gun belts strapped across their shoulders. All three wore similar wide-awake hats and full beards which made them look middle-aged although their eyes were youthful and alert in their grimy faces. Their clothes were shabby and stiff with dust and it was obvious they were bushrangers, living rough.

Callum gave no indication that he was surprised. He just pushed his hat to the back of his head and smiled a greeting when their leader came to crouch at the fire, warming his hands. A warm, rather sickly smell of unwashed body arose from his clothes.

'Goodnight to you, friend, and welcome,' Callum said easily, half-rising to offer his hand as he introduced himself. 'Callum MacGregor. And this is my sister, Maggi.'

Surprised by the lie, she shot him a quick glance. He ignored it.

'Miss.' The man touched his hat briefly although he didn't return the courtesy by giving his own name. His eyes remained on Callum, wary and assessing. 'So, Bullocky. That's a nice piece of horse flesh ye have back there.' He jerked his head towards Bothwell.

Maggi recognised in his speech a brogue thick as her own and was about to remark on it until she remembered Callum had told her she wasn't to speak.

'Yes, he is, isn't he?' Callum said easily.

'Ah, come on.' The man was growing impatient. 'You know why I'm here. Let's cut the cackle and get down to business. Ye wouldn't be carrying money, by any chance?'

'Money? Not me.' Callum laughed softly. 'I'm just a cocky going back home with a few supplies.'

'And home? Where might that be?'

'A few miles to the north of here,' Callum lied. 'So unless you can use a bag of flour or a roll of twine . . .'

230

'The bag? What's in the bag?' The man pointed to Callum's overnight grip, perched on top of everything else in the dray. 'Bit flash for a bullocky, isn' it?'

Callum shrugged. 'It's only the clothes I wear in the city and dirty linen I'm taking home. You can look if you like.'

'What would I be wantin' with a man's dirty clothes?' The visitor hawked and spat into the fire. '''Tis poor pickin's we're gettin' from you tonight. But we can always do with an extra horse. An' that stallion looks like he can go like the wind.'

'He does. But he's my sister's horse and doesn't take kindly to strangers – particularly men.'

'Go on.' The man gave a snort of derision. 'Pull the other leg, it's got bells on. That great brute is no pony for a lady.' And he gathered another mouthful of saliva, preparing to spit again.

'Don't take my word for it. Get up and ride him then, if you're game. He'll only throw you and probably break your neck.' Callum's eyes almost disappeared as he fixed the man with a steely look. 'Now, beat it. You've had your fun. I've been civil enough and you've warmed yourself at our fire but that's as much as you'll get. I'm beginning to find your company rather tiresome.'

'Tiresome?' The man laughed. 'You're no bullocky, that's for sure. A bullocky would tell me to bugger off.'

'Bugger off then,' said Callum without turning a hair. 'Unless you prefer to stay and risk getting shot?' Only now did he let the bushranger see the pistol tucked in his belt, the silver of the barrel glinting in the firelight.

Maggi held her breath, thinking of the two armed men on horseback behind them in the darkness. Without turning, she could imagine herself in the sights of those rifles, the dark holes of the barrels trained on her back.

'I didn' come here lookin' for no trouble.' The man was still smiling but his eyes had grown wary. 'An' there's no call for talk about folks gettin' shot. I bid you goodnight, sir, an' the young lady as well.' With exaggerated courtesy he tipped his hat and walked slowly back to his horse.

He rejoined his companions and exchanged a few remarks

231

as Callum sat tensed, gun at the ready, waiting to see if they'd challenge him again or open fire. They did neither. At a signal from their leader and without a backward glance all three rode off into the darkness.

Dry-mouthed, Maggi realised she'd been holding her breath. She didn't speak until she was quite sure they were gone. 'You took an awful risk,' she said. 'They could have jumped you easily. Three against one.'

'What did we have to lose?' Callum's smile was wry. 'Men who prey on other people are nearly always cowards. They could have killed us, sure. But they knew I'd take one of them with me if they did. Nobody wants to be the one who is shot.'

'Why did you tell them I was your sister?'

'Men like that have their own peculiar code of honour. They'll show more respect for a man's unmarried sister than for his woman or wife.'

'Why's that?'

'Do you never tire of asking questions?'

'I'm sorry. But are you sure it's safe for us to stay, now they know we're here?' Maggi pulled the rug more closely around her as she peered into the darkness. 'What if they come back and catch us while we're asleep?'

'I don't think so. They'll be halfway to Melbourne by now, looking for easier pickings.'

'I hope you're right,' she said. There was silence between them for a moment or two while she mulled over these events, surprised that he seemed unconcerned. 'Callum?'

'Yes?'

'Would you really have shot him – in cold blood?'

'If it came to it, yes. And you, too, rather than let you fall into the hands of the others.'

Maggi shivered as she looked at him, realising he meant what he said. The planes of his face were taut and grim as he stared into the last embers of the fire, disquieted by the closeness of her gaze. So there was more to this Callum MacGregor than she had seen at first glance. He wasn't at all the pampered son of a gentleman she had taken him for. He knew how to handle firearms and was capable of murder, if only in self-defence. She gave him a small, tight smile in the

232

hope of easing the tension which had sprung up between them.

He got up, went to the dray for more blankets and threw one to Maggi. He rolled himself in the other and turned on his side. Soon his regular breathing told her he was asleep. Maggi lay awake, peering into the darkness, imagining she saw horsemen moving in the shadows. It was a long time before she could relax and compose herself sufficiently to go to sleep.

Chapter Eighteen

As they travelled on, Maggi's respect for Callum increased. She became more at ease in his company as she discovered they had much more in common than she'd thought at first. To entertain them as they travelled, they often sang although Maggi had to laugh at Callum's inability to hold a tune, giggling helplessly as he murdered her Irish folk songs and a few of the English ones she had learned since.

Callum opened her eyes to the rugged, unusual beauty of her surroundings which had seemed so harsh and forbidding at first after the soft colours of her native Ireland. Until now, Maggi had seen little of native Australia, apart from the sea. She would rather forget the months she'd spent at Bullivant House, and the rest of her time had been spent in or around the city where the small squares of cottage garden behind the houses reflected the homesickness of the settlers, doing their best to recreate what had been left behind. Native trees and plants had been torn out to make way for plum and apple trees, roses and foxgloves, primroses and daffodils; everything to remind them of home.

Maggi had been unprepared for the sheer size, the sometimes breathtaking majesty of a land for the most part untouched by the hand of man. The plains were much as she expected, the heat oppressive when they had to travel in the glare of the sun without any shade. The coolness of the hills was a welcome change although Callum skirted them wherever possible to save the bullocks a climb. Here, massive eucalypts stretched to the sky, trees so huge that Maggi felt dizzy when she tilted her head back to look at them. Giants spreading their branches to protect the lush greenery which sprang up beneath. They saw a branch fall off without warning, making a loud crack just as it fell. Callum said this happened regularly, sometimes a branch just died. He pointed out others, lying where they had fallen, now covered with mosses and other parasitic plants, gradually to be reabsorbed into the forest. Small waterfalls tumbled from rocks into clear, swiftly running creeks with tree ferns growing on either side. Sometimes there was a flash of bright scarlet or green; a parrot on the wing, screeching a warning to its fellows as it flew overhead. Rain forest, filled with so much fresh air it was almost heady and dressed in every possible shade of green. Refreshed and enlivened, Maggi was reluctant to leave it. She found the dry scrub they passed through afterwards somehow depressing with its sun-scorched grasses and dusty, stunted trees. There was an airless expectancy about it, almost ticking with menace, smelling hot enough to burst into flame at any time. Easy to believe in bush fires here.

Even the insects seemed larger than life to Maggie: grass-hoppers big enough to have faces and bull ants, almost an inch in length, which arrived at their camp sites to feast on crumbs and other morsels of food.

She had a fright one day, mistaking a big blue-tongued lizard for a snake until Callum picked it up to show her its stunted body and small feet, assuring her it was harmless so long as she left it undisturbed.

'Why is it hissing, then?' She recoiled from the lizard which was puffing itself up and opening its mouth to display the bright blue tongue that gave it its name. 'I wouldn't touch the slimy old thing.'

'A common mistake,' he laughed. 'A lizard's not slimy at all. It isn't a slug. It'll feed on garden pests. My mother encourages them to stay in her garden at home.'

Still regarding it with suspicion, Maggi wrinkled her nose. She would never like reptiles. Callum pointed out wedge-tailed eagles gliding on the currents, searching for prey, and she laughed with childlike pleasure at the antics of the grey and pink galahs which would appear in flocks out of no-where, filling the air with their raucous, parrot cries. Callum didn't welcome the birds as she did. He said galahs were destructive, capable of stripping the seeds from a newly planted field in a matter of minutes.

More at ease in each other's company with each passing day, they didn't stay overnight at any of the guest houses or inns they encountered on the way, stopping instead at the village stores to buy fresh provisions for the animals and for themselves. Maggi became so used to walking with Callum beside the dray or sitting alongside him, singing, that she was beginning to wish the journey would never end. But while he was quite happy for her to ride his mare, he remained stubborn in his refusal to let her ride Bothwell.

'If something happened to you or the horse, I'd blame myself,' he said. 'He's a big brute and you're not strong enough to hold him.'

'How many times must I tell you? I can ride. It isn't a matter of strength.'

'What if he bolts with you then? Or trips on a root, breaking a leg?'

'Oh, an' what if the skies fall down?' she mocked. 'Nothing will happen, will it, old fellow?' She kissed the horse, offering him a lump of sugar. He snatched it greedily, nipping her fingers.

'You shouldn't spoil him with sugar, you'll make him fat,' Callum grumbled, jealous of the way she could charm his horse. She raised one finger in an urchin's gesture of contempt, showing several inches of healthy, pink tongue at the same time. 'And don't let my sister see you do that. She'll think you've no manners at all.'

'You're full of *don'ts* this morning.' Maggi tossed her head in a manner very similar to the horse. 'And I don't care what your sister thinks – she can take me as I am.'

In fact she sounded a lot more confident than she felt. Mention of those who awaited them at the end of the journey reminded her that soon it must come to an end. During the past few weeks she had learned to admire Callum's quiet confidence and skills as a bushman and she was happy to be sharing her days with him. There were times when he reminded her of somebody else and she was impatient with herself for being unable to place him.

To prepare herself for the changes which would take place

when they arrived, she kept reminding herself that soon this easy-going, everyday relationship must come to an end. Callum was master in that house and she would be no more to him than any other of his mother's maids.

And the more she considered the prospect of housework, the less it appealed to her. The chores at Bullivant House had been irksome enough and they had been shared among many. Besides, she was used to pleasing herself now, being free to go and come as she pleased. The idea of wearing an apron and a mob cap again didn't appeal to her. As a horse trader's daughter, she was more at home picking stones out of horses' hooves than starching clothes or making a tidy bed. And it would be hard to pretend to be meek, to speak only when she was spoken to and lower her eyes. Only now, as they were drawing closer to Lachlan's Holt, did she realise she was embracing the very lifestyle she had gone out of her way to avoid. And Callum would be glad to be rid of her, no doubt of that. Soon as he had delivered her to his mother, he'd consider his responsibility at an end.

From her seat on the dray, she watched him covertly, strong and tall as he strode in front of her, keeping pace with his bullocks. He seemed almost a part of the scenery, at home with himself and his surroundings. For the first time she considered her own actions. Why was she here? Was it the man himself who attracted her as much as the haven he offered? No. He was wholesome rather than handsome with that strong jaw which made him look unusually solemn and serious. But he had good hands – strong, well-shaped and practical. She liked a man to have good hands.

Becoming conscious of the intensity of her gaze, he turned to look at her. 'What?' he said. 'What is it? Anything wrong?'

'Nothing,' she mumbled, shamed at being caught staring at him and screwing up her eyes to squint at the horizon instead.

And now she looked for it, she could fancy a subtle change in his attitude towards her when he was almost home. Already he was preparing to distance himself. His face came alive with pleasure as he pointed out various landmarks which told him they couldn't be more than a day's travel away from Lachlan's Holt. The flat lands gave way to rolling hillsides, the trees and grasses became greener and more luxuriant. And, for the first time since they left Melbourne, Maggi sensed he was looking at her with critical eyes. He had something on his mind and was looking for a way to put it without offending her.

'Maggi,' he said at last when they were seated boiling the billy at lunchtime, 'I have to talk about this. And if you're embarrassed, I'm sorry. But you haven't taken a bath since you left the city – for that matter, neither have I, but first impressions are important and I think my mother would receive you more kindly if we could present you in clean clothes.'

'I have no other clothes. I left them all behind.' She looked down at the well-worn muslin, yet another of Peg Riley's castoffs. Faded now and with sweat stains spreading from the armpits, it was covered in red dust from her travels.

'Please, Maggie, I don't want you to fly off the handle and take this the wrong way – but if I give you one of the cakes of scented soap I have for my sister, would you wash them perhaps? And your – er – your person at the same time?' He glanced at her, preparing to avoid her flailing hands if she were to take the suggestion amiss. Instead, he saw her face lighting up with pleasure.

'Scented soap? I can have real scented soap and smell like a lady?'

He nodded and smiled, surprised at her simple pleasure in something he took so much for granted.

'Oh. Oh, Callum, nobody ever gave me real soap before. It was always coal tar or some horrible stuff made from sheep fat and eucalyptus we had at the home.'

'Home? I never knew you were in a home?'

'It wasn't for long,' she muttered, not yet ready to talk about Bullivant House. 'Real scented soap? Does it smell of roses or violets? Can I see it now?'

'No, you can't.' He grinned. 'This afternoon, I'll show you the falls and the swimming hole – the water's not deep.'

'I don't care if it is, I swim like a fish.'

'Well, I don't.' Callum frowned. 'The water's clean, it

comes from a spring. A waterfall flows into the pool. And it's off the beaten track. We can bathe in comfort without being seen.

'We shall bathe together, you an' I? At the same time?'

'Of course not.' His eyes widened at the suggestion. 'What are you thinking of, minx?'

'I could scrub your back for you. I used to do it for Tully. We always bathed together when we were small.'

'Well, I'm not your brother. Nor am I small.'

'No,' she said, suddenly thoughtful. 'But what about bush-rangers? Surely, it isn't wise to . . .'

'I doubt we'll see any this far north. They find easier pickings closer to town.'

'Real scented soap an' a whole cake of it to meself!' Maggi whooped with glee. 'Oh, Callum, I'll love you forever for this.' And she hurled herself at him, giving him a smacking kiss on the cheek. He stopped smiling and stared at her, taken aback.

'Steady on,' he said, passing off the awkward moment by making a joke of it. 'Your affection is easily bought. Do you have a comb?' He inspected the hopeless tangle of her bright red locks. 'I've never seen you use one.'

'It's torture. Like tryin' to tame a hedge.' She pulled a wry face. 'But I do have this.' She drew a well-worn piece of tortoiseshell from her pocket. Once it might have been expensive, forming part of a matching set, but now it was broken, minus most of its teeth. 'It belonged to Peg Riley. She was going to throw it away.'

'It'll do. For now.' He smiled. 'But when we get home I'll speak to my sister – she must have dozens of combs. I'm sure she'll be able to spare one.'

Mention of Callum's sister brought all Maggi's misgivings flooding back; the doubts she was trying to suppress. 'Oh, Callum, I do hope your sister will like me.'

He laughed shortly. 'Don't you worry about Lil. It's my mother you have to impress.'

Looking down at her stained and tattered skirt, Maggi chewed her lip, wondering how she could impress anyone, let alone these well-bred MacGregor womenfolk who were certain to see her for what she was. An Irish peasant; a tattered gypsy for whom there would be no place in their orderly, well-run household.

Later, when the sun had risen high enough to bring warmth to the air around them, they arrived at the promised waterfall and the natural pool. As Callum promised, the water was clear as crystal, in contrast to the brackish creeks and muddy billabongs they had encountered along the way. It looked cool and inviting as it cascaded from the rocks above, scattering sparkling crystal droplets as it did so.

When Callum unpacked his bag, he complained that his clothes were now smelling of attar of roses because of the soap. In its expensive pink wrappings it was decorated with a gold crest, proclaiming it to be favoured by Royalty, maybe Queen Victoria herself. Maggi closed her eyes, savouring the perfume and wondering how they managed to get it to smell like real flowers. Before leaving her to bathe at her leisure, Callum gave her a linen bath towel and a clean shirt to put on while she was waiting for her own clothes to dry.

She stripped quickly and waded into the water, gasping as it was cold in contrast to the warmth of the day. Before giving herself up to the pleasure of swimming, she washed her clothes. Standing beside the rocks, she examined her petticoat, bulky and quilted with its bundles of stolen money stitched into the pockets and the hem. Quickly, she folded the petticoat and tucked it into a crevice in the rocks where it would remain dry while she bathed.

Her camisole and drawers responded to soap and water more readily than the dress which, if anything, looked worse than when she started. The stains all ran together to make it a uniform ochre and the fabric, whatever it was, managed to shrink. She tugged at it fiercely, hoping to stretch it back into shape but at last she gave up the struggle and spread it out on the rocks to dry.

At last she gave herself up to the pleasure of washing herself, humming at first and at last bursting into full-throated song. Her voice echoed off the rocks which magnified the sound, giving it an almost theatrical volume.

'All round my hat I will wear the green willow
All round my hat for a year and a day.

240

'And if anyone asks the reason I wear it
I'll tell them my true love is ten thousand miles away –'

Callum had already heard Maggi sing and joined in the
same song with her before but this time it sounded different.
He found it hard to believe this mature, confident singing
voice came from the same girl.

She had been exceptional at the Silver Star, but this was a
voice of almost operatic proportions. Such a voice must
belong to an Ondine, a water nymph or a witch of the sea.
And like more than one man before him, he was drawn to
the sound as if he had no will of his own; the sound of a
woman at peace with herself and the world, singing as she
bathed and for nobody else's pleasure but her own. He
listened again as she launched into *The Black Velvet Band*,
her voice soaring and poignant with emotion as she sang of
the young man's unrequited love and betrayal.

Until now, Callum had been contented to turn his back on
the pool. At no time had it been his intention to spy on her
like a peeping Tom, behaviour be would have condemned in
anyone else. But the singing was irresistible and he convinced
himself he was only acting in her best interests to make sure
no danger threatened. He would take a quick glance from
behind a tree and she'd never know. He would make certain
she was safe and he'd go away. But when he peered down
into the pool and saw the girl waist deep in the water, diving
and splashing with unconscious joy, all his good resolutions
left him. Here was innocence; a maidenly beauty so unexpected it brought tears to his eyes, making him catch his
breath.

Her skin gleamed pale as marble against the contrasting
dark red of her wet hair. She couldn't know it but she was a
natural courtesan, every movement a seduction and all the
more enchanting because it was unstudied. The girl was
slender but strong and there was nothing child-like or fragile
about her body. Her breasts were small, high and more
rounded than had been suggested by the unflattering dress.
Her nipples were large, rose pink, and they peaked as she
lathered them, making Callum close his eyes against an
unwelcome stab of desire. What was he thinking of, to gaze

241

at that slender body and imagine it writhing beneath his own? He should remember she was a young girl, not much more than a child. A child who trusted him and looked to him for protection. He should leave at once before she discovered him spying on her. How could he ever explain himself, if she did? But his limbs refused to obey these commands and he remained as if rooted to the spot, feasting his eyes on her as if he had never seen a woman naked before.

When she had finished washing her body and her hair, she swam up and down the shallow pool and submerged herself to wash off the soap. When she surfaced, she turned to swim on her back, kicking strongly, her arms milling gracefully as her long hair spread out around her. On the return trip she seemed to be swimming directly towards Callum and he cursed, pressing himself against the back of the tree, hoping against hope that she wouldn't have seen him. She stood up, waist-deep in the water to wring out her hair.

Suddenly and without warning she screamed, making him leave his hiding place without a second's thought. He ran into the water fully clothed to reach her as quickly as possible.

'A snake! Oh, Callum! There's a big black snake!'

He snatched her up in his arms as if she weighed nothing and carried her out of the water. She buried her face in his neck and sobbed, not only with fright but with shame that he should have seen her without her clothes.

'Forget about false modesty, sweetheart,' he whispered urgently, realising he was shaking as much as she was. 'I need to know about the snake? Did it bite you? Was it swimming on the surface or was it under the water between the stones?'

'There!' She pointed to the creature which was wriggling away through the water, unconcerned. 'There it goes!'

'An eel!' Callum almost dropped her as he laughed his relief. 'Only a harmless eel. Oh, Maggi, my dearest girl! The fright you gave me. Don't you know an eel when you see one?'

'Only the little ones they peel and sell on the wharf. I didn't know they could grow that big,' she muttered, pink with shame and mortification, unable to meet his gaze. The moment he set her down, she seized the linen cloth he had given her and wrapped it around herself. She was chilled, shivering with cold as well as reaction to her fright.

'But how – how did you manage to get here so quickly?' she said. 'I was afraid you wouldn't hear me.'

'Never mind that,' he snapped. 'Just get yourself dressed.'

'I can't. My clothes are still wet. What's the matter? Why are you angry with me?'

'I'm not.'

'Then what are you shouting for?'

'Just – just put on my shirt and dry out your hair. I'm going to bathe myself.'

The coolness of the water soothed and calmed him and he swam in the shallows until he was clean and his inexplicable rage had left him.

When he came out he had to shake himself dry like a dog as he'd given his towel to Maggi. Quickly he put on his trousers before rejoining her, unprepared for yet another assault on his senses. Sitting cross-legged on the ground, she was the Maggi he knew, his shirt hiding her womanly curves and making her childlike again. She was pursing her lips and wincing as she dragged the comb through her hair which was drying quickly in the sunlight. But what hair! Filthy and full of dust it had been an unusual, startling red but now it appeared as a nimbus of flame around her delicate, heart-shaped face. Hearing his approach, she looked up at him, greeting him cautiously.

'What is it? Why are you staring at me now?'

'Nothing. Just you. You and that hair . . .'

'It's a fright, isn't it?' She gave a small pout and shrugged. 'But there's not a thing I can do about it. Runs in the family. My father had "carrots" too.'

'Oh, no,' he breathed, speaking so softly it was almost to himself. 'No one could call that "carrots". That hair is a red-gold web, a snare, a trap to drive men crazy –'

She eyed him, wondering if he had a touch of the sun and giving a nervous laugh. He looked so solemn, so serious, and she didn't know whether his words were intended as a compliment or not.

243

As she continued teasing the tangles out of her hair, Maggi discovered her hands were shaking. She was unnerved. She didn't understand him in this strange mood. Brown-skinned, stripped to the waist and with his hair wet and clinging to his head, he looked dark and a little threatening, unlike the man she had grown used to. He stood over her with an almost feral look in his eyes, legs splayed, hands on hips, and staring at her as if he would like to eat her. He could have no idea how the sight of his half-naked body disturbed her, robbing her of breath and leaving her heart thumping painfully in her chest. She let her gaze progress from his navel to his mouth, suddenly reminded of the one time she had experienced such an expected stirring of passion before. Reminded of that other man, she closed her eyes for a moment, almost weak with longing as the two men seemed to fuse together in her mind. Was it Callum provoking these feelings or that other, now lost to her forever? She couldn't be sure. But the intensity of Callum's gaze was disturbing. Why didn't he speak?

She licked her lips and swallowed, realising her mouth was dry. She looked at his hands, resting at ease on his hips, and experienced a sudden urge to feel them on her body, exploring the length of it from her breasts to her thighs. And more. She wanted to feel his mouth at her breast. On board the ship where there had been no privacy for the steerage passengers, she had stumbled across a couple making love. She had never forgotten the images left in her mind. The man unfastened the woman's bodice to kiss her breasts. Instead of pushing him away as Maggi expected, the woman had welcomed his attentions with little cries. Maggi had been puzzled, wondering why. Now she knew. If you loved a man you could never get close enough – you wanted him all over you, inside and out.

Was it Callum she loved? Or was there something about him which put her in mind of that other man? Responsible for her feelings today was a natural curiosity about sex; a desire to have done with innocence and know more. But if she gave way to her instincts and let him make love to her here by the pool, what would he think of her? Would he despise her when he was done, rejecting her as Parker rejected

244

Ginny? While Callum seemed to accept, perhaps even forgive her for being a thief, it wouldn't do for him to think she was loose as well.

Returning her gaze to his face, she saw he was staring at her with a fascination equal to her own, his body rigid with tension. She gave a small cry as he caught hold of her wrist, jerking her none too gently to her feet. He pulled her close and took a handful of her hair, tilting her head back, exposing her throat and making her close her eyes against the brilliance of the sun. Unable to breathe already, she gasped and her lips parted naturally as she waited for his kiss. A kiss which never came as he let her go so suddenly that she almost fell.

'No, Maggi. We can't do this. It's all wrong.'

'But why?' She gave him a sleepy smile, still a little drunk with unrequited passion.

'Ah, for God's sake, do I have to spell it out? You – me – here alone. Get your clothes on, girl, wet or dry, I don't care. I'll see to the animals. Just get yourself dressed and join me as soon as you can.'

'Callum, please. You mustn't think – I didn't mean –'

'I don't think anything, Maggi,' he snapped, snatching up the rest of his clothing and striding away.

She stood where she was without moving, shaken by the force of his rejection and waiting until she could no longer hear his retreating footsteps. She sank down with her back to a tree, put her head on her knees and wept. She knew there was no need to hurry. No matter how long she took, how long she kept him waiting, he wouldn't come back. In her eagerness to please, she had handled it all wrong. Now he would despise her, thinking her more experienced than she was. Instead of melting into his arms, she ought to have smacked his face. He would have respected her then.

When she came to put on her dress, her worst fears were realised; it was badly shrunk. By breathing in, she could draw together most of the laces and buttons but the garment clung to her body like a second skin, flattening her breasts and gripping her arms so tightly she couldn't raise them. All the same, she didn't forget to retrieve her petticoat from the crevice between the rocks and put it on, comforted by the rustling of her money. By the time she made her way back to

245

Callum at the dray, she had dried her tears, plaited her hair into a single fat tail and even managed a smile as she apologised for making him wait.

He was leaning against the dray, his hat pulled forward over his eyes to hide their expression.

'You took your time.' He nodded curtly without returning her smile and swung himself up into the driving seat, leaving her to scramble aboard as best she may. Hampered by the dress which was still damp, she heaved herself up to sit beside him, too proud to ask for his help.

He can't bear to touch me now, she thought. He won't even soil his hands with me. And she kept her eyes cast down so that he wouldn't see the tears which blinded her, threatening to spill over and roll down her cheeks. The cicadas were in full cry, assuring them of a hot day, but they could take no pleasure in it.

Maggi flinched as Callum cracked the whip, shouting at the bullocks with more force than necessary to get them to move, and the journey progressed in silence, neither caring to speak. They rode on like this for miles, formal as a pair of strangers, travelling together aboard a public coach.

Were it not for the unfinished business and tension between herself and Callum, Maggi's first glimpse of Lachlan's Holt would have been a pleasure and a surprise. Red gums parted to reveal a modest but comfortable homestead surrounded by young trees from the old country, lovingly planted where they would provide the most shade. More of a farmhouse than a mansion, the homestead was constructed mainly of timber and with a shingled roof – a solid brick chimney providing support at either end. A verandah running the length of the building provided protection from the sun and Maggi concluded there must be a similar structure at the rear. Positioned alongside the river to take advantage of magnificent views, the homestead was dwarfed by its outbuildings – two huge barn-like structures, the wool shed and the bunk house for visiting shearers beyond. Closer to the main homestead but not adjoining were the stable block and the kitchen quarters, in the foreground several stock pens and also a smithy.

Callum had told her Lachlan's Holt was a busy, working

246

homestead. As the bullocks approached the stable yard, slowing as they scented home, two little boys ran out to greet them, waving their hats and whooping to cheer Callum home.

'The Hegarty kids,' he explained to Maggi, reaching among the boxes to dig out a bag of boiled sweets which he tossed to the children. The boys fell on them, squabbling over them like hungry birds.

But it was the two women standing on the verandah who attracted Maggi's attention and held it. If she had imagined Callum's mother to be a stiff, gracious old lady dressed in a widow's black bombazine, she couldn't have been more wrong. Although Elizabeth's features and colouring were completely different, she had the same smile as her son, the same crow's feet around the eyes which made them crinkle and disappear. Her hair, once dark, was now liberally sprinkled with grey and she wore it drawn away from her face and piled on her head with the minimum of fuss. Her figure was lean and lithe as that of a girl and her face was unfashionably tanned. Clearly, she preferred to be out and about around the property rather than sitting indoors, sewing or pursuing more ladylike pastimes. She was dressed in riding breeches like a man, her only concession to femininity a full-sleeved blouse of soft cream linen, stock tied and secured with a gold pin at her throat. Over this she wore a tailored waistcoat of fine leather. While on many women such clothes could appear aggressive, on Elizabeth MacGregor they were only elegant. Maggi stared in admiration, warming to the woman, perhaps because she was so different from her expectations. She remained seated on the dray while Elizabeth ran down the steps to greet her son who sprang down from the dray to catch his mother in his arms, almost lifting her off her feet.

'Callum! Welcome home, my dear, we looked for you over a week ago. We were beginning to be concerned. Is everything all right? Did you see Carpenter? And is the clip safe aboard the *Sally Lee*? D'you think they'll reach England before the end of the wool sales?'

'Yes. Yes to all questions, Mother. But let me get my breath.'

'And what are you doing, driving the team?'

247

'All in good time, Mother. Lilias – hello. You're looking bonnier than ever. And, yes, I have letters from Harley and Constance, before you ask.' He whirled his sister off her feet, making her giggle.

'Callum! Oh, Callum, you're filthy! Put me down!' she squealed. But her actions belied her words as she flung her arms around his neck, hugging him close and planting a smacking kiss on his cheek.

Turning her attention to Maggi who was watching these exuberant greetings, Elizabeth addressed her for the first time.

'Forgive us, my dear. It's such a relief to have Callum home I scarcely noticed he wasn't alone. You must think us very rude.'

'Oh no, ma'am, not at all.' Maggi smiled shyly, enchanted by Mrs MacGregor's soft Highland accent which was much more pronounced than Callum's. But out of the corner of her eye she could see Lilias frowning and biting her lip as she looked Maggi up and down. Tidy and well-groomed as she was, Lilias would be quick to criticise shabby clothes.

Unlike his mother, Callum's sister was exactly as Maggi had pictured her; every inch the stylish young lady. While Callum and Elizabeth were dressed in keeping with an active, outdoor life in the country, Lilias was not. She took up an unusually large amount of space with her hooped skirts and, if anything, was more grand than Amelia Bullivant in her elegant afternoon gowns. Lilias's was composed of many tiers of pink and white muslin – even the sleeves were extravagantly flounced and trimmed with pink satin. Her fine, dark hair had been parted in the middle and drawn back into a complicated bun on the top of her head. To complete the picture of cool, freshly laundered elegance, she was wearing a crisp, white collar of handmade lace. More than ever conscious of their differences, Maggi found the contrast between herself and this vision of regal loveliness almost too hard to bear.

And Lilias was beautiful, too; her features small and perfect with a pair of grey-green eyes enormous in an oval face. Her complexion was milk and roses, making Maggi feel so freckled and plain that she let out a long sigh. Perfect as

248

she was, Lilias would expect perfection from all who served her. Suddenly, Lilias seemed to make up her mind about something and smiled. It was a lovely smile which lit up her whole face as she tucked her arm in Callum's and giggled up at him. She seemed to giggle a lot.

'Well done, Callum, you've excelled yourself this time. A red-headed gypsy! Where on earth did you find her?'

Tired of the conversation flying back and forth over her head, Maggi decided it was time to assert herself.

'If you please, sir,' she addressed Callum with as much dignity as she could muster, 'will ye help me get down?'

With great ceremony Callum handed her down. They both knew she could have sprung to the ground as easily as he did but he was willing to humour her. Safe on the ground, she nodded her thanks, straightened her shoulders and addressed herself to Mrs MacGregor.

'My name is Marigold McDiarmit, ma'am. Mister Mac-Gregor persuaded me I could make meself useful here.'

'How lovely – a leprechaun! A real Irish leprechaun.' Lilias copied Maggi's accent with wicked accuracy. 'Sure an' begorrah! How many wishes do I get? Is it two or three?'

Maggi's eyes narrowed and she was on the point of saying that if she'd been gifted with magical powers, it would have been her pleasure to strike Miss Lilias MacGregor with the ugly stick and turn her into a toad. Fortunately, Elizabeth came to her rescue before she did anything so rash.

'Stop your teasing, Lilias. Let the poor child be. Can't you see she's exhausted after the journey and quite at the end of her tether?'

'I am sorry.' Lilias had the grace to look shamefaced. 'I didn't think. I bid you welcome to Lachlan's Holt.'

Maggi nodded her thanks but her knees refused to bend in the curtsy she knew Lilias was expecting and which she had been taught at the home. Lilias opened her eyes, slightly surprised, but it was Elizabeth who covered the awkward moment.

'Go to Mrs Hallam in the kitchen, my dear,' she said, nodding in the direction of a building behind the main house. 'Tell her I sent you and you're to have a hot meal, a bath and some clean clothes.'

249

Maggi bent her head and nodded again, not trusting herself to speak. The moment had come. She was being dismissed to the servants' quarters already. Callum wouldn't even trouble to accompany her and make the necessary introductions. Too late she realised she wasn't cut out to be anyone's servant and would never be able to live up to Lilias's exacting standards. What a fool she'd been to think she could! She should never have come here. It was all a terrible mistake.

Chapter Nineteen

All three watched Maggi until she disappeared around the side of the building. Callum's mother didn't speak until she was certain the girl wouldn't hear.

'All right, who is she? No ordinary servant, that's for sure.'

His smile was mild. 'She's a little thief, Mother. On the run from the law.'

'Oh, very funny,' Lilias giggled. 'Now tell us the truth, Cal.'

'I have.' He shrugged.

'Then what in the name of heaven possessed you to bring her here? What about Mother's jewellery? My clothes?'

'Your clothes?' Callum laughed shortly. 'I don't think Maggi's first thought will be to steal your clothes.'

'Oh? Why was she staring at them then, with such greedy eyes?'

'I don't know. Maybe she thought you overdressed.'

'Callum!'

'Relax, Lilias. She's not going to steal from us. If she did – where would she go? Five minutes out of here and she's bushed; hopelessly lost.'

'Well, I know that but does she?' Lilias wasn't ready to let it go. Callum groaned, knowing how much his sister enjoyed these arguments which went round and round, going no-where. Bone weary, he dropped into his old basket chair on the veranda and pushed his hat to the back of his head. Too late he wished he'd had the sense to lie about Maggi or at least save the truth until later.

'So I wasn't so wide of the mark when I called her a gypsy?' Lilias was thinking aloud. 'Maybe she'll liven things up around here.'

'Not that we need it,' Elizabeth chimed in. Her complaint was a little more subtle but still there. 'What were you thinking of, son? And what are we to do with her now she's here?'

'I don't know, Mother.'

'Poor old Cal,' Lilias giggled. 'You always were a soft touch. It's the same every time you come back from the city. You always bring us some lame duck to take in and nurture. Last time it was that puppy with a thorn in his foot. Who'd know it was going to grow into a creature the size of a small lion!'

'Yes, Bruno! Where is the old fellow?' Seizing the opportunity to change the subject, Callum brightened and sat up, looking around for his dog. 'I haven't said hello to him yet.'

'He's not here. Gone off on some jaunt with Hamish, I think.' Lilias exchanged a quick glance with her mother as Callum's expression darkened.

'Oh, and where to this time? I told him to stay close to home. He ought not to go off and leave two women alone and unprotected while I'm away.'

'Come on. We're not so helpless as you think. We could look after ourselves if it came to it, Mother and I.'

'I don't know.' Callum frowned, thinking of the hard faces of the bushrangers they had encountered on the way. 'I'll have a few words to say to young Hamish when he gets back.'

'Never mind Hamish. What about this gypsy of yours?'

'There's nothing to tell.' He shrugged. 'Nothing I haven't told you already.'

'You've told us nothing.' Lilias folded her arms to confront him, making Callum groan, raising his eyes to heaven. His sister might have the appearance of a Dresden shepherdess but she had a core of steel. 'And I mean to get to the bottom of it. Not content with bringing home flea-bitten mastiffs, this time it's a girl. By your own admission a thief and probably with a temper lively enough to match her hair.'

'Come on, Lil, Mags can't help the colour of her hair,' he

252

said. 'And do you wonder she's out of sorts? A fine welcome she had from you – giggling at her Irish accent and calling her a leprechaun. Why can't you think for once before you open your mouth? She's only a child, for heaven's sake – a little girl.'

Lilias gave a rich chuckle. 'A little girl? Oh, no. If that's what you think, you're a bigger fool than I thought. Little girl, indeed! Little tiger more like. Devouring you with those great yellow orbs.'

'Rubbish.'

'Is it? Then why are you sitting there, positively thrumming with irritation?' She glanced at his fingers, drumming the arm of the chair. He stopped at once, glaring at her. 'You're so naive with women, Cal. It's easy to see how it is – she's got you twisted around her little finger already.'

'Shut up, Lil. You know your trouble? You read too many cheap novels and fill your head with too many stories from women's papers. Nothing's going on – nothing at all. It's all in your mind.'

'Why are you yelling, then?'

'I'm not!'

'And instead of worrying about what's going on in my head, perhaps you should concern yourself about what's going on in hers. Look at it from her point of view.' Lilias chewed her lip in thought. 'Swept off her feet by a handsome landowner and whisked away to spend three weeks alone on the road. Three whole weeks, Callum. Quite long enough for two healthy people to fall in love.'

'Now stop it, Lilias, that's quite enough.' Elizabeth felt bound to intervene. 'Have done with your teasing and leave your brother alone. He's not home ten minutes before you're making mischief again.'

'Sorry, Cal.' Lilias relaxed and grinned. 'I only do it because there's nothing else to do here and I'm bored.'

'Well, it's unattractive in you, Lilias,' Elizabeth warned.

'I did say I was sorry, Mother.'

'That's all very well but you get carried away and saying you're sorry won't mend the results every time. You'll have to be careful of Harley's sensitivities when you're married and have a home of your own.'

'God, yes. Poor Harley,' Callum rallied again. 'Perhaps I should tell him what he's letting himself in for? The nagging tongue, the little worm of cruelty in his otherwise perfect rose. He might even want to back out before it's too late.'

'Harley loves me!' Tears sprang to Lilias's eyes. Fond as she was of teasing others, she didn't like it so much when the tables were turned. 'And he wouldn't dare. You'd think that was funny, wouldn't you, Cal? To see me jilted. Shamed and left on the shelf.'

'On second thoughts, no.' He grinned. 'Because we'd have to put up with you here for the rest of our days.'

'Stop it, the pair of you.' Elizabeth was exasperated. 'You should hear yourselves – bickering like a pair of children in the school room.'

'I'm sorry, Mother.' Callum leaned forward to take her hand. 'But Lilias would try the patience of a saint.'

'I know, but this time she does have a point. Why did you bring this girl to us, Callum?'

'Oh, I don't know.' He squirmed in his seat, uncomfortable in the face of her honest, inquisitive gaze. 'To be honest, I didn't give it much thought. Her brother had sailed away with the *Sally* and she had nowhere else to go. I felt sorry for her, that's all. Surely Hallie can make use of an extra hand in the kitchen? There must be something the girl can do?'

'Yes, but what?' Elizabeth looked thoughtful 'Hallie's set in her ways, and besides she's used to working with Cassie – I won't have her upset. I don't see this girl as a maid of all work and we've never had anyone wait on us at table. Unless . . .' She glanced at Lilias. 'Weren't you talking of hiring someone to train as a personal maid?'

'Oh, no, don't wish this one on me.' Lilias gave a small shiver. 'I *am* looking for a maid, yes. But I want someone who knows how to handle a goffering iron, not some renegade Irish peasant with a reputation for being light-fingered. Sorry, Cal. I'd like to help out but I need a sensible, biddable girl who knows her trade.'

'Please, Lil, won't you give her a chance? She's bright enough. All she needs is someone to take her in hand and show her what to do.'

'Well, it's not going to be me. Sorry.' Lilias's eyes danced with mischief. Callum would have risen to the bait once again but they were diverted by the arrival of Mrs Hallam. Red-faced and breathing heavily, she was mounting the steps of the verandah, not at all her usual, immaculate self. Grey hairs were escaping from beneath her starched white cap, and she had a determined look in her eye.

'O-oh, here comes trouble!' Lilias muttered.

'Begging your pardon, madam, but it's about the young person you sent to the kitchens –'

'Yes?' Elizabeth sighed. 'What is it now, Hallie?'

'She said as she weren't hungry so I showed her to the bath house an' give her a towel an' some clothes like you said. I hope I did right, madam, but the only clothes as would suit were Miss Lilias's old school smocks and aprons. Bit on the fancy side for the likes of her but . . '

'That's all right, Hallie, go on.'

'Well, while she were in the bath, I thought to give that old dress of hers a turn in the tub – bein' as I had some other washin' on the go. An' – oh, madam, I wouldn't want you to think ill of me. Sarah Hallam has never been one to pry –'

'I know that, Hallie. Go on.'

'I picked up the petti – filthy it was and seemed a bit on the heavy side. An' when I looked you could've knocked me down with a feather!' and she dropped Maggi's travel-stained petticoat into Elizabeth's waiting hands. 'Didn't half give me a turn. Never seen so much money in my life, not all in the same place at the same time.'

But before Elizabeth could say anything reassuring, they were stopped by a howl of rage from somewhere at the back of the house, making them all start in alarm. Seconds later, Maggi herself came flying around the corner of the building and stormed up the steps of the verandah, barefoot, her clothes flung on in haste, drops of water flying from wet hair.

'Where is the ould witch? How dare she take my petticoat? An' what's she done with it, that's what I'd like to know?' She glared at all of them, deflating a little when she saw the garment in question lying in Elizabeth's hands. Callum groaned and fell back into his chair, letting his hat fall over his eyes while Lilias draped herself against one of the supports

255

of the verandah and folded her arms, biting her lip to prevent herself from laughing out loud.

'Is this what you're missing, Maggi?' Elizabeth was firm but gentle. 'And would you care to tell us how you came by so much money?'

'Oh, Mother, don't ask.' Lilias gave a breathy laugh. 'She'll only make up a juicy lie. Your gypsy's full of surprises, isn't she, Cal? A little bit more than a petty thief.'

'Thank you, Hallie, that'll be all for now.' Elizabeth had the sense to dismiss the housekeeper who was becoming fascinated by this turn of events. 'And not a word to Cassie or anyone else about this.'

'No, madam.' Clearly disappointed, she gave Maggi a long and searching look and went away muttering to herself, 'Don't know what the world's a-comin' to.'

Callum stood up and stretched his back, weary from more than too many days on the road.

'I'll deal with this, Mother, if you don't mind. After all, I am responsible for Maggi and for bringing her here.'

'Indeed an' you're not.' Far from being repentant and hanging her head, Maggi stood up to him. 'No one's responsible for me but myself. And when you've done with admiring the weight of me petticoat, I'd like it back.'

Elizabeth passed it to Callum. 'Here, son. You know the history and the circumstances – I'll leave you to deal with this. Come on, Lilias.'

'Oh Mother, no,' said Lilias, backing away as she realised she was to be cheated of this prime entertainment. But Elizabeth wasn't to be denied. Taking her daughter by the arm, she bundled her into the house and closed the door firmly behind her. Callum waited a moment, to make sure it remained so, before addressing himself to Maggi.

'Now then, young lady,' he said. 'What do you have to say for yourself?'

'You can't pretend you didn't know – didn't you see me stealin', your very self? An' it's no good goin' all prissy on me now because I can't give it back. I haven't the first idea who it came from.'

'But, my dear girl, there's a small fortune here. Have you any idea how much?'

'No. Not for certain I don't.' Maggi twisted her hands in her apron, unwilling to admit her knowledge of numbers was sketchy.

'Five hundred – perhaps as much as seven hundred pounds.'

'That's a lot, is it?'

'Oh, Maggi, Maggi.' Callum winced. 'You could be sent in chain's to Van Dieman's Land or to the hulks for stealing a fraction of this. Why take such a risk, when you don't even know what you want it for?'

'I knew what I wanted it for, all right,' she said, stung by his criticism.

'Then tell me, Maggi, because I'm trying to understand. What mattered so much that you were willing to sacrifice your freedom and your future for it? What was it you wanted? Pretty clothes?'

'Pretty clothes!' She almost snorted with disgust. I suppose you think all women are vain as that sister of yours?'

'Leave Lilias out of this.'

'All right, I'll tell you. I can see I'll have no peace 'til I do. I wanted the money for Tully. To pay for his education. I wanted to send him to a good school.'

'On stolen money?'

'Why not? What good was it doin' the miners? Every day I had to watch them fritter their money on painted women an' cheap booze. Lightin' their pipes . . '

'. . . with five pound notes. I know, you said so before.'

'An' it seemed such a waste when I needed it for my Tully.'

Callum nodded, at last beginning to understand. 'But, Maggi, it takes more than just money to give a boy a good education. A home and a stable background, too.'

'Which I don't have?'

'It isn't a criticism. But you can't buy a boy an education and expect him to put it on like a Sunday hat. For one thing, the student has to be willing to learn. And your brother didn't strike me . . .'

'What would you know about Tully? You didn' see him for more'n five minutes at most.'

'I saw enough. I saw a boy achieving a life-long ambition. He was thrilled to be going to sea.'

257

'What are you saying, then? He was glad to be rid of me?'

'No, never. But I think he'll fare better as an honest seaman rather than a nervous thief.'

'Oh, yes. I wondered how long it would take for you to get back to that.'

'Don't you see? You were risking your neck for nothing. Tully would never have let you send him to school.'

Maggi said nothing, perhaps because she knew he was speaking the truth. 'He could be a musician,' she said at last. 'He can still go to college when he comes back.'

'I don't think so, Maggie.' Callum tried to break the news gently. 'He's part of a ship's company now. He won't want to go back to school.'

'He will, if I say so. I'll make him see it's for the best.'

'Then he'll be doing it to please you. Is that what you want?'

'Yes. No. Oh, I don't know any more.' Impulsively she tried to give him the money. 'Take it, then. I don't want it. I don't know what to do with it any more.'

'I can't keep it either. But I may be able to suggest a solution; a way to dispose of the money where it'll do the most good.'

Callum's suggestion was to divide the money between several charitable institutions devoted to the care of the widows, deserted wives and children of miners. Callum and Elizabeth wrote the letters and Maggi tucked the money into the envelopes and gave them to Callum to take to the post.

She had been at the homestead for more than a week and still she hadn't set eyes on the younger brother, Hamish. It was almost the end of January and summer was here with a vengeance, the heat of the sun oppressive and the thrumming of insects promising more hot weather to come.

While Lilias referred to Maggi as 'our little gypsy,' treating her as an amusing novelty, Elizabeth was more understanding. It was she who suggested Maggi should rest and do nothing for the time being; a few weeks' holiday with no strings attached. Also this would give her time to assess the girl's abilities while she decided how best to employ her.

Mrs Hallam's rule was absolute in the kitchens, hindered

rather than assisted by her scullion, Cassie, who wasn't very bright. Cassie resented Maggi, fearing she had come to cheat her of her position. Maggi stayed out of her way as much as possible although she was forced to share sleeping quarters with the girl. The last thing she wanted was to deprive Cassie of her position and take over the boring repetitive work in the kitchen. Sarah Hallam regarded herself as a 'good plain cook' and kept the household supplied with porridge, beef or mutton stew and the occasional suet pudding if she felt like it.

Molly Hegarty, the overseer's wife, had charge of the laundry and she cooked for her own family, visiting shearers and any casual workers employed on the property. When Maggi showed no more enthusiasm for working with Molly than with Mrs Hallam in the kitchen, Elizabeth despaired of finding a use for her until Maggie asked to look over the stables.

Elizabeth stood in the doorway and wrinkled her nose at the acrid smell of horse manure and neglect emanating from the stalls. 'Oh, dear. I tend to forget that when Hegarty isn't here, there's no one left to look after them but myself.'

'What about Callum?'

'No. Not at this time of year. He's out mending fences and rounding up any stray sheep. He expected Hegarty to be here to do the job with him but ...' Elizabeth sighed and shrugged. 'That'll be something more to hold against Hamish when they get back.'

'They don't get on, Callum and his brother?'

'No, I'm afraid they don't.' Elizabeth sighed again, her expression bleak. 'They never have.'

'But caring for the stables is a full-time job on its own. For this many horses, you should have a full-time groom.' Maggi walked along the line of stalls, wrinkling her nose at the swarms of bush flies congregating on the fresh droppings around the horses' feet. 'I'd say you need more than the help of one man, part-time.'

'Not even that.' Elizabeth's smile was wry. 'Hegarty has so much else to do. We used to employ a groom, Silas Crabbe – a horrible man. More than lived up to his name. I can't say I was sorry when he left us to go to the gold fields.'

259

'So you have no one to help you take care of the animals now?' Maggi thrust aside recent cobwebs to peer down a row of stalls where she could see the Clydesdales which did the heavy work around the property and on the opposite side those containing the saddle horses. Bothwell, recognising her voice, lifted his head and whinnied a greeting.

'Then look no further,' Maggi crowed, clapping her hands. 'I'll be your groom. I'd sooner muck out after horses than humans any day o' the week.'

Still Elizabeth hesitated. 'You, Maggi? I don't know. Taking care of the stables is back-breaking work. To expect a girl to cope with it single-handed doesn't seem fair.'

'Of course it is. I wouldn't offer if I didn't think I could. Oh, please, Mrs MacGregor. I'm good with horses – I was raised with them. There isn't a horse alive can get the better of me, not even Bothwell there. It's the only worthwhile thing Da ever taught me – the love of good horses an' how to manage them. Mrs MacGregor, please!'

'Well . . .' Elizabeth smiled, beginning to weaken.

'You'll let me do it, so you will? You'll give me the charge of your stables?'

'It's a big responsibility for anyone, Maggi, let alone a young girl. Maybe we should discuss it with Callum first.'

'No!' Already aware of his views on women and horses, Maggi was certain he wouldn't agree. 'He thinks a woman's place is at the kitchen sink – that a female is good for nothing but sewing and making food. These horses need someone to care for them now. To ride them. Put them out in the paddocks for an hour or so, to get some fresh air and to graze. Let me try it for just a week, that's all I ask. And at the end of the time, if you don't like what I've done, you can pay me a week's wages an' give me the sack. I can't say fairer than that now, can I?'

'No,' Elizabeth said slowly, realising she was being pushed towards a decision she might regret.

'Settled then.' Maggi shook Elizabeth's hand to seal the bargain. 'Oh, an' there's one thing more.'

'What's that?' Elizabeth asked, looking apprehensive.

'I'll need to wear trousers like you do. Da never taught me to ride side-saddle an' it's a terrible hardship for me to ride in a skirt.'

Elizabeth agreed, providing Maggi with shirts and some trousers she used to wear a few years ago when she was more slender still.

In a ferment of anxiety, Maggi waited to hear if Callum was going to veto his mother's decision. To her relief, he didn't. In the hope of winning his total approval, she treated Bothwell with special care, cleaning his feet and brushing him until his coat gleamed like polished ebony. While she longed to ride the stallion, testing his abilities to the full, she wouldn't do so unless Callum gave his permission. She didn't want to put her new position at risk. Bothwell was temperamental. Strong-boned and well-muscled, he needed more exercise than Callum had time to give him. The mare remained his choice for the day to day work around the property because she was used to it and could be trusted, when he dismounted, not to run away.

Mrs Hallam voiced her disapproval when Maggi insisted on moving from the bedroom she shared with Cassie to the traditional groom's quarters – the attic over the stables. Maggi insisted that she was responsible for the safety of the horses and if she was to do her job properly, she should sleep close to them. Elizabeth saw no harm in it but Lilias sided with Mrs Hallam.

'I hope you don't live to regret it, Mother. You're spoiling that girl. Let her have far too much her own way.'

'That's funny.' Elizabeth smiled. 'I have one or two friends who used to criticise and say exactly the same thing about you.'

'Well, I am the daughter of this house. While Maggi – Maggi is only –'

'An upstart little Irish girl? Oh, Lilias. I do believe you're jealous of the child.'

'And how many times must I tell you, she isn't a child? She shouldn't sleep out there over the stables. She should be downstairs with Cassie where Mrs Hallam can keep an eye on her.'

'Why? I can hardly blame her for not wanting to sleep in the same room as Cassie whose personal hygiene isn't the best.'

'That isn't the point, Mother. She'll make herself much

too comfortable. She could entertain men up there and you'd never know.'

'What men?' Elizabeth laughed. 'Opportunity's a fine thing. There's only Hegarty – and I think Molly would have something to say about that. And you can't be suggesting that Callum . . .'

'No, Mother, we already covered that.' Lilias sighed, her words heavy with portent. 'But you're forgetting Hamish, aren't you? It's Hamish I'm worried about.'

Chilled to the marrow, Tully was up in the crow's nest, hunched against winds that made icicles form on his nose and hoping he wouldn't get so numb he'd fall out. Ropes and sails creaking in the freezing temperatures, the *Sally Lee* moved cautiously towards the Antarctic on the way to Drake Passage and Cape Horn. Anxious to make up the time he had lost in Melbourne, Captain Carpenter was using the Great Circle Route, following the curvature of the earth. While it would cut many miles off the journey, it would also bring the *Sally* perilously close to the Antarctic region.

Having boarded the ship with nothing suitable for visiting such climes, Tully was wrapped in all the warm clothing Jem and Hobley could spare. His duty today was to keep his eyes peeled for icebergs. If the cold threatened to creep into his brain and send him to sleep, there was always fear to keep him awake. Some of the older seamen told tales late at night; tales of boys who had fallen asleep and frozen to death in the crow's nest or whose inattention had allowed them to miss an approaching iceberg. And it wasn't only the prospect of colliding with a submerged giant, there was the worse prospect of becoming embayed – stuck fast and frozen in the underwater extensions of a huge berg. Most of the time an experienced captain and crew could take action to avoid such perils but sometimes a ship was caught, frozen in time with all hands. This, then, was the price to be paid for speed. Tully felt as if he were freezing to death right now as the chilling sea mists rolled in all around him, making it difficult to see more than a few yards ahead.

It was hard to be turned out of a warm bunk to take a turn at the watch while everyone else but himself and the helmsman was safely tucked up in their blankets below. The work of a seaman was much tougher than he'd thought it would be. Every man aboard had to pull his weight; the safety of the ship depended on it. And the *Sally* was badly maintained; something he hadn't realised before. Sails split without warning, cleats gave way and ropes snapped, leaving her to the mercy of screaming Antarctic winds and icy, mountainous seas. Hell wasn't always hot.

As the most junior member of the crew, he was kept on his toes and at every other seaman's beck and call. There seemed so much more to do than when he had been a passenger, helping his friends when it suited him. Jem and Hobley did their best to keep an eye on him but there wasn't much they could do to make his life any easier; they couldn't be seen to be showing him any favouritism. The ship carried no passengers on this leg of the journey – the steerage quarters being crammed with bales of wool.

Captain Carpenter was a disappointment to Tully as well. Far from being the jovial skipper of his memory, the man was aloof and distant this time, very conscious of his rank and careful not to become too familiar with any member of his crew.

There were other less subtle changes and not all for the best. In place of the former Mate, an easy-going, cheerful fellow who had struck it rich at the gold fields, the Captain had engaged one Joshua Herring, who joined the ship's crew in Melbourne at the same time as Tully. A well-built, swarthy individual in early middle age, Herring sported a huge gold earring which made him look more like a stage pirate than a genuine man of the sea. He spoke with a confusing mixture of accents from both the old and new worlds and was disliked by everyone, the old hands in particular resenting the change. Tully felt sure he'd seen Herring before and was bold enough to say so. The mate denied it at once, insisting he had never been anywhere near Ballarat or the gold fields.

'An old sea dog from way back, that's me,' he said, thumping himself on the chest to add force to his words. 'You won't catch old Joshua Herring too far from the sea.'

Tully was certain the man was lying but he couldn't prove

it and the more he cudgelled his brains, the more the truth evaded him.

Having realised his dearest ambition, he ought to have been on top of the world but he wasn't. His work as a seaman was hard, maybe ten times harder than he'd expected, but that wasn't all. His conscience continued to nag him about Maggi. Now his anger had cooled, he realised he should have been more honest with her and given her time to adjust to a future that didn't include him. At the time he'd thought he was making a grand gesture; taking charge of his life. Now he saw himself as a selfish coward, running off and leaving his sister in the lurch. No matter that Peg Riley had urged him on, saying: 'Go on, Tully. Your sister's all right with me.' But was she? Peggy meant well but her emotions were sometimes shallow and she had her own career to look out for in the challenging world of the stage. No, he wasn't at all sure his sister would be all right. But lost in the frozen wastes of the Antarctic, it was too late to be having second thoughts.

Life could have been bearable were it not for Joshua Herring. He seemed to bear Tully a special grudge. If ever there was something extra to be done, some filthy or dangerous chore, it was always Tully McDiarmit he singled out.

'Leave it for Irish,' he'd growl. 'Build up those muscles – do the boy good.'

And Tully had done what was asked of him with never a word of complaint. From the outset Herring had warned his men that he was a hard taskmaster and would make it his business to keep a tight ship. Any reluctance to follow orders would earn a seamen three strokes of the lash. The older crew members exchanged glances, shaking their heads at this news, certain Captain Carpenter would permit no such violence on his ship. They were wrong. Carpenter grew more and more remote, leaving the day to day running of the ship to Herring.

These days the Captain spent most of his time in his cabin, eating little and poring over his charts. He never came on to the bridge unless the ship was about to change course and the only order he delivered in person was to request more

264

speed. He wanted to raise as much canvas as possible to make use of the following winds.

Tully voiced his concern to Jem and Hobley at the breakfast table after keeping watch on a particularly turbulent night. The three friends were fortunate that seasickness never troubled them although others, some experienced hands, couldn't face any food while the ship bucked and plunged, fighting her way through the heaving seas. Herring also was present, never ill.

'The Captain – he isn't the man I remember, not at all,' Tully said, glancing at the chair at the head of the table, empty once more. Carpenter hadn't sat there at mealtimes for days, even before the weather turned foul. 'Is he quite well, d'ye think?'

'Shut up an' keep that thought to yourself,' Jem whispered out of the corner of his mouth, turning a wary eye on the Mate to see if Tully's remark had been overheard. 'He'd bloody well better be! We'll never get round the Horn in one piece, let alone up the Azores, if that bastard has to take over command of the ship.' As usual Hobley nodded, eyes rolling comically as he agreed with his friend. 'I bet he don't even know the basics – not he. I got more seamanship in my little finger than he has in the whole of his fat, ugly body.'

'He's got a Captain's ticket. I seen it,' Hobley joined in, having an opinion for once.

'What if he has?' Jem grabbed his mug to stop it sliding away from him down the table on a particularly violent lurch of the ship. He took a gulp of the strong tea, narrowing his eyes as he looked over the rim at Herring. 'It's not that hard to pick up a Captain's ticket – probably not even his own.'

'What's your problem, Jem Burden?' Herring was sharp enough to guess that he was the subject of the seamen's gossip at the other end of the table. 'Idle hands an' all that. I'll soon find you something to do.'

'Oh, no need for that, sir.' Jem leaned back and grinned, though there was no friendliness in it. 'I got to take over the helm from Watson in half an hour.'

'Then you should be eating, 'stead of talking, Burden.' Herring sat back to watch them, idly picking scraps of food from between his teeth.

265

Pieface, under the table, gave a low growl. He had good cause to dislike Herring who never failed to kick him in passing; a recent encounter had left him lame. Tully slipped him a piece of ship's biscuit under the table to quiet him, scratching the rough hair of the dog's back with his bare foot. He could feel the sharp ridge of the spine; Pieface was getting thin.

'And as for you Irish, if you've finished feeding your greedy little face you can lend a hand pumpin' the bilges. This ship is beginnin' to stink like a blocked drain. We shan't have time later on. We'll need all hands on deck to get round the Horn.'

'An' how many times have you been round the Horn, sir?' Jem's query was mild but some of the older men grinned, sensing the mockery behind it.

'Enough times to have some respect for it, Burden. Hop to it then, Irish. What are you waiting for?'

'McDiarmit has to take up the Captain's breakfast, sir,' Jem put in, giving Tully a quick wink. 'Cookie gave him his orders not five minutes ago.'

'Then stir your stumps and get on with it, lad.' Herring was determined to have the last word. 'No good sittin' there like a shag on a rock. You can make a start on the bilges when you've done.' And he formed his right hand into the shape of a pistol, pretending to fire at the boy's feet as he stood up.

Tully felt the colour leave his face as the gesture made the man suddenly familiar, allowing the pieces of the puzzle to fall into place. He could remember him now. The man's name wasn't Herring at all and he had been at the gold fields. He had been with the Californian Rangers, one of McGill's men. One of the group of trained soldiers on whose expertise the miners had depended and who, at the last minute, had let them down. Giving way to political pressures, McGill and his rangers had marched out of Eureka, leaving the miners to face experienced soldiers on their own. More than ever he was certain Herring was an imposter. How could he be a fully ticketed ship's officer and a member of the Californian Rangers as well? Herring must know this, too. That it was only a matter of time before he was remembered and exposed.

266

Tully concentrated on keeping his expression bland while his mind raced, coming to terms with what he knew. With Herring sitting across the table and straining his ears to hear what they were saying, he couldn't pass on this information to Jem and Hobley. That would have to come later. But he had been given the perfect opportunity to pass on his suspicions to Captain Carpenter. It would then be up to the Captain to decide what to do.

With Pieface slinking at his heels, he made his way to the galley where the meals were produced for the ship's crew. Cramped, airless quarters, filled with a miasma of steam and presided over by a volatile Chinese cook.

Avoiding the cook's attempts to swat him with a dirty towel while shouting insults at him in pidgin for being late, Tully seized the pot containing the Captain's breakfast and ran for the ladder. He hoped he'd be able to negotiate the deck without stumbling and dropping it on the way. The Captain kept his own plates and eating irons in his cabin as well as a case of good quality bourbon which was his favourite tipple.

As he knocked and entered the Captain's cabin, Tully had no reason to suspect there was anything wrong. He heard no command to come in but that didn't surprise him; the Captain's voice would be muffled by the howling winds and the straining of the ship's timbers. He noticed the darkness first; that the oil lamp attached to the ship's rafters was flickering and burning low. Then the smell hit him so suddenly that he gagged. The room stank like a privy. Thirdly, he saw the Captain, slumped over his desk as if he had fallen asleep over his charts, his head on his arms. The man's eyes were open, fixed on nothing, and his complexion had already deteriorated to a mottled, unhealthy grey. Even with the corkscrewing motion of the ship, he had stiffened in death, the expression on his face was of mild surprise. A trickle of blood had emerged from his nose to congeal on the charts. He had been dead for some hours.

After all he had seen in the aftermath of the battle of Eureka, Tully was case hardened enough to take the old man's death in his stride. There was no sign of violence; nothing to indicate he had died from other than natural causes. It was only odd that he should have been lying up here dead while Tully and his friends had been discussing just such a possibility only moments before. With the Captain dead it was too late for him to voice his suspicions of Herring. To do so now would only cause panic among the crew. As the only other ship's officer with a Captain's ticket, stolen or no, he would have to assume command of the *Sally Lee*. They were in his hands. It was Herring they would have to trust to bring them safely to England now.

Chapter Twenty

Maggi had been sleeping over the stables for only two nights when she was woken by the creaking of one of the outside doors. Someone had come in. Nerves tingling, she sat up in bed, straining her ears to hear more. A visitor this late at night could be a bushranger or some other person desperate enough to steal a horse. But after listening to the movements below a while longer, she let go a long breath and relaxed. A bushranger wouldn't be whistling and banging doors as if he had every right to be there. A horse thief would be sneaking about, doing his best to be quiet. Clearly, it was someone who didn't know anyone was trying to sleep in the bedroom over the stables. Wide awake now and consumed with curiosity, she wanted to see who it was. Quickly, she threw on a pair of moleskins and an old shirt. She was about to put on her boots but she changed her mind, deciding to go barefoot. That way she could have the advantage of the intruder and give him a fright, paying him back for disturbing her rest. It was, after all, well after midnight.

She opened the trapdoor without making a sound and crept down the ladder, avoiding the rungs which creaked. One of her vacant stalls was now occupied by a chestnut stockhorse and beside him a big grey, snorting and shaking themselves as they waited to be rubbed down. The interloper, whoever he was, had his back to her and, still whistling softly, was inspecting his saddle and harness for any weakness or damage before he put them away. All she could see was a tall, broad-shouldered figure in dusty work clothes and a broad-brimmed leather hat.

She picked up the shovel she used for mucking out the stalls and stalked him, waiting until she was right behind him to let him know she was there.

'All right then, Mister, who are you? Don't you know better than to come crashin' about in the middle of the night disturbin' my horses?'

A seasoned fighter, the man's action was automatic. He whirled to face her, assuming a crouched position, ready to defend himself. He relaxed, grinning, as soon as he saw it was only a girl who menaced him, and a small one at that. He held out his hand for the shovel.

'I'd better take that. Before someone gets hurt.'

She stared back at him, too astounded to offer any resistance as he took the shovel from her nerveless fingers.

'And where did you spring from?' he said conversationally. 'Fresh off the boat by the sound of you. Who hired you? And why are you threatening me with a shovel in my own stables?'

'*Your* stables?' Maggi whispered.

'I'm Hamish,' he said, introducing himself. 'Hamish Mac-Gregor. Now tell me, who are you?'

'The groom.' Still she couldn't speak above a whisper. 'Your – your mother put me in charge here.'

'Did she now?' He raised one eyebrow, looking her up and down.

Too late she wished she had taken the trouble to dress more carefully before coming down. She was painfully aware of her hastily buttoned shirt and mop of unruly hair now coming under his critical gaze. For a moment she wondered if she could be still asleep in her bed. Standing before her, as so often in her dreams, was the same dark-haired young man who had addressed himself to her father on the steps of the Post Office. The young man he had robbed and who had haunted her girlish fantasies ever since. And his name was Hamish. Hamish MacGregor. She would have known him anywhere, even without the smart city clothes. Tall, rugged, handsome, and here in the confined space of the stables, much bigger than she remembered. An old saying of her mother's flashed into her mind: 'Small people like big things.'

270

But Hamish was no figment of her imagination. He smelled real, as if he had been working with animals. A mixture of horses, good leather and honest sweat – pungent, yes, but certainly not unattractive. Being grubby, he was somehow more human, more accessible. With those looks he would otherwise have been too perfect. She would have liked to amaze him, charm him with her wit, but she could think of nothing to say. And while she was calling herself all kinds of an idiot for gaping at him like a moron, he was lighting a kerosene lantern and hanging it on the wall, the better to see her, looking her over with a practised eye.

'Well, I'll be . . .' He let out a soft whistle of appreciation, pushing his hat to the back of his head. 'Things are certainly looking up around here. How liberal of my mother to think of setting a girl to work in the stables. What a good idea.' He took her hand in his own to give it a firm shake.

'So you're Hamish?' She let go a long sigh, not realising until then that she had been forgetting to breathe. Chance remarks from Elizabeth now fell into place. 'I've been hearing so much about you,' she said, wishing she could stop saying the expected, conventional things.

'None of it good, I'll be bound.' He smiled up at her under his brows in a gesture so blatantly flirtatious that her heart set up a new irregular rhythm. 'I'm the black sheep of the family. I have a bad reputation round here.'

'And do you live up to it?' Maggi smiled, hoping he wouldn't see how his charm affected her.

'Oh, I expect so.' He grinned, his teeth very white in a tanned face. 'My brother's the paragon, of course. The plaster saint who can do no wrong.' He said this with bitterness and a wry twist to the lips. 'But you probably know that already?'

'I like Mister MacGregor. He's a gentleman,' Maggi felt bound to defend him. 'He's shown nothin' but kindness an' consideration to me.'

'A perfect gentleman, eh? That'll be Callum.' Hamish laughed, turning her words against her. 'And do you repay his kindness with consideration in return?'

'I have no idea what you mean,' Maggi said, revealing all too clearly that she did. Until then, Hamish had seemed to be all she admired most in a man, the unshaven face and the dust of his travels only adding to his attraction, giving him a piratical, rakish air. She was disappointed to find him so mean-spirited towards his brother and it diminished him in her eyes. To hide her conflicting emotions, she picked up a handful of dry straw and started to work on the stockhorse, rubbing him down.

'Here, let me do that.' Hamish stopped teasing and set to work, grooming the horses. 'You shouldn't have to work at this time of night.'

Maggi shrugged and went on with what she was doing. They worked together in a silence broken only by Hamish's soft whistling. He seemed unconcerned, unaware of the cauldron of emotions he had set boiling in Maggi. When both horses were dry, she fetched clean blankets to keep them warm. Although it wasn't a cold night, the pair had been sweating after their travels and she didn't want them to take a chill.

'I made you angry, didn't I?' He was watching her through narrowed eyes. 'Was it something I said?'

'Doesn't matter.' She avoided his gaze and picked up a bucket, meaning to go and draw water for the horses.

'I can finish off here if you want to go back to bed?' he offered. Maggi shook her head.

'I like caring for horses.' She could hardly tell him she wouldn't be able to rest until he was out of the stables. Sleep would be impossible while he was moving about below.

'Just a moment.' He peered at her. 'Let me look at you.' He caught her by the chin, turning her face to the light to take a closer look. 'I know you from somewhere, don't I? Red hair and a cat's yellow eyes – an odd combination of colours. I could swear I've seen them before.'

'That's very unlikely, sir,' she said, wriggling free and turning her face away. Her skin tingled pleasantly where he had touched her but she didn't want him to remember where he'd seen her before.

'Never mind, it'll come to me. I never forget a face.' He picked up a second bucket, ready to follow her outside to the trough. 'I should go out and about more often.' He laughed.

'If it encourages my mother to fill the place with pretty women while I'm gone.'

Knowing how scruffy she looked, Maggi blushed, not knowing how to respond to his particular brand of teasing. Fortunately, she didn't have to. Another man loomed in the doorway, speaking to Hamish. He had a Southern Irish accent, not unlike her own.

'Well then, Mister Hamish,' he said. 'I thought you'd be needin' a hand with the horses.'

'Thank you, Paddy, but I have all the help I need.' Hamish grinned, pulling Maggi forward to be introduced. 'Look what the wind blew in while we were away. A fellow country-woman – a little Irish lass to take over the stables. Sorry,' he said to Maggi. 'Didn't catch your name?'

'McDiarmit,' She frowned, not sure if she liked his patronising attitude. 'Maggi McDiarmit.'

'Patrick Hegarty,' the man mumbled his name in return, not entirely pleased. He didn't look like a man much given to smiling. There were deep lines etched in his face from nose to mouth. Maggi knew the meaning of such lines in a face; she'd seen them often enough before. This man had experienced famine, hardship and tragedy before escaping to make his way in this new land. He was marked forever. He might never go hungry again but his face would never fill out. It would remain a testimony to the years of suffering, compounded by the fact that he worked out of doors under the relentless Australian sun. Hardship had taught him to expect little of anyone, fellow countrywoman or no, and Maggi sensed he was assessing her, wondering if she were a threat to his own position or not. He dismissed her with a nod and a thin smile.

'So if you've no further use for me, Mister Hamish, I'll bid ye goodnight.' He edged towards the door. 'An hour or two's shut-eye in me own bed won't come amiss after sleepin' rough. I've still to square things with the wife. Ye said we'd be gone for two days an' it's more like two weeks.'

'Don't you worry about Molly.' Hamish gave him a playful punch on the shoulder. 'She'll soon change her tune when she sees how much money you've made. And if she doesn't, tell her to come and see me in the morning.'

273

'There'll be no need for that, Mister Hamish.' The man pursed his lips. 'I hope I'm man enough to be able to handle me own wife.'

Maggi gave a slight shiver, sensing the threat behind those words and gaining some insight into his relationship with Molly. A relationship similar to that of her own parents which used to hover on a knife edge – love on one side and violence on the other. Such a relationship between Hegarty and his wife might well account for the boisterous, war-like behaviour of their two little boys.

Weary now, she longed to go back to her bed, wondering how best to excuse herself. Before she could do so, Callum loomed behind Hegarty in the doorway. He, too, must have heard them arrive and had also thrown on some clothes in haste, moleskins and boots over a flannel nightshirt. Without offering his brother a greeting, he came straight to the point.

'I thought it would have to be you. So the bad penny has turned up again? And making enough noise to waken the dead, let alone Maggi here. All right, Hamish, let's have it. Where the hell have you been?'

'Oh, not that far afield.' Hamish shrugged, still inclined to be flippant.

Hegarty cleared his throat. 'I'll be sayin' g'night to ye then, Mister Callum.' And he tipped his hat, anxious to get away. Having witnessed such arguments between the brothers before, he wasn't anxious to be drawn in again. Certainly not at this time of night.

'Goodnight to you, Patrick,' Callum nodded. 'We'll talk in the morning.' He leaned in the doorway, blocking Hamish's exit and waiting for Hegarty to be gone before he repeated his question.

'Out with it, Hamish. I want to know where you've been.'

'To London to see the Queen?' he said lightly, still mocking.

'What have you been doing? I want to know.'

'None of your business, Cal. Maybe you're content to doddle along with your sheep, scraping a living from one year's end to the next. Well, I'm not.'

'Sheep farming is our livelihood, for God's sake.'

'For God's sake, Callum? Or is it yours?'

274

'Wool is our business. It's a tradition at Lachlan's Holt.'

'Tradition be blowed! Much good tradition will do for us with the price of wool going up and down like a toilet seat. We can't even be sure we'll get enough hands for the shearing, not these days.'

'Somehow we manage. We always do.'

'No, Cal. You're relying on too many variables. Too many other people. The ships, to name but one. Sailing into Antarctic waters – cutting corners to reduce speed. Dangerous. You can never be sure they'll make it to England at all, let alone in time for the wool sales.'

This last remark produced a gasp from Maggi, reminded that Tully was somewhere out there on the open ocean. Out there where she couldn't help him, aboard the *Sally Lee*. Everyone had assured her he would be safe with Captain Carpenter. No one had spelled out the dangers – not until now.

The gasp also reminded Callum that she was still there. 'Maggi, you'll be exhausted. You shouldn't be up at this time of night.' Her cheeks reddened; she didn't care to be spoken to as if she were a child. 'Go back to bed at once – try and get some sleep.'

'You lied to me,' she accused. 'You said my brother would be safe. You promised!'

'Please, Maggi, not now.' He sounded weary rather than impatient 'We'll talk about it in the morning. Go back to bed.'

She would have liked to stay and hear more. To ask if he had word of the *Sally Lee*. But she knew that tone; it invited no argument and she had no choice but to do as he said.

Upstairs in the familiar haven of her attic, she was too restless to sleep. Her first thought wasn't to eavesdrop on the brothers but it was impossible not to overhear what they were saying as the sound of their voices, raised in anger, floated up from below.

'If you want to stick to sheep farming, Cal, that's all right with me.' That was Hamish's lighter tone. 'But that doesn't give you the right to interfere – to stop me making a quid.'

'I don't want to stop you doing anything, Hamish. Long as you stay inside the law.'

'Inside or outside the law, I still say it's not your affair.'

'But it is. I'm the head of this household and I pay Hegarty's wages. You make it my affair when you divert him from his duties to take off on some fool's errand of your own. You do realise you left a household full of women, alone and unprotected, to fend for themselves? Irresponsible, that's what you are.'

'I might say the same thing of you. You were away so long this time, we thought you'd sailed away with the wool.'

'Oh, you wish!'

'Callum, it's late and I'm tired. Nothing happened. Mother and Lilias are both safe. What are we arguing about?'

'Your attitude. Your total lack of responsibility towards anything or anyone. So what was it this time? Not sniffing around the gold fields again, I hope?'

'Not for the reason you think. There's an easier way to make a fortune than grubbing about in the mud for a few grains of gold. I've hit on a lucrative little sideline.'

'An honest sideline, I trust?'

'Always ready to think the worst of me, aren't you, Cal?'

'You so rarely disappoint me.'

'All right. If you must know, we've been rounding up wild cattle to sell to the gold fields. The butchers are so desperate for fresh meat, they'll pay whatever we ask – cash up front – sometimes ten or twelve pounds a head. And if we can deliver some thirty or forty at a time – well, work it out for yourself.'

'I see. And you've involved Patrick in this madcap scheme? Selling off our prime cattle to the shambles at the gold fields?'

'Not *our* cattle, no. The wild cattle on the fringes of the property. You said yourself the herds needed to be culled before they increase and become a danger, breeding disease and clearing the feed we want for our own stock.'

'And what makes you so sure these cattle are wild? Do you check them for brands, to be sure they don't belong to anyone else?'

'Hell, no. Not at the risk of getting an arm torn off. Callum, take my word for it, these are wild steers – sinewy old beasts. They put their heads down and ran us off the first time we attempted a muster. It took old Yellagonga to show us how to get them.'

'He'd know. That old sheep stealer!'

'Not any more. He's a reformed character. He said to use only experienced horses – the kind that won't panic at a stampede – and no dogs unless they've the sense to keep quiet. That Bruno of yours turned out to be ideal.'

'I was wondering where he was. Go on.'

'No noise at all – no hallooing or cracking of whips. We don't even try to budge them until they're surrounded. That's the tricky bit. One wrong move and they panic. You can find yourself in the thick of it, cattle bearing down on you from all sides. It's exciting but not for the faint-hearted. The boys work damned hard for every penny they get.'

'What boys?' Interested at last, Callum forgot to be critical. Maggi heard them leave the stables and close the doors, meandering across the yard in the direction of the kitchen. In a moment they'd be teasing Hallie who was always up early, flattering her into cooking them early breakfast. She sat on her bed, reliving the past hour. Sleep was out of the question now; she had too many thoughts and misgivings, churning like an old-fashioned merry go round in her head.

So his name was Hamish. Her unknown love. The last person in the world she'd expected to find living here. He who had figured so largely in her dreams, helping her to survive the long months of boredom and drudgery at Bullivant House. She found she was hugging herself as excitement welled up inside her. Did this mean fate had taken a hand, throwing them together again? Surely, something would have to come of it now?

And then there was Callum. Callum who had been there when she needed him most. Callum who had been her friend and protector on the long journey from Melbourne and whose cruel rejection had left her with a dull ache in her heart. Of course, she reminded herself, she had nobody but herself to blame for that. No doubt she had startled him by playing the wanton and being so forward. Surprised by the intensity of their emotions, both had been taken unawares. He had never laid a hand on her until then; never treated her as other than a travelling companion and a friend. And she had so nearly been in his arms – so nearly – but there was little point in pursuing that. The moment was gone if not entirely forgotten and these days he didn't care for her even as a friend. Worse, he did his best to avoid her. Most likely he regretted bringing here at all. To salve her pride, she had made up her mind that she didn't care for him, either; Mister Nose-in-the-air MacGregor, full of his own importance and mindful of his position as master of the house. He thought of her as his mother's servant, if he thought of her at all. And he had lied to her, too, which was harder to bear. He had promised her Tully would be safe with Captain Carpenter aboard the *Sally Lee*.

A tear escaped to roll down her cheek at the thought of him in danger, shipwrecked even. Still so young and he'd had no life of his own. Would she see him again? Ever? She shivered, remembering how the ocean had already swallowed her mother. Was it hungry enough to take her brother as well?

Captain Carpenter's death brought a hush to the *Sally Lee*. The crew exchanged anxious glances, taking little comfort from the surgeon's pronouncement that he died of natural causes. A bursting of some blood vessel in the brain, he said, brought on by a tumour perhaps – without carrying out a post mortem, it was difficult to say. Joshua Herring vetoed a post mortem, ordering the ship's carpenter to build a box in a hurry for a speedy burial at sea. Anxious to obliterate all evidence of his predecessor, he allowed the crew little time to brood. Little time even to pay their respects to their Captain whose passing was marked by a few mumbled words and the mournful tolling of the ship's bell.

'A heathen, that's what he is,' whispered Hobley, finding his voice for once. 'Probably a limb o' bloody satan hisself.'

Jem frowned, aware of the practical reasons for the hasty burial. All hands would be needed for the approach to Cape Horn where there would be no respite from the high winds and treacherous seas until they were safely clear and travelling up the west coast of the continent of South America. There they would touch the coast to take on fresh water and food enough to sustain them for the next leg of the journey.

278

The *Sally* was not sufficiently provisioned to make the entire journey without stopping at all as did the more modern clippers.

Chapter Twenty-One

As the days passed into weeks at Lachlan's Holt, no one was more surprised than Maggi when it was Lilias who became her closest friend. Hamish treated her with his own brand of teasing condescension, calling her 'Little Irish' or 'Little Leprechaun', giving her playful punches on the shoulder and treating her like a boy. If anything, this irritated her more than when he was flirtatious, particularly as she felt that same breathlessness and fluttering in the stomach whenever he was near. It didn't matter how she tried to get over it, reminding herself that he was arrogant, self-opinionated and much too sure of his own attractions, her heart refused to be told. Against her better judgement, she carried a torch for him still, although she would have gone through the torments of the damned rather than admit to it.

Callum was equally impossible but in a different way; so careful to be polite that this built an even greater barrier between them. What had become of her carefree companion of the road? He had been reserved, yes, but there had been none of this awkwardness between them.

There was Patrick's wife, Molly – she might have been a friend, Molly Hegarty who was broad as she was tall and had an infectious cackle to go with her build. But Molly was busy, taking care of the laundry on the property, and spent her days in the wash house which echoed to the sound of her tuneless singing as she went about the never ending tasks of boiling, washing and starching of sheets and clothes. Then there was all the ironing to do afterwards. If she had any spare time, it was spent chasing after her two mischievous little boys.

Sometimes Elizabeth would ask Maggi to ride with her but more often her duties as mistress of the property kept her indoors. To keep up with the needs of the animals as well as the humans on the station, she would spend most of her mornings in the ration house, bringing accounts up to date and taking stock of groceries, making sure nothing would be forgotten when Patrick drove into Beechworth to pick up supplies.

So Lilias was the only one with time on her hands; time to become Maggi's friend. Lilias whom she disliked at first because of her superior manner and sly ways. Lilias whose talk was always of the city, despising everything that went with living in the country.

Maggi had been the one to take the bull by the horns and make the first overtures of friendship. Not on her own account but for the sake of Lilias's neglected white pony, Toby. Lilias had ignored him for weeks and what had been a willing, spirited little horse was turning into an ill-tempered nag. When he turned and kicked his back legs at Maggi for the second time that week, she decided to speak out on his behalf. Rather as she expected, she found Lilias draped in a basket chair on the verandah, a footstool under her slippers and her nose in a book.

'If it's my mother you want, she's resting inside,' she said without looking up. 'You'll have to come back.'

'I'm not here to see your mother, I'm here to see you.' Maggi planted herself in front of the girl, arms folded and legs astride, ready for battle. 'Are you going to spend some time with your pony or leave him to rot? Because if you don't want him, I think you should sell him.'

'Who asked for your opinion?'

'No one. But it's not fair to keep a pony and neglect him, day after day, week after week.'

'But I don't want to go anywhere.' Lilias shrugged. 'He's only a means of transport, not a pet. You can ride him if you want.'

'I don't want. I have eight other horses to look after apart from the Clydesdales. I haven't the time.'

'Get Hegarty to help you then, I don't care. You're the one who wanted to work in the stables. Don't come moaning to me if you've too much to do.'

'I'm not moaning and I don't have too much to do. I'm begging you to spend some time with your horse. He misses you, Lilias. He's pining for you to pay him some attention.'

'Oh, rubbish!' Lilias put down her book and looked up. 'Toby's greedy, that's all. He isn't pining for anyone – not so long as he has water and feed. What else can he want? He's only a horse.'

'And you're just a stupid girl who doesn't deserve him.'

'How dare you!' Lilias jumped up, tossing her book aside. 'I'll tell my mother how rude you are and have you dismissed. How dare you come here, telling me off and speaking to me as if we were equals?'

'We are. Jack is as good as his master here, or so I've been told.'

'Well you were told wrong!' Lilias tossed her curls.

Maggi grinned. Suddenly, she wasn't nervous of Lilias any more. 'That's good. I've shaken you out of your seat. You can probably do with the exercise as much as your horse. I can have Toby saddled and ready in five minutes. Are you comin' with me or not?'

Half an hour later, the two girls were walking their horses together, beginning to like each other better by the minute. Toby, who had caused a few anxious moments until he had worked off some excess energy, was now walking quietly. Maggi was riding one of the spare stockhorses. While he lacked the spirit of a thoroughbred, he was a good choice for today, happy to amble along and keep pace with Toby. For the first time in her life Lilias began to appreciate the countryside around the homestead which she had taken so much for granted, seeing it afresh through Maggi's eyes.

'I love it here – so much space and fresh air.' Maggi breathed deeply, filling her lungs with the scent of flowering eucalypt as they reached the crest of a small hill and paused to look back at the sloping roofs of the homestead, spread out before them in the valley below. 'I can't believe there aren't more people living here. Just the MacGregor sheep and a few cattle. In Ireland a place like this would belong to ten farms instead of just one.'

'Oh, there are people here all right, even if you can't see

282

them.' Lilias nodded into the distance. 'Dozens of them, on the other side of those hills, digging for gold at Spring Creek.'

Both girls were pleased to discover they had more in common than they'd thought and their afternoon rides became almost a daily ritual. Lilias entertained Maggi with tales of the pranks and snobbery at the 'seminary for the daughters of gentlefolk' where she had been a boarder until recently, while Maggi amused her with tales of life at Bullivant House. Soon she had Lilias giggling as she imitated Miss Prunella and the Matron, portraying them as buffoons. She made no mention of Kitty or Ginny.

One afternoon, when they had dismounted to sit by the creek in the autumn sunshine, leaving the horses to graze, she told Lilias about the Silver Star, her friendship with Peggy and her singing career, cut short when her brother left with the *Sally Lee*.

Lilias leaned back against a tree, nibbling a stem of grass.

'How I envy you, Maggi, I really do. You've seen so much more of the world than I have. And I wish I had a real talent like yours. Oh, I can strum the piano a bit but I can't sing – Mother says I've a voice like a crow with a sore throat. How can you bear to give it up?'

'I haven't. I practise my scales every day and I often sing when I'm working. The singing will still be there for me; I've just shelved it for a while.'

Lilias considered this for a moment and sighed. 'Oh, well, I don't suppose I'll do anything half as exciting as you. I'll just get married to Harley and that'll be that.'

'Don't you want to marry him, then?' Maggi's eyes strayed to the magnificent solitaire diamond Lilias always wore on the third finger of her left hand. Following the direction of her gaze, Lilias turned the diamond in the light, examining it.

'Of course I do. I've no intention of being an old maid.'

'But you don't love him?'

'Did I say that? No!' Lilias looked at her and blushed, put out by Maggi's question. Unconsciously, she began to pluck at her riding skirt, pleating and unpleating it between her fingers. 'Of course I love Harley. I adore him. He's the brother of my dearest friend.'

Maggi shrugged, knowing better than to argue with Lilias in such a mood. It struck her that while they were much of an age, Lilias had led a more sheltered life than she had and was still unsure of her own mind. Disturbed that Maggi had deduced her own doubts with such accuracy, Lilias glanced at her out of the corners of her eyes, unable to resist a moment's spite.

'How is it you know so much, then? I suppose you've been in and out of love dozens of times?'

Maggi should have expected the question but all the same it took her by surprise, making her blush. The last thing she wanted was for Lilias to find out about her foolish, unrequited love for Hamish. How she would laugh.

'I don't know about that,' she said, casting about for a way to get off the subject. 'Look! Isn't that a kookaburra, down there by the creek?'

'Probably. They're everywhere.' Lilias didn't even trouble to look. 'What do you think of my brothers, then? Are they attractive to women or not?'

'How should I know?' Maggi frowned, cursing the surge of colour heating her face. 'I haven't thought about it.'

'No? I've had more than one friend swooning at Hamish – I suppose he is rather dark and dashing. He doesn't care, though. He despises girls who throw themselves at his head. And Callum . . . don't let's forget Callum. D'you think he's good-looking or not?'

'I don't know,' Maggi snapped, wanting to put a stop to this outpouring of Lilias's thoughts.

'Then what are you blushing for?'

'I'm not blushing. It's just that it's hot.'

'You'll get used to it.' Lilias smiled.'Which one, Maggi? Which one of my brothers do you like the most?'

'Does it matter?' She looked down at the water running swiftly over the stones in the creek. It reminded her vividly of that last morning at the falls with Callum and her own foolish behaviour. Embarrassment coloured her cheeks again. 'I don't think it would be proper for me to say. A servant in your mother's house.'

284

'Bull-dust!' Lilias said, unexpectedly pithy. 'Didn't you say to me yourself that Jack was as good as his master? Or Jill for that matter. Maggi, I want you to speak your mind. Feel free to say what you think.'

'I think – I think we should be going if we want to be home before nightfall.'

'That's not fair. I won't let you wriggle out of the question like that. And I'm on to something, aren't I? Or why would you blush?'

'Lilias, please! Can't you just let it alone?' Maggi scrambled to her feet and jammed her straw hat more firmly on her head, hoping to hide her expression.

'All right, I'll make a bargain with you. If I let the family skeleton out of the cupboard, you must tell me which one of my brothers you like?'

'No.'

'Aren't you the least bit curious? Wouldn't you like to know why they hate each other so much?'

'Hate each other? They do not!' Maggi stared at her. Hate wasn't a word you used to describe family arguments. 'Brothers can't hate each other. You're making it up.'

'No, I'm not. I wish I were. I can't remember a time when there wasn't a feud between them. Ask Mother if you don't believe me.'

'I wouldn't dream of it. It isn't my place. And I don't think you should be . . .'

But Lilias ignored her protests, determined to tell the tale. 'It started ages ago when they were children, before I was born. Mother was expecting me then.'

'Lilias, this is private family business. I don't think you should be telling me.'

'Why not? You live here now and have a right to know. Hamish blames Callum for causing our father's death.'

'He does?' In spite of herself, Maggi's curiosity was aroused. She sat down, hugging her knees, waiting for Lilias to go on.

'Callum was learning to swim and he was showing off. The river was full and Mother told him not to go in. But you know boys – convinced they can do anything. He got caught in the current mid-stream and would have been carried off over the falls and on to the rocks if Father hadn't jumped into the river and saved him.'

'But they were all right?'

'Touch and go with Callum at first. He coughed up a lot of water and weed before he started breathing again. And while they were both on the river bank, recovering, Hamish says he saw Father taken with some sort of seizure or fit. A heart attack maybe – nobody's really sure. But he died in a matter of minutes, right there on the river bank. No time to get any help. Callum was too weak and Hamish too small. He says he'll never forget how helpless he felt, watching our father dying, fighting for breath.

'Poor little boy. Oh, Lilias, that's dreadful.'

'Especially as it's the first thing in his life he can really remember. Callum swimming when he was told not to and causing our father's death.'

'But, Lilias, it was an accident. Hamish must see that now even if he couldn't when he was small.'

'I know. Mother lost her husband and she doesn't blame anyone. But try telling that to a little boy who's just watched his father dying in front of him.'

'In front of Callum, too.'

'Well, yes.'

'But Hamish isn't a child any more. Life must go on. He can't go on blaming Callum for something that happened so long ago. Reasonably, he must see . . .'

'Oh, yes. And reasonably and rationally he does. But he's used to bearing a grudge and it's become such a habit, he doesn't know how to stop. He swears he'll get even one day.'

Maggi shivered and stood up, suddenly chilled. She brushed the leaves and dust from her trousers.

'It's getting cold,' she said. 'We ought to be getting back.' Used to the volatile atmosphere of her own family – flashes of temper, wounds inflicted and quickly healed, Maggi found this hard to understand. The thought of a feud kept alive and simmering over the years was alien to her nature and she found it disturbing. And Lilias's calm acceptance of the situation left her unaccountably depressed. It was as if, in the telling, the burden had been shifted from Lilias's shoulders

286

to her own. 'How can you discuss it so casually?' she said. 'Why aren't you upset?'

'Upset? Why should I be upset?' Lilias shrugged. 'It all happened a long time ago, before I was born.'

Maggi could take no further pleasure in the day. She held Toby for Lilias while she remounted and vaulted into her own saddle with practised ease. Lilias peered at her, seeing the bleak expression.

'Maggi, you're not to worry. I'll be sorry I told you, if you do. There'll be no pistols at dawn – my brothers are far too civilised for that.'

'I hope you're right,' Maggi dug her heels into the mare's flanks, encouraging her into a canter.

'Wait!' Lilias flicked Toby's fat hindquarters with her whip and started in pursuit. 'You were going to tell me which of my brothers you like the most?'

'No, I wasn't,' Maggi called back over her shoulder. 'That was your idea.'

The canter revitalised Maggi, restoring her spirits, and the two girls arrived, laughing and late, just before nightfall. By now the shadows had lengthened and the sun had melted to become an orange lake, about to slip out of sight over the horizon. Darkness would fall as if a candle had been snuffed. A grim-faced Callum was awaiting them at the stables.

'About time. I was getting ready to saddle up and come after you. Have you any idea how late it is?'

'Of course.' Lilias grinned, pulling a face to imitate her brother's thunderous expression. We can see the sun going down just as well as you can. We stayed out late on purpose, Callum – to annoy you.' She held out her arms as she had done ever since she was a little girl, inviting him to lift her down. He did so, still serious.

'It's not a joke, Lil. You don't know who's out there. The bush after dark is no place for girls on their own.'

'Hush! Hush! Here comes the bogey man!' Lilias twisted her back into a hump and pulled a comic ugly face. 'Do you have to be such a bear?'

'Where did you go?' Callum ignored her clowning.

'How should I know? Maggi was leading the way. We ended up at the creek like we always do.'

287

Maggi had already dismounted and was busy unfastening her saddle. While Callum's criticisms seemed to be directed against his sister, she was certain they were really intended for herself.

'I'm sorry, sir. I wouldn't knowingly lead your sister into danger.'

'I know you wouldn't, Maggie.' His expression softened as he turned towards her but deliberately she ignored it. Scrupulous in their dealings now, they had come a long way from their former closeness.

'Come on, Cal, I'm starved and I'd sell my soul for a hot cup of tea.' Lilias tucked her hand in her brother's arm, expecting him to escort her back to the house. 'There's not much to be done here, is there, Maggi?' She wriggled her nose in a childish way, hoping to be excused the chore of looking after her tack. 'You don't need any help, do you?'

Maggi smiled and shrugged, only mildly irritated by the other girl's behaviour. 'If you please, sir. Can you spare me a moment, before you go?'

Callum frowned at the two 'sirs' in as many minutes but didn't want to comment on them in front of his sister. 'Certainly, Maggi. What can I do for you? What do you want?'

To be your friend! To go back to the way it used to be! she wanted to shout. Instead she said something entirely different. 'I was wonderin' if you have any news of the *Sally Lee*? The ship has been gone for months now and you promised to let me know as soon as you have word?'

'So I did, Maggi. But I have no news,' he said slowly, reminded that she was voicing his own niggling concerns. 'Our agents in England won't write 'til the clip has been sold.' What he didn't say was that he had received no word from Captain Carpenter either. Carpenter whose habit it was to post a letter from each port of call as a progress report; his personal reassurance that all was well.

'I'm sure you'll think I'm being silly.' She hesitated, watching him, afraid he would scoff at her fears. 'I think so myself, really. But my brother an I are so close an' I have this sinkin' feeling – an awful feeling that something's wrong.

'Nothing will be wrong,' he said gently. 'Remember the

288

old saying: bad news travels fast. No news is good news, Maggi, I promise you.'

'Yes,' she said, wishing she could have faith in such glib phrases. But she didn't. The feeling of doom persisted and increased.

Tears of self-pity blurred her eyes as she watched Callum leave, Lilias dancing beside him, her butterfly mind on nothing but tea and cakes. It was all very well for the MacGregors, they had nothing to lose but this year's wool. Tully was the only living relative she had in the world. To work off the gloom and resentment that threatened to overwhelm her, she threw herself into the task of grooming Toby, becoming so involved that she was startled when a figure loomed from the darkness at the back of the stables and came towards her. Blinking away her tears, she saw it was Hamish.

'How long have you been standing there? You gave me a fright,' she scolded. 'Do you always lurk in the shadows, waitin' to creep up on folk?'

'Only folk who creep up on me waving shovels.' He grinned. 'I like to see you jump out of your skin. Oh, dear.' He looked at her more closely. 'Those aren't tears, are they?'

'No, they're not,' she snapped. 'I thought I was going to sneeze an' I didn't.'

'If you say so.' He gave a wry smile and leaned against one of the posts to regard her. This close she was very conscious of his lounging, masculine presence and wondered if he knew it. The effect of tight moleskins encasing long legs, muscular from so many years on horseback, the dark blue cotton shirt with several buttons undone at the throat revealing an expanse of tanned, muscular chest, the sleeves rolled up to reveal strong arms covered with soft, dark hairs. Hamish needed no more exercise than his work to make him strong; he was a true cattle man, a son of the outback. He regarded her, shaking his head. 'You're a fool to let Callum upset you. I don't.'

'It's just that he's so – so –' Unaccustomed to any kindness from Hamish, she felt fresh tears pricking her eyes. She scrubbed them away with the back of her hand.

'Critical and overbearing?' He provided the words.

'Yes, and he won't talk to me any more. Not like he did when we were travellin'.'

'Yes, I was forgetting.' Hamish was suddenly thoughtful. 'You're his little protegée, aren't you? Three weeks you spent together. Three weeks all alone on the road.'

'I wish everyone would stop saying that!' Maggi's temper rose. 'We were travellin', you know, not loungin' about. What do you think we were doin'?'

'I don't know.' A slow smile spread across Hamish's face. 'You tell me?'

'Nothing, that's what! Nothing happened at all.'

'All right. You don't have to get so het up about it. Knowing my brother, I believe you. Even if you did take his fancy, he'd never let you know. Now if it had been me . . .' And so saying, he chased her into an empty stall, giving a villain's laugh and twirling his moustache. 'You'd have been left in no doubt of my feelings, me pretty. You wouldn't have been so safe – not at all.'

'Hamish, stop it.' She tried to edge past him. 'I have work to do.'

'It'll keep. I'll give you a hand to finish the chores later on. Why won't you spend some time with me, talk to me, Maggi?'

'Why should I, Hamish? When all you do is tease me.'

'Oh, but I love it. The way you say my name with that lilting Irish accent – Hamissh! Go on, say it again.'

'No.' Once more she tried to push past but he restrained her, blocking the only exit and smiling down into her eyes. She tried to stare him out but was first to look away. 'Ah, will ye stop it? Stop makin' fun of me.'

'You should be flattered. I only make fun of girls I like. Go on, Maggi, say it. "Hamissh" – say it again.'

'Hamish! Hamissh! Now will you let me go?'

'No. The first time it was sweet, like a caress. You're shouting at me now.'

'Yes, an' I'll shout at ye some more if ye don't stop hinderin' me an' get out of me way!'

'You can go if you give me a kiss. Just one. I promise it won't hurt a bit.' He let his hands come to rest on her shoulders but gently, using persuasion rather than force. She was as conscious of his hands as if they were burning through the thin fabric of her blouse.

'But I don't – I don't want to kiss you.'

'Are you sure?' He lifted her towards him and whispered, 'Really sure? If you don't want to kiss me, why are you closing your eyes and quaking under my hands like a trapped bird? Sighing and parting your lips because you can't breathe.'

She felt as if she were drowning in the familiar smell of him – leather, horses, and clean, masculine perspiration. And she wished she could smell of lavender or roses like Lilias. The cake of soap Callum had given her was long washed away. Callum! Why did she have to think of him now? Just as her dreams were about to come true right here in Hamish's arms?

Hamish bent his head and kissed her thoroughly, searchingly, and with enough expertise not to frighten her. For a first kiss it was wonderful, memorable, all she had dreamed it would be. Abandoning all thought of resistance, she surrendered herself with a small sigh, linking her hands on his neck and pressing into his arms as if she could never get close enough. It was happening; it was all coming true. Hamish loved her. He wanted her as much as she wanted him. As their kisses deepened, she threaded her fingers in his thick, dark hair and allowed her body to mould itself more intimately against his own, crushing her breasts against the muscular hardness of his chest.

Treating her gently as if she were a wild bird he had tempted to his hand, he had sense enough not to take this first encounter too far, too fast. He stopped kissing and caught her just as her knees began to tremble and give way. Certain now that this was her first taste of sensual pleasure, he laughed softly, setting her back on her feet.

'Ohh!' She breathed. 'What you must think of me now. I didn't mean . . .'

'It's all right, Maggi.' His smile in the gathering gloom was like a further embrace, soft and conspiratorial as he drew a finger across her parted, still willing lips. 'The blame for this is all mine,' he said as he bent to kiss her again.

*

In total command of the *Sally Lee*, Herring was a worse tyrant than ever, no longer troubling to hide the gaps in his knowledge or lack of seamanship. He cared only that his orders should be obeyed; carried out the moment they were issued. As one man rather ruefully put it: 'The man's a mongrel all right. Somethin' between Blackbeard an' Captain Bligh.'

He handed out stiff punishments for the most minor offences and was incapable of mathematical calculations. He didn't seem to care if the ship stayed on course or not; a matter which would have been of prime importance to Captain Carpenter. The neglected bilges overflowed and contaminated some of the tightly packed cargo of wool, the stink becoming so unbearable that he ordered half the cargo tossed overboard into the sea. When food became short as the ship meandered towards the equator, he ordered Tully three strokes for sharing his rations with the dog.

'I'll make an example of you,' he roared, his face suffused with temper. 'An' don't let me catch you feedin' that filthy cur again – or Cookie can boil the bugger and we'll eat him instead.'

'Pieface is a useful member of the crew, sir.'

'Captain sir!'

'Captain sir. Every day he catches a seagull for the pot. You've enjoyed them yourself, sir.'

'Be damned to your insolence, Irish!' Herring motioned to the seaman who was to deliver the punishment. 'Haul him up now an' get on with it.'

Having seen grown men reduced to tears by the whip, Tully was shaking uncontrollably as the burly seaman roped his wrists to the mast to hold him upright and ripped the remains of a threadbare shirt from his back.

'Sorry, lad,' he whispered.'I'll keep it light as I can but if Herring sees me, he'll mebbe take over an' thrash you hisself.'

Tully nodded and bit his lips, his mouth dry with apprehension. Really, he was too appalled to complain. All he could hope was to bear the beating and give a good account of himself. He prayed he wouldn't shame himself and foul his trousers as did many under the whip. The first stroke wasn't so bad and he thought he could bear it although, for all the seaman had promised to spare him, he felt it split the skin of his back. But when the second stroke landed across the first, the pain was agonizing and he heard himself screaming aloud.

At this point Jem could stand by and watch no longer. Swearing under his breath, he snatched the whip and tossed it over the side to be lost in the sea. It was no use. A replacement was fetched and while he succeeded in obtaining Tully's reprieve, his interference earned him the remainder of the boy's strokes, plus three more of his own. Obliged to watch as his friend took his punishment for him, Tully's loathing of Joshua Herring increased.

The ship's company was appalled by this unjust punishment and later, in their quarters below, Jem whispered of mutiny and how to get the rest of the crew to mutiny with them.

'Ach, careful, Hobley!' he winced as his friend anointed his stripes with stale mutton fat. 'That bastard Herring doesn't deserve to be Captain – time somebody knocked him off his perch.'

He was surprised when the crew rejected his pleas.

'No, no, mate, don't ask – I can't afford the risk.'

'I agree but I got a wife an' kids waitin' back in Plymouth.'

'We will win. We can't afford not to,' Jem tried to urge them. But the story was the same all over the ship.

'Sorry, mate. Can't take the risk.'

Grumbling and planning a mutiny was one thing – putting these plans into action was quite another. In the end nobody had the courage to do anything and Jem had to abandon the idea.

The fierce winds and gales at the tip of South America had already taken their toll of the crew. Now, as the ship wallowed in the doldrums, the men faced trouble of a different nature. The sun blazed down on them without mercy, blistering their skins and sapping their last reserves of energy. Water and rations were short and all the fight had gone out of them. Even the old hands, who remembered the better days under Captain Carpenter, men who might once have rallied to the cause, now looked at one another shaking their heads. They were in no shape to do battle in any case; scarecrow thin and suffering from sunstroke, skin peeling and covered in sores, eyes bloodshot from days of squinting into the tropical sun.

Nobody trusted Herring but no one would risk a flogging by going against him. They prayed only to survive, to get back to England whole and unharmed. And as the *Sally* crept at a snail's pace towards the equator, the weather became unbearably humid and hot. Their remaining supplies of water were stagnant and almost too foul to drink and the wind dropped altogether, leaving the ship becalmed. Morale was at an all time low.

Chapter Twenty-Two

As autumn gave way to a winter of frosts and fog, Maggi felt as if she were living a double life. There was her work of course which took up most of her time in the morning from first light, and then there was the slow progress of her affair with Hamish which occupied all of her thoughts. Following those first stolen kisses, she looked for him to advance the relationship by declaring his love. He didn't. Nor did he make any particular effort to see her, alone or otherwise. He gave her smouldering glances instead, making a joke of it.

The way he kept her dangling was an exquisite torture and her only comfort lay in the fact that no one suspected her feelings, not even Patrick Hegarty who spent more time with her in the stables than anyone else. Lacking the native cheerfulness of most Irishmen, he had little to say and noticed even less but Maggi soon earned his respect for her 'way with horses' as he called it. Doubting her abilities at first, he was now impressed by the way she kept the stables. Caring little for her own appearance, she kept the horses, the tack and the stalls neat as a new pin. No horse was allowed to stand in its own ordure and in the stables the air was sweet, smelling of well-groomed horse flesh, metal polish, beeswax and fresh straw. Hegarty helped her to look after the stock-horses as well as the pair of big Clydesdales which did most of the heavy work around the property. In the absence of a full-time bullocky, Callum had sold off the bullocks and engaged a local carrier to come by with stores from Beechworth. The dray stood forlorn and deserted in a far corner of the stables, waiting for the MacGregors to need it again.

Soon after dawn, Maggi would be up to attend to the horses and turn them out into the paddocks, with the exception of the ones she knew would be needed sooner rather than later that day. On these cool, frosty mornings, sometimes chill as any winter in Ireland, she would send them all out wearing blankets, sometimes better protected against the elements than she was herself. Callum was obstinate, refusing to let her ride Bothwell, and to exercise the big stallion, she had to walk him instead. He wouldn't be budged on this, no matter how often she told him the horse didn't exist who could get the better of her, not even Hamish's Nero, who needed a firm hand. She didn't mention that Hamish himself had been out on Nero most days and she had not yet been invited to ride the big grey.

Had Lilias been less excited about her forthcoming visit to Melbourne, she might have picked up the signals before, recognising how Maggi felt about Hamish. But Maggi was too sharp for her, steering Lilias away from pointed enquiries, encouraging her to prattle about herself instead.

'We'll be travelling by coach from Beechworth – one of the new American coaches, Mother says. They travel so fast they have to change horses every time we stop.' She turned to Maggi, her face lighting up with an idea. 'You could come with us. I'm sure Mother won't mind. Oh, Maggi, do come. We'll have a lovely time.'

'I don't think so, Lilias.' Maggi shook her head. The other girl's view of Melbourne was very different from her own. 'Besides, what would happen here? The place would go to rack and ruin. Somebody has to mind things while your mother's away.'

'But why does it have to be you? Hallie will do all the cooking and surely Hegarty could look after the stables for once? And there's Molly. Molly could help.'

'Molly could not. She has more than enough with her laundry work and those wicked little boys.'

'Horrible, aren't they? I had to stop them chasing Cassie with a spider the other day. Only a huntsman, but she was screaming her head off.' Lilias wrinkled her nose at the memory. 'So you won't be persuaded, Maggi? You'd rather stay behind?'

'I would.'

'Lord knows why. There's nothing to do here. I just love the city – all that bustle, excitement, and the beautiful clothes. I don't even mind the noise. Harley's promised to take me to the Cremorne Gardens – they have an aviary and a zoo there now. And Constance is taking me shopping; she knows all the best places where they have the very latest from overseas ... oh, and she's found a real treasure of a dressmaker – French, I think – rooms upstairs somewhere in Collins Street. And I'm dying to start planning my wedding gown.'

Maggi smiled, not at all sorry to be avoiding it. Fond as she was of Lilias, she could imagine nothing worse than spending hour after hour trailing behind her as she visited the shops. Lilias would be relentless in her search for just the right pair of gloves or the right shade of silk ribbon to match a hat. And she would have company enough with Harley's sister, Constance. After her own experiences with Ginny and Peg Riley, Maggi knew very well that three could be a crowd.

Constance Maitland was an heiress in her own right. The Maitlands owned several parcels of land both at Richmond and Emerald Hill, land which they were now able to subdivide and sell at a profit. Maggi listened attentively, hoping to learn a bit more about Harley, but gained a much clearer picture of Constance instead. The prospective husband remained no more than a shadowy figure in the background. While Lilias enthused about afternoon tea and shopping, she had little to say of the man she was going to marry, the supposed cause of all this frenzied activity. Just as well he was rich, Maggi thought – Lilias wasn't likely to be a thrifty housewife.

On the morning of their departure, Hamish had disappeared. Once again he had been out all night. Patrick Hegarty told her this in rather injured tones. Since Callum had made his objections clear, Hegarty could no longer ride out at night with Hamish in search of wild cattle. He was to spend his time working about the property instead.

When he was finished with helping Callum to round up the sheep, moving them to higher ground away from the plain which was in danger of flooding during the winter months, he helped Maggi with the horses and the day to day work of the stables. In addition, he had some skills as a blacksmith, capable of lighting the forge and re-shoeing a horse when she needed it.

This particular morning he arrived early to help her recapture the pair of horses needed to draw the MacGregors' buggy which was to take the ladies to Beechworth where they would meet the long-distance coach. This wasn't so easy as it seemed. The pair had been running wild for weeks and weren't anxious to find themselves in harness again. After a lot of swearing from Hegarty which sent Maggi into gales of laughter, they were at last caught and harnessed. Then Hegarty returned to the cottage to change into his best clothes, ready to drive them.

Elizabeth came out of the house tightly corsetted and elegant in her dark brown travelling clothes. Today Maggi thought she looked strained and somewhat older, divested of the comfortable casual clothes she wore at home. Lilias as usual was carefully groomed, dressed for the city already and wearing a new bonnet, trimmed with silk roses, which Maggi had never seen before. Callum, waiting to see them off, was looking pained. The cause of the expression was the number of bags Lilias wanted to take. He was suggesting some should be left behind. Elizabeth agreed.

'Lilias, the more luggage you take, the greater the risk of losing it on the way,' she said. 'And don't forget, there'll be twice as much to bring back.'

'We won't have to bring anything back.' Lilias's lips formed a stubborn line. 'Constance and Harley will bring it when they come up for the Spring Races.'

'No, Lilias. It's not fair for us to take advantage of the Maitlands just because they have their own coach.'

'They won't mind. What shall I do in Melbourne with nothing to wear? I can't appear in these travelling rags, not for the whole six weeks.'

'Exactly,' Callum chimed in. 'Six weeks not six months. How many clothes do you think you need?'

'All of them,' Lilias pouted, her forehead creasing into lines of ill temper. 'I packed them very carefully. I need everything, Cal.'

Callum raised his eyes to heaven. As usual with Lilias, the argument could go round and round forever unless he put a stop to it.

'At this time of year, Melbourne is muddy and wet and the streets are awash. There's no point in trying to dress up.' He took out his pocket watch and glanced at it. 'Mother, it's time you were on your way. You should leave yourselves plenty of time – the mail coach isn't going to wait, not even for Lilias and her bags.' And before his sister could argue further, he whisked a hat box and two extra bags from the buggy, leaving only the one big trunk.

Lilias eyed the hat box with longing but she knew she was beaten. She let Callum hand her up into the buggy and offered a cool cheek for him to kiss.

'Learn to be a bit more gracious, puss.' He gave her an affectionate peck. 'You know Mother hates the city almost as much as I do. She's only going on your account. Try not to give her a hard time.'

Lilias's pout remained although her expression softened and while she settled herself on the cushions, pulling a warm woollen shawl more closely around her shoulders, Elizabeth said her farewells. Embracing Maggi with as much affection as if she were her own child, she pushed back the unruly mop of red curls to look into the girl's face, not entirely happy with what she saw.

'You're looking peaked, my dear, and too thin – if anything thinner than when you came to us. And I don't like those shadows beneath your eyes. Are you sure you're getting enough sleep? The work in the stables isn't too hard? It is a man's job after all.'

'No, no,' Maggi blushed and looked at the ground, avoiding Elizabeth's penetrating gaze. How could she say she slept badly because she was suffering from unrequited love? 'Don't you worry about me, Mrs MacGregor. I love the work with the horses and I'm doin' just fine.'

'Well, I hope so, Maggi. But I wouldn't like to think we were taking advantage of you.'

Lilias broke in, impatient to be gone. 'Do come on, Mother. If Maggi says she's all right, then she is. For goodness sake, let her be.' She looked up at the skies, full of

299

cloud and threatening drizzle. 'We don't want to miss that coach. If it rains again we could be held up crossing the creek.'

And there Elizabeth was obliged to leave it. Hegarty stood holding the horses, waiting as Callum handed his mother into the seat beside Lilias and passed them a rug to share between them, spreading it across their knees.

'The stores from Beechworth should be delivered on Friday.' Elizabeth's mind was still running on her domestic responsibilities. 'Make sure you ask Hallie if there's anything else she wants – she can give the carriers another order to take back.'

'Don't worry, Mother, everything's going to be all right.' He squeezed her hand. 'The place won't fall about our ears because you're going away for a few weeks.'

Hegarty flourished his whip and shouted for the horses to move. They responded too well and the buggy lurched forward as they set off at a spanking trot. Both Callum and Maggi stood waving until it disappeared, weaving among the trees.

Left alone with him, Maggi realised Callum was gazing at her with such intensity, she knew he had something on his mind; something he wanted to say.

'That's it. They're gone,' she said, stating the obvious. 'Things will be a bit quiet around here without Lilias. Oh, well.' She turned away to go back to the stables. 'Can't stand here natterin' all day. Not when there's work to be done.' Even to her own ears, the words sounded inane.

'Maggi, before you do . . .'

'Yes? What?' she muttered, shuffling from one foot to another. She had a feeling she wouldn't like what he had to say. He looked at her for a long moment and then relaxed, apparently changing his mind.

'Nothing. It really doesn't matter. Not at all.'

'Until later, then.' Maggi put her head down and hurried towards the stables. She didn't invite him to follow.

Hamish arrived after lunch, looking like a bandit and covered in red dust, unshaven and exhausted from lack of sleep.

'Ruddy bushrangers,' he muttered. 'Must've been watching

us every step of the way. They must've known we had money and followed us all the way from the gold fields – had to split up and double back on our tracks to shake them off.'

She took Nero from him and promised to wash his saddle and tack, noting that the big horse was almost as weary as he was. Hamish murmured his thanks and went off, yawning, saying he was going to bed for a week. It wasn't a week but he stayed there, according to Hallie, for the next twenty-four hours, sleeping the clock around.

When he surfaced at last, he came at once to the stables to thank Maggi for taking care of his horse and surprised her by asking her to go riding with him after lunch when the chores were done. Pink with delight, she accepted the offer, her heart singing as she finished her work in record time. She captured Elizabeth's mare and saddled up, wanting to be ready by the time he appeared.

For the first half hour he walked alongside her with Nero, sedate as if he were with Lilias. They spoke little and Maggi knew he must be as bored as she was. So she slapped Nero on the rump when Hamish wasn't looking, surprising him into a gallop. Whooping like a circus girl, she did her best to catch up with him on Elizabeth's mare. He reined in to talk to her when they reached the swiftly flowing creek and both dismounted to let the horses relax and nibble the fresh grasses which grew on the bank.

'You're a good horsewoman,' he said, regarding her with a respect that was new. 'How long have you been able to ride like that?'

'Since I was six years old.' She grinned, basking in the sunshine of his admiration.

'Have you ever raced before.'

'No.' She shook her head. 'My da wouldn't allow it. But I used to help him break horses when we lived in Ireland. Strange to think it was so long ago.'

He broke in, impatient with her reminiscences. 'But you're good; good enough to race, if you wanted to. Could you handle Nero?'

'I think so,' she said. 'I could handle any horse, even Bothwell, if Callum would let me.'

'Fat chance of that.' Hamish's mouth took on a wry twist

301

as always, speaking of his brother. 'Bothwell is wasted on a plodder like Cal. He wouldn't know a good piece of horse flesh if he fell over one. Has to rely on someone else's judgement instead. Want to know how he came by that horse?

'He bought him from the horse fair – he told me.'

'Yes, but only to spite another buyer. I heard him saying as much to Mother. He can't appreciate anything unless somebody else wants it first.'

Maggi stared at the ground, saddened by Hamish's attitude and wanting to hear no more of his spite towards his brother.

'You should hear yourself,' she said at last. 'It can't be healthy to feel such bitterness towards anyone, let alone a brother. How long are you going to keep it up? This senseless feuding?'

'Senseless?'

'Yes. Senseless. To go on bearing a grudge over something that happened so long ago. D'you think your father's spirit can rest in peace while you do?'

Hamish whirled her to face him, letting her see the full fury of his anger and making her gasp. 'Peace! Oh, I'd like to have peace, I really would. But what peace can there be when I have only to look at Callum to remember what he's done?'

'What *has* he done? It was an accident, Hamish. Nobody's fault.'

But he wasn't listening. 'I shan't forget. I don't want to. I remember everything, clearly as if it were yesterday.'

'Hamish, you were just five years old.'

'How do you know? Who's been talking about it?'

'Lilias.'

'She had no right.'

'She did. She had every right. I live here and I care about you – all of you – as if you were family of my own. As Callum cares about you.'

'Mealy-mouthed rubbish.'

'He is your brother, Hamish.'

'Yeah, yeah! Tell me something I don't know.'

'If you can't care about Callum, think of your mother. You're making her old before her time, breaking her heart.'

'Maggi, that's enough. You're talking through your hat, you know nothing about it.'

'You have a fine, beautiful place here. You should kiss the ground and thank the good Lord that you do, instead of fighting amongst yourselves, tearing each other apart.'

'This fine, beautiful place, as you call it, belongs to Callum, not me. It isn't mine and never likely to be – while he lives.'

'Oh Hamish, you don't – you can't wish him –' She choked on the word, unable to say it.

'How dare you presume to know anything about us, you interfering little bitch? You know nothing! Nothing at all!' His eyes had become slits of blue ice and he was gripping her so fiercely, she was sure he would leave bruises on both her arms. Seeing her wince, he let her go. 'Sorry – didn't mean to fly off the handle at you. If anyone tries to talk to me about Cal, I always see red. Look what he's done today. Succeeded in putting a pall on it even when he's not here.'

'But –'

'Let it go, Maggi. Let's change the subject and talk about something else. Think you can handle Nero, then? Can you hold him while he's going flat out? He's fast and mean with it, too.'

'Trying to scare me, Hamish?' Her smile was taut. 'I'll show you – I can ride him now, if you want?' She was still irritated with him but knew nothing would be achieved by pursuing the earlier argument any further. He held Nero steady with one hand while he assisted her into the saddle with the other. For just a moment, while he was shortening the stirrups to accommodate her shorter legs, she had a few qualms. Nero was unpredictable, he was a big horse and the ground was a long way off.

She set off slowly at first, getting the feel of the horse and resisting the temptation to show off. Nero was testing the limits with herself as well. Used to the heavier weight of Hamish, he discounted Maggi's abilities at first, feeling free to do as he pleased. She reined in quickly, soon as he showed any tendency to bolt, convincing him she was mistress and knew what she was about. Only when they had confidence in each other did she ride him flat out.

'Oh, you're good, really good.' Hamish's spirits were restored by the time she brought the horse back. Nero was snorting and Maggi pink-cheeked and breathless with the effort of holding him. 'Let this be our little secret, eh? We'll practise together as often as possible but keep it under wraps until race day.'

'Why?'

'Because, little goose, we can make a lot more money by keeping our mouths shut. I'm a good rider but you're even better. I want to put you up on Nero for the big race.'

'You'd do that? Trust me enough to let me race him for you? But wouldn't there be more glory in riding yourself?'

'Maybe. But I'm happy to leave the riding to you. More money to be made that way.'

'An' is that all you care about, Hamish MacGregor? The makin' of money?' She jumped to the ground, wanting to show she could do so without his assistance.

'I thought money was all you cared about, too?' He raised a quizzical eyebrow. 'Or so Hallie said. Loves a bit of juicy gossip does Hallie. Couldn't wait to tell me how you turned up here looking like a gypsy with your skirts full of money and mud. That's what reminded me – where I'd seen you before. Outside the Post Office in Melbourne. I lost my purse the same day. Very embarrassing.'

She stared past him at the ground, unable to meet his gaze. 'So if you knew – all this about me – why didn't you say so before. Why wait 'til today?'

'I like secrets.' Hamish's smile was wolfish. 'Gives me an edge. But you weren't alone that day – a father and brother were with you, too. What's happened to them?'

Her lips quivered and she had a horrible feeling she was going to burst into tears. She staved it off by continuing to stare at the ground. 'My brother has gone to sea and my father is dead.'

'Oh! Oh – I –' For once he was at a loss for words. This wasn't the answer he'd expected. Instead of catching her out, he had been caught wrong-footed himself. 'I'm sorry. I didn't know.'

'And the thievin' isn't so much of a secret as you think.' She blinked the tears away quickly, ready to meet his gaze.

'Callum knows about it and so does your mother – Lilias, too.'

'They know you had stolen money, yes. But not that some of it was mine.'

'I never. I never stole from you. That was my da.'

'Yes. But you were his willing accomplice, weren't you? Pretending to eat me up with your eyes.'

'So what will you do with me now? Lock me up in the barn while you send for the troopers an' have me arrested? Maggi the thief.'

'Of course not.' He pushed his hat to the back of his head and grinned. 'Why should I turn you in when I'm just as much of a thief in my own way? I just wanted to show you how much alike we are. Twin souls, that's what we are.'

They were far from being twin souls and she knew it. But Hamish never said or did anything without a reason; he was far more devious than she could begin to be.

Callum was waiting for them when they got back. Patiently, he stood watching while they unsaddled and rubbed down the horses. Sensing his brother wished to speak to Maggi alone, Hamish remained chattering, dawdling and taking as long as he could to clean his tack.

'Teatime already,' he announced consulting his pocket watch when he was done, purposely ignoring his brother. 'Coming to the kitchen, Maggi?'

'Yes, in a while,' she said, deciding not to accept his offer of escape. It was clear that Callum had something on his mind and she may as well hear it now. 'All right,' she said when Hamish was finally persuaded to go. 'What now? Bad news is it, about the *Sally Lee*?'

'No. Still no news, good or bad.' His distracted expression told her he had something else on his mind. 'Maggie I know you must be hungry and I won't keep you long. Mother would have spoken to you but she didn't have time. And I – I hoped there'd be no need to say anything but ...' He sighed, clearly uncomfortable. 'But after today –'

'And just what about today?' Maggi's hunger had been replaced by a tight knot in her stomach. She had a feeling she knew exactly what he was going to say.

305

'Maggi, please. Don't make this any more difficult than it is.'

'What then? I went riding with Hamish today because Lilias is away. What's so wrong about that?'

'Nothing – if that was all. Listen to me, Maggi, and please don't take my advice the wrong way.'

'I don't recall that I asked you for your advice,' she muttered, folding her arms across her chest as if to protect herself from his words. 'But I suppose I'm going to get it, anyway.'

'I have to talk to you about my brother, you see. You're so vulnerable, especially now while my mother's away. Hamish isn't – that is, he doesn't – oh, dammit all!' Here Callum took off his hat and scrubbed his fingers through his hair, as if it would help him to find the right words. 'Hamish doesn't live by the same moral code as most people. He doesn't set store by the same values. Just don't get too close to him, that's all. Don't take him too seriously.'

'And why shouldn't I?' Maggi's temper flared as she leaped to the wrong conclusion. 'I'm not good enough for this family, is that it? What happened to "Jack is as good as his master", eh? We don't see too much of that here. It's all right for me to work 'til I drop, yes. But don't get too close. Don't taint the pure bred MacGregor blood with a mongrel Irish strain. That's why you're chokin' over your words an' findin' them hard to say.'

'No, Maggi, you have it all wrong.' Callum's face twisted in an agony of mixed emotions. 'It's you I'm worried about – you I'm afraid will be hurt. I know Hamish of old. He'll take every advantage, making the most of it while our mother's away.'

'Hah! And to think I didn't believe it when he told me how jealous you are. How you never covet anything unless it is prized by somebody else.' She had a bitter taste in her mouth. 'To think I respected you, looked up to you even. But no more Callum MacGregor. Not any more.'

'Oh, Maggi.' He could only shake his head in despair, unable to make her understand.

'You must think you're so clever. Always in charge, playing

the puppet master, pullin' the strings, meddlin' in all our lives.'

'Is that how you see me? Is that how you interpret my concern?'

'Yes. Yes, I do. An' you needn't stand there with your jaw dropped, pretendin' to be so innocent. Who persuaded me to let my Tully go off to sea? Who said it was a good idea for me to come here?'

'Where else were you to go?'

'You said I could make meself useful – and I have. I see your game, Mister MacGregor. It's fine if I make friends with your sister, no harm in that. But now I make friends with Hamish, you don't like it so well.'

'Friends, yes. If I thought that's all it would be.'

'Then what are you so afraid of?'

'Hamish, of course. He has the morals of an alley cat.'

'Is that so? An' while we're talkin' of morals, you should look to yourself before you start on somebody else. Was it Hamish who hid in the bushes, watchin' me when we stopped at the waterfall to bathe?'

'You knew? You knew all the time?'

'An' was it Hamish, risin' out of the water like a sea god, eatin' me up with his eyes an' admirin' me hair? Oh, you're a fine one to talk about morals, Callum MacGregor.'

His eyes narrowed and his colour intensified under his tan. 'I never touched you, laid a hand on you, Maggi.'

'Not because you didn't want to. You made me feel like a trollop who'd led you on.'

'Oh, Maggi – I never meant to do that. To hurt your feelings that way.'

'Well, you did.' Tears of self-pity pricked at her eyes.

'How is it we've come so far from understanding, you and I? We used to be friends.' He sighed. 'My fault again. I don't express myself very well.'

'I wouldn't say that.' Her voice was husky with bitterness. 'I'd say you've made your feelings all too clear.'

'Just listen to me, Maggi. Listen and try to be fair.'

'Fair? That's rich, coming from you. I'm not a complete eejit, you know. I've travelled half round the world an' I do have some experience of life.'

307

'I know. But you haven't come up against anyone like Hamish before. Hamish has lots of women – he collects them like feathers to put in his cap. I wouldn't like to see you becoming one more.'

'Is that it, then? Have you done?'

'Yes,' he said slowly, hoping she would give some thought to his words.

'Then if you'll excuse me, Mister MacGregor, there's supper waitin' for me in the kitchen.'

'Maggi. Maggi, please –'

But she pushed past him, ignoring his wounded expression, determined to keep him in the wrong. She would give him no chance to reinforce his arguments and didn't want to hear any more. Drawing herself up to her full height, she stalked off in the direction of the kitchen. She might manage a cup of tea but with the knot of misery clenching her stomach, she knew she wouldn't be able to eat a thing.

Following this brief but upsetting interview with Callum, the chasm between them could only grow wider. And it seemed that the more she fell under the spell of Hamish and his dark good looks – his mocking laugh and raffish, heart stopping smile – the more impatient and irritated she became with Callum. Unlike Hamish who treated the world as his playground and life as a joke, Callum seemed too solemn and serious by far, almost middle-aged in his attitudes. Nothing he could say or do ever pleased her and the sound of his voice or the sight of him herding a flock of sheep into the yard, was sufficient to set her teeth on edge. She never stopped to wonder if it might be Hamish who was influencing her feelings. Callum was out of favour and likely to stay that way.

The *Sally Lee* was becalmed for so long that Tully thought he would never feel a sea breeze on his face again. But even as the seamen prayed to their various gods for some wind to fill the ship's sails, they received more than they bargained for. Joshua Herring, not enough of a sailor to look into the skies and read the change in the weather, left it to the old hands to decide how and when to gather in sail.

'Fast as you can, lad, we don't have much time,' Jem

yelled, showing Tully how to secure the hatches and tie down anything likely to move in the storm. If it was fierce enough, everything on deck which wasn't secured, including the seamen, would be swept away into the sea.

They were too late. Even as they strapped the helmsman to his position at the wheel, forked lightning danced across the sky which had darkened to become an ominous blue-black. The sea which had been calm as a lake only minutes before was now whipped by the rising gale to a boiling fury. The wind screeched around the ship like an angry demon, tearing through rigging and rending the sails as if they were made of paper. Mountainous waves tossed her back and forth as if she were a child's toy. Tully watched, appalled, as several men at the prow were washed overboard and lost as the *Sally Lee* plunged into the waves. The main mast cracked and fell across the deck without warning, killing the helmsman outright and injuring one or two more. The ship's timbers which had suffered a battering in the journey around the Horn, were able to stand no more. The ship groaned and shuddered like a creature in its death throes. She was breaking up.

Unable to make himself heard over the howling gale, Jem signalled Hobley to keep a tight hold on Tully.

'To the lifeboats!' he shouted, although his words were lost in the wind. 'Before we go down with the ship!'

On the other side, they could see Herring and his cronies already scrambling into lifeboats and shoving others aside, concerned only with saving themselves.

Jem was trying to lower the boat into the water without capsizing it, which had to be done between the assaults of the waves. Soon it would be all up with the *Sally Lee*; with a broken main mast she was at the mercy of the elements, wallowing and becoming waterlogged, well on the way to breaking up. Nothing short of a miracle would save her now.

Following Jem's orders, Hobley seized Tully by the belt and held on. He in turn was clinging to Pieface, almost choking the dog, determined he shouldn't be swept away.

'No!' Jem made a pantomime of it, shaking his head and crossing his hands. 'Too dangerous! Let him go!'

Close to tears, Tully glared at Jem, defying him and

309

clinging to his dog, shouting to be heard over the noise of the storm.

'He goes or I stay!'

'Don't be a fool, boy!' Jem roared. 'Let him go.'

'No!'

In the midst of the argument none of them saw the big wave until it slammed over them, drenching them and making Hobley cough. It was a shock but somehow Jem held on to the lifeboat and Tully to his dog. Hobley jumped down into the boat and was doing his best to hold it steady, waiting to receive them. Tully did hear a rope snapping behind him but didn't realise what it meant.

'Mind the boom!' Jem's shout of warning came too late. The boom slammed into the back of the boy's head. Tully felt Pieface slide from his hands as everything went black.

Chapter Twenty-Three

Hamish rode out with Maggi so often that she began to regard it as a daily routine. She would rise an hour earlier each day to make certain of completing her chores and be ready to go out after lunch. Hamish knew the property, the boundaries and the surrounding countryside so well that he could show her a different landscape almost every afternoon. Flattered by his attention, yet warning herself not to build too much on it, she couldn't believe her luck. He made every day special, familiarising her with this beautiful corner of the state that he loved. Would he do this, spending so much time with her, if all he wanted was to see her competent enough to ride Nero for him at the race meeting to be held in the spring at Lachlan's Holt?

If they made a late start and time was short, they would go on wild gallops across the open plains where the wind would play havoc with hats and hair. Sometimes they saw grey kangaroos and once a pair of sandy-coated native dogs.

'They don't *look* wild.' Maggi felt sad when Hamish told her they would have to be hunted down and shot. 'They're just dogs. They could be somebody's pets.'

'I assure you they're not.' Hamish gave a wry smile. 'And you'd soon change your mind if you saw what they can do to a flock of sheep.'

They didn't always go to the plains. Sometimes, if they could escape early enough, Hamish would take her on long, meandering treks up, up past the falls and the dwindling scrub, past granite outcrops and sometimes climbing so high that she felt as if they were becoming lost in the clouds as the

311

mist swirled about them in this wild place where people rarely came and where there seemed to be nothing but moss and bare stones. Sometimes he took her to sheltered valleys at the foothills of the mountains; cool, damp places of fern and shade, frequented by birds so exotic they might have been creatures from another world. The gang gang cockatoo, distinctive with its dark grey plumage and beautiful pink head, so fearless of humans it would allow them to come quite close, although Hamish warned her never to touch. Once they were lucky enough to see lyrebirds, the male stately as a peacock, making loud cries to attract the female while spreading his shimmering tail feathers into the shape of the lyre for which he was named. They heard whip birds, hidden in the undergrowth, identified only by their soft yet piercing cries which sounded like drops of water falling a long way into a deep, underground pool. In another direction would be forests of eucalypts, massive old trees which had been allowed to grow undisturbed for centuries, stretching hundreds of feet towards the sky. In these woodlands, brightly coloured rosellas swooped between the branches, usually in pairs, shattering the silence with their shrill, argumentative cries.

Maggi couldn't help but be aware of Callum and how he bristled with disapproval if he happened to see them ride out. He spoke to her hardly at all these days, and he never mentioned her friendship with Hamish again.

It was rare for them to postpone a ride although the weather was often inclement, the odd fall of snow coming down although it didn't settle or stay. A mud winter, Dermot would have called it. Warmly dressed and with a stockman's waterproof over her clothes, Maggi was always ready and waiting after lunch, rain or shine. She tried to ignore Mrs Hallam's comments that it wasn't proper for a hired girl to spend so much time with a young master of the house. She knew Lilias and her mother would come back from Melbourne quite soon. And much as she looked forward to seeing them, she knew it meant these days and hours of freedom would come to an end. She had to make the best use of whatever time she had left.

'And there's another thing.' Mrs Hallam wasn't about to

312

let her off the hook so easily. 'I don't know that you should be a-wearin' down Mrs MacGregor's mare – ridin' her every day as you do.'

'It's my job to exercise the horses,' Maggi sighed. 'Not that it's any business of yours. I don't try to tell you how to make cakes, do I?'

'An' we'll have less of your lip, cheeky.'

'Mrs MacGregor said I was to take Roma any time I liked. Besides, I take one of the stockhorses if we're going to the hills.'

'No need to tell me the ins an' outs of it.' Mrs Hallam brandished her rolling pin, making her point. 'But Mrs MacGregor said I was to look out for you an' so I am. An' I'm tellin' you, it's not right. You an' him. Out there. Day after day. By yourselves.'

Maggi laughed, looking out into the driving rain. 'What do you think we'll get up to in this? It's hardly the weather for rollin' around on the ground.'

Mrs Hallam's eyes widened and she pursed her lips, puffing her chest like a pigeon fluffing its feathers. Having tangled with Maggi and come off second best, she would say no more.

Hamish remained an enigma to Maggi. While she was sure he enjoyed her company, he made no effort to advance the relationship, happy to leave things as they were. He smiled and flirted, teasing her, but he never kissed her again although she tried to let him see she would welcome it. Certainly, his actions didn't measure up to the character Callum had given him; a lusty young man whose only interest lay in ravishing her. He paid her no more attention than if she were his sister. Gloomily, she began to wonder if the old saw could be true – did familiarity indeed breed contempt? Certainly, he seemed to be taking her for granted.

During her months at Lachlan's Holt, Maggi began to understand the opposing natures of the two brothers. They would have rubbed one another the wrong way even without the stimulus of a long-term feud. While Callum liked to make full use of the land, taking a farmer's pride in building a solid home, a sheep station to be proud of, always looking for ways to expand, Hamish was a dedicated cattle man who

313

saw his brother's efforts as a waste of time. He hated the silly sheep who grazed the land to a dust bowl in summer and whose little feet turned it into a quagmire in winter. And he despised the fences Callum raised to contain them, preferring to look out on the rolling countryside, the natural unspoiled beauty of the bush. He scoffed at Callum's long–term plan to build a bigger and better homestead. Nothing but stupid pretension, he said. The MacGregors had always been farmers first and gentlemen second. What was the point of building a mansion out here in the bush? They had a roof over their heads, what need for another? While Maggi could see both points of view, she knew it would be hopeless to suggest a compromise.

Hamish himself was never happier than seated on a rock looking down at some panoramic view across a valley or watching water tumbling and cascading over a fall. He could find beauty anywhere, even on the banks of a meandering, muddy creek. And while he sat there, communing with nature and lost in his thoughts, Maggi studied him in turn, memorising every curve and line of his face and realising as she did so that she had fallen hopelessly in love. With growing impatience she waited for him to declare himself. To gaze at him with such longing, waiting to speak, was a sweet yet almost unbearable pain. Without literally hurling herself at his head, how could she make her feelings any more plain? How could he be so insensitive? So blind.

At last, when she was on the point of despair, convinced he had changed his mind and his earlier interest had waned, he turned and looked at her through his lashes, smiling that lazy smile of his and taking her by surprise. Today they weren't far from home but at the same creek where she used to sit with Lilias, daydreaming and gossiping through so many sun-filled afternoons. July now, the wind was chill and it was always damp under foot. Although they dismounted to give their horses a well-earned rest, there was nowhere to sit down. Hamish lounged against a tree, looking at her and smiling that slow, heart-stopping smile. 'We'll have to do something about this, won't we, Maggi?'

'What? What did you say?' She was cautious, afraid of mistaking his meaning, her throat suddenly dry.

'Oh, come on. No need to be coy. That isn't like you.'

'I'm not. I just want to be sure what you mean.'

'Then let actions speak louder than words.' He took her by the elbows, pulling her close. 'You've been looking at me too long with love in your eyes. We know each other too well to pretend. So what are we going to do about this feeling, this attraction, you and I? A shame let it go to waste.'

'Oh. Well.' She could hardly breathe, unable to believe her luck. It was here. The moment had come. Hamish was going to ask her to marry him. All he needed was a push in the right direction. 'What do most people do?'

'You tell me?' His face was very close to her own. 'I want to hear it from your own lips.'

'Well, most people get married, I suppose, and they –'

'Live happily ever after?' He gave a hoot of laughter. 'Oh, Maggi, not you too! I thought – I hoped – you'd be different. You'd be a bit more original than that.'

She bit her lip, feeling foolish, suddenly less than sure. 'Why, Hamish, I want – I hope for the same things as most girls.'

'Oh, what a shame. And I was thinking you were a renegade. One of life's pirates, like me.'

'Well, of course. So I am.' She gave a shaky laugh, anxious to cover her mistake.

'That's more like it.' He put a finger under her chin, tilting her lips towards him 'Oh, I want you, Maggi. I've wanted you since the first day I set eyes on you. That's why I chose to wait, the better to savour the moment when it came.'

'Oh, Hamish.' She pressed into his arms and closed her eyes, giving herself up to the joy of kissing him. Her hat fell back, caught on its string, displaying hair which was a mass of tendrils, curling in the damp air.

'So sweet, so fresh,' he murmured against her lips. 'Oh, Maggi, I need you. Maybe more than I've needed any girl.' He caught her hair in his hands and tilted her head back to look into her face, his eyes dark with intensity. 'And I thought – I dared to hope – that you felt the same?'

'I do. Yes, yes I do.' Maggi surrendered herself to his embrace although she was surprised and a little shocked at the confident way in which he fondled her breasts, hunting

315

his way through the layers of clothes. No one had ever touched her so intimately. Carried along by his avowed if rather calculating passion, she felt as if it was all happening too fast. Without her wishing it, another image rose before her of Callum, gazing at her with equal intensity, his hair lying flat to his head as he rose from the pool at the falls to stand over her, brooding and critical. She banished the image immediately to concentrate on Hamish instead.

'Pity it's so cold,' he was saying. 'Not much we can do about it here.' He smiled wryly, glancing at the wet ground, his eyes sleepy with passion. She sensed rather than felt his arousal through the many layers of clothes. 'I'll have to come to you – to your room at the stables.'

'Oh – oh, Hamish I don't know –' She hesitated, feeling rushed and a little cheated. She'd been expecting a betrothal, a declaration of his intentions in front of everyone and their smiling congratulations. Not a sordid, hole in the corner affair. But she loved him, didn't she? And she was her own woman, answerable to no one; her own woman, to do as she pleased.

While she paused, thinking, he kissed her with such a mixture of tenderness and passion that she relaxed. Of course he wanted her, loved her; these kisses were proof of it, weren't they? And he was a man, with desires more urgent than her own. Wasn't it only natural that he should want to come to her bed? He was right, it was early days to be thinking of marriage, she'd been a fool to talk about it so soon – there'd be plenty of time for that later on.

They rode home in what to Hamish was a companionable silence. Maggi was lost in her thoughts, full of doubts.

''Til tonight then,' he whispered, dropping a kiss on the tip of her nose as he left her to see to the horses alone. 'Leave the stable door open and go up early to bed. I'll get away just as soon as I can.'

'Hamish. Hamish, wait!' She caught him by the sleeve. 'Now I've thought about it, I'm not at all sure I can do this . . .'

'Ssh!' he said, trying to stifle her misgivings with another kiss. 'A little reluctance is sweet. I find it attractive in you.'

316

'But I'm not trying to be sweet, I'm trying to think it through. To be sensible for once in my life.'

'Well, don't. You'll make your brain hurt.' And he took off her hat and tried to ruffle her hair which she'd plaited tightly to her head. 'Look at this. No wonder you're so tense. Relax, Maggi, and let down your hair. The rest will come quite naturally, you'll see.'

The early part of the evening seemed to creep at a snail's pace. After supper she went upstairs to her sleeping quarters and looked at them critically, as if seeing them for the first time. Really, they were far from comfortable; stifling in summer, chill in winter when the slightest breeze created a draught. It was draughty now but Elizabeth's thoughtful provision of a firm, down-filled mattress, warm blankets and a faded patchwork eiderdown kept Maggi from feeling the cold. She combed out her hair and studied her reflection in the small cracked mirror which she kept on a stool beside her bed. Worried eyes looked back at her, reflecting all her uncertainties. If the weather had been kinder and they had been able to make love on the spur of the moment and out of doors, she could have fooled herself and said it was bound to happen; they had been swept away by the force of their emotions. But to plan it in cold blood, to invite him up here for the sole purpose of letting him have his way with her – *his* way, she reminded herself, not hers. She knew it wasn't right; it felt sordid and shameful somehow.

Not that she didn't love him. She did. She had lived with the pain of loving Hamish for so long that she could scarcely remember a time when it hadn't been there. But she had looked forward to courtship, a gradual unfolding and expressing of love. Not a hasty coupling just to quench their desires.

Full of doubts and anxieties, she had eaten so little at supper that Mrs Hallam frowned, asking her if she were unwell. Maybe she was. Certainly, she felt queasy now. Should she bolt the door, preventing anyone, Hamish included, from coming in? No. He'd take it as a slap in the face. She could lose him forever, then.

Her heart stepped up its beat as the main door creaked open and several of the horses stirred and shuffled, whinnying a greeting to the person who had come in. Those few seconds

317

told her she couldn't go through with it. Disappointed or not, Hamish would just have to understand. But instead of the stealthy tread on the ladder she was now dreading, she heard someone in heavy boots moving about below. Callum, was it? Or Patrick Hegarty? Neither was likely to disturb her but she quivered under the bed covers, hugging them close, beginning to feel like one of those painted trollops who sometimes came into the Silver Star. One thing this adventure had shown her: she certainly wasn't cut out to play the whore.

Moments later she identified Patrick Hegarty's smoker's cough and heard him leave, having found what he wanted, closing the door softly behind him.

She didn't know how long after that she lay there in silence. It might have been minutes or hours. At last she realised she wasn't the only one to have second thoughts; Hamish must be having them, too. Perversely, now she was certain he wouldn't be coming, she felt let down. She punched her pillows into submission, turned over to lie on her stomach and closed her eyes. In a matter of seconds, she was asleep.

She was awoken by a weight on her back. Someone was lying astride her, pinning her to the bed. She wriggled round to find herself staring into Hamish's cool blue eyes. He smiled, placing a hand across her mouth.

'Don't scream,' he said. 'It's only me – come to ravish you as I promised. Callum must have suspected something, I swear he has a sixth sense. He took an age to go up to bed and I didn't want to leave the house until I was sure he was asleep. I'm sorry, Maggi, I'll try to make it up to you, make it worth the wait.' And he took his hand from her mouth and kissed her soundly, setting her nerves a-tingle. Afterwards he leaned up on one of his elbows to look at her with such warmth in his eyes that the little speech she'd prepared to discourage him flew out of her head.

'My God, Maggi, you look good enough to eat, lying there with your hair spread out around you like a curtain. So much of it, and like saffron-coloured silk.'

She smiled shyly, very conscious of being naked under her worn silk robe. Only her eyes showed over the eiderdown

318

which she was still clutching, pulling it firmly up over her chin.

'Don't keep burrowing down in that quilt and hiding from me. I want to see you, look at you.'

'I can't let you look at me, Hamish. I'd be shamed.'

'Why? You don't have to be so nun-like. Beauty like yours should be shared, not hidden. Come on, Maggi, let me see.'

'How can you tell I'm beautiful? I might –'

'Ssh! I just can.' And with a movement so quick she had no time to prevent it, he tweaked the eiderdown away, leaving her curled in a foetal position, quivering in the robe.

'Please, Maggi. Take it off,' he whispered, the words gentle as a caress.

'No. It's too cold.' She shook her head, curling up on her side to hide herself.

'Only for a moment, a few seconds, Maggi, and then I'll give you the covers back – let you get warm. Better still, I'll warm you myself.'

'Hamish, I'm sorry, but I can't do this.' She hid her burning face in the pillows. 'I'm just not ready. An' it seems so – so brazen, makin' a peep-show of meself.' Without wishing it, she had a vision of Ginny Luckett, sitting up in bed and removing her nightgown, proudly showing off her breasts. Ginny would have no such qualms; she would revel in displaying herself.

He leaned forward to kiss her on the shoulder which she kept hunched against him. 'Please, Maggi. As you love me. Do this for me.'

'All right.' Her voice broke, betraying her nervousness as she took off the robe and threw it away, hoping she was throwing her doubts and inhibitions with it. She took a long, shuddering breath before she dared to look at his face to see his reaction, wondering why the sight of a woman's naked-ness should mean so much to a man. She watched, seeing his face change, softening as he looked his fill at every inch of her strong, young body. Encouraged by his pleasure, her nipples responded to his gaze as if he had touched them, swelling and hardening in the cool night air.

'Good Lord, Maggi, you're lovelier than I thought,' he whispered, almost to himself. 'Someone ought to paint you there, lying against the background of your own hair. A skin like milk and roses and the marmalade-coloured silk of your bush . . .'

Her cheeks burned that he should discuss her so intimately and she turned her head away, covering her mound with her hands.

'Don't do that,' he said. 'Don't shrink from me as if you're afraid. What is it, Maggi? What's wrong? I thought you wanted me, too?'

'I do – I do, only –'

'Only what?' His eyes hardened and a faint crease appeared between his brows, warning her he was tired of the delay and coming to the end of his patience with her.

'I'm sorry, Hamish, but it's too soon. I love you but I feel rushed, swept off my feet.'

'We kissed. I touched you. You knew how I felt.'

'Yes, I did. But still . . .' She chewed her bottom lip, searching her mind for the words to make him understand.

'I was a fool, wasn't I? To think you'd be any different.' He made to rise from the bed until she stopped him, clinging to his hand.

'Please, don't be angry with me, Hamish, I can't bear it.'

'I thought you were like me. Too down to earth to lead a man on and play games. Now I see that you're not. You're just a little prick tease – fickle as any other foolish girl who doesn't know her own mind.'

'I do love you, Hamish. I've already told you that.'

'Then what are we waiting for? Why must we tie ourselves up in the trappings of courtship and pretence?'

Gently now, so as not to scare her into retreat, he took her by the shoulder and bent his head, seeking her lips. Hamish liked kissing; he'd had a lot of practice and he was good at it. He kept kissing, giving her no time to speak, not even to draw breath until he felt her respond, relaxing in his arms. Only then did he let his hand fall quite naturally to her breast, rolling the sensitised nipple between the tips of his fingers until she sighed and lay back, offering the other for his attention as well. Satisfied she was ready for more, he took her nipple into his mouth, teasing it with his tongue and teeth. A small moan of pleasure escaped her and he began

320

casually stroking her thighs, working his way towards her sex as her body responded to his seduction. As a natural progression to the lovemaking, she spread her legs, opening to him like a flower, letting him explore her body with his fingers. With her eyes closed she sighed, squirming against those teasing, questing fingers, enjoying the sensation which was entirely new. Surprised when he stopped and withdrew them, she opened her eyes, fascinated and a little repelled to see him sucking the moisture from his fingers; the same fingers which had been inside her a moment ago.

'Hamish, what are you doing?' she whispered.

'Tasting you,' he said. 'One day, when you're ready, I'll taste you with my tongue and you'll taste me, too. It is one of the ways of pleasure between red-blooded men and women. I look forward to teaching you – oh, everything. And now, will you hold me, help me, Maggi?'

While he was speaking he had been unfastening his trousers to release his member which had been uncomfortably confined. Maggi stared at it, thinking how large it seemed and wondering how his body was supposed to fit her own. Half-afraid she held it gingerly as he instructed until he became impatient and showed her how to exert a little more pressure, working her hand under his own. His penis felt warm and silky, less threatening now, and he closed his eyes, gasping his pleasure as she did so.

Suddenly, the touch of her hands was no longer enough and he pressed her back against the pillows, parting her legs to feel the core of her yet again.

'Now, Maggi,' he murmured against her lips. 'You must be ready for me now.'

But when he placed his aroused member where his fingers had been and made the first thrust, she gasped and tensed as her body rejected him. It wasn't just the physical pain as membranes began to tear but a mental rejection, too. Her muscles spasmed, trying to repel him. Lost to his own pleasure, he ignored her when she slapped him, trying to get his attention.

'Hamish, please stop! You're hurting me . . .'

'Not now,' he grated through clenched teeth. His face was dark with passion, his eyes a pair of blue slits, hard and

321

merciless as those of a demon. 'I won't – I can't – let you cheat me now!'

She tried to see where their bodies were joined, at the suntanned darkness of his body, thrusting between her thighs and couldn't believe she was actually doing this. It hurt so much and she was sure she was bleeding. He was killing her and he didn't care. What misguided fool had ever called this making love? This painful rhythm, this rending of her body, could have nothing at all to do with love. Ignoring her protests, he thrust himself deeper, making her give a small whimper which he interpreted as passion. He was panting against her ear, intent on gratifying himself, and all she could do was hold on to his shoulders and ride it out, biting her lips as she waited for it to be over; for him to be done. Hot tears pricked at her eyes and she squeezed them shut, unwilling to let him know how he disappointed her.

At last Hamish shuddered to fulfilment and was still. When she opened her eyes and looked at him, he was looking so pleased with himself that she wanted to strike him; to wipe that self-satisfied smirk from his face. All too clearly now, she saw what she had done. She had given herself to a man who didn't love her. So far as Hamish was concerned, she was nothing special at all. In a day or so he'd be telling his friends, winking and saying what a good sport she was.

She had expected her first lover to prize her virginity, accepting it as the crowning glory of their love. Or so her mother had always led her to believe.

'I don't say you have to wait for marriage, Maggi – that's not always the way. But do be careful where you bestow the gift of your love. You'll know when the time is right.'

But she hadn't known. And there had been no one to ask. Now all she felt was hollow and spent when she should have been feeling cherished and appreciated, full of joy and fulfilled by their love.

Insensitive to her feelings of misery and remorse, Hamish rolled away, grinning sheepishly and wiping semen from himself with the tail of his shirt. He who had been so anxious to see her naked, hadn't even bothered to undress.

'Sorry,' he said, still catching his breath. 'Too anxious –

322

couldn't wait for you to come. Poor little Mags.' He ruffled her curls, misinterpreting her reason for turning away from him. 'Don't be too disappointed. It was only a first attempt. Better luck next time, eh?'

'Didn't you hear me, Hamish? I asked you to stop.' She was beginning to tremble as reaction set in. 'I said you were hurting me an' I asked you to stop.'

'What if I had?' He shrugged. 'You'd only have been more nervous the next time.'

She stared at him, hoping, waiting for him to put everything right. It would take only a few words. She needed to know she was loved; that she meant the world to him as he did to her. Maybe then she could stop feeling so bereft. Before the act, he had been so tender, praising her and saying she was beautiful. Why couldn't he say so now?

'What is it? What do you want me to say?' He was irritated, sulky now, sensing she wanted more than he was prepared to give. 'Lots of girls say it hurts the first time. You don't have to make such a fuss.'

'What girls?' Maggi felt a surge of anger, only now remembering that Callum said Hamish collected women as feathers for his cap.

'Come on, Mags, don't be jealous. You can't pick a quarrel over a man's past. Fine thing if I was as innocent as you are. The pair of us fumbling about getting nowhere.'

'Well, I'm not so innocent now, am I?'

A pained expression passed over his face. 'Losing your virginity isn't the end of the world. You can't make me feel guilty for that. You went into this with your eyes open. Lord knows I gave you time enough to back out. No, Maggi, you were hot for it as I was.'

'It seems to me you have a lot to say about heat and very little about love, Hamish. You didn't consider my feelings at all.'

'You're a feast.' He grinned, catching a lock of her hair in his fingers and tugging it gently, trying to tease her out of her dark mood. 'A feast of marmalade and milk.'

'Let me go, damn you!' Shivering, she pulled herself free and rolled up in the quilt, angry with herself as much as with him.

323

'Oh, come on, Mags.' He chucked her under the chin. 'This is only virgin's remorse.'

'And you'd know all about that, wouldn't you?' She reared up to look at him, wanting to wipe the smug look off his face and hurt him in return. 'Just how many virgins have you spoiled?'

He pulled her back into his arms and murmured, 'How many? Only a couple of hundred or so.'

'Oh, you –' Too upset to realise he was joking, she raised her hand to slap him. He caught her wrist before she could deliver the blow.

'But none, my darling Maggi,' he murmured, 'to match up to you.' He took the time to kiss her as before, using all of his tenderness and expertise until he felt the tension go out of her. 'That's more like it. Nobody wants to make love to a little shrew.' He moved his lips from her mouth to her throat and she winced as he gave her a fierce love-bite, leaving a bruise. 'There. Now I've marked you as mine.' His lips continued their downward path. 'And do you like this – and this?' He opened his mouth and teased one nipple with his teeth while his fingers played with the other, reminding her how much she had liked it before.

'You do love me, don't you, Hamish?' she murmured as she dug her fingers into his hair, pulling his head more closely into her breast and making it impossible for him to answer her with words.

This time she knew what he wanted when he guided her hands to his member which had swelled once again. She did as he asked, hoping that this time he'd let her bring him to satisfaction outside her own body. She was sore and felt sure she was bleeding. So she tensed when she felt him separating her thighs, preparing to thrust himself inside her again.

'Relax!' he ordered, making it impossible for her to do so. 'Of course it's going to hurt if you hold yourself tense as a spring.'

Fortunately, with the edge taken off his desire, he was more considerate this time and she could begin to see how it could be pleasurable for herself as he said.

This night was to set the pattern for the future. But for Maggi, who delighted in the kisses, the foreplay and the words of love, something was always missing from the act itself. She could never achieve that same level of abandonment, the same groaning, shuddering, open-mouthed climax as he did. Proud of his sexual prowess, Hamish thought himself a magnificent stud. How was she to tell him he fell short of her expectations and she gained little satisfaction from this nightly union of their bodies?

After a week and more of these furtive encounters, she felt as if she were caught in a treadmill – worn out from working all day and spending her nights with him. And there was something else. Coupling as often as they did, she was afraid of falling pregnant. She knew Hamish wouldn't want to accept the responsibility of a child and he had made his views on matrimony only too clear. That far at least, he had been honest with her.

She tried asking him to give her some breathing space, some time to herself, but he laughed, refusing to believe it when she told him she was exhausted and needed her rest.

'Nonsense. Strong as an ox you are, Mags,' he said, dropping a casual kiss on her lips and pinching her cheek. 'See you tonight.'

Although he was thoughtless, insensitive and sometimes cruel in his demands, she loved him still, too stubborn to put an end to the affair and admit she'd made a mistake. She kept telling herself he would change when he fell more in love with her but in her more rational moments, she knew she was fooling herself. Hamish would never change. He would never become the considerate lover she wanted him to be, nor would he ever ask her to be his wife.

Tully was awake, wincing up into a cloudless sky, not quite sure where he was. For a moment he thought he must be lying on the deck of the *Sally Lee*. Then he remembered and raised his head, trying to see where he was. The storm was over and the ocean was calm again but there was no sign of the ship. Various boxes and pieces of timber and other flotsam were bobbing about on the surface of the water and at a distance he could make out what looked like a group of men clinging to a mast but the vessel was gone. Most of the crew had been drowned and her cargo lost.

325

He seemed to be lying in an awkward position in the bottom of a lifeboat. Jem and Hobley were with him and there wasn't very much room. He was also wet as water seemed to be seeping into the bottom of the boat. He struggled into a sitting position, ignoring the insistent throbbing at the back of his head. He felt for the source of the pain and found a lump there, big as an egg.

'What? What happened?' he said to Jem who was at the oars, trying to ride the waves and stop the boat from shipping any more water.

'Welcome back to the land of the living,' he said. 'An' the way things are shapin' up, it won't be for long.'

'The dog? Where's my dog?' Tully recalled with chilling clarity the argument before he was hit on the head. He stood up, rocking the boat dangerously as he stared around in panic.

'I'm sorry, lad.' Jem screwed up his eyes, unable to meet the boy's accusing gaze. 'I dunno that we'll get out of this one ourselves without worryin' about a stupid dog.'

'He's not a stupid dog.' Tully's voice broke with emotion. 'He was my dog and he trusted me. You let him die.'

'I said I was sorry.' Jem shrugged, helpless in the face of the boy's misery and rage.

'Sorry! An' that's supposed to make it all right, is it? You never wanted him here. Easy enough for you to say sorry now.'

'But he is here! There he is!' It was Hobley who spoke, pointing at the dog who was paddling briskly towards them, holding his head above the waves.

'Well, I'll be . . .' Jem's face flushed pink with relief.

It was so unlikely for the dog to survive a fall from the sinking ship that Tully rubbed his eyes, unable to believe that Pieface was really there, swimming briskly towards them. He shouted, encouraging him. 'Here, Pieface! C'mon, good boy! Good dog!'

But other eyes had caught sight of the dog on the surface of the water. At a distance still but slicing through the waves as it sped towards him was the dorsal fin of a shark.

'No! No! Get away from him, you brute! Leave my dog alone.' The sight of the shark was too much for Tully. It

326

would be too cruel if Pieface were to survive the shipwreck only to become a meal for a fish. With no thought for his own safety, he spread his arms, taking a moment to get his balance as he prepared to dive into the water to rescue him.

'Don't be a fool, boy,' Jem growled. 'Don't throw your life away on a mangy cur.'

Hobley, as usual, said nothing. But while the others were arguing, he slipped quietly over the side and into the water, his angular body swimming expertly across the surface of the dark blue water.

'Hobley, come back here, you stupid bugger!' Jem's voice rose to a wail as he realised there was nothing he could do for his friend.

Hobley reached Pieface at the same time as the shark and they could see him stabbing at it with his knife, colouring the water with its blood. Pieface kept on swimming towards Tully in the boat and with the shark out of action, Hobley followed.

Jem said nothing but his expression was grim as Tully hauled the dog aboard to land in a heap with him in the bottom of the boat.

'There's blood on him,' Tully said, a tremor in his voice.

'From the shark,' Jem growled. 'An' keep bailin' will you, unless you want us to sink.'

Hobley was almost there, his hands reaching out to grab the side of the boat and heave himself aboard. Then everything went wrong. He gave an awful, high-pitched scream, suddenly cut off as something took hold of him and pulled him strongly downwards under the water. He surfaced again for a moment, choking and sobbing as he fought to beat the predators away with his hands, jerked this way and that as the sharks pulled his body apart, fighting over him. Jem and Tully could only watch in horror, unable to help, imagining rather that seeing what must be happening beneath the waves. Tully thought he saw a few bubbles rise to the surface but they never saw Hobley again. Soon there was no sound other than the regular slap of the waves on the side of the boat. Unaware of the sacrifice that had been made for him, Pieface stood up and shook the water from his coat. It seemed awfully quiet when he stopped.

Chapter Twenty-Four

Maggi turned her head to look at Hamish, lying beside her, sprawled on the untidy ruin of her bed. He was sleeping soundly, one knee bent and his arms flung loosely above his head as he slept. His face was relaxed, lips parted and dark eyelashes fanned on his cheeks. Asleep he looked younger, more vulnerable, and she couldn't resist leaning forward to give him a kiss and breathe in the warm, healthy young-man smell of him, musky after their lovemaking. As she did so, a heavy lock of her hair fell forward and tickled his cheek. 'I love you so, Hamish,' she whispered. 'And I wish – I wish you really loved me, too.'

He gave a small shiver, muttering something in his sleep. Shifting position without waking, he turned away. She couldn't make out what he said but she knew it wouldn't be an answering declaration of love. That would be too much to hope for. Hamish was too wily for that, even when he was half asleep.

'Hamish! Hamish, I know you're up there!' An urgent, piercing whisper intruded on her reverie. 'Get down here at once.'

It was Callum, calling loudly enough to get their attention but not to disturb anyone else. It was, after all, the middle of the night, the cold, bluish light of dawn only now beginning to steal through the wooden louvres which served as windows up here in the loft. Wide awake now and trembling with the shame of being found out as much as the cold, Maggi sat up in bed, shaking Hamish awake.

'Come on, Hames.' Callum was speaking from the bottom

of the ladder now. 'Your horse is home so I know that's where you are. No use skulking up there trying to hide under Maggi's bed.'

Hamish groaned and leaned up on one elbow, making no effort to get up. 'Go away, Cal,' he called, his voice still husky with sleep. 'We'll talk about it in the morning, if you must.'

'We'll talk about it right now. I'm waiting outside.'

'Oh, bloody, bloody hell!' Swearing under his breath, Hamish lurched to his feet and put on his clothes. 'No need to look so worried, and don't bother to get up.' He kissed the air towards Maggi. 'I'll get rid of him quick as I can and come back.'

Maggi felt sure he wouldn't dispose of his brother so easily. Having caught them in exactly the situation he'd warned her about, he would have plenty to say. She hurried into her clothes, hoping to forestall a confrontation.

'I thought as much,' Callum said as they came out, closing the stable door behind them. 'Hamish, how could you? How could you take advantage of Maggi while Mother's away?'

'Much more easily than when she's here.' Hamish grinned, slinging an arm across Maggi's shoulders and trying to laugh it off. 'You shouldn't be so surprised, Cal. After all, this is what people do when they're in love.'

'In love!' Callum snorted, unconvinced. 'You've never been in love in your life. You wouldn't know the meaning of the word.'

'Maggi offered and I accepted. What's so wrong about that?'

'What's wrong? She has no parents – no one to protect her from people like you.'

'Ah, but who could resist it?' Hamish picked up a lock of Maggi's hair and kissed it. 'She's delicious, Cal. Sweet as honey. Soft and pliant as a lily . . .'

'My God! I ought to knock your head off!'

'Steady on.' Hamish laughed nervously, letting Maggi go. 'You'll have me thinking you're jealous next.'

That last jibe was too much. Callum hurled himself at his brother and punched him full in the mouth, grappling with him as they crashed to the ground. Maggi screamed.

'Stop it!' Her voice was shaking, full of tears. 'Stop it, the pair of you. You're family, for God's sake. An' I'll not have you fightin' like dogs – not over me.'

With reluctance Callum stood up, brushing the mud from his clothes. Hamish took a few moments more to recover before he scrambled unsteadily to his feet, wiping his mouth on his sleeve. It came away covered in blood.

'Don't you worry, Maggi. I'll make him marry you.' Callum was watching his brother through narrowed eyes. 'You can be certain of that. He'll buy you a ring and you'll have a proper betrothal when Mother comes back. I'll pound him into the earth if not.'

'Callum, no.' She was so wretched, she could hardly get the words out. 'I don't want him. Not if it's like that.'

Hamish tried to laugh and found that he couldn't. He contented himself with landing a gob of blood mixed with spittle at Callum's feet.

By now the commotion had roused the Hegartys who had come out of their cottage to see what the fight was about. They stood huddled together, shivering, their coats over their nightclothes, enthralled by the drama unfolding before them. Maggi was thankful that Hallie and Cassie seemed to have heard nothing. Or didn't show their faces if they had.

'So what do you want me to do with him, Maggi?' Callum squinted at her, puzzled by her refusal. 'Don't you want me to make him face up to his responsibilities?'

'No. No, I don't.' She was still shaking. 'And you can serve me best by pretending all this never happened. It's been upsetting enough as it is.'

'You see?' Hamish managed a snort of laughter, earning himself a look of loathing from Callum.

'Very well, Maggi.' He gave her a curt nod. 'If those are your wishes, I have to respect them. There's no more to be said.'

'Callum, please.' She started to run after him. 'You expect so much of people. Too much. Nobody's perfect – least of all me. Please try to understand.'

He gave no sign that he heard her and she could only stare at his retreating back as he strode towards the house.

330

'Hah! You said it. That'll teach him to poke his nose in where it's not wanted,' Hamish crowed. 'God blast the miserable sod, let him stew. We're going back to bed.'

'No, we're not.' She was irritated that Hamish should expect her to go on as if nothing had happened. 'I have work to do even if you don't.'

'Let it wait. Oh Maggi, Maggi!' He took her face in his hands, meaning to kiss her and forgetting the blood on his lips. Wincing she avoided it, turning her head away. 'You know I can't resist making him savage, winding him up. It worked a little too well this time.' And he fingered his bruised jaw which had stiffend and hurt when he tried to smile.

'Serves you right. I hope it hurts.'

'Thanks a lot. Come on, Mags. Forget about Cal, he's just an old kill-joy. Nothing's changed between us.'

'Oh, but it has. I'm ashamed of us, Hamish. Myself just as much as you.'

'But that's what he's hoping for, what he wants you to feel.'

Maggi shivered, pressing her lips together to stop them from trembling. 'I'll never forget the look on his face – so hurt. As if I'd disappointed him somehow, let him down.'

'I told you, forget about Cal. He's jealous, that's all. Getting to be a dried up old bachelor. Probably not had a woman in ten years.'

'Well, I'm sure you've more than made up for it! Taking his share as well as your own.'

He stared at her, unable to fathom her mood. 'Get on with it, then. I can't talk to you. Not in this mood.'

'Then don't.' Beset by conflicting emotions, all she wanted was to get back inside and be alone where she could heal the dull ache of her misery in a fit of crying.

'See you tonight.' He tried to give her a playful slap on the bottom but she saw it coming and avoided it. 'You'll see things differently then.'

'Don't count on it, Hamish.' She spoke quickly, breathlessly, before her courage failed. 'I don't want this again – tonight or any other night.'

'I don't believe this.' He was still smiling, not yet

331

convinced. 'You're actually trying to give me the brush off. Oh, you're not serious, Mags?'

'Yes. Yes, I am. Besides, we've been running too much of a risk, making love all the time. We could have a baby. Is that what you want?'

'Good God, no!' A glimmer of fear showed in his eyes, gone as quickly as it had appeared but there long enough for her to see it. 'Maggie, you've not missed already? You're not – not –?' He choked on the word, unable to say it.

'Of course I'm not,' she snapped, impatient with his concern which she knew was all for himself. 'Better to be safe than sorry, though, don't you think?'

'Yes. Yes, better safe than sorry,' he repeated, making no attempt to disguise his relief. That in itself was far from flattering. Now he knew there wasn't a problem, his mind was already running on something else. A certain boarding house in Beechworth, perhaps? Where, in an unguarded moment, he had told her there was an accommodating girl. For a moment Maggi almost wavered in her resolve. Did she really want to drive Hamish into that other girl's arms? It was a risk she would have to take. He would never value her if she didn't stand up to him. She would never let him take her for granted again.

That same day, while the atmosphere fairly crackled with tension between the two brothers as all their old animosity was revived, Lilias and her mother came back.

While Elizabeth was quick to size up the situation and surmise that all wasn't well in her household, taking note of Hamish's split lip and Maggi's red eyes, Lilias remained blithely unaware. She could scarcely wait for the man with the hired waggonette to drive away before she regaled Maggi with a detailed description of her holiday.

'You should have been there – it was so exciting! We wrapped ourselves up and went to the Cremorne Gardens. Nobody minded that it was cold. It was wonderful – like a fairyland. Oh, and I spent a fortune in the shops! I can't wait to show you all my new dresses. I have one for you, as well . . .'

332

'Lilias, you shouldn't. Where will I ever go to wear a new dress?'

'Here, of course. You'll need something pretty to wear to the party after the races. I'll not have you dressed in rags.'

'If I come to the party at all,' Maggi muttered, biting her lip. What would happen if Elizabeth were to hear of her recent behaviour? No parties for Maggi then.

'Of course you'll be there. It's a tradition. Everyone comes to the party on Saturday night – the Hegartys, Hallie and Cassie. Besides, I've told all my friends about you. You're going to sing.'

'But, Lilias, I can't! I haven't practised my scales in weeks.'

'And why not? What have you been doing while I've been away? You used to practise every night before going to bed. It was lovely. I used to open my window to hear you.'

'I never knew that.'

'Oh, there's not much escapes me,' Lilias grinned, wagging a finger. 'Not much about you that I don't know.'

Hearing this, Maggi blushed, grateful that Lilias had been absent during the past few months.

Her mind and heart remained in Melbourne and she could talk of little else. Over the next few days, Maggi did her best to seem interested and attentive but found her mind often wandered as Lilias chattered of people and places she'd never seen. And when Maggi didn't enthuse enough to please her, Lilias shrugged and said: 'You should have been there.' She showed no interest in anything that had happened during her absence from Lachlan's Holt and believed Maggi when she said nothing *had* happened. Nothing she wanted to discuss, anyway.

Lilias described in detail the house Harley had bought for her; the house they would live in when they were married. Even now, workmen would be swarming all over it, decorating it to her taste. How difficult it had been to decide on the colours, peach vying with pink for the bridal bedroom. How she wished she'd chosen a cheerful colour for the kitchen rather than green. Too late to change it now. Maggi listened to all this but learned no more about Harley Maitland than before. He was still a shadowy figure in the background. She thought he must be very preoccupied with business to spend so little time with his future bride. Either that or deadly dull.

With her head full of plans for her official betrothal and writing letters and invitations, Lilias decided it was time to let Toby go. He left Lachlan's Holt to go to a hotel keeper in Beechworth whose daughter needed a gentle ride.

The departure of Toby left Maggi's afternoons free. She waited, wondering if Hamish would lay claim to them as before. He didn't. During the early days of their affair, she had been exhausted, rushed off her feet. Now she had time on her hands. Callum largely avoided her and Hamish, denied the comfort of her bed, now treated her with a kind of brotherly familiarity; a cheerfulness with an edge of mockery, building an even greater barrier between them. He would demand his horse at odd hours of the night and disappear without saying where he was going – sometimes for days. He would return looking like a gypsy, covered in filth and with several days' growth of beard, hair matted with dust and eyes swollen from lack of sleep.

She found it hard to believe he could cut her out of his life so easily and it served only to confirm her worst fears. He had taken up with her because he thought she was easy, his feelings had never been deep. Nor did he care that he was deprived of her company now.

She went over that terrible scene a thousand times during many sleepless nights. Could she have said or done anything to make it turn out differently? If only there could be a second chance. If she could turn the clock back to the time when her relationship with Hamish was new; when they had exchanged no more than kisses and the act of love lay ahead, something to be savoured later on. That's how a normal courtship would have progressed. Too late for that now. Passion and greed had bypassed romance and love never stood a chance. It was over and she had nothing, not even his friendship. And she had lost Callum's respect as well.

Attempting to fill this emotional vacuum, she threw herself wholeheartedly into her work. She rode to the ironmonger's in Beechworth and purchased horseshoes and nails enough to re-shoe all the horses in the MacGregor stables. Then she spent the whole day at the forge, working the bellows for

334

Patrick Hegarty until he saw she was ready to drop from exhaustion when he told her to stop.

'Are you after killin' yourself, girl?' he said, shaking his head. 'You're goin' the right way about it, if so.'

In his own gruff way, Patrick was kind. The only mention he made of the fight was to offer a quick word of advice.

'Stay out of their battles, girl, an' never take sides. Always been bad blood between those two.'

Intuitively, he seemed to know that for Maggi that morning had been a turning point, having a profound effect on her life.

She practised her singing again, shocked to find out how much ground she had lost. Her voice wavered on scales which had been effortless before and she cracked on some of the higher notes, having no breath to sustain them. She went back to basics, to some of the earliest scales her mother had taught her, and did breathing exercises to strengthen her lungs. 'I'll make you proud of me yet, Mam,' she whispered. 'See if I don't.'

In the mornings she slaved as if her life depended on it, spring-cleaning the stables, shovelling deep muck out of every stall and taking it, a barrow load a time to put on Elizabeth's rose gardens, ready to nourish the trees when they bloomed again in the spring. She scattered fresh bedding throughout the stables, relishing that special fragrance of well-groomed horse flesh and clean straw. The MacGregors visitors were to be impressed. No one should be allowed to doubt her capabilities as a groom.

She dismantled and cleaned all the tack she could find. She washed the stirrup irons, bits and metal rings in warm water, dried them and polished them with a soft cloth until they gleamed. She cleaned all the saddles, working saddle soap well into the leather to feed it. She dragged out even the old-fashioned high-backed saddles which must have belonged to Elizabeth's husband, lying covered in dust and neglected for years. She drove out several spiders, so huge she thought she could see their eyes. She knew they were harmless but still they horrified her because of their size. And when she was done, the stables looked as if an army of grooms had been hard at work there rather than one girl.

This exacting, manual work made her lean, tough and strong as a boy. Her figure, including her breasts, diminished, becoming boyish as well. Only her hair, that most arresting and glorious claim to beauty, was left to advertise the fact that she was a girl.

If Elizabeth thought it strange for Maggi to throw herself into her work with such demonic energy, she didn't say so. She had enough to worry about with the revival of the old quarrel between her sons. Before she went away, she had allowed herself to hope that matters were mending between them. Not so now. And if she suspected the new rift had anything to do with Maggi, she had the tact and good sense not to mention it.

Had she been anyone other than Hamish's mother, Maggi might have confided in her. But how could she ask for advice when she knew she was in the wrong? She had taken advantage of Elizabeth's absence to sleep with her son. And while Elizabeth didn't strike her as being old-fashioned or prudish, Maggi didn't dare risk the recriminations which might follow such a confession.

The MacGregor ladies had been home for three weeks and, according to the calendar, it was officially spring. Although it was still cold at night, winter was losing its grip. The sharp, sometimes frosty mornings, heralded fine weather later in the day. Gradually, the sun was regaining its warmth, although the wind could still penetrate thick clothes and bring tears to the eyes if it blew down from the mountains where there was still some snow. But Elizabeth's jonquils and daffodils were already showing up bright green spears, showing they, too, believed in the coming of spring.

In the early part of the evening the wind dropped; the gale force wind which had been making work so difficult during the day. Patrick Hegarty returned the Clydesdales and left, anxious to get to his supper and set his feet before a fire. Maggi was feeding them and making them comfortable, humming softly, practising a scale. She thought herself alone until Hamish spoke up behind her, giving her a fright.

'Hello, Mags!'

She gave a little shriek. 'Hamish, don't do that. You scared ten years off of me.' And she pressed a hand to her

336

chest to still the leap of her heart. It would still betray her when he turned up unexpectedly, smiling that lazy, impossible smile and taking her breath away.

'We can't go on like this, Maggi. It's silly. Here we are in the same household, behaving like a pair of strangers. Can't we bury the hatchet and start over again?'

Wasn't that what she wanted? A new beginning? She hesitated, wondering whether he meant the same as she did. She wanted to take things slowly this time.

'I'd like that, Hamish. I'd like us to be friends again.'

'Friends, Maggi? I was hoping for more.'

'I can't go back to the way we used to be. Not yet.'

'All right.' He shrugged. She waited for him to argue but he seemed to have other things on his mind. 'Look, Mags, I know it's an imposition at this time of night but can you give me a hand? I need Nero in a hurry – I'm running late.'

'Yes. Yes, of course.' She ran to get his saddle, letting her hair fall across her face so that he wouldn't see how he affected her. She managed a bright smile when she came back.

'Where to, then? Where are you going tonight?'

'Where d'you think?' His grin became sly. 'The wind's dropped, there's a perfect hunter's moon and we're after wild cattle again. I say,' he said as if it was only now occurring to him, 'you wouldn't like to come with me, would you? Patrick's housebound since Molly went sour on it – won't let him out at night any more. Left us in a bit of a fix.'

'Oh, I would – I will, if Mrs MacGregor doesn't mind.'

'No. For heaven's sake, don't involve Mother in this!' He wrinkled his nose. 'Besides, there's no time. Decide for yourself, Maggi. Are you with me or not?'

'Yes. Yes, I am.' She was thrilled at the prospect of going out at night as well as spending the evening with Hamish. She was happy again for the first time in weeks. She had been right, after all. Right to assert herself. Now he wanted her for a friend, a helpmeet, as well as a bedfellow.

'Right. And not a whisper to Mother or Callum or I'll never hear the last of it.'

337

'No.' She returned his smile which drew her back into the old intimacy so that it was almost like old times. 'What do we have to do? I've never been gully rakin' before.'

'Ssh!' He glanced around, suppressing a laugh. 'You mustn't call it that. Callum's on tenterhooks as it is. If he ever finds out and quizzes you, we were moonlighting, that's all – mustering scrubbers as they come out in the open at night to feed.'

'I don't think he will. He ignores me these days.'

'Don't take it personally. He's just crabby, too busy to talk to anyone, wearing himself to death mending fences to keep in his precious sheep. I'd like it fine if he'd mind his own business and let me mind mine but he's always at me to help him. Says he'd be through it in half the time.'

'Why don't you, then? Help him – meet him halfway. Maybe then you would –' She paused, biting her lip.

'Mend our quarrel? Why should I?' He looked at her out of the corners of his eyes. 'Besides, it suits me better to have him occupied, out of my way.'

'You've never got on,' Maggi was speaking half to herself.

'No. And you don't know the half of it.' Hamish's jaw was set and even in the gloom of the stables, she could see his eyes glittering, bright and hard as diamonds. 'Callum owes me, Maggi. And I'm just about ready to collect.'

'What do you mean?' She shivered, daunted by the wild-eyed, haunted look on his face that made him suddenly a stranger.

'Nothing,' he said. 'It's not important.'

Maggi shot him a sidelong glance. Something which triggered such rage could not be dismissed as unimportant.

'Lets go. I don't want to be late.' Hamish adjusted his stirrups, preparing to mount. 'Which horse will you take?'

'One of the stockhorses, I suppose.'

'Too old and too slow. You can take Bothwell tonight.'

'Without askin' Callum? Oh, no. That would be askin' for trouble. I couldn't do that.'

'Why not? He'll never know.' Hamish gave a short laugh. 'Don't worry. Cal doesn't care about Bothwell. He has no feeling for a good horse at all. I bet he hasn't taken him out in weeks.'

338

'He has. But I still have to walk him each day to make sure he gets enough exercise.'

'All the more reason to give him an outing, then. Callum won't care – he's on to the next enthusiasm already. Spends every spare moment with the architect and the builder, poring over his plans. You know he wants to build a bigger and better Lachlan's Holt?'

'What for? You have a nice enough house already?'

'Because Callum doesn't want a "nice enough house". He wants a mansion grand enough to rival anything in the American South,' Hamish's face took on the sneer he adopted whenever he was speaking about his brother. 'A wool baron. Callum MacGregor, master of all he surveys.'

'And you? Do you see yourself as a cattle baron?'

'Maybe,' said Hamish, bringing a saddle to put on Bothwell. 'But one thing I do know. I can't stay here playing second fiddle to Callum indefinitely. And I'm not telling him how much I get from my cattle or he'll be after the money to spend on his silly sheep. I want to make sure I have a fat purse when I'm ready to leave.'

'And – and when is that likely to be?' Maggi shivered, suddenly certain there was no place for herself in Hamish's long term plans.

'You'll find out. So will everyone.' He dropped a kiss on the end of her nose. She felt a stab of anger when he treated her thus, like a child. Sensing her mood, he caught her by the hair and pulled her into his arms, kissing her thoroughly to stifle any further queries. Hamish had always been a good kisser and when they drew apart, her heart was thundering and she was breathless. She smiled up at him, reassured and happy that their differences had been mended.

Although Nero was snorting, impatient to leave, Hamish secured the big grey and made him wait while he helped Maggi to saddle Bothwell. She knew it was wrong to take him without permission but she had to agree, there was no other suitable horse in the stables. She must ride Bothwell or let Hamish go out alone.

'Wrap up warmly,' he told her before she attempted to mount. 'It might not seem so cold now but it can be damp and chilly out in the bush at night.'

339

Maggi shivered, half in anticipation and half because she was already feeling the cold. She tucked her hair up into one of Patrick Hegarty's old hats, wrapped a clean horse blanket about her shoulders and let Hamish give her a leg up into the saddle. Bothwell accepted her without complaint and she kept her hands steady and firm on the reins, communicating her confidence. He was a tall horse, even taller than Nero, and the ground seemed a long way off. Hamish took a quick look outside to make sure there was no one around to see them set off and, signalling her to follow, led the way out and into the night.

Chapter Twenty-Five

At night the bush seemed grey and eerie, quite different from the way it looked with the sun shining on it in daylight. Near the creek there were pockets of mist, hanging in the air like wraiths and gum trees shone white in the moonlight, well named 'ghost gums'. Making no concessions to Maggi for not being used to Bothwell or riding at night, Hamish maintained a brisk pace, expecting her to keep up. They travelled far and fast and she came to realise he was right; there would have been no point in embarking on such an adventure on a slow horse.

She was more aware of the wild creatures than in daylight; dingoes howled to each other and to the moon, mournful desolate cries which made the horses snort and flatten their ears. Bothwell almost shied at a movement in the trees and Maggi suppressed a shriek, startled by a fierce gutteral grunting which she took to be a wild pig. Her heart lurched painfully as she imagined some hoary tusker, bursting from the undergrowth to confront them, making the horses panic.

'Only a koala in search of a mate,' Hamish assured her, laughing as he pointed out the chubby marsupial responsible for making so much noise and which was out of all proportion to its size. Maggi too laughed in relief when she saw it, feeling foolish for being frightened of something that looked like a cuddly child's toy with its rounded ears and comic, pin-toed walk. Awkward as it was at ground level, it moved swiftly when it took to the trees, using its strong claws to gain a foothold as it climbed. On reaching the safety of a fork in the tree, it sat gazing down at them, watching their every move until they were out of sight.

'I am a true son of this land,' Hamish boasted. 'Like most of the native creatures, I do my hunting at night.'

Maggi smiled but she hoped there would be no more such surprises. Bothwell, quick to pick up on her own anxiety, pranced sideways, spooked by any sudden movement in the bushes as rats and other small nocturnal creatures fled from their path. She wondered how he would fare when they got down to the real business of the night. The rhythmic creak of leather and the cry of an occasional night bird was the only accompaniment to the beat of their horses' hooves. Hamish was keeping Nero on a tight rein, unwilling to let him gallop at night for fear he might stumble or trip on an exposed tree root. Unlike Bothwell, the horse was used to working at night but he had a mind of his own. More than once she heard Hamish cursing aloud, cuffing the big grey about the ears for trying to run him into a tree or into a bush full of thorns.

Happy just to be near him, to be included in his life again, Maggi had given no thought to the men they would meet, expecting they would be competent stockmen, tidy and respectful like Patrick Hegarty. She was surprised when Hamish skirted the gold fields and met up with a party of men who hailed them from the bushes at the side of the road.

Having spent some time as a traveller herself, Maggi knew the world contained all sorts but she felt a frisson of alarm on seeing Hamish's friends. They reminded her all too vividly of the three bushrangers who had accosted Callum and herself that first night out of Melbourne; just as heavily armed and carrying extra bullets across their chests in the manner of brigands. Four pairs of eyes glittered from beneath four wide-awake hats and they wore coloured handkerchiefs over their noses and mouths, supposedly to avoid breathing dust but which made an effective disguise. Each man carried a rifle and enough ammunition to start a small war. Seeing Maggi, they looked her up and down, unimpressed.

'This the best you can do, Hames? Where's Pat Hegarty? Still playin' the henpecked husband?' one of them quipped, producing sniggers from the others. 'Where'd you find this one, then?' He peered at Maggi in the darkness. 'Sure he's up to it, Hames? Horse looks useful enough but I'm not so sure about the lad.'

'Ah, don't worry yeself about the McDiarmit.' Hamish affected a comic Irish accent, giving Maggi a broad wink. 'Take my advice an' leave the creature alone – it's a lot meaner an' tougher than it looks.'

'He'd better be.' The man hawked and spat, letting them know he disapproved of this latest addition to their ranks. 'I'm lookin' to make a few bob tonight an' he'd better not let us down.'

'He won't,' Hamish said.

They rode on into the night, the horses maintaining a brisk walking pace until it occurred to Maggi that they had been travelling for hours. She hadn't the slightest idea where they were, not even if they were still on MacGregor land. They encountered several isolated groups of cattle quietly grazing but Hamish rode on, ignoring them. Hearing rather than seeing movements and the scratching of claws as something ran up the trees, she looked up expecting koalas and saw small, wide-eyed animals rather like squirrels staring down at them, apparently frozen in fear. Some had babies, tiny copies of themselves, clinging with strong paws, resembling little hands, to the thick, grey fur on their mothers' backs.

'Only brushtails – possums,' Hamish said. 'And a damned nuisance they are, too. Get into the orchards and take one bite out of each piece of fruit, leaving it to rot on the ground.'

Maggi looked at them, unable to think badly of these doe-eyed, innocent-looking natives of the bush. She and her mount both flinched when one of the men took aim and shot one. He retrieved the possum, still dripping blood, swinging it by its long, bushy tail. The animal was larger than she had thought at first, more the size of a hare than a squirrel. The man grinned, seeing her looking at it.

'Tough as old boots and not much of a taste to them,' he said. 'But you'll put anything in the pot if you get hungry enough.'

Suddenly, Hamish held up a hand for silence, motioning Maggi to stay out of sight underneath the trees, his eyes on a fair-sized herd which was ambling ahead of them. These must be the wild cattle they were searching for.

Used to working as a team the four men rode in formation to round up some of the bullocks, isolating them from the rest of the herd. The animals lowed their complaints, unused to being mustered or doing anything other than please themselves. When they had half a dozen cattle separated from the main herd, they steered them towards Maggi and Hamish asked her to keep them together and prevent them from escaping and joining the main herd, much as a sheep dog controls a small flock of sheep. Hamish and his friends rode off to divert a few more and after what she took to be another hour or so, they had collected some thirty or forty cattle and one of the men stayed to help her contain them. She realised Hamish was skilled as any circus rider, particularly in the use of the whip he used to keep the cattle travelling in the direction he wanted.

He paused at last to count them, saying he was satisfied to call it a night.

'Doesn't pay to be too greedy,' he said, giving Maggi a sly wink. She let go a long sigh, grateful to be relieved of responsibility. Determined the men should have no cause to complain or criticise, she had lost none of the cattle left in her care, although some of the younger bullocks had been frisky, testing her to the full and looking for an opportunity to run away. Fortunately, Bothwell responded quickly and was equal to the task.

The five men took over from Maggi when it was time to move the herd. That, too, was a relief. By now the excitement and novelty of the adventure had worn off, she was tired and her stomach growled reproachfully, reminding her of the supper she had missed. Did Hamish mean them to travel all night without a break? She couldn't ask him as he was riding at the side of the mob while she remained at the back and she didn't want to cause any comment by holding them up. If Hamish's friends chose to think she was an ignorant dolt, she was happy to leave it that way.

They travelled a long way, this time on a downhill curve until Hamish raised a hand, calling a halt. Maggi stared at him, exhausted, hoping he would ask no more of her tonight.

But the men knew the routine. Two of them took charge of the cattle while Hamish and the others dismounted, leaving their horses with Maggi while they collected enough wood to start a small fire. When it was warm and glowing, Maggi secured the horses and the four of them sat down beside it to relax and have something to eat. Mrs Hallam had provided Hamish with huge slabs of cooked mutton between doorsteps of freshly baked bread and when she smelled it and sank her teeth into it, Maggi discovered she was more ravenous than she thought. The old leather hat she had pulled on to contain her unruly curls now felt like a tight band about her head, giving her a headache. Without thinking, she took it off and shook down her thick mane of red hair.

'Stripe me, Hames!' The younger of the two men whistled appreciatively. 'Why didn't you say the nipper was a girl?' And he offered Maggi what he imagined to be an encouraging smile. It wasn't a pretty sight. His teeth were broken and uneven and there was a huge gap between the two front ones which looked as if they had been punched out of shape.

Hamish responded with a shrug. When they had finished eating, Maggi expected them to change places with the other men who were minding the cattle. They didn't. Instead, Hamish produced a pouch of tobacco and offered it around. Taking a large pinch himself, in the expert manner of a bushman he rolled himself a smoke and sealed the paper delicately with his tongue. Leering at Maggi, the younger of the two men changed places to come and sit beside her, making her aware of the stale, sickly odour which arose from his clothes. She knew that smell; it brought back memories of their worst days in Ireland and of travelling steerage aboard the *Sally Lee*. It was the stink of poverty; of people who haven't the means to wash their bodies or their clothes. Once she wouldn't have turned a hair, being none too clean herself. Now the smell of this man made her stomach turn.

'Pretty little thing.' He stretched out a grimy finger towards her. She recoiled before he could touch her cheek. 'Useful with cattle, too. Don't have too much to say for yerself, do yer?' He thrust his face into hers, giving her a whiff of bad breath and a closer view of that gap in his teeth. She smiled briefly and shifted away. He was Hamish's friend and she'd

345

prefer not to offend him but she wanted him to go away. She sat hugging her knees, making herself as small as she could and fixing her gaze on Hamish in a silent plea for his help. He must see she was far from comfortable with this man? Why didn't he come to her rescue? Following the direction of her gaze, the man raised his hands shoulder-high in a gesture of surrender.

'Oops. Sorry, Hames. No offence. Didn't know she was your girl.'

'Oh, she used to be.' Hamish yawned and stretched as if he found the matter too boring to discuss. 'But not any more. Maggi's her own woman now. She can do as she likes.'

She was grateful for the darkness as well as the flickering firelight for hiding the colour which swooped into her cheeks. This then was the ultimate betrayal. This was to be her punishment for asserting herself and trying to win his respect.

'So, ah, what are you saying?' The man licked lips which showed moist and red in the tangled nest of his beard. 'You don't mind? You wouldn't shoot a bloke in the toes for tryin' his luck?'

'Go ahead, Pete.' Hamish's smile was cool. 'It's up to Maggi. Far as I'm concerned, she can choose for herself.'

She stood up promptly before the situation could get out of hand. 'No!' she said sharply, leaving Pete in no doubt of her feelings. 'Hamish. I want a word with you. In private. Away from these friends of yours.'

Head high, she walked away to the trees where their horses were tethered, hoping the darkness would disguise the fact that her legs were trembling so much she could hardly walk. She didn't dare to look over her shoulder to see if he'd followed. Seconds later she gasped as he seized her, turning her to face him and grasping her by the upper arms, almost lifting her off her feet.

'Now maybe you understand,' he whispered fiercely. 'Now you see the sort of trouble you can get into if I'm not around.'

'If it wasn't for you, Hamish, I'd be in no trouble at all. I'd be tucked up safe in my bed.'

346

'You didn't need much persuasion. You wanted to come. I never twisted your arm.'

'No. But I didn't know you had it in mind to pass me on to your friends like a cast off coat.'

'A cast off coat? Oh, very poetic, Maggi.'

'Poetic be damned! This is serious, Hamish. I'm in danger here.'

'From Pete? No. These lads might look a bit rough an' ready but they're all right. They just don't get to see many white women. Come to think of it, they don't see any women at all – unless they steal them from the blacks.'

'And that's supposed to make me feel better, is it? To know I'm in the company of men who steal women from helpless savages?'

'Not that helpless. They're pretty accurate with their spears and can fight like wild animals when they're roused.'

'Against men with guns?'

Hamish shrugged. 'No use groaning about it, Maggi. It's been going on for years.'

'And that makes it right, does it?'

'Don't be too hard on Pete and his mates. We all have the same needs, you know.' So saying, he took her by the elbows, meaning to lift her into his arms. She stiffened, resisting the embrace. It would be so easy to give in, to fall back into the same old ways, but she wasn't ready to do that. Not yet. She loved him, yes. But she was determined not to let him take her for granted again. This time she would wait until he said the right words and meant them.

'I love you, Maggi,' he said, lifting her into his arms and kissing her lightly, without passion. 'Surely you know that by now?'

'Do I?' she said coolly. The words had slipped off his tongue too easily and she didn't believe them. 'Tell me, Hamish – tell me the truth. You wouldn't really have stood by and let him . . .?'

He laughed aloud then, his teeth very white in the moon-light. 'It's your own fault. You encouraged him.'

'How?'

'You gave the game away when you pulled off your hat. I'm not the one who told them you were a girl.'

347

'Don't you dare laugh at me!' She struck out at him and the blow landed on his arm, making him wince. 'You're a beast, Hamish MacGregor, and I hate you!' Her temper flared as she sprang at him, trying to hit him again. This time he was ready and caught her by the wrist, holding her off.

'Everythin' all right back there, Hames?' The men at the camp fire sniggered, misinterpreting the sound of their struggles. 'Give us a yell if yer need any help!'

Hamish took advantage of this diversion to pull Maggi into his arms, kissing lips that still trembled under his own. 'That's more like it,' he said. 'Still my girl?'

She nodded and he smiled, placing an arm across her shoulders as he led her back to the camp fire.

'You stole my horse!'

Maggi sighed. The accusation wasn't unexpected. She let Bothwell put down the hoof she had been examining for stones and stood up, straightening her back to face Callum. Not caring if he startled the horse or not, he had flung open the stable door, letting the light shine in her eyes, blinding her.

Worn out after her night's adventures, she was full of remorse for taking the horse without permission and also for riding him so hard. She had hoped to sneak Bothwell back into his stall before Callum missed him but, being both large and noisy, the big stallion wasn't built for sneaking. It was hopeless, anyway. Callum already knew. He must have been keeping an eye on the stables, watching and waiting for his horse to return.

And Hamish wasn't here to support her. How like him to dodge the issue, taking off with his friends and the cattle, leaving Maggi to face Callum's wrath on her own. Outlined against the blinding rays of the early-morning sun, he resembled nothing so much as an avenging angel, his fair hair standing out like a halo, his arms folded across his chest.

She looked at the horse and back to Callum again, realising there was no point in trying to deny it. The animal's exhaustion was plain for all to see. He was still sweating and shaking under the blanket she'd lain on his back to stop him from taking a chill.

'I didn't steal him, Callum. I borrowed him.' She spoke slowly, playing for time. Time to think up an acceptable lie. She was too tired to face up to the kind of confrontation the truth would provoke. 'You neglect him, you know. You don't ride him nearly enough. He'll turn wild if you don't give him more exercise.'

'Turn wild?' Callum repeated her words, his voice heavy with sarcasm. 'So that's what you were doing – exercising my horse? In the middle of the night? I don't think so, Maggi. You'll have to think up a better explanation than that.'

'All right, I'm sorry. I shouldn't have taken him without asking. What else do you want?'

'The truth, for a start. You've been out gully raking with Hamish, haven't you?'

'Of course not, I –' she broke off, seeing his raised eyebrows. He could always see through her lies and defences.

'And don't bother to make up another lie. I saw you when you were leaving last night.'

'Then whyever didn't you say so?' She seized on the smallest opportunity to put him in the wrong. 'And save all this fencing about.'

'I thought you'd taken one of the stockhorses. I didn't find out 'til this morning that Bothwell was gone.'

'I am sorry. I know it was wrong but what more can I say? Please, Callum, can we talk about this later? I'm ready to drop.'

'Where's Hamish? Why didn't he see you home?'

'He's taking the cattle straight to the gold fields.'

'Where did you go?'

'I don't know.' Tiredness made her irritable. 'It was dark. I just followed Hamish and the others.'

'What others.'

'Bushmen. Hamish's friends.'

'And when you left here, did you strike out for the east or the west?'

'I told you, Callum, I don't know. I wish I'd never gone. It was very hard work.'

'Did you round up many head of cattle?'

'Some.' She shrugged.

349

'And did you – did they – examine these cattle for brands – marks? And don't keep saying you don't know.'

'But I don't. Honest, Callum, you're worse than a magistrate with all these questions. Those cattle are wild – strays that nobody wants. Hamish said so.'

'And you believe everything he says?'

She frowned, rubbing her eyes.

'And just how wild were they, these wild cattle? Dangerous? Difficult? Easy to keep in a mob?'

'Easy enough, I thought.'

'Little fool!' He smacked his fist into his hand, more angry than she had ever seen him. 'What if there had been men in charge of those cattle, guarding them? You could have been fired upon, killed outright or your horse shot from beneath you.'

'Aha, now I see where this is leading,' she said, trying to keep it light. 'It's not that you're concerned about me at all. Only Bothwell. Well, you don't have to be. He's a good cattle horse is your Bothwell. Knows when to shift and when to keep quiet.' She chose her words carefully, avoiding mention of Pete and the others. Really, they had scared her far more than anything else which came out of the bush. It had been a relief to part company with them when Hamish had thanked her and sent her home from MacGregor's Creek. He and his companions would drive the cattle straight to the gold fields. The butchers were waiting for them, he said. Now she wondered if it was because he wanted to see them slaughtered as soon as possible. After all, one bullock looked much like another, skinned, beheaded and hung up on a hook outside a butchers' shambles. Callum was quick to sense her doubts.

'I suggest to you, Maggi, they weren't wild cattle at all. They belonged to our neighbour, Sir Athelstane Gurney.'

'Sir Athelstane Gurney?' Maggi smiled at the name. 'He sounds like a right English milord. I don't mind robbin' a man with a name like his.'

Callum frowned, refusing to see the joke. 'You don't, do you? You don't mind robbing anyone. You've never been any different, not since I've known you. Life is a joke to you, isn't it, Maggi? You're only happy when you've got your

350

hand in a man's back pocket, robbing him, thumbing your nose at the law.'

'I don't do that. Not any more.' She blinked, stung by the criticism.

'Fool that I was, I thought you'd changed. I hoped – no I believed – that when you turned that money over to charity you were turning over a new leaf. But you weren't, were you? You haven't changed at all.'

'Does anyone, deep down? No, I don't think so. You haven't changed either, Callum MacGregor. You're still the same self-satisfied prig I met on the wharf.'

'What's that? What did you say?' By now she had closed Bothwell into his stall, leaving him to feed. She made her way to the back of the stables, the saddle and tack in her arms. Callum followed, chasing her into a corner.

'Put that down and talk to me,' he ordered, a muscle twitching in his jaw, warning her that she'd pushed him too far. 'A prig, am I? That's what I get for treating you properly, is it? For treating you with respect and concern. But you don't care for that, do you? You despise good manners. To you they're a sign of weakness in a man. You'd rather I treat you roughly – like Hamish.' And to her astonishment he seized her by the elbows, jerking her off her feet and into his arms. His kiss was hot, punishing and unenjoyable, his teeth clashing against her own. But his nearness was something else. She loved the smell of his clothes, of his skin, his long fair hair on her face and the sureness of his hands under her arms.

'Callum?' She said his name with a sense of wonder, eyeing him cautiously as they both came up for air.

'Oh, Maggi,' he groaned, burying his face in her untidy hair.

It should have been all right. It would have been all right. Except she remembered what Hamish had said.

'Let me go.' She wriggled in his embrace, like a cat held against its will, spitting and struggling to be free. 'You don't want me for myself at all. Only because you think I belong to Hamish.'

He blinked at her. This time it was his turn to look astonished. 'What do you mean? What are you talking about?'

'He told me. He said you never want anything unless it is

351

prized by somebody else. And it's true. First it was Bothwell. Now me.'

'And you believed him, did you? Believed what he said.' Taking her by the shoulders, he shook Maggi until her teeth rattled and she felt like a rag doll in his arms, about to faint.

'Callum!' It was Elizabeth who spoke from the doorway, shocked at the scene before her. 'Callum, what are you thinking of? Let go of Maggi at once. What's going on here?'

'Nothing, Mother,' he said through gritted teeth, releasing Maggi so suddenly, her knees buckled and she slumped to the floor, burying her face in her hands. 'Absolutely nothing at all.' And without offering any further explanation, he stormed out, slamming the stable door and making the horses stamp and whinny in fright. Bothwell turned and kicked the door of his stall.

'Maggi.' Elizabeth held out her hands and the girl took them, allowing herself to be hauled to her feet. 'My dear, whatever happened to bring that on? Are you all right?'

Maggi nodded, too beset with conflicting emotions to speak. Elizabeth stared after Callum, shaking her head.

'I've never seen him like that before. Callum was never one for losing his temper, not even when he was small. Had it been Hamish now . . . But what happened? What could have provoked him to –?'

'A misunderstanding,' Maggi croaked. 'Something I shouldn't have said.'

'It's all right, Maggi. You don't have to tell me if you don't want to. But my son needn't think he's heard the last of this. His behaviour was unforgiveable, whatever you said.'

Maggi was suffering from mixed feelings herself. The kiss had been clumsy, born of his rage. But why should it feel so right? As if she belonged there in Callum's arms. Why, when it was Hamish she loved? Or did she? Dismayed by the fickle nature of her own heart, she tried to dismiss the incident and forget it. But she couldn't. In the quietest moments and when she least expected it, she would remember the unexpected sweetness of that embrace; the sureness of his hands, the warmth of his body and the way she felt when he said her name as he buried his face in her hair.

*

Unpacked at last and spread out on Lilias's bed, the dress exceeded Maggi's wildest dreams.

'This is for me? Oh, Lilias, I can't, it just wouldn't be –'

'Don't you dare say it's not suitable,' Lilias cut her short. 'This party's for everyone and I mean you to look your best. I won't have you appearing in anything drab. You are our prima donna, after all.'

'Prima what?'

'Our principal artiste.'

Maggi fingered the cream silk taffeta and matching lace, wishing her fingers were less work-worn, that her nails could be transformed overnight into ladylike pink ovals. When Lilias had promised her a dress, she had expected something plain and fitting to her station as a girl of the servant class. A schoolgirl's party dress – something girlish and high-waisted with puffed sleeves. But this was a ball gown for a lady of fashion, a sophisticated confection with a plunging neckline and a tiny waist. Thoughtfully, Lilias had provided much more than a dress – there was a froth of petticoats and a corset to wear underneath. Maggi held up the corset, pulling a face and shaking her head.

'Sure an' I'm thin as a stick already. Why would I be wearin' a cruel thing like that?'

'Pride must bear a pinch – or so Mrs Hallam always says.' Lilias laughed at Maggi's forlorn expression. 'Of course you must wear a corset to hold your figure in the right place. It pushes up the bosom and cinches the waist.'

After much complaining and swearing on Maggi's part and gales of laughter from Lilias who didn't know the meaning of half the words – fortunate indeed as most of them were from Ginny Luckett – the corset was in place and laced to Lilias's satisfaction.

'It's impossible,' Maggi gasped. 'Lilias, I can't move in this thing. I can't breathe, let alone sing.'

'Relax. You'll get used to it.'

'Never. And I won't be able to eat a thing.'

'Ladies aren't supposed to eat very much.'

'Now I know why. But Lilias, all that lovely, lovely food.' Sighing, Maggi stepped into the hooped petticoat, tied the

353

tapes at her waist and wriggled impatiently as Lilias played lady's maid and hooked her into the dress.

'Be still, Maggi,' she grumbled. 'You're slippery as a fish.'

Turning to look at herself in the full-length cheval mirror, she found it hard to believe the young lady looking back was indeed herself. Featherbrained as she was for most of the time, Lilias couldn't be faulted for her taste. The cream of the silk flattered Maggi's colouring without detracting from the vibrant colour of her hair. The skirt was composed of three tiers of silk taffeta which rustled as she moved and each of the tiers was trimmed with heavy embroidery and fine lace. It was a beautiful dress, fit for a debutante, and Maggi had never possessed anything so lovely in the whole of her life. Her waist hauled in to a mere nineteen inches, seemed impossibly small and, as Lilias promised, the corset lifted her bosom, giving the impression that she was better endowed than she was. There was also a wide lace collar attached to the scooped neckline which somehow managed to stay in place without slipping off her shoulders.

'I look – oh, I don't look like meself at all,' Maggi faltered, for once at a loss for words.

'Yes, you do. Your very best self. What shall we do with your hair?' She frowned at Maggi's tangled mane, which refused to be tamed. 'We can't just let it hang.'

'A bun?'

'Ringlets, I think.' It was Elizabeth who spoke. She had slipped into the room unnoticed while the girls were absorbed with Maggi's reflection. 'Not that you don't look quite lovely as you are, but ringlets would make a nice change. It is a gala occasion, after all.' She frowned slightly, her head on one side. 'I have but one reservation. That neckline might be just a little too revealing.'

'Oh, Mother, no,' Lilias wailed.

'It's Maggi's first party and we don't want her to give the wrong impression,' Elizabeth insisted. 'I brought some gloves that might match and I thought this might add the final touch.' She flung a fine, oriental silk shawl across Maggi's shoulders.

The cream of the shawl matched the colour of the dress exactly and it was embroidered with a design of orange

354

chrysanthemums and green leaves.

'It's lovely.' Tears pricked Maggi's eyes as she touched the fabric, her roughened fingers catching a little in the fine silk. 'But, Mrs MacGregor, I can't possibly.'

'Yes, you can, because it's only a loan.' Elizabeth hugged her. 'It was a gift from my husband so I can't part with it. But it'll be nice for you to give it an airing.'

Maggi was still smiling when she passed through the kitchens on her way back to the stables. Seeing her, Mrs Hallam sniffed, having heard all about Maggi's dress and the excitement it had created.

'Yes, an' if you'll take my advice, young lady, you'll not let all this attention go to your head. You're still a servant in this house, remember. No more to the family than we are. For all Miss Lilias makes such a pet of you, dressin' you up in fine clothes.'

'It's only because she wants me to sing for her guests.'

'Sing, is it? Whatever for? I dunno why they set so much store by your caterwauling. What about me, then? Who gives a toss about me? Bakin' meself to a frazzle in front o' the stove all day. I don't get no new dress, do I? No.'

Maggi didn't wait to hear any more. Life was good again and she wouldn't let even Mrs Hallam's jealousy dampen her spirits. Not today.

Chapter Twenty-Six

'So what are you saying? You're still punishing me? I'm still
to be banished from your bed?'

'It's not to punish you, Hamish. I wish you wouldn't think
of it like that.' While Maggi was talking, she was fastening
Nero's girth.

'Come out and talk to me properly,' he said. 'I can't see
you, hiding behind the horse.'

Reluctantly, she came out to face him. It was no accident
that she had given him this news while they were saddling
Nero. She knew he wouldn't shout or do anything to startle
his horse.

'But Maggi, why? I thought all our differences were behind
us?'

'They are. There's no reason why we shouldn't be friends.
It's just that I –'

'I want us to be more. I love you, Maggi, surely you know
that?'

'Do I? I could have done with the words of love before,
Hamish. Now I'm thinkin' they come too late.'

'Of course it isn't too late!' Frown lines appeared between
his brows, telling her he was losing patience fast. Hamish
was used to getting his own way. 'So what do you want from
me, Maggi? What can I say to put things right between us –
to get us back where we were before?'

'I'm not sure I want to be back where we were before.'

'I see.' He nodded, folding his arms. 'I see where all this is
leading. You're going to starve me out; force the issue and
get me to marry you.'

'I've already refused an offer to force you, Hamish. I don't want to push you into anything. Least of all a marriage you don't want.'

Nero was snorting, feeling the tension between them, and Maggi broke off to calm him, patting his neck and whispering reassurance.

'Leave him alone and talk to me!'

'I am. I can't help it if you don't like what I say. I have my pride, Hamish. And I can't keep my pride and take you back to my bed.'

'Your pride!'

'You'd better go.' She twitched her lips into a small tight smile as she handed him Nero's reins. 'Remember the Maitlands. Won't do to keep them waiting.'

'Do them good. Harley's a stuffed shirt and Constance is a bore.' He sighed, seeing Maggi's raised eyebrows. 'Well, they are. I'd like to see how much time Lilias would give them if they weren't so filthy rich. All right,' he responded to her shooing, 'I'll go. If I don't that fool of a coachman will probably miss the track. He took them almost to the border last time before he woke up.'

'Go, then. Stop wasting time.'

'This isn't the end of it, Mags. I'm not done with you, yet. We'll talk about it some more when I get back.'

'Hamish, really, there's nothing –' She paused as she realised he wasn't listening. He vaulted into the saddle, giving Nero such a kick that the big grey leaped towards the open stable door as if he'd been stabbed. Maggi had to flatten herself against the doorpost to avoid being knocked to the ground. She stared after them, hands on her hips and shaking her head. Hamish was leaning forward, riding low over the horse's neck as Nero pounded the earth, kicking up lumps of mud as he galloped away.

The truth was that she was just as confused about her feelings as he was. The physical attraction remained, yes. The sight of Hamish riding in on Nero could still make her heart turn in her chest. But she was no longer blindly, hopelessly in love. While she loved him, she wasn't at all sure that she liked him and the more she learned of his character, the more this view was reinforced. Her feelings for Callum were

357

just as difficult to fathom. She pressed her fingers to her lips, remembering that one kiss which had gone so wrong. It was all too much to cope with, too much to bear. If she wasn't sure of her own feelings, what chance did she have of understanding theirs? So she decided for the moment to do nothing; to make no sudden moves.

Mrs MacGregor also was giving her cause for concern. While Lilias bloomed, her mother looked pale and strained, lacking in vitality. In a quiet moment she confided to Maggi that she was worried about her sons and that it upset her to see they were at each other's throats again, just as she had been hoping they might have outgrown it. Maggi listened, feeling guilty about the part she herself might have played in fanning the flames. Meanwhile, Lilias sailed through the days in a cloud of lavender water and smiles, blissfully unaware of the undercurrents and absorbed in the preparations for her betrothal which was to be announced at the party after the Spring Races. She was already wishing the days away. While the engagement was common knowledge in Melbourne, it had yet to announced to the MacGregors' nearest neighbours and friends.

With the racing and the party less than a week away, Sarah Hallam was baking as fast as she could place pies in the oven. House guests would need food and her own cakes and pastries must take pride of place at the party after the races; the event of the year, overshadowing even Christmas at Lachlan's Holt.

In the midst of all these culinary activities, Maggi tried to slip in for her supper unnoticed. The kitchen was in an uproar – a broken bowl on the floor, Mrs Hallam screaming at Cassie who was in tears. Not wishing to be drawn into their argument, Maggi cleared herself a space on one corner of the kitchen table and helped herself to mutton stew from a pot hanging over the fire. She took a chunk of bread from the crock, not surprised to discover it wasn't fresh.

'Can I do anything? Want any help?' She offered, munching on the bread and hoping the answer would be no.

'Help? What can you do? You'd be no more help than stupid Cassie.' And Mrs Hallam shot her kitchen maid a look of such malice that the girl threw her apron over her head and fled to hide herself in a corner of the pantry, her renewed sobs floating back to them. 'See what I mean? Tears. Broken dishes. Useless. Totally useless in a crisis. I don't suppose you can cook?'

'No.' Maggi shook her head. She didn't say that for the greater part of her childhood, food had been so scarce that it didn't matter how it was cooked.

'Shut your face an' let us get on with it, then,' Mrs Hallam said rudely. She was under far too much pressure to be civil. 'Oh, yes. I've done the lion's share of the cookin' for this turn ever since Mrs MacGregor started it. I suppose I'll go on doin' it 'til I turn me toes up an' go to me grave.'

'But all this – this baking.' Maggi waved a hand at the rows of pies, waiting to be glazed and put in the oven. 'It seems an awful lot for one person to do.'

'Oh, it isn't so bad.' It was surprising how Mrs Hallam's temper improved when she thought she had a sympathetic ear. 'Cassie can chop up some more vegetables soon as she's over the sulks.' She glanced at the pantry door. 'Time was when the missus used to lend us a hand. Don't think she's up to it these days.'

'No.' Maggi frowned, reminded that Elizabeth was looking far from well. 'Why not see Callum about it? I'm sure he wouldn't mind getting you some help.'

'Ho, no thanks. Not after the last French chef – so-called. Burned jam all over me stove an' couldn't have turned a hand to make pastry to safe his life. An' d'ye know, while my back was turned, he polished off the last of our vintage port. Should've known that great red nose of his wasn't for nothing. No, Maggi. If that's the sort of help I get, I'd sooner do without.'

She nodded, chewing through her meal which wasn't up to Mrs Hallam's usual standard, the meat tough and floating in a watery gruel which tasted mainly of salt. A sample of Cassie's cooking, she supposed. But she listened, nodding from time to time, which was all Mrs Hallam needed to keep up her one-sided conversation. 'You'll see. There'll be food enough on the day when the pubkeepers come from Beechworth an' set up their tents. All the beer and vittles you could wish for – pedlars with toffee apples, pies for the hoi-polloi. But I'm a'thinking of Mrs MacGregor and her guests. I take a pride in the food we set on the table here at Lachlan's Holt.'

'And you do all this by yourself? Every year?'

'Without fail. In good times or bad. The mistress wouldn't dream of letting her charities down.'

'Charities?'

'Yes, silly. Who did you think it was for?'

Maggi shrugged. 'Lilias's betrothal, I suppose.'

'That's just the occasion this time. An' it's *Miss* Lilias to you. Mrs MacGregor started the race meetings after the big floods – can't remember the year. Soft-hearted, she is. Likes to do her bit for the widows and orphans. Become a tradition now – an annual event – people look forward to it. A full day's racin' an' a big party after on Saturday night. Folks come from miles around.'

Maggi nodded, waiting for her to go on.

'An' if you're sittin' there waitin' for Cassie to wash your dishes, you'll have a long wait. She'll be in there howlin' for hours.'

'I'll do them.' Maggi stood up.

'Not that I mind the extra work.' Mrs Hallam blew ineffectually at a lock of grey hair which had fallen out of her cap, obscuring one eye. 'I like guests – 'specially when it's the Maitlands. Miss Constance is a lovely girl, no trouble at all. An' as for her brother, Mister Harley – well, he's a real gentleman. Never forgets to leave a nice "thank you" in good hard cash when he leaves.'

Maggi smiled, amused that Mrs Hallam should judge a person's character by the size of the tip he would leave.

'What's she like then, this Constance? Lilias talks about her all the time but she's never . . .'

'Pretty enough.' Mrs Hallam shrugged. 'But she's shy. You know Miss Lilias, not likely to pick a friend who's goin' to stand in her light. Miss Constance is a serious sort of girl. Time was when we thought Callum would make a go of it with her.' And she paused, glancing at Maggi to make sure her words would have the maximum effect. 'But nothin' came of it. Now we're thinkin' she's sweet on young Hamish instead.'

Maggi's heart gave a sickening lurch. While she was still unsure of her own feelings for Hamish, she wasn't ready to hear she had a rival in Lilias's best friend; a rich girl, so much more eligible than herself.

'Why should I care if she's sweet on Hamish or not?' She spoke more sharply than she intended. 'What's it to me?'

'What indeed?' Mrs Hallam smiled into her mixing bowl as she concentrated on kneading her pastry, gratified by the girl's reaction to her gossip.

Leaving her dishes unwashed, Maggi headed for the door. 'I must get back to the stables.'

'What's your hurry? You haven't had your sweet.' Mrs Hallam watched her thoughtfully, sucking a hollow tooth. 'Bit of apple pie goin' beggin' if you want it?'

'No, thanks. I'm full up.'

'If you was to ask me, you're lookin' a bit peaked.' Mrs Hallam peered at her. 'Not sickenin' for anythin', are you? Hope not. You'll have your hands full when the visitors get here – everyone wantin' in an' out all the time. An' there's the Maitlands' coach an' four.'

'A coach and four? Nobody's told me to expect a coach and four. But won't the coachman take care of that?'

'Wouldn't count on it.' Mrs Hallam smirked. 'You haven't seen Mister Moxton. Thinks he's a cut above the rest of us. A professional coachman, he calls himself, not a groom. Very partic'lar about what he will an' won't do.'

'So am I.' Maggi stuck out her chin and straightened her shoulders, ready to do battle with Moxton even before he arrived. 'If Mrs MacGregor asks me to look after the coach an' four, then I will. Otherwise Mister Moxton can do for himself.'

'Hoity!' said Mrs Hallam as Maggi headed for the door. 'And don't go bangin' . . .' She raised her eyes to heaven as the request came too late. Maggi had already slammed it. 'The draught'll put paid to my scones!'

With the Maitlands' arrival imminent, Maggi didn't go to bed at her usual time. Instead, she occupied herself by preparing stalls for the visitors' horses and wasn't all that

361

surprised when Elizabeth joined her after supper, praising her work.

'It's just wonderful, Maggi, the difference you've made here.' She looked around at the collection of supple leathers and polished tack. 'I'd not be ashamed to invite the Governor himself to come in here.'

Even the oil lamps were shining brightly. Maggi had dismantled them one by one to wash the flues and free them of dark, oily grime and polished the brass reflector plates to make them give twice the light. A light bright enough, as it happened, to let her see how tired and haggard Elizabeth looked. Slender before, she was now fragile and suffered from shortness of breath. A vital, energetic woman had left for Melbourne and only her shadow had returned. She had aged ten years in the few months she had been away. Maggi was puzzled by this deterioration which seemed to go unnoticed by everyone else. At the risk of being told to mind her own business, she asked Elizabeth if she were ill, expecting a vehement denial. Elizabeth sighed instead.

'Oh, dear. I was hoping it didn't show. Is it so obvious, Maggi?'

'Maybe only to me. Because I'm so fond of you.'

'And my own children aren't?' Elizabeth smiled gently.

'Oh, no, I didn't mean it to sound like that.' Maggi paused. 'I lost my own mam, you see. I knew she was ill but I didn't want to face up to it. I thought if I ignored the signs, refusing to see it, then maybe she wasn't so sick, after all.'

'Lilias is young. She's to be married soon. She has so much else to think about.'

'No, she doesn't. Everything's being done for her while she's away.'

'Do I detect a note of criticism, Maggi? A little envy?'

'No, I don't think so.' She frowned, examining her feelings and wondering if it was true. Did she envy Lilias her orderly, pampered life? She pulled out a stool and brushed the straw from it, inviting Elizabeth to sit down. 'Tell me. Tell me about your illness, if it will help?'

'I'm not sure that it will.' Elizabeth ventured a small smile. 'Maybe I'm a bit like you – hoping that if I ignore the symptoms, they'll go away.'

'What symptoms?'

'My heart. I had a few pains, you see. I put them down to indigestion but I did see a doctor while I was in Melbourne.' She was doing her best to sound matter-of-fact about it but Maggi sensed her distress. 'He says I've had a small attack – nothing serious as yet but it's a warning. I could go on for years if I take things easy and get plenty of rest. If not . . .' She shrugged. 'And on top of that worry, there's Sir Athelstane – our nearest neighbour, you know. He's been buying up everything. Now he's at me to sell him Lachlan's Holt.'

'But you wouldn't do that?'

'I don't know. I've not even mentioned it to the boys. But sometimes I wonder if it might not be better to sell up instead of leaving them tied to the station and to each other. Perhaps it would be better to sell the place, split the money between them and let them go.'

'But they love Lachlan's Holt. Both of them. And where would you go?'

'I don't know.'

By now Maggi was kneeling at the woman's feet, holding both her hands. 'And you've kept all these worries to yourself?'

'Yes, until now.'

'They should know you're unwell. All of them. Callum, Hamish and Lilias too – you'll need their support. An' if you're not goin' to tell them, I will.'

'No, Maggi, please. I don't want them to start treating me as an invalid. Peering at me as if they expect me to fall down dead any minute. I want to lead a normal life for as long as I can. And this time is for Lilias. I want no clouds on her horizon; nothing to mar her happiness now.'

There was no time for further discussion as one of the farm dogs began barking outside. This set off the others, heralding the arrival of the coach. Elizabeth carried a lamp outside, raising it as a beacon for her visitors. Maggi followed, meaning to watch from the shadows. Shocked and upset by Elizabeth's news, she didn't want to see anyone until she had come to terms with it.

Nero pounded into the yard ahead of the coach. Hamish sprang to the ground and gave Maggi the reins, expecting

363

her to lead him away. Not wanting to miss the arrival of the coach, she started walking him instead, to let him cool down.

The coach arrived with its matched four, colourful as a scene from a Christmas card – all that was missing was the snow. In a top hat and with his many-collared cloak flapping, the coachman was hauling on the reins yelling,'Whoa! Whoa!' and less acceptable expressions under his breath. He pulled up the team outside the open stable door and from what Maggi could see of him in the darkness, he was just as florid and full of himself as Mrs Hallam had said.

On hearing the coach arrive, Lilias and Callum came out of the house to greet the visitors. The door of the coach opened and a young man alighted. He was dressed in a heavy winter coat over a tweed suit – country clothes chosen by a man from the city. He turned to hand down his companion, a young lady who put Maggi in mind of a young Queen Victoria, if only from the pictures she'd seen.

'Connie! Oh, Connie, you're here!' Squealing like a school-girl, Lilias hurled herself into her friend's arms, for the moment ignoring the young man who was frowning slightly at this noisy display of emotion. Pale and weary after her long journey, the girl submitted to Lilias's embrace although she appeared to be looking for someone else. She had beautiful eyes – doe-like brown eyes with long lashes; her best claim to beauty, Maggi thought.

Constance's gaze settled at last on Callum and colour suffused her cheeks. She released Lilias who promptly offered her cheek to Harley. Constance held out her hands to Callum, closing her eyes and offering her lips to be kissed. Maggi could see none of the shyness Mrs Hallam had mentioned. Callum accepted the outstretched hands, giving them a little shake to make her open her eyes, his mouth scarcely touching the proffered lips.

'Welcome to Lachlan's Holt, my dear,' he said, clearly doing his best to sound much older, like an uncle. 'And Harley, too. What a pleasure to see you both again.'

The doe-like eyes reproached him for the formality of his greeting. 'Oh, I assure you, Callum, the pleasure is all mine.' She had just the sort of voice Maggi expected her to have.

Breathy and with a cultivated lisp. 'I think you've grown more handsome than I remember.'

While Elizabeth and Hamish joined in the general greetings and queries about the journey, Maggi led Nero away to the stables. Waiting for her there was the Maitlands' coachman. Tired and dusty after his journey, he wasn't inclined to be civil.

'Someone to talk to at last – an' not before time. Things are pretty slack around here. Where's the groom?'

'I am the groom,' Maggi snapped. 'Moxton, isn't it? What can I do for you?'

'Rub down the team, o' course, an' get them some feed. An' it's *Mister* Moxton to you, cheeky.'

'And Miss McDiarmit to you,' she answered with equal dignity. 'Well, Mister Moxton. I've saved the big stall at the end for your team – they should be comfortable there. You can get them settled and rub them down while I go for the feed.'

The man's eyes narrowed to become a pair of glittering slits. 'I'm a coachman, dammit. Not a groom. I don't rub down –'

'Why not?' said Maggi, pretending innocence. 'Did nobody show you how?'

'Why you – you little –' the coachman spluttered, going brick red with fury.

'Don't upset yourself, Mister Moxton,' she said sweetly. 'It's not good for a man of your age.'

And she turned on her heel, leaving him speechless and gasping like a fish, the bubble of his dignity neatly pricked.

Chapter Twenty-Seven

Awake early as usual, Maggi looked out from her window high over the stables, surprised to see how many people there were already, swarming all over MacGregor land. Land which only yesterday had lain empty apart from the odd flock of sheep. Overnight an assortment of booths and tents had sprouted like mushrooms around the piece of ground which had been marked out as the race course and the scene resembled a travelling carnival.

One by one the members of the family rose and went out, Callum driving the MacGregors' sturdy, four-wheeled buggy, Lilias and Constance behind, facing the horses and Harley perched on the box beside him. Smiling and attractive, their faces flushed with excitement, the two girls looked well in their new bonnets trimmed with silk ribbons and flowers, colourful shawls thrown around their shoulders to protect them against the wind which was cold for all it was supposed to be spring. Hamish had ridden out early on Nero, and Elizabeth, smart and dignified in her best burgundy-coloured riding habit and matching top hat, was last to leave. She was irritated when Maggi asked her if she was sure she was well enough to go.

'Of course I'm well enough, Maggi. Don't fuss.'

'I'm not fussing, Mrs MacGregor, it's just that you look so pale. You will let me know if you start to feel tired?'

'I'm not going to feel tired,' she hissed, glancing around to make sure they weren't overheard. 'I'll have plenty of time to feel tired next week when the party's all over. And if you're going to stand over me like a nursemaid, Maggi, I shall be sorry I told you about my illness at all. Now you can see why I don't want people to know.'

Maggi nodded, shrewd enough to realise that Elizabeth was having a bad day. Her mouth was pinched against incipient pain and her face scored with deep lines from nose to mouth. In other circumstances, she would have stayed in bed. To suggest she did so now would only irritate her further. So Maggi brought out Roma, her gentle mare, and helped Elizabeth into the saddle. The formal riding habit called for a side saddle which she knew would tire Elizabeth even more. Maggi adjusted the saddle to make it as comfortable as she could. Sheer determination would have to carry the woman through the day as she played the part of the gracious hostess, mingling with neighbours and friends. Maggi watched her slow progress on the mare, hoping her strength would hold out over the long day ahead.

The day before, Patrick Hegarty, together with some men hired from Beechworth, had cleared rocks and obstacles from the ground chosen for the course and constructed a rough rail to mark out the boundaries. In addition they put up a covered stand for some of the spectators, opposite the winning post.

Clouds scudded across the sky, threatening the odd shower, but most people agreed the day was set to be fair. The first race was scheduled for noon and the races would continue every two hours for the rest of the day.

Maggi went out to the paddock to capture one of the stockhorses and took him back to the stables to look for a saddle. With nobody left at the homestead but herself and Mrs Hallam, she wanted to leave before that lady captured her and prevailed on her good nature to make her stay behind and help to set out the food for the coming guests. Cassie had already made her escape. Maggi had seen her running towards the racecourse, her best red shawl flapping about her shoulders and laughing like a child with one of the Hegarty boys attached to each hand.

Maggi had just saddled up and was about to ride out when she heard someone arrive on horseback outside and dismount, pausing to secure his horse to the rail outside. She leaned out of the stall, trying to see who it was.

'Maggi?' It was Hamish, calling softly, 'Maggi, are you still here?'

'Yes, but I won't be for long.' She came out of the stall, arms folded, ready to do battle if necessary. 'What is it, Hamish? What do you want?'

'No need to be edgy – I won't eat you, Mags. I just came to remind you, you're entered as my rider in race three.'

'On Nero?'

'Come on, Mags. You can't have forgotten?'

'But you haven't mentioned it for days. I was thinkin' you'd changed your mind.'

'Why should I? Just because we don't see eye to eye about our relationship doesn't mean –'

'We don't have a relationship.'

'Yes and whose fault is that?'

'I don't want to argue, Hamish. Not today.'

'Nor do I. I just want you to do as you promised and ride Nero for me in race three.'

'I can't. Girls aren't allowed to compete, Patrick Hegarty says. They'll turn me away.'

'No, they won't. Not if you keep your mouth shut and hide your hair under a hat.'

'Oh no, I'm not doin' that again.'

'I put you down as M. McDiarmit, that's all. You could be a Martin or a Michael for all they know.'

'Hamish, I can't. I won't. Besides, Nero isn't used to me any more. We haven't worked together in weeks.'

'Rubbish. He knows what to do. All you have to do is stay on.'

'Fine. If it's so easy, ask somebody else.'

'I don't want anyone else, I want you. I've got a hundred pounds riding with you, right on the nose.'

'Then more fool you, Hamish MacGregor, to part with your money so easily. You should have made sure of me first.'

'That's what I'm doing now. Oh, Maggi, please. Do me this one favour. For old times' sake.' As he crowded her into the stall, she felt her temper rise. Did he think she could be so easily bought? With a few compliments and hastily spoken words of love?

368

'Hamish, listen to me.' She was dangerously quiet. 'Whatever you say, whatever you promise, the answer is no.'

'Ah, you don't mean it, Maggi. And I still love the way you say Hamissh. Nobody says it quite the way you do.'

'I'm not sure of Nero, either. Hegarty says he's not used to crowds. He's a good night horse but he may be too unstable and skittish to take part in a race.'

'Hegarty! What does he know? Nero isn't nervous, he's a stockhorse, for God's sake. You've seen him in action yourself.'

'Yes. Trying to run you into a tree.'

'He's a bit mischievous, that's all.'

'Mischievous? Downright dangerous, I call it. How do I know he won't shy at the crowd? Pitch me over the railings an' break me neck?'

'He won't. You're a better horsewoman than that. Ah, well.' He shrugged, watching her under his eyelashes. 'I must say I'm surprised. I wouldn't have taken you for a coward, Maggi.'

'I'm not.' She rose to the bait for a moment and then she laughed. 'Time was when you could have caught me with a cheap taunt like that. I'm wiser now. Learn to accept when you're beaten, Hamish, an' give in with good grace.' And giving him no chance to put forward any more arguments, she vaulted on to the stockhorse and pushed past him, calling back over her shoulder as she headed for the door, 'Are you with me or not? We don't want to miss the first race.'

'To hell with the first race!'

Since dawn the innkeepers and piemen had been arriving from miles around to set up their stalls and tents, expecting to make a lot of money from the crowds. Tipsters and gypsies appeared on the scene as if by magic, strange and outlandish in their colourful clothes and adding to the carnival atmosphere as they moved through the crowd.

Maggi also rode through the crowds, far less at ease than she thought she would be and feeling shabby in her muddy riding boots and workaday clothes. Thanks to Hamish's arrival, she hadn't even taken the time to pull a comb

369

through her hair, let alone change. Every other woman was dressed to the limit of her resources and sported a new hat if not new clothes. Even Molly Hegarty, her arm linked in Patrick's, was wearing her best Sunday black. She called after Maggi with a smile and a wave.

'Exciting, isn't it?'

Maggi smiled and nodded but she didn't join them. With Cassie in charge of the children for once, the Hegartys could have the day to themselves.

For a while, she was bemused by the size of the crowd, not having seen so many people gathered in one place since she left the city. Not many were on foot. As most of the racegoers had come in carriages, carts or on horseback, most of them were riding or driving up or down, greeting neighbours and friends, exchanging pleasantries with those they may not have seen since this time last year.

Hamish kept Maggi in sight, following her at a distance, as yet unwilling to say farewell to his hundred pounds. His hundred pounds which might yet become a thousand if Maggi could be persuaded to change her mind. Irritating as she was, he had to admire her for taking a stand. This new, independent Maggi excited him as never before; she intrigued him much more than Maggi tearful and lovelorn. Perversely, the more she tried to ignore him and keep him at arm's length, the more he desired to have her back in his bed. Like most men, Hamish enjoyed the thrill of the chase.

It wasn't difficult to keep her in plain sight. That cloud of unruly red curls shone out like a beacon. Other girls might be more beautiful, better dressed, yet Maggi made them seem colourless and insipid, hiding under their discreetly flowered hats. He saw her pause to exchange a few words with Lilias and Constance, before moving on. Lilias practically fell out of the buggy, trying to get Maggi to stay, but she smiled, made her excuses and rode away. Hamish was about to kick Nero into a canter and ride after her but he was hailed by a well-dressed, middle-aged man on an overweight hunter. He groaned but there was nothing for it but to pause and pass the time of day. It was Sir Athelstane Gurney, their nearest neighbour, whose lands lay adjacent to their own. Hamish couldn't avoid him without being rude.

370

'Good day to you, young feller! Fine day for it, eh?'

Hamish nodded, hoping to be brief and get away. Full of ponderous self-importance, Sir Althelstane was a well-known bore. He was a handsome man whose even, patrician features gave him an air of being intelligent and fair-minded; an impression enhanced by a leonine mane of silver hair. In fact he had none of these attributes and his smile today also belied his true nature. Although he had twice the land of the MacGregors he was ever greedy for more, forever disputing boundaries and erecting fences without telling his neighbours. He even went so far as to annexe MacGregor Creek, insisting it was on his land, which led to a rare event of another kind. The MacGregor brothers joined forces for once to get it back. Neither of them had any time for this man. It was one of the few things on which Callum and Hamish agreed. Both despised men of wealth who were graziers in name only and because they owned vast tracts of land. Exiles, city dwellers who grabbed the profits from their country properties while spending as little time in the country as possible, having no real love of the land. All these thoughts churned through Hamish's mind as he tipped his hat, hoping to pass the time of day and move on.

'Sir Athelstane,' he said, trying to avoid the man's gaze. But he wasn't to escape so easily.

'Excellent turn out – excellent. Your mother must be well pleased.'

'Yes, sir. No doubt she is.'

'And that's a fine-looking grey you have there, quality horse. Part Arab, I'd say, except he's so big.'

'Maybe.' Hamish shrugged, hoping to kill the conversation and get away. Sir Athelstane had other ideas. He frowned, consulting his race card.

'Wait a minute. This is your Nero, eh? You have him down for the third race?'

'That's right, sir.'

'Close-mouthed young feller, aren't you? Don't give much away. Worth a pound or two on the nose, is he? What d'ye say?'

'Maybe. There's a lot of good horses in that race, sir.'

'Yes, but there's not so many as big as he is and strong

371

enough to go the distance. Who's this jockey of yours – McDiarmit? Can't say the name rings a bell. A professional, is he?'

'I'm sorry, sir, I – you must excuse me.' And Hamish cantered away leaving the older man staring after him, blinking at his rudeness. Used to being courted for a few moments of his time, Sir Athelstane was piqued to be treated with such scant respect. And there was something else that now niggled at the back of his mind – some superstitious nonsense from his men. Cattle duffers. Cattle duffers led by a man on a big grey phantom of a horse . . .

But so far as Hamish was concerned, Sir Athelstane was forgotten. Kicking Nero into a canter, he set off again after Maggi. He had one last trick up his sleeve. His last chance of saving the day.

The first race wasn't meant to be taken seriously and offered only a token purse. A mixed bag of horses and riders lined up to take part. Farmers, middle-aged shopkeepers and teenaged boys, mounted on short-legged, overweight ponies. All the same they thought themselves fine fellows. Stockmen if only for a day. They went riding off to the gate like experienced hands, whooping and waving their hats at the crowd as they wasted energy, stretching their ponies to the limit even before the start. People sang out to them, cracking jokes as they rode past.

'Garn! A three-legged donkey's goin' to run faster than that, Tom!'

'Be lucky to get that ole nag past the post at all.'

'Where'd you win yours from, Fred? The knacker's yard?'

The race was run in the midst of a lot of good-natured teasing, the winner a skinny, teen-aged boy. Unused to attracting so much attention, he blushed to the roots of his sandy hair as Elizabeth presented him with his ribbon and purse.

'Thank you, Mrs MacGregor,' he whispered, too shy to make a proper speech. Something in his manner reminded Maggi of her brother. So involved had she been in her own affairs, she hadn't thought of Tully in weeks. Callum must have news of the *Sally* by now. Why hadn't he said anything?

372

Conscience-stricken, she was determined to find him and ask him, right here and now. It was easy to pick out the Mac-Gregors' buggy – Lilias's pretty parasol was like an orange flag, standing out in the crowd. But this time she was alone, being driven by Harley. Callum and Constance were nowhere to be seen.

Maggi found a few coins in her pocket and bought a toffee apple from a pedlar who was pushing his way through the crowd with a tray. It was delicious; the toffee brittle and the apple sweet. She munched it greedily and leaned forward to give the core to her horse. There was a booth with a perform-ing puppet show, attracting children and adults alike. She dismounted for a moment and stood watching, cheering and jeering with the little ones at the antics of demons and angels until her horse became restless and anxious to move on.

The runners lined up for the second race. No shopkeepers' ponies this time. Nothing but quality bloodstock. Dainty, high-stepping mares, their riders colourful in their tight-fitting trousers, silk shirts and brightly coloured caps. The finish was so close that a heated argument between the two riders ensued, resulting in the race being declared a tie.

As the afternoon wore on, it was almost time for the third and last race. Maggi had been careful to avoid Hamish, wanting no further argument about the race. She saw Con-stance walking beside Elizabeth who was still mounted on Roma. She was pleased to see her mistress seemed to be bearing up although she was still looking tired. Maggi would have suggested the lady dismount and sit down for a while but she was well aware that Elizabeth wouldn't thank her for drawing attention to her weakness. Before Maggi could ride up to join them, a pair of elderly ladies in a governess cart managed to beat her to it, halting to pass the time of day with their hostess. Maggi could see the effort it cost Elizabeth to remain bright and cheerful as she drew Constance forward to be introduced. The ladies exclaimed and twittered.

'Such a pretty girl is Lilias – your brother must be very proud.'

'We shall expect an invitation to the wedding! Will you be a flower girl?'

Maggi turned her horse and rode away.

373

'There you are! I've been looking for you. Maggi, wait!' She closed her eyes in frustration and muttered a curse. Hamish had caught up with her at last and after she had been so careful to keep out of his way all day. She drew a deep breath, steeling himself to refuse him yet again.

'Let me alone, Hamish. And you can save your breath because the answer is still no. I'm not riding your horse.'

'That's a pity. I'll have to scratch him them.'

She turned and saw he was no longer riding but leading Nero, wincing and favouring his right foot as he lurched across the turf, struggling to catch up with her. 'Land sakes, Hamish, what have you done to yourself?'

'Piece of damned bad luck – you wouldn't read about it. Dismounted for a moment to buy me a beer, fell into a bloody pot hole an' twisted my foot.'

'Drunk on just one beer, Hamish?' Her lips twitched. 'You're losing your touch.'

'Oh, trust you! I wasn't drunk, I tell you. Wouldn't matter if I was – I'm out of the race. Can't even bear any weight on this foot.'

'Do you want me to pull off your boot? If you leave it, the ankle might swell.'

'Too late. It already has. Probably have to cut through the leather to get it off.'

'Oh, Hamish, I am sorry. What a shame.'

'A shame for old Nero, too.' Affectionately, Hamish patted his horse. 'He was all set to win. Looking forward to it as well.'

'All right. All right, I give in. You don't have to go on.'

'What?'

'I'll do it. I'll ride the old brute. Just stop hopping around, looking pathetic. Give him to me.'

'Maggi, you're a real trouper, that's what you are. One out of the box!' A slow grin took over Hamish's face spreading from ear to ear. 'I owe you for this. I'll never forget what you've done for me today.'

'Oh yes you will. Soon as you've got your prize money tucked in your belt.'

'Tell you what – we'll give the whole lot to Mother's charity.'

374

'We haven't won anything yet.'

'But we will!'

'And the money from the bet?' She raised a quizzical eyebrow.

'The bet? Come on, don't let's get carried away.'

'This is against my better judgement, Hamish, and I'm only doing it because you can't ride yourself.'

'I know – I know.' He looked at her under his eyelashes in that special way of his. Her heart lurched and stepped up its beat, mocking all her good resolutions. To cover her confusion she became crisp and businesslike.

'D'ye think you can take this horse back to the stables?' She jumped down and offered the stockhorse. 'If you can heave yourself into the saddle you might ride.'

'Don't worry about me, I'll manage. But go on, Maggi. Quickly, before they say you're too late. The stewards have already called for the riders to be weighed.'

'But –'

'Not now.' He handed her his bright yellow silks with their matching cap. 'Put this on over your clothes. You've no time to change.'

'What shall I say?'

'Nothing. They're expecting you.'

'Oh, are they?' Her smile faded. 'Very sure of me, weren't you, Hamish?'

'Tick me off later – not now. Maggi, do go on. Some of the starters are already mounted and lining up.'

'But, Hamish –'

'Whatever you do, don't let Nero get out in front – he musn't set the pace. Keep him behind the leaders and stay on the outside until you've made the last turn and get into the straight. Don't let them bail you up on the inside or get close enough to upset him. Nero likes plenty of room.'

'I have to be crazy to –' Maggi muttered, pulling on the shirt and stuffing her hair into the jockey's cap. Then she rode over to join the others in the queue to be weighed on a butcher's steelyard which had been brought out for the purpose.

'Good heavens, lad, you're the lightest weight of the lot.' The man shifted the weights, hardly able to believe she could

375

register so little. 'I only hope you're strong enough to control that big feller. Don't want any accidents, do we?'

Maggi narrowed her eyes and said nothing, knowing her voice would give her away if she spoke.

'Nervous, are you?' The steward misinterpreted her silence. 'I'm not surprised. Here.' He attached some weights to her saddle. 'That'll even things up a bit. Watch yourself, lad. There'll be some stiff competition out there.'

It was true. Lining up with the other competitors, Maggi felt more than one or two qualms. She was flanked by horses as big and as fit as Nero, ridden by spare-looking men with a steely look in their eyes. This was the longest race of the day, the major event, and it carried a fat purse. No quarter would be given; there'd be no gentlemanly behaviour, not today. Not with this much at stake. On the outer edge of the field, she thought herself well placed for the start although she knew she would need every ounce of advantage she could get. Looking along the line she saw ten starters in all and realised, with a jolt of surprise, that one of them was Callum, seated on Bothwell. No one had bothered to mention that he would be racing today. He sat easily in the saddle, waiting for the race to begin, his white silks contrasting with the coal black of his horse. His eyes widened a little as he recognised Maggi on Nero and his jaw set, showing her that he didn't approve. It was Callum's attitude that strengthened her resolve. If he didn't want her there, it was just too bad. She'd give all these men a run for their money and do her best to bring Nero in first.

So involved was she in her own thoughts she almost missed the starter's orders and suddenly they were off. Nero leaped out in front of the others, starting wide. Remembering Hamish's instruction, she eased him back, careful not to discourage him or break his stride. Deliberately, she let two other horses pass her on the inside. Then she settled down for the long haul, seeing nothing but a blur of waving hands and faces, open-mouthed and yelling on the other side of the fence. The crowd had become a monster, crying out with a single voice. She saw Elizabeth near the winning post when they passed it the first time and Hamish, cheering her on at his mother's side. Maybe his foot didn't hurt him so much, after all. He must have decided to watch Nero's progress instead of taking the stockhorse back to the stables.

Nero continued, running smoothly and refusing to be put off, even when there was some bumping and jostling while they were on the far side of the course, away from the stewards' eyes. Soon she realised he had it in him to win. Having plenty to spare, Nero was thundering home, while many of the horses around them were beginning to fail and drop back. She made the last turn and came into the final stretch, Nero well out in front, set to be a clear winner, showing the rest of the field a clean pair of heels. The crowd roared its approval, cheering her on. And, as she approached the winning post, she could see Hamish himself at the fence, leaping up and down, yelling and waving his hat in the air. Leaping? Suddenly, her hard won victory turned to ashes as she realised he had deceived her and taken advantage of her once more. He had been determined that she would ride Nero and here she was, his puppet, dancing to his tune yet again. Nothing was the matter with his ankle. Would he be able to jump up and down like that if there was?

All this went through her mind in a matter of seconds. She took the pressure off Nero at once, rising in the stirrups as if the race was already won. With seconds to spare, Callum streaked past her on Bothwell to win by half a length, leaving the rest of the field to finish a poor third. Out of the corner of her eye, Maggi could see Hamish throwing his hat to the ground in temper and crushing it with his foot.

Anxious now to get away as fast as she could, Maggi decided she had seen more than enough of racing for one day. She shrugged, pretending to be too embarrassed to answer any queries and when the weighing was over and the weights returned, she left the field on the pretext of returning Nero to his stable. She wasn't surprised to find Hamish already there, waiting to confront her.

'Why, Maggi? Just tell me why? You had the race in your pocket and you threw it away.'

'You know very well.' She dismounted from Nero and took off his saddle, occupying herself with the needs of the horse, rubbing him down with vigour. 'You tricked me, Hamish. You made a fool out of me.'

377

'Not as big a fool as you made out of me. D'you realise what you've done? You've lost me a thousand pounds.'

'No, it was only a hundred. You wouldn't have had a thousand unless Nero won.'

'He would have done, too. He was going like a beauty. He wanted to win and you cheated him.'

'No more than you cheated me.'

'And Callum of all people. You let Callum pip you to the post.'

'Ah? So we're back to that again are we? The famous MacGregor feud.'

'I'm serious, Maggi. This isn't a joke.'

'No, more's the pity. I wish it were.'

'What are you trying to do to me? Drive me mad?'

She ignored him, humming under her breath to hide her nervousness as she continued to work on the horse. She had seen him lose his temper before but never angry like this. Even Nero was beginning to quiver, taking his cue from Hamish's mood.

'Will you stop scrabbling about with that bloody grooming and pay attention when I'm talking to you.'

She stood on tiptoe to hiss at him over Nero's back, 'Shut up, Hamish. Can't you see you're upsetting your horse?'

'You little bitch. I ought to wring your stiff, arrogant little neck!'

She anticipated his lunge and dodged away, keeping Nero between them, afraid of what he might do if he caught her.

'Stop that, Hamish. Leave Maggi alone.' It was Callum who had come up on them, talking to his brother as if he were still a small boy. This didn't endear him to Hamish who transferred all his pent up rage to Callum instead. Leaving both of them staring after him, Callum led Bothwell to his stall and calmly attended to his horse's comfort before returning to address them again.

'Is it too much to ask that you keep your sordid little squabbles to yourselves for once?' he said. 'We have guests here today.'

'To hell with our guests and with Maggi McDiarmit, too!' Hamish was in no mood to be rational. 'Hell, Callum, you

378

know what this is about. Maggi threw the race. Deliberately threw the race and let you win.'

'Did she?' Callum laughed shortly. 'And I thought I was going so well. I ran a good race and so did she. She mistook the finish, that's all. Easy enough if you don't know the course. Can happen to anyone.'

Hamish gave a snort of derision. 'Oh, yes. You can afford to be gracious and make excuses for her – now that you've won.'

'Hamish, you can't go on blaming Maggi. It isn't her fault.' Callum was trying to cool his brother's temper and make him see reason. 'If you had to be so sure of it, you should've ridden Nero yourself. Why didn't you?'

'I had a hundred dollars on Nero with Timmy O'Rourke – I wanted to be sure the little shyster didn't sneak off without paying.'

'Oh, Hamish.' Callum was smiling ruefully, shaking his head.

'All right, what is it? What's so bloody funny about that?'

'You'd have collected nothing, even if Maggi had won. I saw Timmy O'Rourke and that shifty-eyed sidekick of his – they were packing their bags and leaving before the last race was run.'

'Why didn't you stop them? Say something?'

'And get a knife in the ribs? No thanks,' Callum said. 'No skin off my nose. I'm not a gambling man.'

'You wouldn't be, would you?' Hamish was squinting at his brother, his face twisted with bitterness. 'Not good old reliable Callum MacGregor. Always playing it safe. We can always depend on Callum to do and say the right thing. Not like that worthless brother of his. Don't you ever take a chance, Cal? A single risk in the whole of your boring life?'

'I did. I took a risk once.' Callum's expression was suddenly bleak. 'And because of it, our father died.'

'You killed him. You took him away from me, from Mother, from all of us.' Hamish was lashing out, determined to wound.

'I didn't mean – I –' Callum's face drained of colour.

'Hamish, don't. Don't do this to him.' Maggi sensed that

379

the argument could only get worse. But Hamish wasn't to be silenced.

'You took him from me.' He spoke clearly, driving home his point. 'So I made myself a promise a long time ago. I promised I'd take someone away from you.'

'What do you mean?' Callum whispered, suddenly very still.

'Maggi, of course, who else?' Callum seized her by the arm, literally dragging her into the argument. 'Why did you bring her here, Cal? Out of the kindness of your heart? Because the poor little girl had nowhere else to go? I don't think so. I know how your mind works – what makes you tick. You were waiting for Mother to take her in hand, add a little polish and turn her into a suitable grazier's wife. But I didn't want a wife. I was happy to take her as she was. She was ripe for it, too, so ready to fall in love. Sorry, Cal. Sorry I had to ruin your plans by getting in first.'

'You worm!' Callum spoke softly but he was shaking with suppressed anger. 'And I stood back because I thought you loved her, really cared for someone for once in your life. But you've never cared for anyone or anything, have you? Only your pathetic revenge. Why, you pathetic, sadistic little bastard!'

'That says it all, doesn't it? How you really see me. Always little – always lesser than you.' Hamish put a hand on his brother's chest and shoved. 'Feel that? I'm at least as big as you are and probably tougher, too.'

Goaded beyond endurance, Callum began shoving back.

'Will you stop it! Stop it, the pair of you!' At last Maggi found her voice, although it fluted on the edge of hysteria. 'I'm sick and tired of it, do you hear? Tired of being the meat in the sandwich between you two. Havin' you fight over me like two dogs growlin' over a bone. As if all the decisions are yours and I'm just a thing – a creature who has no say in it. No will of her own.'

'Oh, Maggi. Maggi, I –' Callum started towards her but she held up a hand to stop him. Concern was the last thing she wanted, that would be too much to bear.

'No! I want you out – out of here, both of you! Just get out and leave me alone.'

380

Hamish's shoulders slumped and he stood biting his lips, looking shamed. All the fight had gone out of him and he deeply regretted his words. His tongue had run away with him and he'd spoken without thought. It was Callum he wanted to injure but he'd hurt Maggi instead. Once more she was the victim, caught in the crossfire.

'Maggi.' His voice was no more than a whisper as he shook his head. 'Maggi, it wasn't like that – like I said. Not at all. I didn't mean . . .'

'I know, Hamish, I know,' she sighed. 'You never do.'

'But –'

'Just don't say any more. You'll only make it worse.' She turned her back on both of them and bowed her head. She wanted them to be gone before she gave way to the luxury of tears. Both men shuffled to the door, neither wanting to be last to leave, but she didn't move until she was sure they'd both gone. Even then, she held back her tears. Old habits die hard and she made sure that both Nero and Bothwell were fed and watered and even checked on the Maitlands' four before she climbed the ladder to her attic bedroom and fell face downwards on her bed, the sobs shaking her whole body as she wept as if her heart would break. Never had she felt so alone in the world as she did at this moment. Her parents were dead. Her brother was gone. Elizabeth was desperately ill and Hamish's love for her was only a sham. And Callum? She was too numb with misery to consider her feelings for him. Her last thought before she fell into an exhausted sleep was that still she had been unable to ask him for news of the *Sally Lee*.

Chapter Twenty-Eight

When Hamish rode out that night, he had no idea where he was going and no clear purpose in mind. He knew only that he would be no fit company for Lilias or her friends. While his brother might be sufficiently mature and self-contained to put the quarrel behind him, Hamish could not. Today, for perhaps the first time in his life, he was seeing himself in the wrong. He who had always considered that *he* was the injured party; *he* was the one who had been deprived of his father and wronged. Only now did he realise Callum must feel the loss of their father as keenly as he did and how futile it was to cripple their lives by harking back to that old feud. Lachlan MacGregor had died of a heart attack – everyone said so. His father had had a serious illness which must have overtaken him sooner or later whether he overexerted himself in the water or not. Even his mother said so.

But after the scene which had just taken place he needed some time to himself and the thought of attending a party made him cringe. He was in no mood to smile and make small talk, pay compliments to elderly ladies or dance with his sister's friends.

Today he had succeeded in taking his long-awaited revenge but could he take any pleasure in it? No. He remembered only the stricken expression on Maggi's face. And that wasn't the first time he'd hurt her. But it would probably be the last. This time he had gone too far. Nothing he could say or do would restore her confidence in him now. She would never trust him again and such a thought left him feeling bereft. He didn't know if he was in love with her or not – he had no means of measuring such feelings. But he hadn't set out to seduce her with such cold-hearted purpose as he said. He couldn't pretend his emotions were never involved.

With all these thoughts churning in his mind, Hamish kept riding steadily, hardly aware that the light was fading around him. Soon Lachlan's Holt and its evening of festivities had been left far behind. A true son of the country, he was comforted by the emptiness and silence of the bush, content to be on horseback and out of doors. Tonight there was only a gentle breeze to stir the scent of the wattle and rustle the leaves; the track was easy to follow in the light of a moon which was still almost full.

Without being directed, Nero left the track at the usual place, taking Hamish to the bushmen's camp in the hills overlooking MacGregor Creek. They occupied the piece of no-man's land which had been the subject of the dispute with Sir Athelstane Gurney a few months ago. Only now did it occur to Hamish that in laying claim to MacGregor Creek, Sir Athelstane might have been trying to rid the district of 'undesirables' as he called them. Men who acknowledged no master and who came and went as they pleased, having no visible means of support.

When Hamish rode into camp he found it deserted. Only Pete sat hunched, staring into the flames of a dying fire. A pall of smoke hung in the air, giving off the acrid stink of fat and burning bones; the tell-tale aftermath to a supper of stolen sheep. Pete tensed, peering into the darkness to see who approached, relaxing only when he recognised Nero.

'Blimey, Hames. You didn' half gimme a fright. You never said you was comin' – not tonight. The others is off to Beechworth, some big card game at Maisie's. I can take it or leave it. Not so much of a gambler meself.'

'It's still a full moon, Pete. Don't we always go out when the moon is full?' Unreasonably, Hamish was disappointed to find his friends weren't ready and waiting for him as usual.

'Yes, but we didn't think you'd be comin' tonight. Not with your sister's party an' all.' Pete smiled broadly, showing his ruined teeth. 'Thought you'd have other things on your mind. Like gettin' your fingers up a bit of upper-class Melbourne skirt.'

'Well, I'm not.' Hamish scowled, irritated by the younger man's preoccupation with sex. 'Come on, Pete. What say we catch a few strays on our own? Nice enough night for it. Gully raker's moon.'

'Ooh, I dunno about that.' Pete considered it, rasping the stubble on his chin. 'The others've gone off with all the guns.'

'Guns? What do we want with guns? I've got my whip.'

'Hah! Fat lot of use that'll be if we run into trouble.'

'Why should we run into trouble? We never have before. Besides, the world and his wife's at my sister's party. There won't be any lookouts posted – not tonight. Half a dozen bullocks will never be missed. Let's see. Ten quid a head split two ways – makes us thirty quid for the night. Not a bad pick up for a couple of hours' work.' Shrewdly, Hamish guessed Pete stayed away from the card game not so much because he wasn't a gambler but because he was out of funds.

'You're on.' Pete grinned as he threw some dirt on the camp fire and stamped on it to make sure it was out. 'I'd like to show those bastards I can do well enough on me own. They're always havin' a go at me, sayin' I'm wet be'ind the ears.'

An hour later Hamish and Pete were circling, wondering how to separate a few stragglers from a herd of prime, well-fed cattle. Hamish raised a hand for Pete to keep silent as he edged Nero slowly towards them.

'Blimey, Hames.' Pete was hanging back, shaking his head. 'Better leave this lot alone. They're his breedin' stock – look at the brands. Nobody's goin' to believe they're stewin' beef.'

'I don't care,' Hamish growled, flourishing his whip and riding in to separate a couple of bullocks from the main herd. 'We've found them and we're having them, prime or not.'

Isolating them from their fellows wasn't as easy as he thought. Pete lacked skills and his horse didn't react as quickly as Nero. It might have been easier with a dog but Hamish had come out on the spur of the moment and didn't bring one. He would separate a bullock from the main herd, only to have it dodge past Pete and rejoin it from another direction, disturbing the others and making them noisy and restless, likely to stampede. Hamish cursed softly under his breath, only now seeing how idiotic it was to attempt this with only one other rider; a job which would have been easy with four men or five.

The sudden baying of a dog was a shock to everyone. The cattle took off, crashing away through the bush. Pete's horse started to bolt and Nero reared up in fright, almost spilling Hamish out of the saddle.

'Halt! Halt or I shoot!' a man called to them out of the darkness, firing a shot in the air without waiting for a response. The shooting upset Nero who flattened his ears, snorted and turned to kick his back legs at a hound which came plunging towards them out of the undergrowth. Short, vicious kicks which must have connected as the dog took off, yelping, and didn't return.

'Stand. Stand where you are and with your hands up!' came the order. 'Hands high and you won't get hurt.'

'Don't – don't shoot!' Pete called out to them before Hamish could warn him to keep silent. 'We're unarmed.'

Now he had given away their position, several more shots followed the first, one whistling past Hamish's ear and another volley of shots depriving Pete of his hat.

'Jesus, Hames. They're shootin' for real. They'll bloody kill us.' Pete's voice quavered on the edge of hysteria.

'Nah. Probably only bird shot, trying to scare us off,' Hamish growled. 'Just shut up and ride.'

But by now the men were closing in and their shooting became more accurate. Being a grey, Nero was clearly visible in the moonlight, unlike Pete's dark chestnut which could disappear into the shadows. Nero screamed as shot connected with his hind quarters. This time he was successful in dislodging Hamish and, whinnying in pain and fear, he lurched away into the bush. Hamish lay where he was for a moment, winded and staring after him.

Pete rode close, leaning out of the saddle with the intention of collecting Hamish and swinging him up to ride behind him.

'Come on, Hames. We gotta get outa here.'

'Bastards,' Hamish said. 'Nero will die out there – bleed to death if he doesn't get help.'

'An' they won't think twice about murderin' us. That's not bird shot. Come on, Hames. We have to get out of 'ere. Now!'

'On the one horse? Not a hope. We wouldn't stand a chance.'

'Yes. Get up.'

'No, mate. I got you into this and I'll have to get you out of it. I can hold them off for a while – you ride.'

'No. I ain't leavin'. Not on my own.'

'Suit yourself then. Stick around and see the fun.' Hamish retrieved his whip which had fallen close by and rose to his feet, planting himself squarely in the path of the oncoming riders. He cracked the whip to warn horses and riders alike that he was prepared to use it. The moon illuminated the scene with an eerie, silvery-blue light, making it nightmarish and unreal.

'Hames, are you nuts? Tryin' to get yourself killed. A whip ain't no use against guns!'

Hamish thought about it. Was that true? Was he trying to get himself killed. He didn't know. Only that he was filled with a cold hatred against these men who had made a target of his horse.

'Just stay out of this, Pete.' Hamish bared his teeth and growled, cracking the whip at their pursuers again. There were two of them, both armed with rifles, but seeing what looked like an angry madman in the path before them, they paused to exchange glances, for the first time less than assured.

'Come on. You can come closer than that.' Hamish's smile was a grimace. 'I want to see your faces, you bastards. The faces of brave men who'll shoot down a man's horse.'

'That was an accident –' one of them began.

'Shut up, Tom,' the other cut him off. 'This bastard's in the wrong, not us. You are on land belonging to Sir Athelstane Gurney,' he said to Hamish. 'I'm placing you under arrest. You have committed trespass and been caught in the act of stealin' cattle. Now, are you goin' to put down that

386

whip an' come in like a good lad or do I have to shoot you in the leg?' He fired at the ground close by, illustrating the point.

If Hamish had been in a cold fury before, his temper took over now. In a reflex action to those shots, he cracked the whip again, so that it snaked out viciously clipping the man about the face. He might not have expected his aim to be so accurate and so cruel but it was. Weighted with shot, the whip was designed to be felt through the thick hide of a bullock, never a man's face. The man gave a hoarse scream and dropped his gun. He fell from his horse to the ground, clasping his hands to his lacerated and bleeding face. 'My eyes! Oh God, you've put out my eyes. I can't see.'

Everything happened very quickly after that. Seeing his companion so brutally wounded, the other man panicked, firing shot into Hamish at close range, loading and firing several times. Seemingly impervious to these wounds, Hamish kept coming until he secured his whip firmly about the other man's waist, hauling him from the saddle to land with a sickening thump on the ground. Thick-set as he was and of middle years, the man couldn't take such a fall without breaking some bones and he lay there, groaning, unable to get up.

'Help me,' he whimpered. 'I can't move. I think you've broken my back –'

Hamish's answer to this was to land him another crack of the whip, making him roar.

'Hamish! For God's sake, stop!' It was Pete, his voice breathless with shock. 'Jesus an' Mary, what have you done? One man blinded – another crippled. And, ah, God love us, look at yourself. You're wounded all over the place an covered in blood.'

'Nobody . . .' Hamish coughed, realising his face was damaged and his mouth had filled with the coppery taste of his own blood. 'Nobody hurts my horse –' And he succumbed to his injuries at last, pitching forward and landing full on his face, losing consciousness as he hit the ground.

Maggi awoke to the sounds of music and revelry coming from the house. She knew she must have slept long into the evening. She had no idea of the time but it had to be late. How many hours had she slept? Impossible to guess. No one seemed to have missed her which was just as well. Having wept so long and so hard, she knew she must look a fright. She shivered, cowering in bed, feeling chilled although the night wasn't cold. She'd removed her boots but was otherwise fully dressed and still wearing the yellow silk shirt she had worn in the race, crumpled now and spotted with dried mud. She pulled it off and flung it across the room; it reminded her too much of Hamish.

Her nose was blocked and she was sniffling as if she had a bad cold. Her eyes felt swollen and uncomfortable, like a pair of ripe plums, ready to burst.

Physically and emotionally exhausted, she knew she ought to have slept until morning. What could have woken her? Her nerves tensed as she heard movement below. If that was Hamish, thinking to creep back into favour after all he'd said – all he'd done! Anger revived her and her hands curled into fists, ready to deal with him.

'Maggi?' It wasn't Hamish who called but Elizabeth, standing at the bottom of the ladder, the only means of entry to the attic. Maggi let go a long breath of relief. She didn't think Elizabeth would come up, not if she was already dressed for the party; it was enough that she must have picked her way across the mud in the stable yard. Elizabeth's scent drifted up to her, a mixture of expensive lavender water and soap. Maggi sniffed appreciatively, enjoying the contrast to the smells of the stable.

'Maggi, please talk to me.' Elizabeth sounded tired, making her feel all the more guilty for not answering at once. 'Surely you're not going to hide yourself away all night? Just because of what happened about the race?'

'It's not that, Mrs MacGregor.' Maggi lifted her voice, trying to sound more cheerful than she felt. 'I don't think I'd better come down – I'm getting a cold.' And she sniffed loudly, trying to confirm it. 'I don't feel well at all.' That wasn't a lie. She had a headache which was keeping pace with her heartbeat, pounding behind her eyes.

'Think of Lilias then, if not of yourself. She's going to be terribly disappointed if you don't appear in that dress.'

388

No, she won't, was Maggi's first, uncharitable thought. Since the arrival of the Maitlands, Lilias seemed to have no time for anyone else. Not even her mother, exhausted and ready to drop after playing hostess all day.

'Well, if you're not coming down, I'll have to come up. Maybe you should see a doctor if you're really sick.' Agile, in spite of her voluminous skirts, Elizabeth soon mounted the ladder, joining Maggi in the loft.

'You're not sick, are you? You've just been crying your eyes out all night.' Elizabeth made a quick assessment of Maggi's health. She spread her skirts and settled herself on the side of the bed, taking one of Maggi's calloused, work-worn hands into her own. 'Won't you tell me why?'

'I'd rather not,' Maggi whispered, feeling more guilty than ever when she looked at Elizabeth and saw the dark circles beneath her eyes. Sick as she was, she could find time to concern herself with the troubles of somebody else.

'It's Hamish, isn't it?' Elizabeth sighed. 'I know what he's like. He's been jealous of Callum all his life and blamed him for my husband's death.'

'Lilias told me.'

'Lilias wasn't there.' Elizabeth placed a hand on her stomach, reminded of those dark days and the baby girl she had been carrying at the time. 'It's a wonder she was born such a carefree baby. Maybe because I kept myself busy, fulfilling my husband's plans. I didn't give myself time to grieve. Hamish was most affected although I didn't see it at the time. I should have spent more time with him, explaining it was an accident and not Callum's fault. Hamish. A beautiful boy, then a beautiful man, and I let him grow up flawed, full of bitterness.'

'How could you know?'

'They're my children. I ought to have known, ought to have seen. Callum can never have anything but Hamish must spoil it or take it away from him. Not just things. Friends, people as well.'

Maggi frowned. 'But – but that's what Hamish always says about Callum.'

'He would. He's clever, you see. He'd know just how to set you at odds with his brother.'

'He tried to warn me – Callum – and I wouldn't listen. I believed Hamish instead.'

'Why not?' Elizabeth gave a sad smile. 'I suppose you thought you were in love.'

'I don't know. I don't know what to think any more.'

'Then don't. And don't let either of my boys spoil this special night for you. You must dry your tears and make an effort to buck yourself up.'

'I'm not sure I can.'

'You must. And you'll have to come down after supper, you've promised to sing.'

'But I can't,' Maggi wailed. 'I can't possibly sing in public, not now. I look awful and I'll sound as if I've a frog in my throat.'

'No, you won't. Please do this for me, Maggi. Because if you don't they'll ask Lilias and Constance to sing a duet instead. And to be honest, I wouldn't inflict that on anyone.'

'Are they really so bad?' In spite of herself, Maggi smiled.

'Worse. Individually, they're not so good. Together it's a refined form of torture. Constance can hold a tune but she won't sing out, while Lilias is loud – she has the voice of a sick parrot. I was saving them for the end of the evening when I want to clear the place and send everyone home.'

Maggi giggled.

'There, you see? You're smiling again – things aren't as bad as you thought. Be brave, Maggi. Screw up your courage and join us.'

Still she hesitated, chewing her bottom lip.

'And if it's Hamish you're worried about, then don't.' Elizabeth was quick to divine the real reason for Maggi's hesitation. 'He's not here.'

Half an hour later Maggi was looking at herself in the elegant cheval mirror in Elizabeth's bedroom, feeling like Cinderella herself and unable to believe such a transformation had taken place. In the absence of Lilias or anyone else to help her – even Cassie was already at the party – Elizabeth helped Maggi into her clothes and groomed her.

The tousled red curls had been civilised and brushed 'til

390

they shone, drawn back from a centre parting and gathered into two neat bunches on either side of her face.

Convinced that artificial enhancements to the complexion should be saved for the stage, Maggi was surprised when Elizabeth opened a drawer and produced a box of French powder for the face and a small pot of rouge.

'Oh, no, Mrs MacGregor,' she said. 'I can't. Mam used to say only bad girls wore paint.'

'Well, I haven't time for such scruples now,' Elizabeth snapped, too weary to be gentle after such a long and tiring day. 'Do you want everyone to see you've been crying for hours? No.' She answered the question herself before Maggi could get a word in edgeways. 'No more than I want them to see that I'm tired and sick. Think of this as part of our battle strategy, Maggi. It's only to help us get through the night.'

So Maggi screwed up her face like a child as Elizabeth put a dusting of powder all over it, paying special attention to her nose and eyelids. Cautiously, she opened her eyes to peep at herself in the mirror, complaining she looked like a ghost.

'I haven't finished yet,' Elizabeth reassured her, applying rouge to the girl's chin and cheekbones with something that felt rough and scratchy. 'My lucky rabbit's foot,' she answered Maggi's unspoken question. 'I've had it for years. My old nurse gave it to me when I was a girl and I've kept it ever since.'

The final touch was a little oil which she applied to Maggi's eyelashes to remove the excess powder and add a sparkle to her tear-washed eyes.

Resigned to this prelude to her performance, Maggi composed herself as Elizabeth laced her into the corset, helped her into several layers of crisp white petticoats and finally the gown. With her hair tamed and dressed, the effect was stunning and she peered at herself in the mirror, scarcely able to believe this elegant lady with the sparkling eyes and flawless complexion was indeed herself. The freckles across her nose had faded if not entirely disappeared. With a pair of gloves to conceal her less than ladylike hands and Elizabeth's embroidered shawl across her shoulders, the illusion was complete.

Chapter Twenty-Nine

When Elizabeth rejoined the party with Maggi in her wake, few people remained in the main hall where the dancing had been taking place. The big dining table which usually took pride of place in that room, together with a rug which was a family heirloom, had been transferred to a large tent outside where refreshments were being served. The dining chairs now surrounded the walls to allow room for dancing and provide seats for those who preferred to watch. A mirror over the fireplace reflected the lamp and candle power, giving the impression of a room twice its actual size. A fire burned in the grate to give cheer although the night wasn't cold. Doors leading to the verandah stood open and secured to allow revellers to spill out of the room and dance outside on the verandah if they were so minded. It was quieter than it had been all night. While most of the guests were enjoying Mrs Hallam's food outside, the musicians were taking a break. Fortunately, the showers which had threatened earlier in the day had come to nothing and the clouds had rolled away to leave the night fine and clear.

As they entered the hall which had been cleared for dancing, Maggi blinked, finding the lights too bright for eyes which were still sore from weeping. A quick glance in the mirror reassured her there was no outward sign of this except a moist look which only added a sparkle. Suddenly shy, she drew the borrowed shawl more closely about her shoulders, not merely because she was feeling the cold. She was receiving speculative glances from one or two men who had returned from supper and who were already seeking new partners for the dance. Never had she been so conscious of herself, not even on the stage at the Silver Star. There it had been Ginny who received all the burning looks. Ginny with her fruity giggles and whose humour relied on her sex appeal. Although everyone had recognised Maggi's superior talent, she had always been treated as something of a prodigy, a little girl. And only as a child had she felt confident enough to move so freely among the men in her audience. Not so tonight. Tonight she could be assured that she was completely grown up. Tonight, men stared at her openly and with thinly concealed desire while the womenfolk frowned and whispered, raising their eyebrows and assessing the value of her clothes.

She waited for Elizabeth to explain; to say she was only the hired girl who worked in the stables. But Elizabeth sailed through, introducing her only as Marigold McDiarmit, a close friend of the family, who would shortly be entertaining them with a song. As soon as Elizabeth left her, she was surrounded by a crowd of eager young men. Someone provided a chair, settling her in their midst as if she were a rare and precious jewel. And so far as they were concerned, she was. For the first time she realised how hard these men must compete for unattached women as there was a severe shortage of females of their particular age and class. Most of them faced the prospect of sending to England for unseen, unknown brides, resigning themselves to wait months, sometimes years, for these girls to arrive. For Maggi to appear in their midst like a Cinderella – young, attractive and beautifully dressed – was a bonus for all of them. They bombarded her with questions and ponderous compliments, competing for her attention.

'Marigold, eh? A lovely name for an even lovelier girl.'

'Where do you live? Does your father own a property somewhere near?'

'Go on, Freddie. Make yourself useful for once. Go and get the young lady a glass of wine.'

'You go. I want to talk to her myself.'

'McDiarmit? I say, you're not related to that fellow who threw the race?'

'I love that red hair –'

393

Maggi looked from one eager face to another, wondering how to escape these over-attentive swains. Someone put a small glass of wine in her hand and, without thinking, she swallowed it at a gulp. Her eyes watered as it caught in her throat, making her cough.

'I say. A girl who can hold her liquor. I like that,' somebody quipped.

The wine warmed her stomach and went to her head, reminding her she'd had nothing to eat but a toffee apple all day. She didn't dare to eat anything else – not if she was to sing. The wine boosted her courage and made even that prospect less daunting.

Anxiously, she peered past the young men for a glimpse of Hamish or Callum and didn't see either. Lilias was there, holding court on the verandah and hanging on Harley's arm. On her left hand glittered the expensive solitaire which looked too heavy on her slender hand and she was laughing as she showed it to her friends, allowing it to catch the light. The girls admired it with varying hoots of envy and delight while Constance stood to the left of the couple, looking bored.

The musicians returned, tuning up and conferring as they arranged the programme for the rest of the night. More and more guests wandered back from the tent outside, ready to dance off the effects of their over-indulgence. Mrs Hallam and Cassie passed close to Maggi on their way to the kitchens without recognising her, surrounded as she was by the crowd of young men.

'Keep your sticky paws off them leftovers, Cassie an' leave the sherry trifle alone. There'll be work enough for us both in the mornin' an' I don't want to hear you've been up with a belly-ache all night.'

Poor Cassie. Even tonight, when she should have been having fun, she couldn't escape Mrs Hallam's nagging tongue.

At that moment Elizabeth returned, drawing Maggi away from her admirers who sighed and protested, reluctant to let her go. Now that supper was over, it was time for the entertainment to begin. Maggi had a brief chat with the band leader, pleased to discover he knew most of her old favourites, including *The Black Velvet Band*. She told him she'd begin with some ballads and finish with *Reilly's Daughter* if she needed an encore. It was a saucy song with a catchy tune and a rousing chorus which everyone would soon pick up and join in.

Born to sing, she filled the room with sound, her voice echoing off the walls. Unlike the patrons of the Silver Star, Elizabeth's guests could appreciate a good singer and when she was finished, curtsying gracefully to the floor as Peggy had shown her, she was rewarded with a storm of applause and cries for more.

She sang two more songs and still her audience refused to let her go. People crowded the room and the verandah outside to watch and listen. She sang *Reilly's Daughter* intending it to be her final encore, and the whole roomful of people joined in, yelling the chorus. Afterwards they were still applauding, calling for more. Maggi decided to break the mood and finish by bringing them down to earth with a sad song.

> *All round my hat I will wear the green willow*
> *All round my hat for a year and a day*
> *And if anyone asks me the reason I wear it*
> *I'll tell them my true love is ten thousand miles away.*

She bent her head to more thunderous applause when she finished, appalled to discover she was close to tears. How foolish to have chosen that particular song, especially when her emotions were still so fragile.

A florid, middle-aged man in a frock coat elbowed his way through her admirers to press a card into her hand.

'Never heard anythin' like it in my life.' He had a warm smile and a direct manner which, together with his accent, placed him as a man from the North of England. 'I could put you on t'stage an' have my theatre filled every night o' the week, lass. Long time since I heard a voice like that in the halls. Right lovely you are – fresh as the mornin'. Brought tears to me eyes. Don't lose that card, mind. It's your passport to see me an' I don't give 'em out easy – not these days. If ever you come to Melbourne an' are lookin' for work . . .'

'Sure an' I'm honoured, Mister –?'

'Meacham – Perry Meacham. 'Fraid I didn't catch yours.'

'It's Marigold,' she whispered, turning the card in her hand and wishing she had been able to read. 'Marigold McDiarmit.'

'Oh, well.' He rolled his eyes. 'We can soon do something about that. I've got it! The Southern Songbird, that's what we'll call you.'

'But I don't think . . .'

'Don't say it, lass – you just never know. Keep that card safe now. Show it an' ask for me any time at the Queen's Theatre, Melbourne.'

Maggi stared at him. The Queen's Theatre. This man was important. A theatrical manager. She would remember that. Meacham smiled, saluted and disappeared, quickly as he had come. Maggi tucked his card into her bosom to make doubly sure she didn't lose it.

Meanwhile the musicians were striking up with a lively tune and as soon as they saw Meacham leave, the young men crowded around her in force, all asking her to dance. She looked from one pleading face to another, not knowing what to do. How was she to tell them she didn't know how? She could hear Da's voice in her mind even now.

'Dancing? Waste of time. Who wants to watch a lot of brainless fools jiggin' about?'

'Miss Maggi, this is my dance, I think.' Suddenly, Callum was there, reaching past the others to offer his hand. She stared at him, for the moment at a loss for words – he'd never called her 'Miss Maggi' before. 'You must remember?' he smiled, prompting her. 'You promised me the first dance after supper, as soon as you'd finished your song?'

'Oh, yes. Yes, of course.' She smiled her relief and grasped his hand as if it were a lifeline, thankful to be delivered from the young men. Flattering as it might be, she was beginning to find their attentions suffocating.

'You were in good voice tonight,' he said as he led her on to the floor. 'And after that upset with Hamish –'

'Please. I'd rather not talk about that.'

'Don't worry, I won't. But I was afraid you might cower up there in your attic and miss the party entirely.'

'I would have, too, but I wasn't allowed.' Briefly, she explained his mother's part in making sure she came down.

'Sensible woman, my mother,' he nodded. 'She knows we're going to need all the pretty girls we can get. As you see,' he nodded towards the young men who were still following their progress, some glaring with open hostility, 'there are never enough young ladies to go around.'

'But, Callum, I can't dance. Da wouldn't allow it. He said dancin' was only for gypsies an' fools.'

'But you must have a sense of rhythm if you can hold a tune?'

'I know how to keep time, if that's what you mean.'

''S easy, then. Come on. You don't have to look so scared – I won't bite. Just step into my arms and I'll lead you. I'll teach you to dance as we go.'

'Oh, Callum, with everyone looking?' Still she hesitated, biting her lip.

'Yes,' he laughed. 'The lovely Miss Marigold can't be a wallflower tonight.' And he placed his right hand firmly on her waist to guide her while clasping her own right hand in his left, shaking it to make her relax. 'Don't be so stiff and tense. Do as I do and above all enjoy yourself – go with the flow.'

'How long have you been a dancin' teacher, Callum? Does your mother know?'

'And we'll have less of the cheek, young lady. One two three, hop – one two three, hop. There you go. Simple isn't it? Easier than you thought.'

Laughing, Maggi let him whirl her round in the polka, exhilarated by the music and beginning to enjoy herself for the first time that night. Hamish and his treachery, if not entirely forgotten, had been banished to a dark corner of her mind. She wouldn't think about him again, not tonight. Some of the young men continued to wait, hoping to partner her, while others had gone off in search of easier prey. Even the demure Constance was out on the floor. Over her partner's shoulder, Maggi saw her watching herself and Callum through narrowed eyes. She looked far from pleased.

Tonight and for perhaps the first time in her life, Maggi felt like the belle of the ball – cherished, feted, desirable even, and it was balm to her wounded pride. They danced two vigorous polkas in quick succession and when the music stopped, she stood holding her side.

'I have a stitch,' she said as soon as she could speak. 'Can we go outside for a breath of air? I'm not used to wearin' a corset at all, let alone dance in one.'

Callum led her out on to the verandah where he rolled himself a cigarette and leaned against one of the supports, drawing the smoke into his lungs as he regarded her, unsmiling. His curls, which had been barbered severely in honour of the occasion, clung damply to his head, shining like dark gold in the lamplight. Not as handsome as Hamish, his face was too long and his jaw too pronounced. But his eyes were wide-set and now studied her candidly with an expression she found impossible to read. She looked away at last, embarrassed by the intensity of his gaze.

'Callum, I know we said – I said – I didn't want to talk about what happened today. But why did you bring me to Lachlan's Holt? It isn't – it wasn't true, was it? What Hamish said?'

Mention of Hamish brought the shutters down at once and Callum's expression darkened as he shrugged. 'Who knows? Is anything ever true that Hamish says? I don't think he can lie straight in bed.'

'Please. Don't avoid the question, Callum. I need to know. You didn't bring me here because – because –'

'Oh, God, I don't know, Maggi.' He took a long pull at his cigarette, betraying his nerves. 'Does it matter any more? I didn't bring you here to take up with Hamish, that's for sure.'

'No,' she said slowly, peering into the crowd as if talking of Hamish might conjure him out of the darkness. 'Where is he tonight? I thought he'd be here.'

'Why? Do you want him to be?' Callum snapped, his eyes suddenly dark as the sea at night. 'To admire your success? To make him fall in love with you all over again?'

'Of course not,' she said, suddenly miserable that he could think her so shallow.

He let go a long breath. 'Forgive me, Maggi. I shouldn't

398

have said that. Hamish brings out the worst in me even when he's not here.'

'Will you excuse me?' Torn by conflicting feelings, all she wanted now was to get away. 'I haven't spoken to Lilias all night or thanked her properly for this lovely gown.'

'Lilias will keep. She's in a whirl – she won't remember who's spoken to her and who hasn't. Please Maggi, don't rush off in a huff. Lets talk about something else.' The musicians chose that moment to strike up, playing a lively military tune. 'Another polka. Are you rested and ready to try again?'

'Yes, but I'd rather stay here. You did say we could talk about something else.'

'Yes?'

'The *Sally Lee*. She must have reached England by now and there's still no word. Am I – is it foolish of me to be so concerned?'

'No, it isn't.' His expression clouded. 'I've been thinking the same thing myself. I wrote to the ship's agents three times but they seem to be no wiser than we are.'

'Ten whole months and she still isn't there? Oh, Callum! And she took only four to sail right round the Cape to come here. Where is she? Where can she be?'

'South America maybe. I don't know, Maggi. I only wish I did.'

'So what will you do?' She hesitated, unwilling to put her real fears into words. Surely she would know it, sense it, if Tully were lost? 'You'll be wantin' to send another clip before summer's out.'

'I'm afraid not. Without the money from last year, we can't afford so much as a shearer's cook, let alone a team.'

'Couldn't you shear the sheep yourself, then? I'd help.'

'Would you, Maggi?' He smiled. 'You don't know what you're letting yourself in for. We can wash them ourselves – we've done that often enough before. But we'll need a dozen good men who know what they're doing to shear the sheep. No. Without the money from last year's clip, we'll be in trouble with the bank.'

'Does Mrs MacGregor know?'

'Not the whole story, no. Not how serious it is.'

'The ship will get there, Callum.' Maggi spoke with certainty and for her own comfort as much as his. 'It *will* get there because it must.'

Whatever Callum was going to say, his words died on his lips as a man came riding out of the darkness, calling out as he skirted the big tent which was taking up most of the empty space at the front of the house. The guests fell back to make way for him and one or two women screamed, thinking the party was about to be held up by bushrangers. It wasn't surprising that they should think so. The man's hair was long and unkempt, his eyes wide and staring, his face filthy above a matted beard and the dust of months in his clothes.

'Help us! For God's sake, somebody help us, please!'

Maggi recognised him immediately as lights from the verandah illuminated his face. It was Pete, one of Hamish's bushranging friends. But why had he come in alone? Where was Hamish himself? Beset by a sudden, horrible fear Maggi picked up her skirts and ran down the steps of the verandah towards him, Callum hard on her heels. Pete appeared to be holding a bundle of torn and bloodied rags flung over the saddle before him. It took Maggi only seconds to realise it wasn't a bundle of clothing at all but the broken and bloodied form of a man. *Please God*, she thought, *not this. Don't let it be Hamish.* But when they went to lift him down, they could see at once that it was.

'Is – is he –?' She couldn't bring herself to voice her worst fears. Together she and Callum lowered him to the ground and Maggi sank down beside him, cradling the limp, unconscious form in her lap, careless of the blood and filth which was ruining her dress.

'Alive? He was the last time I looked.' To hide his embarrassment, Pete hawked and spat. 'Full of shot, but – mebbe enough lead to poison him.'

'But who did this to him – and why?' Callum began.

Pete cut him short, in no mood to be quizzed.

'I promised I'd get him home an' I have. We left more'n a bit in the way of trouble back there.' He glanced up the track behind him as if expecting pursuit and began turning his horse. 'You'll take care of him, eh? I gotta be off.'

'Wait!' Callum put a hand on his bridle to keep him. 'A crime has been committed here and –'

'Not by me.' The man jerked himself free from Callum's restraining hand. 'You want to know anythin', you ask Hamish. I done the best I can. Now I gotta look out for meself.' So saying, he yelled at his exhausted mount, kicking it into action.

'A doctor,' Callum said, looking at his brother's pallid, unconscious face. 'We need a doctor.' He raised his voice to address the crowd. 'Is there a surgeon present? Someone – anyone with some medical knowledge?'

A circle of onlookers had gathered, appalled yet at the same time fascinated by the sight of the lovely songstress with what seemed to be a tattered bushman lying in her lap. There was no medical man among them and they exchanged glances, not knowing what to do. As yet unaware of the drama taking place just a few yards away, the musicians continued to play, entertaining the revellers.

Maggi saw and heard nothing, oblivious to everything but Hamish, lying in her arms, badly wounded and shocked. She couldn't bring herself to look too closely at his wounds; she was too afraid. Her knowledge of medical matters was small. The trouble was she didn't know how many wounds there were. He was fainting and weak from loss of blood which continued to ooze through his clothes and she knew he was full of shot which would have to be removed. Suddenly, he coughed a mouthful of spittle and blood as he opened his eyes, trying to focus on her. He attempted a smile which was a travesty on that ravaged face; he would be scarred for life if he managed to live. His voice was no more than a hoarse whisper and she had to lean close to his lips to hear what he said.

'My God, Mags. They've got you done up like the Queen of the May.'

'Hamish. Oh, Hamish, thank God. You're alive.'

'Am I? Thought I might've died already an' gone to heaven.' He started to laugh and winced instead because it hurt.

'Hamish, save your strength. Don't try to talk. Callum's gone to ask for a doctor. He'll be here soon.'

'Doctor? He can fetch all the doctors he likes – won't do any good. Must've stopped enough bullets to fell an ox. I'm finished this time, Mags.'

'No. All you have to do is hold on.'

'Bastards killed Nero. Shot him from under me. My brave horse.'

'Oh, Hamish,' Maggi breathed. Nero had been a character; a horse with a mind of his own. A horse she had learned to love. It was hard to accept he was dead. 'But who – who would do such a –?'

'Saw red after that. Didn't care what they did to me.'

'What are you saying? They shot Nero first and then you?'

'No. I – I hurt them, too. Pulled a man off his horse. Be a cripple if he lives. Better off dead – like –' Hamish paused, fighting for breath.

'Where's that doctor? Why isn't he here?' Maggi stared at the party guests, silent now, standing around them in a crowd, the men grim-faced, the girls wide-eyed with their hands covering their mouths. By now the band had been told to stop playing and everyone realised something was wrong.

'Promise me, Maggi.' Hamish was once more making an effort to speak, his grimy, bloodstained hand grasping her by the chin, drawing her back to face him. 'As you ever loved me, Maggi – promise this one thing?'

Maggi's lips trembled and tears blurred her eyesight. Death-bed promises and the smell of blood – vividly the images returned: her mother's last moments aboard the *Sally Lee*.

'Promise!' he insisted again, his grip surprisingly strong.

'Yes,' she whispered, letting her tears splash unheeded on to his face.

'Find Nero and bury him for me. I can't bear to think of him out there, meat for the crows.'

Maggi promised without hesitation, although she wondered how she was going to dig up the hard, unbroken ground to bury anything as big as a horse. 'I'll do it, Hamish. I promise. I'll go at first light.'

'Well, well, well. What have we here?' The doctor appeared at her side, taking charge. He was a short, balding man in his fifties and had that irritating, jovial manner adopted by some medical men. Maybe they thought it put heart in their

402

patients, inspiring confidence. He smelled of whisky although he didn't appear to be drunk and his hands were steady as he examined some of Hamish's wounds. 'Oh, dear, we have been in the wars. Shall we see if we can get you inside and to bed?'

'I'm sorry, everyone.' Once more it was Callum who raised his voice to speak to the party guests who were standing around looking embarrassed, wondering what was to happen next. 'As you see, my brother has had a bad accident and the party cannot go on. We appreciate your attendance and your contributions to the charity but now I must ask you all to leave and go home.'

Condolences were murmured as the party began to disperse. The doctor, aided by Callum and two other men, lifted Hamish to get him indoors. Slowly, Maggi dragged herself to her feet and followed them.

'Maggi!' Hamish called out, his voice on the edge of panic. 'Maggi, don't leave me.'

'I'm here,' she said as people fell back to make way for her, appalled by the sight of Hamish's blood, spreading like dark flowers on the cream of her gown. Grim-faced, Elizabeth fell in to walk beside her.

'What's the matter? What's happened now?' This was Lilias as the crowd parted to let her pass. She took one look at Hamish and then at the stains on Maggi's dress. A small sigh escaped her as she fell backwards, fainting gracefully into Harley's arms.

Chapter Thirty

The doctor was at work on Hamish for more than an hour. Callum, Elizabeth and Maggi took it in turns to hold the lamp aloft for him to see what he was doing. The bullets were small and individually might not have amounted to much. Together they made a punishing assault on his body. After the torture of so much surgery, Hamish fell into a deep sleep, verging on coma, his face pale, almost grey, under his tan.

'Best thing that could happen,' the doctor tried to allay Elizabeth's fears. 'He's young and strong – sleep is the best restorative. Don't forget, though, he was bleeding unchecked for some time. We can't rule out the possibility of fever or a poisoning of the blood. If he can survive the next few hours, he'll probably live.'

'Probably?' Elizabeth stared at him. Until that moment she had never considered the possibility that Hamish might die. Hamish, always so full of life and energy. 'You will return – if we need you? If he takes a turn for the worse?' The man was already packing his bag, ready to go.

'Yes,' he said. 'But there's not much more I can do. I've given him a little laudanum to help him sleep and it's up to his own powers of recovery now. No.' He held up a hand to stop Callum who was already moving towards the door. 'I can see myself out.'

'I'll sit with Hamish, Mrs MacGregor,' Maggi said, quick to observe the dark circles of tiredness under Elizabeth's eyes. 'It's the least I can do.'

'I'll sit with him, too, Mother,' Callum offered, making

404

both women turn to look at him in surprise. 'He is my brother, after all.' He picked up a chair to seat himself on the opposite side of the bed. 'And I've done precious little to help him before today.'

'Oh.' Elizabeth's expression cleared. If this scare was what it took to bring her two sons together, it might not be such a bad thing after all. 'I'll watch over him just now, Maggi, if you want to go to my room and take off that dress. I'm afraid it's ruined.'

'It doesn't matter now.' She looked down at the dark stains which had eaten into the fabric of the gown. 'I'd not have the heart to wear it again. Not after today. And I wouldn't like him to wake up and find me gone.'

'No.' Elizabeth glanced at him fearfully, his hair so dark it made his skin look even paler against the white of the sheets. She had an awful premonition that, for all their brave talk, Hamish would never wake again.

'I'm staying at least until first light. I promised him I'd go out and look for his horse. He wants me to bury him.'

'You can't be expected to do that.' Callum frowned. 'He was raving, Maggi. He didn't know what he asked of you.'

'I gave him my word, all the same. I have to try.' She returned his gaze steadily, defying him.

'Not alone, you won't. I'll go with you.'

'As you wish.' She shrugged.

'You look exhausted, Mother.' Callum turned to Elizabeth, taking her hand in his own. 'Why not go to bed for a few hours? You can take over here when we leave.'

'No, Callum,' she protested weakly. 'I wouldn't sleep a wink.'

'Then lie down and rest at least. We'll tell you at once if there's any change.'

Elizabeth looked from Hamish to Maggi and back to her eldest son. If it crossed her mind to wonder about the girl's relationship to either of her sons, this wasn't the time to question it. Reluctantly, she had to give in to her total exhaustion and withdraw. It would help no one if she made herself ill.

Maggi turned down the lamp to stop it from shining in Hamish's eyes and, for a while, there was silence in the room

405

as they sat with only their own thoughts for company on either side of his bed.

After what seemed like a long time but was probably only an hour or so, Callum rose and yawned, groaning with the effort of remaining seated in one position for so long.

'Would you like a glass of wine to refresh you, Maggi? I need to get a breath of fresh air and stretch my legs.'

Her first instinct was to refuse in case the wine made her sleepy but she changed her mind. A little alcohol might calm her and still the anxious beating of her heart. She kept hearing the doctor's words in her mind: *'If he gets through the next few hours, he'll probably live – probably live.'* Only probably. Was the doctor too much of a coward to tell them the truth?

As soon as the door closed behind Callum, she leaned forward to kiss Hamish on the temple. She would have kissed his lips but they were broken and bleeding from his fall.

'Please, oh please, come back to me, Hamish,' she whispered. 'Don't die.'

He groaned in his sleep and opened his eyes, taking a moment to focus on her, trying to smile.

'Sweet Maggi,' he said. 'Why are you done up to look like one of Lilias's friends?'

'I'm sorry, I didn't mean to wake you.'

'Why not? Kiss me again. And put more into it this time. I'm not made of china, you know. I won't break.'

She could have wept with relief. If he could smile and make jokes, he couldn't be close to death. 'Oh, Hamish,' she said. 'You're such a fool.'

'I know.'

'I just wish –'

'No, Maggi.' He tried to shift position and stopped at once because it hurt. 'Too late for wishes. Too late for regrets.'

'Don't say things like that. You're frightening me.'

'*You're* frightened?' He grimaced and screwed up his face, with pain she thought until she realised he was laughing without making a sound. 'I'm the one who has to account for his sins tonight – face up to the unknown.'

'Oh, Hamish, if only it could have been different. If only you could have loved me as I love you.'

'Don't fool yourself, Maggi. You never really loved me.'

'Of course I did. I still do.'

'No. I let you think so. You were dazzled and I took advantage – like I always do.'

Suddenly, his body arched and began to shudder. She held him tightly in her arms, thinking he was having some kind of fit and she closed her eyes in relief when his body relaxed and was still. She was still holding him when Callum returned, bringing the two glasses of port wine.

'Oh, good God,' he said, setting them down on the table beside the bed.

'He'll be all right now,' Maggi murmured, her face still buried in Hamish's shoulder. 'He was shakin' somethin' awful but he's quiet now.'

'Maggi.' Callum took hold of her gently by the shoulders. 'Maggi, let him go.'

'No.'

'Look at him.' Gradually, Callum made her let go of his brother's inert body. 'His eyes are open but he's not breathing. He's gone, Maggi. Hamish is dead.'

'No!' Her cry of anguish must have been heard all over the house. Suddenly, Lilias, her mother and the Maitlands were all there, crowding into Hamish's small bedroom; the room he had so rarely occupied when he was alive. While the members of the family were looking at one another, stunned into silence, unable to believe it, Maggi took the opportunity to slip away. She remained dry-eyed, like the others. It was too early for grief. Only Cassie was bawling into her apron as Maggi sped through the kitchens, fearful of being stopped and questioned by Mrs Hallam. But, as usual, Sarah Hallam was taking out her spite on the kitchen maid.

'Stop that caterwaulin', you stupid creature. Do you want to waken the dead?' Mrs Hallam gasped and sat down heavily, her hands clasped to her mouth as she realised what she'd said. Cassie's wails began anew.

Numb with shock and unable to think, Maggi tore off the ruined dress and struggled out of the corset with difficulty. A card fell out. The card she had tucked away in her bosom

just a few hours ago. Those few hours which had meant the
difference to Hamish between life and death. She looked at
the card, remembering what it represented. It was her passport to the Queen's Theatre, Melbourne. A corner of it was
dark with Hamish's blood. She set it carefully among the
small collection of treasures beside her bed.

'Maggi, where are you going? You don't have to do this.' It
was Callum who intercepted her as she rode out on one of
the stockhorses.

The aftermath of a party can be sad at any time but in the
pale light of dawn, the wreckage of this one seemed worse
than most. No one had bothered to clear anything away.
Chairs lay scattered and overturned, streamers drooped and
the Chinese lanterns, which had made such a pretty feature
of the verandah, were now limp and forlorn.

'I have to look for Nero.' Maggi's voice was only a croak
through dry lips. 'I promised him.'

'But the horse could be anywhere, Maggi. You don't even
know where to start.'

She shrugged. All she wanted was to get out for a while;
she would feel as if she had something useful to do as well as
collect her thoughts. 'I promised him,' she insisted, a stubborn twist to her lips. 'I shall start at MacGregor's Creek.'

'Then I'll go with you,' Callum said. 'Wait while I saddle
the mare.'

It was a lucky guess. Nero was at MacGregor's Creek. He
had been trying to come home.

'But he's alive,' Maggi breathed. 'And he looks all right.
Why on earth did Hamish think he was dead?'

'Careful, Maggi. Take care how you approach and don't
startle him,' Callum warned. 'He's wounded, d'you see?
Blood on his hind quarters, running down his leg.'

'Nero!' she whispered, hoping the grey would respond,
recognising her voice. He lifted his head to regard her although he remained where he was. Making no sudden moves
which might frighten him off, she urged the stockhorse a
little closer, holding her breath in case the big grey should
panic and take off, making his injuries worse. Instead, he
seemed to be waiting for her, standing quietly while she

approached and reached for his reins. Slowly, she walked him back and forth, asking Callum to watch his gait to see if he was lame but the horse moved easily, making them smile their relief. It would have been doubly hard to find him alive and still have to destroy him.

'If Nero recovers from this, Maggi, he's yours,' Callum said. 'Hamish would have wanted it so. Nobody else can handle him anyway.' He threw in this last to lighten the mood. Her lips were trembling and she was close to tears. But she was doing her best to smile as they turned their horses for home. Nero would live. She would nurse him night and day, if need be, to make sure of it.

They had gone no more than a few yards when three men on horseback broke cover to face them, blocking their path.

'Oh, no, not now,' Maggi groaned, thinking they were to be set upon by bushrangers. She was surprised when Callum greeted the older of the three who was obviously their leader.

'Morning, Sir Athelstane,' he said easily. 'You're up and about your business early after such a late night.'

'I could say the same of you.' The man ignored Callum's greeting. 'I thought someone had to be coming back for that grey. Belongs to your brother, doesn't he? I have to say I'm surprised, MacGregor. Didn't expect to find you covering the tracks for that young rogue. Whoever was riding that horse last night is a thief. Caught red-handed in the act of trying to run off some of my prime beasts.'

'Sir Athelstane, I hardly think –'

'No, and I don't think it either, sir. I know. I've one man lying dead back there and another blinded in one eye. Doubtless he'll be able to open the other wide enough to identify your brother as his assailant. I've put up with this long enough, I mean to make an example of that young man. He shall hang from the highest –'

'You can save yourself the trouble, sir.' Maggi could keep silent no longer. 'Because you're too late. Hamish is dead.'

'Dead, you say? And why should I take your word, you little red-headed hellion? How do I know you're not trying to throw me off the scent?'

'Believe what you like, sir,' Callum snapped. 'But you'll be civil to this girl. She has committed no crime and neither have I. It is you and your men who are the trespassers, here on MacGregor land. My turn, I think, to ask you to leave.'

'Oh? And how long do you expect to keep your precious MacGregor land? I gave you some good advice and you chose to ignore it, sending your clip to England on the *Sally Lee*. Now I hear the ship's lost – what a terrible shame.' He sounded far from sorry.

'The *Sally* is late, that's all. I'm not concerned. It's a pity we've missed the sales but we'll manage. It's happened before.'

'Not concerned and the ship over nine months late?' the man sneered. 'Then you must be a bigger fool than I took you for. Talk to your mother, MacGregor. Remind her of my offer and say it's the best she'll get. She should take advantage of it while the price is still high.'

'What offer?'

'My offer to buy Lachlan's Holt. She didn't even bother to mention it?'

'Because she knew she'd be wasting her breath. Lachlan's Holt is our family home and it isn't for sale. And if it were, I wouldn't urge her to sell it to you. I'd give it away rather than sell it to a land-grabber, a city farmer like yourself.' And turning his back on Sir Athelstane, who was making sounds like a kettle boiling over, Callum rode over to Maggi and fell in on the other side of Nero, signalling her to move on. They walked the big grey between them, Callum morose and distant although there were a dozen questions Maggi wanted to ask. What could have happened to the *Sally Lee*? What was the meaning behind Sir Athelstane's words?

Nero lived. The bullets which had proved so fatal to Hamish had scarcely pierced the animal's hide. There were flesh wounds in his rump and he had lost some blood but no vital organs had been affected. Maggi held him, whispering softly to reassure him, while Patrick Hegarty demonstrated his veterinary skills, removing the shot so gently the big grey didn't feel a thing. When he was done, he instructed Maggi to keep the wounds clean while they were healing and, still more importantly, prevent them from getting fly blown.

For Maggi and everyone else who had loved him, Hamish's

410

funeral was a nightmare. She stood at the graveside looking from one face to another, seeing how each family member was affected by the loss. His expression sombre, only Callum remained dry-eyed. He and his brother might never have seen eye to eye but he had always believed there would be plenty of years ahead during which their differences could be resolved. Nobody could have foreseen it would end this way.

Hiding under a thick veil and with a handkerchief pressed to her mouth to suppress her sobs, Elizabeth leaned on Callum, her frailty obvious as she watched her son's coffin lowered into the ground and tossed the first grains of earth after it. Earth which had been difficult to dig, having lain undisturbed for so many years. Callum, Patrick Hegarty and even Harley Maitland had taken turns, sweating over the task on the previous day, the womenfolk doing their best to comfort each other, trying to close their ears to the sound of spades scraping and chopping their way into ground which was rock hard.

Maggi and Lilias stood together, shivering and hunched as if feeling the cold, clutching each other's hands for mutual support and rigid in their determination not to break down. The Maitlands, while affected by the family's grief, had not been well acquainted with Hamish and were less emotionally involved. Together they stood side by side, gazing with unseeing eyes at the ground while the minister, a Scot hastily summoned from Beechworth, cleared his throat and opened his prayer book to intone the last rites. No mention had been made of Maggi's relationship with Hamish but by tacit agreement she was accepted as part of the family now. In dying, Hamish had elevated her to the status of widow although, had he lived, she was sure he would never have made her his wife.

And there was an uninvited guest. Sir Athelstane Gurney was at the graveside, determined to see for himself that Hamish was dead; that a real funeral was taking place and a body being laid to rest in the ground. Shamed by Elizabeth's tears, he was now wilting under Callum's stare. Until he had seen for himself the genuine and unaffected grief of the MacGregor womenfolk, he had been inclined to believe the funeral was a sham; an elaborate smokescreen to allow the miscreant to escape, to hide in the mountains perhaps.

Maggi was most concerned about Elizabeth who seemed to have diminished, ageing visibly during the past few days. Lilias, too, had grown up almost overnight in response to her mother's needs. With her hair pulled away from her face and dressed in black, she was no longer the simpering school-girl. Grief had matured her.

When the ceremony was over and Patrick Hegarty began filling in the grave, people started to move away. Fearing he was about to be ignored, Sir Athelstane placed himself squarely in Elizabeth's path.

'Dear, dear lady, what can I say?' he began.

'Spare me your condolences, Sir Athelstane.' She swept her skirts aside, wishing to avoid the slightest contact with him. 'I know they are not sincere.'

Anger coloured his cheeks. Used to people fawning on him, he was unused to such lack of respect, particularly from a woman. 'You want the truth, dear lady, then you shall have it. Your son was a cattle duffer – a murderer – a thief in the night. And he received no more than his just deserts. I am the injured party here.'

'Is that so? Then how is it you are not six feet under the ground as he is?' She faced him, her voice suddenly strong. 'Sir, we have just buried my son. I can't talk to you now. This isn't the time.'

'You'd better go.' Callum reinforced his mother's senti-ments, taking her by the arm to support her. 'Forgive us if we don't invite you in. Today our home is open only to family and close friends.'

'You won't be able to stand on your dignity for long.' The man was too thick-skinned to be put off. 'You'll need to speak to me, and sooner than you think. You won't get a better offer than mine.'

'You are despicable, sir!' Anger put new heart into Eliza-beth. 'Only you would attempt to discuss matters of business with us, today of all days. I have to tell you, you're wasting your breath. I'll grub vegetables from the ground on my hands and knees like a dirt farmer before I'll sell you so much as an inch of MacGregor land.'

412

'You won't be so proud in a week or two – you wait and see!' he yelled after them as they turned away. 'Your clip is lost. Gone down with the *Sally Lee*. You'll have to sell up and go. You won't be able to stay.'

'He's right, you know,' Callum said some time later when they were fortified with hot tea and Mrs Hallam's funeral meats. 'We have to make plans.'

'Oh, Callum,' Elizabeth sighed, setting her teacup down in her saucer with a crash. 'Do we have to talk about this today?'

'I'm sorry, Mother.' He rubbed the back of his neck, equally ill at ease. 'I like it no more than you do but we have to face up to the future while we're all here. While Harley is present to give us the benefit of his advice. If we're to have a lawyer in the family, we might as well make good use of him.'

'Please do.' Harley's rather ordinary features lit up and became eager at the prospect of being useful. 'What seems to be the problem here?'

'There isn't one,' Elizabeth said.

'Now, Mother.' Callum was gentle but firm. 'No point in burying our heads in the sand –'

'Maybe the *Sally* isn't lost!' It was Maggi who blurted the words, making everyone stare at her. 'My brother's not dead, I'm sure of it. I'd feel it, if he was.'

Callum shook his head. 'I'm sorry, Maggi. You're just saying that because you can't bear to face up to the truth. You're believing what you want to believe.'

'No! Oh, I know you think it's all foolishness but I promise you – I'd know if my brother was dead.'

'I hope you're right. But whatever the case it won't solve the problem here – what to do about this year's clip. I could go down to Melbourne, I suppose, and put the problem before the bank. Jameson's a good sort. He's helped us out of tight corners before.'

'I told you, Callum.' Elizabeth managed a tiny smile. 'There is no need. And please stop looking at me like that – I'm not losing my mind. Hamish had money. A lot of money. He gave it to me for safe keeping.'

413

'Hamish? Hamish had money?' Callum scratched his chin, finding it hard to come to terms with this idea. 'But whatever from? Not gully raking? Stealing cattle?'

'Perhaps.' Elizabeth shrugged. 'I never liked to ask. He wanted me to look after his savings. He wouldn't put them in the bank in Melbourne, in case he was tempted to use them while he was there and gamble them away. He said he was saving up to buy a place of his own. He wanted to breed horses –' Her voice trembled and she wiped her eyes.

'But –' Callum frowned. 'He never mentioned any of this to me.'

'Was he likely to?' Elizabeth was becoming impatient with her eldest son. 'When you disapproved of everything he did. He said the money was to be mine, to dispose of as I wished if – if anything happened to him. Almost as if he was expecting it.'

Lilias burst into noisy tears.

'Stop that, Lil!' Callum spoke through gritted teeth, making her stifle her sobs in a handkerchief. 'You promised you weren't going to do that. Mother, go on.'

'So I see no reason why Hamish's money shouldn't be put to good use. We must use it to save Lachlan's Holt.'

'Mother, I don't want you to think I don't appreciate the offer – I do. But Hamish's savings won't be enough. A drop in the ocean, I'd think.'

'If you say so.' Elizabeth shrugged. 'If you call something over three thousand pounds a drop in the ocean.'

'Hamish had three thou – Good God!' Callum sat down, looking wide-eyed. 'All that out of selling his wild cattle to the gold fields?'

'I don't think so. Sometimes he made money out of gambling as well.' Elizabeth gave a wry smile. 'But I find it hard to sympathise with our noble English neighbour over the loss of a few of his beasts. Not when he's barking at our gates, hoping to capitalise on our misfortune. So, Callum, what do you say? Is it enough? To pay for your sheep to be sheared and –'

'More than enough.' He was still solemn and thoughtful. 'But that money belonged to Hamish and he wanted you to have it, Mother. Not me. I'll borrow as much as I need to get

414

the job done but when the money returns from the auctions, I'll pay you back.'

'Callum I don't need it. I don't want –'

'Otherwise I won't take it at all. Hamish will come back and haunt me. You know he never had time for sheep.'

Elizabeth did weep, then. But these were cleansing tears, not the sobs of misery and grief which had racked her before. It was Harley who spoke when her paroxysm of weeping was over.

'My sister and I have trespassed on your hospitality long enough,' he said. 'It's time we went home. My father's leniency has been stretched to the limit already and he'll be expecting me back at the practice before too long.'

'Oh, Harley, no!' Fresh tears sprang to Lilias's eyes as she took his hand. She had scarcely troubled to get to know him while she had been on the social merry go round in Melbourne but here, in her own home, she had learned to love and value him for his quiet strength and support and the way he had rolled up his sleeves and taken to country pursuits.

'The months will fly, love.' He dropped a kiss on the top of her head, flattered by her distress. 'And I must go to make certain our house is quite ready to welcome its new mistress.'

'But, Harley, I need you here.'

'As your mother needs you. I must tell Moxton to have the horses shod and be sure they're fit and ready to make a start on the journey tomorrow.'

'Then may I go with you, Mister Maitland?' Maggi startled everyone with her request. 'While it may no longer matter to Callum to learn the fate of the *Sally Lee* –'

'Maggi, I didn't mean –' he began but she tossed her head, ignoring him.

'I shan't be able to rest 'til I know what has become of my brother.'

'I understand.' Harley smiled. 'By all means travel with us. I'm sure my sister will welcome the company of another girl.' His answer was generous and given without hesitation but his smile faded when he saw his sister's frown. It was noticeable that she didn't confirm his invitation.

Chapter Thirty-One

Until they set out for Melbourne together, Maggi had given no thought to Constance Maitland or her opinions, unaware that the girl considered her to be a scarlet woman. Constance kept her under surveillance, peering at her through those large, slightly myopic brown eyes, certain Maggi wouldn't be satisfied with the conquest of just one of the MacGregor brothers. Surely, now he was gone, she would be setting her cap for somebody else? Harley perhaps or any other man she could get. Taking it on herself to protect the interests of her friend, Lilias, Constance never lost an opportunity to remind Harley of his commitments and his betrothed.

'What a pity Lilias isn't here to see it,' she would say if Maggi tried to point out a landmark or release the tension by making a joke. Harley did his best to be pleasant to make up for his sister's lack of friendliness but small talk didn't come easily to him; he wasn't a natural wit.

Maggi was left in no doubt as to Constance's feelings when she returned to the carriage one afternoon after a late lunch at a makeshift hotel. She was the last to return to the carriage, after a hasty visit to the privy.

'But she's dreadful, Harley – quite dreadful.' Constance spoke in an agonised whisper. 'Oh, she may look the lady, dressed up in Lilias's old clothes – but to be forced to share a carriage with a woman of those morals and that class!'

'Be fair, Connie. She's a brave little spirit. I have nothing but admiration for the way she's pulled herself together and rallied after all she's been through.'

'Trust a man to take her part. But she *slept* with Hamish,

416

I'm sure of it – Lilias good as told me so. How do you know she won't want to sleep with –'

'With me? Don't be silly, Connie. She isn't like that.'

'How do you know?'

'Look at her now, her concern is all for her brother. I wish I could be as sure you'd come chasing after me, if I should be missing at sea.'

'The question's purely academic, Harley. You wouldn't be such a fool as to run off to sea.'

'No.' He managed to put a lot of feeling into that small word.

Hearing him, Maggi had the impression that he, too would have liked to kick over the traces, pleasing himself for once. Anything to escape his sister and her nagging tongue.

Aware now that Constance disliked her, she wished she'd been in less of a hurry to alienate Mister Moxton. Had they been friends, it would have been natural for her to sit up on the box beside him. Impossible now. She had injured his pride and he would never forgive her for that. No. There was no alternative but to put up with Constance and her thinly veiled malice. There were the brief respites when they paused at some hostelry overnight but for the most part the journey was awkward and uncomfortable for all of them and there were many long hours when conversation flagged and they rode in silence. The last thing Maggi wanted was to be accused of flirting with Harley so she placed herself by the window, looking out, immersing herself in daydreams. Sometimes her thoughts were of Callum, recognising creeks and billabongs where they had paused to catch fierce-looking fresh water crayfish – yabbies – for lunch. But more often her thoughts were of Hamish.

Believing that someone should know of Elizabeth's illness besides herself, Maggi confided in Lilias. At first this set her at odds with both of them. Lilias, angry with her for keeping her mother's illness a secret, Elizabeth for betraying it. Fortunately, they came round to the view that she'd acted for the best. Lilias celebrated by throwing open the doors of her wardrobe, insisting that Maggi should take some clothes.

'But, Lilias, I can't,' Maggi protested at last, unable to see over the mounting pile of dresses in her arms.

417

'Yes, you can. And you're not to worry about Hamish. He wouldn't have wanted you trailing around in black.'

'I know. But so many! And I haven't a bag.'

'Take one of mine. Look at them – look at these hats – I'll never wear them again. Riding habits – underskirts –'

'Lilias, no!'

'Yes! Take as many as you like. Take them all, I don't care. Will you look at this?' She held up a froth of green silk with puffed sleeves. 'Too, too ingenue! Green doesn't suit me anyway, it'll look much better on you. Besides, I'll be an old married woman soon. I'll never be able to wear it again.'

Maggi had no idea what Lilias meant by 'ingenue' but the clothes were irresistible and she allowed herself to be persuaded. How else would she come by so many beautiful things? It was a generous gift and she wasn't too proud to wear second-hand clothes. Even as she accepted them, she knew Lilias wasn't acting entirely without selfishness. Married to Harley, she would demand a whole new wardrobe, to reflect her status as the wife of a successful lawyer.

Elizabeth embarrassed her by offering money.

'But I can't possibly take it,' she said. 'Mrs MacGregor, you'll need all this and more – to keep the property safe.'

'I don't care. I won't let you leave us without it.' She closed the girl's hand around the crisp new bank notes. 'Think of it as your wages. You've earned it, girl. Why, you've been working for us for months and taken nothing but small change.'

'But I've taken so much from you already. I can't let you give me money as well.'

'How are you going to live in Melbourne without it?'

'I don't know. But Mister Meacham –'

'I'd rather not have you dependent on Perry Meacham. I know him of old. Always handing out those cards and promising the world.'

'Oh,' Maggi said, her hopes suddenly dashed. Until that moment, she'd thought herself particularly singled out.

'Don't look so downcast. I'm sure he meant what he said – at least at the time. Maybe he does have a place for you but I'd rather know you have means of your own to fall back on.

418

How are you going to live while you wait for your money? You can't expect to be paid before you perform.'

'I have other friends,' she said, thinking of Peg Riley.

'And have you heard from them of late? Have they been in touch?'

'How can they?' Maggi blushed, painfully reminded of her own inability to read or write. 'They don't even know where I am.'

'Then how do you know they'll be there for you now? You do realise you've been out of circulation for the best part of a year? A lot can happen in that time. I'll rest much easier if I know you can afford proper food and a decent bed.'

Whether or not he planned it that way, Callum's farewell was conducted in public, in front of Lilias and his mother.

'You will come back to us, won't you, Maggi?' He took her by the hand, holding it against his heart; an unconscious gesture, she thought. Somehow he had been able to read her mind, sensing that in the wake of so much heartache and tragedy, she might never come back. She could be leaving Lachlan's Holt for the last time. 'You don't have to worry about Nero, he's mending nicely now – he'll be back to his old, dangerous self by the time you return.'

Nero! In the midst of her concern for Tully, Maggi had forgotten him. How could she bear to leave that beautiful horse? Since she found him and nursed him back to health, the bond between them had strengthened and he had become more dear to her than ever.

'Callum – oh, Callum, I –' There was so much she wanted to say but she didn't know how to put it into words. Looking up, she saw the silent plea in his eyes, begging her not to say too much, not to speak of feelings that were still too raw.

'I – I just wanted to thank you for being so good to me. All of you.' This time she included Lilias and Elizabeth in her smile. 'You've been like a second family to me.'

That was how she had left Lachlan's Holt. Not quite sure she would ever return. And now here she was in the Maitland's carriage, every jolt of the wheels taking her further away from the place she had come to think of as home and the burial plot of Hamish, the first man she had ever loved.

419

Oh, Hamish, Hamish! His name returned like a litany in her head. Why, oh why, did you have to die? Why did it have to end like this? When she was being honest with herself, she had to admit he had never treated her well. It was of little consequence now. She would forget the bad times and remember only the good. He would always occupy a special place in her heart. She'd come to love the other members of his family, too. Lilias for her generosity despite her selfishness – that was all part of her charm. Elizabeth for her wisdom and quiet strength. And Callum? What did she love about Callum? Her mind veered away from that question, unwilling to follow the thought to its natural conclusion. She wasn't ready to think about Callum and what he could mean to her. Certainly, he wouldn't be wasting his time on thoughts of her. He would be far too busy organising the shearing of his sheep and saving the fortunes of Lachlan's Holt.

Past experience should have prepared her but the noise and manic activity of Melbourne still came as a shock, especially after so many months of living in the quiet of the country. Even the suburbs on the way to the city teemed with twice as many carriages as she remembered as well as horsedrawn omnibuses and people on foot. For most of the journey, which had taken just under a week, Constance had remained prickly and ill-tempered, never relaxing her guard. Maggi had worn herself out, trying to be polite to the girl and doing her best to keep the peace. Now she was anxious to take her leave of the Maitlands, asking Harley to set her down in the eastern outskirts of the city at the top of Bourke Street Hill. He did so, at the same time looking anxious, reluctant to let her disappear into that seething metropolis, unchaperoned and alone. He handed her down from the carriage while Moxton unstrapped her bag and tossed it to land with a thump beside her on the ground. Conduct which earned him a sharp look from Harley.

'Are you quite sure you're all right?' He glanced down the hill at the noise and bustle which was Bourke Street. 'I really don't care to leave you on your own.'

'Oh, I know my way round.' Maggi smiled bravely. 'I used to live here, remember?'

'I'm sure the MacGregors would never forgive me if – '

'Harley, if the girl wants to leave, let her go.' It was Constance who spoke, leaning out of the carriage window and glaring at them. 'I'd like to get on home. Mother's expecting us.'

'No, she isn't. When I wrote I said I wasn't sure when we'd arrive.'

Constance retreated with a sigh.

'Maggi, take my card.' He pressed a gold-edged visiting card into her hand. 'And please don't hesitate to call on me if I can be of service to you. Ever. And – I'm sorry – sorry about –' He wrinkled his nose and jerked his head in the direction of the carriage where Constance sat fuming, waiting to leave.

'It isn't important, Harley. I do understand.'

'Poor old Connie. Try as she will the fellers just don't seem to take to her. 'Fraid she's all set to be an old maid.'

'Harley!' Constance called again from inside.

Maggi gave him a peck on the cheek which made him smile bashfully and blink. 'Thank you,' she said. 'Thank you for everything. You'd better go.' And without looking back, she pushed her hat more firmly on her head, picked up her bag and set off down the hill towards the city.

Her footsteps slowed once she was sure the Maitlands' carriage was gone. Really, she didn't know where to begin. She wanted to go straight to the wharf, to the place where she had last seen Tully, to see if she could pick up the threads from there. But her first priority was to find a room – somewhere to spend the night and also keep her bag, heavy with Lilias's gift of clothes.

Almost without thinking she followed familiar paths and found herself knocking at the door of Mrs Hennessy's boarding house. She was holding fast to the hope that Peg Riley and the other dancers might still be living there. A familiar blast of carbolic greeted her as the door swung open and there stood Mrs Hennessy herself, wiping her gnarled, workworn hands on her apron.

'Good afternoon, madam.' She almost dropped a curtsy, seeing a lady on her doorstep and not recognising Maggi in Lilias's smart, russet-coloured riding habit. 'What can I do for you?'

'Mother Hennessy, don't ye remember me?' Maggi laughed, reverting at once to a strong Irish accent similar to the woman's own. 'I was here last Christmas with you – ye must recall me brother an' his horrible dog?'

The woman peered at her for a moment until her homely features broke into a smile. 'If it isn't herself! Little Maggi McDiarmit? Well, I'll be – an' wasn't I thinkin' about you only the other day? My, you certainly fell on your feet by the cut o' your clothes. Come in, come in an' sit down – I'll brew us a nice dish o' tea.'

Over the tea Maggi gave Mrs Hennessy an edited version of her adventures, saying she was back in Melbourne to ask after Tully. The woman shook her head, saying, 'Dear, oh dearie me,' when Maggi told of the possible loss of the *Sally Lee*. Maggi said nothing of Hamish nor did she touch on the subject of why she left Melbourne before and in such a hurry. Mrs Hennessy had her own version of the tale.

'I never believed you was robbin' the diggers, never. An' I kept saying so to the end. I know my Maggi, I said. She wouldn't take nothing from no one – a girl like that. She has honest eyes.'

Maggi stared into her teacup and smiled. She couldn't afford the luxury of unburdening herself and telling Mrs Hennessy the truth. Not when she needed a place to stay. So she changed the subject instead.

'Peg and the girls? They're not still here with you?'

'Lor, bless you, no! Not for months. Not since they all split up an' went their ways. Some of them went to play Ballarat – very good money for dancers these days. Peggy got married. I was forgettin' you didn't know.'

'No. No, I didn't.' Maggi tried not to show how much the news set her back. She had relied on Peg to be here when she needed her.

'Love at first sight it was,' Mrs Hennessy went on. 'A whirlwind romance.'

'But she's here? Living in Melbourne still?'

Once again Mrs Hennessy shook her head. 'Not her. Married a bloke from London – some kind of entre – entrer – oh, I dunno. Arranges for theatricals to go all over the world. They married one day an' sailed for London the next.

422

'Oh. Oh, I see.' Maggi's lips trembled and she felt her eyes filling with tears.

'There now, don't take on. She wanted to let you know but there was no time – you so far away, an' all.'

'I'm sure.' With an effort Maggi produced a bright smile. 'Do you have a room for me, Mrs Hennessy? I can pay.'

Mrs Hennessy gave her a small but sunny room at the back of the house and within a few hours, apart from missing Peggy and her friends, Maggi began to feel as if she'd never been away. Mrs Hennessy also gave her Tully's mandolin which Peggy had left behind. She sat on her bed, cradling it in her arms, fingering the beautiful inlaid wood and touching the strings her brother had touched, too emotionally drained to shed any more tears. At last she lay down on the bed, meaning to rest for only a short time but, more exhausted than she thought, she fell into a deep sleep. Sometime during the evening Mrs Hennessy crept in and covered her. She slept the clock around and didn't rise until noon the next day.

She wore the least flamboyant of Lilias's clothes and, scraping her hair back in a bun, did her best to make herself look like a companion or a governess. It wouldn't do to attract the wrong sort of attention when she visited the wharf. During the months she had been away, a railway had opened, making the four-mile journey from Melbourne to Sandridge much simpler and the wharf much more accessible than before. The advent of the railway meant there were many more sightseers crowding the wharves in addition to those who had legitimate business there.

An hour later, she was no wiser and beginning to think she had been foolish to come; to pin so much on the slim hope that somebody here must have news of the *Sally Lee*. Seamen and shippers alike shrugged off her queries with a complete lack of interest. Most had not even heard of a three-masted clipper which went by the name of the *Sally Lee*.

After spending a futile hour at the wharf she went home and changed into the russet-coloured riding habit, aware that the colouring suited her well. She dressed out her hair to look less severe and when she was satisfied with her appearance, went back to Bourke Street and stood outside Harry

Napier's Silver Star, trying to screw up the courage to go in. Cowardice prevailed and she didn't. If Ginny and Harry were married now they wouldn't be pleased to see her; she would be an unwelcome reminder of the past. Not only that, there was still the danger of being pointed out as a thief. And worse than any of it, the prospect of telling Jinks she feared that Tully was lost at sea. Lost at sea. How final it sounded. She shrugged off the thought, unwilling to believe it.

So she walked up the hill to the Queen's Theatre instead. It was one of the newer buildings in Melbourne. An imposing venue on which no expense had been spared. To Maggi it might have been a palace, comparing favourably with the opulent music halls of the old world. Here and in abundance was the rich red carpet, red plush and gold braid she had always imagined; the setting her mother dreamed about so long ago, certain there would be a place for her daughter behind the footlights and at the top of the bill.

It was late-afternoon and the front of the theatre was empty apart from a manager, already dressed and ready to welcome people to the evening's performance. As he started towards her, Maggi avoided him, dodging out into the street again to go in search of the stage door. The doorman frowned when she presented him with Perry Meacham's card and fingered the bloodstain on the corner. Hamish's blood, she reminded herself, feeling a little queasy.

'Oh, not another one,' he muttered, half to himself, rolling his eyes to heaven.

'Tell him it's Maggi, Maggi McDiarmit,' she said.

'Wait here an' I'll ask.' The doorman scratched his head with a blunt pencil. 'But don't get your hopes up too high – he's got one on him today.' So saying, he sniffed and creaked off down a corridor, shoes squeaking every step of the way. A party of girls came in, laughing and squabbling like a pack of starlings as they ran off down the same corridor without sparing Maggi so much as a glance. One or two men followed them, sharp-featured dramatic-looking men who stared her up and down before disappearing into the recesses of the theatre. Feeling very much an outsider, she was beginning to wish she'd never come. She considered leaving before the

424

doorman returned, avoiding the rejection before it came. He arrived before she could do so.

'Mister Meacham will see you now,' he said, sounding almost as astonished to give the message as she was to receive it. 'Second door on the right.'

Maggi drew herself up and took a deep breath as she knocked at the door. This was her best chance. She needed this work. Mister Meacham would have to live up to his promise and give her a place. If not the future looked bleak. It would be traipsing round third-rate bars and theatre-cafes looking for casual employment or returning to Lachlan's Holt, admitting defeat. And she couldn't do that; not before she found out what had happened to Tully.

'Thought it was you, lass.' Mister Meacham's smile was welcoming as he held the door wide for her to come in. 'The Southern Songbird, isn't that what I said?'

'You did.' She returned his smile, grateful he had remembered her. She looked around and saw she had been invited into a comfortable room which resembled a middle-class parlour rather than a businessman's office. Tea and a tempting array of biscuits had been set out on a table before the fire.

'I have just the spot for you, starting the week after next,' he said when they had become reacquainted and Maggi had consumed two cups of tea in quick succession as well as most of the biscuits.

'Oh?' She was taken aback. 'Not right away?'

'Patience, lass. I have to do up the posters an' bang the drum a bit. Folks has to know that you're here – otherwise they won't come.' He took a pencil and paper from a drawer under the table and began a rough sketch of a theatre bill. 'What did you say your name was?'

'Marigold. Marigold McDiarmit.'

'Oh, lord, yes, I remember now. Supposin' we call you Mary instead? Mary Gold the Southern Songbird – that rolls more easily off the tongue. And we'll have you dressed all in gold as well.'

'Oh.' Maggi chewed her lip. 'Wait a minute. I have several lovely dresses – none of them gold.'

'No matter, lass. You have the dress an' I'll stop the money out of your fee.'

'Yes, I was coming to that. The fee. What will it be?'

'You can leave the money side of it to me, lass.' He winked and leaned forward, patting her on the knee. 'No need for you to worry –'

'– my pretty head about it?' Tartly, she finished the sentence for him. Suddenly, she didn't like him so well. But nor did she want to ruin her chances entirely by brushing his hand away.

'No doubt my lawyer will deal with it,' she said comfortably, suppressing a smile as his hand left her knee at once as if it were stung. 'Mr Harley Maitland. He's getting married to Lilias soon – you met him, perhaps, while you were visiting Lachlan's Holt?'

'No. No, I didn't,' Perry Meacham said slowly, steepling his hands and regarding her with a new respect.

'So, if you'll have the contract drawn up, I'll get Mister Maitland to look it over.' Maggi stood up, pulling on her gloves and preparing to leave.

'Contract, you cheeky little madam?' Meacham also sprang to his feet and for a moment she thought she might have overplayed her hand. Then he laughed, showing he was surprised rather than offended. 'I don't give contracts to casuals, lass. Most girls are only too happy to get half a chance to go on.'

'But I am not most girls, Mister Meacham, as you very well know. I am a first-class singer, you said so yourself. And if I am to work for you, I shall expect a proper contract, a dressing room to myself, tea and coffee whenever I want it, and first-class treatment all the way.'

'The devil you do!' Meacham subsided into his chair.

'Don't bother to get up,' she said sweetly. 'I'll show myself out.'

Maggi was an unqualified success. The Queen's Theatre, only half-full on the first night of her performance, was packed to the rafters by the end of the week. Her insistence on star treatment from the outset had paid off. Nobody remembered Maggi McDiarmit, the little Irish thief, and if

426

they did, they wouldn't connect her with Mary Gold the Southern Songbird; an artiste important enough to have her own lawyer to look over her contracts and who was all of a sudden the toast of the town. Meacham had been shrewd enough to recognise her talent but even he could not have forecast the universal nature of her appeal. She was everyone's sweetheart, whimsical, funny and often sad. Women wept and men cleared their throats when she sang to them of lost loves, her voice vibrant with emotion.

Sometimes she had to slip out of the theatre via the side door to escape the hordes of young men who wanted to ask her to supper or simply to offer her flowers and kiss her hand. Had anyone told her six months ago that by Christmas the name of Mary Gold would be on everyone's lips and she would hold Melbourne theatre-goers in the palm of her hand, she would have laughed and said they were mad.

For all her success, there was still a ritual she never missed. However late she went to bed, she would get up early and go to the wharf, dressed in very plain clothes and wearing a veil. If people assumed that she was a widow, she didn't trouble to disillusion them. She would talk to the new arrivals, particularly seamen, but she never came across one person who could tell her what had happened to the *Sally Lee*.

Weary of visiting the wharf to no avail, she would go to the Post Office also, talking to those returning from the gold fields in the vain hope that Tully might have returned unnoticed and gone back there to stake a new claim. Still her enquiries turned up nothing. In a matter of weeks it would be Christmas again and the approaching festivities made her all the more conscious of her orphaned state; she had no family, not one person of her own flesh and blood. Without that, the adulation of all these strangers meant nothing. What was the point of success if there was no one to share it?

And today was the last day of November – her birthday. Today she was twenty years old. Last year she had shared her birthday with Ginny, celebrating with a few precious imported nuts pinched from Mother Bullivant's fruit bowl and some early apricots stolen from the kitchen garden. At the time it had seemed like a feast and they had been careful

427

to dispose of the stones and the nutshells so that Miss Prunella wouldn't find them out. Here, surrounded by acquaintances who wished to bask in the reflected glory of Mary Gold, she had no real friends other than Mrs Hennessy who guarded her front door like a watchdog, dealing with the more persistent of her admirers. Remembering Ginny with her coarse humour and wicked monkey grin, she could almost miss the Londoner and her abrasive friendship.

Maggi took off the shimmering gold dress she always wore for her last number on stage, removed the heavy greasepaint and put on her street clothes. Then, in the manner of all women celebrating a birthday, she leaned on her elbows, regarding herself in the dressing-room mirror, searching for the first tell-tale signs of lines on her face. There weren't any, of course. She was only twenty years old. While she was doing this, there was a brisk tap at the door and one of the dancers came into the room.

'Ooh, Mary, whatever's the matter?' The girls at the theatre never called her Maggi. 'Why the funeral face?'

'Nothing, Jenny. It's my birthday, that's all.'

'Birthday?' Jenny gave a shriek of delight. 'Well, why didn't you say so? We must celebrate – can't have you looking so glum.'

'Oh, I don't know,' Maggi sighed. 'I'm not sure I feel like it. Not tonight.'

'So what are you going to do? Sneak off to old Mother Hennessy as usual an' treat it the same as any ordinary night? I dunno. You have more invitations to supper than the rest of us put together an' you never go. Why not?'

'Let's just say I have other things on my mind.'

'Come out with us tonight. Oh, Mary, you must. Just for half an' hour – long enough to get merry. There's a cosy little place down on Bourke Street. Ever so friendly, nothing flash – just a piano player there.'

'I'm not dressed for going out.' All Maggi had with her apart from her stage clothes was the plain, rather governessy navy suit she wore to go to the wharf. There was one other item of clothing which caught Jenny's eye. A beautiful shawl Maggi had bought from a travelling Chinese pedlar who had visited the theatre a few days before. It was so perfectly suited to her colouring; cream silk, embroidered with tiger lilies to match the startling colour of her hair. Jenny picked up the shawl and arranged it, flinging it around Maggi's shoulders.

'There you are – wonderful.' And refusing to listen to any more murmured protests, she opened the door and clapped her hands for attention, yelling to her friends in the chorus dressing room. 'Party time, girls! It's Mary's birthday tonight.'

The girls responded with a cheer and Maggi found herself borne out of the theatre and along the street in the midst of a crowd of laughing theatre people bent on enjoying themselves. It was equally impossible to refuse when she stood outside Jenny's 'cosy little place' and saw it was Harry Napier's Silver Star.

Inside, at first glance, the place appeared unchanged. There was still a noisy crowd at the two mirror-backed bars which ran the length of the room on either side. But there was less standing room these days. More space had been devoted to individual tables, surrounded with chairs, encouraging people to make themselves comfortable and stay. The rickety, make-shift stage was no longer there, replaced by an upright piano and a pianist – a broad-shouldered young man who sat at the keys in a bowler and shirtsleeves, his back to the room. He strummed the piano, clearly self-taught and not up to concert standard but with a good sense of rhythm, playing fluently and with ease; tinkling American tunes which set the feet tapping. The rather raucous, vaudeville atmosphere which had been so much a feature of the Silver Star, was no more. The dancers were gone. The extra seating encouraged more ladies to patronise the bar and waiters went back and forth serving food as well as hard liquor and beer.

Maggi peered through the pall of cigar smoke but there was nobody she recognised standing behind the bar. Maybe Harry and his daughter were no longer there. Maybe the Silver Star had changed hands.

She sat down, accepted a glass of champagne and began to relax. But it wasn't long before she was recognised and surrounded by a dozen eager young men.

'Sing us a song, Mary!'

429

'Let the songbird sing for her supper!'

'Ladies and gentlemen!' A man who seemed to be a head waiter, in the absence of a master of ceremonies, stood up and clapped his hands, calling for silence. 'We are honoured tonight by the presence of the Southern Songbird herself, Miss Mary Gold. Shall we see if we can impose upon her good nature and ask her to give us a song?'

A roar of approval greeted the remark. Submitting to the inevitable, Maggi rose to her feet to a storm of cheers and applause. Smiling people fell back to make way for her to join the pianist on the far side of the room.

'All right, what'll it be?' he said, continuing to watch his hands and doing a little riff on the keys. 'I don't read sheet music, I'm afraid.'

'Nor do I,' she said. 'Do you know *The Black Velvet Band?*'

He did turn to look at her then and the world seemed to stop for a moment as they stared into each other's eyes, the shock of recognition robbing them both of speech. He was first to recover himself. 'My God, Maggi, it's you!'

'Tully! Oh, Tully,' she whispered, falling into his arms.

430

Chapter Thirty-Two

There was a concerted sigh, breathed by the young men still hovering around Maggi's table, waiting for her to return. This was hard for them to bear. Here was the songbird, who had eluded their advances for so long, subsiding gracefully into the arms of the bronzed young man at the piano.

'My brother!' she announced to the room at large, unable to resist sharing the drama of the moment, although her joy and surprise were genuine enough. 'The longlost brother I have been searching for.'

'Not so hard as I've been searching for you,' he said, shaking her hand to regain her attention. 'I expected you to be with Peg Riley. How do you think I felt, coming back to find everyone gone? I've torn Melbourne apart trying to find you but nobody knew where you were. Not even Jinks.'

'Oh, Tully! And with my likeness staring down at you all over town?' She hugged him again, smiling through her tears. He was taller, rangier, and his face had lost the look of wide-eyed innocence she remembered. He was a man now; she could feel the strength of him even in the clasp of his hands.

'Marigold – Mary Gold – but of course! Everyone's talking about the Southern Songbird and her wonderful head of red hair but I never thought for a moment it would be you. I thought she'd be someone from Europe, come out to visit the colonies.'

'The family reunion can wait!' someone yelled from the back of the room. 'Come on, Mary, you promised us. Give us a song!'

And Maggi did sing. Not one song but three of their old favourites, smiling all the while into her brother's eyes. And he smiled back, justly proud of his famous sister and her success.

By the end of the third song, Jinks Napier had joined them; an angry Jinks Napier, her little pointed features twisted into a scowl. As a tavern keeper she was used to visiting celebrities, mostly renowned for leaving trouble in their wake. Clearly, she was less than enchanted to see the famous Mary Gold so taken with her pianist.

'What's all this then, Tully McDiarmit?' She stood looking Maggi up and down, her hands on her hips. 'Just 'cos the lady's famous, you needn't think you can forget your marriage vows.'

'Marriage vows?' Maggi was so astonished, she reverted at once to her Irish brogue. 'What marriage vows? To be sure an' the boy's only seventeen. Too young to be thinkin' of gettin' married at all.'

'Well, married he is, Miss – an' I've got the papers to prove it. So you can piss off back to your fine theayter, Miss Gold, an' leave him alone. This one's mine.'

Maggi frowned. Jinks must have been busy and missed the announcement that Tully was her brother. All the same her rudeness and use of coarse language was unforgiveable, whatever the case.

Tully caught his wife by the arm, trying to calm her.'Jinks, wait a minute. I can explain –'

'Explain? Explain what?' she said, irrational in her jealousy. 'Here we are married less than two weeks an' you're makin' sheep's eyes, gettin' ready to betray me with some trollop from the stage.'

'Don't you know me then, Jinks?' Maggi said softly.

Jinks peered at her, taking the trouble to look at her properly for the first time. Until then she had seen only a young woman worthy of her envy – a star of the theatre, wrapped in an expensive shawl. Her eyes widened and she clapped her hands to her mouth. 'Maggi!' she said. 'It is you! But you look so different – so elegant – not like yourself at all.'

Maggi smiled at the back-handed compliment. 'And what's

this I hear?' She gave her brother a teasing punch on the shoulder. 'What do you mean by gettin' married behind my back?'

'But I thought you liked Jinks?' Tully was deflated by his sister's criticism which she had voiced as soon as they were alone. By now it was past three o'clock in the morning and the doors of the Silver Star had been closed for half an hour. The theatre people and Maggi's admirers had gone on to other places or to their homes. Having seated her sister-in-law in their comfortable parlour at the rear of the Silver Star, Jinks had left them to talk while she went to the kitchen to make a fresh pot of tea.

'Of course I like her. I always did. I'm just sayin' you're too young to be wed.'

'Good women are scarce here in the colony. I couldn't afford to do the sensible thing and wait. Look around you, Mags. You've men hangin' round you likes flies after honey an' they're not all stage door johnnies, you know. Some of them want to get married. They'll chase after any girl who's single and halfway pretty.'

'Thanks for the *halfway!*'

'Oh, you know what I mean.'

'I think so. But don't change the subject. It's you we're talkin' about. Not me.'

'I was coming to that. Jinks happens to love me an' she's willing to have me now, today. Not in three years time when I'm twenty. She might've got tired of waitin' an' found somebody else.'

Would that she had, Maggi thought, watching her brother's expression soften and his eyes grow sleepy with remembered passion.

'An' I find I'm far too fond of the married life. Sometimes I think I'm addicted – we do it three, maybe four times in a night.'

'You see what a child you are? To boast so of your manhood.'

'An' you'd know all about it, wouldn't you, Mags? An elderly virgin like yourself?'

She gave a tight smile, unwilling to discuss her virginity or

433

the loss of it. But the more she heard of her brother's marriage, the less she liked it, fearing that a union built on a boy's teenage lust couldn't last. Jinks was already unsure of her youthful husband and inclined to be jealous. Delighted as he was with the bargain now, how would he feel in one year or two? How would be cope with the responsibility of children? But before she could say as much, Jinks pushed aside the curtain over the door and returned with a fresh pot of tea and three cups and saucers, rattling cheerfully on a tray.

'My father died, you know.' She started a new conversation when they were all seated and she began pouring the tea. Maggi sensed criticism in the remark. In the excitement of her reunion with Tully, she had neglected to ask after Harry.

'I'm sorry to hear that, Jinks. I didn't know.'

'That woman. She killed him.'

'Jinks, we don't have to talk about this – not now,' Tully began.

'Oh, I don't mean she killed him like sticking a knife in him. She married my father and wore him out. To put it plainly, she fucked him to death.'

Tully frowned. He might be used to coarse language at sea but he didn't care to hear it from the lips of his pretty wife. 'Jinks, you know that's not true. Harry died of a heart attack.'

'Yes. Brought on by –'

'Don't. Just don't say it again.'

'Why shouldn't I?' She gave him a cat-like smile. 'Don't be such a hypocrite, Tully. You like fuckin' well enough. Didn't I hear you tellin' your sister we do it all night? Why not tell her everything? Describe it in detail? Better still, let her watch –'

'Stop it, Jinks. I was only tellin' her how much I like married life.'

'Oh, I know what you like.' Jinks kissed the air towards him, giving a lewd wink. 'But your sister's a woman of the world – she must be, by now. A girl doesn't get to the top of the bill by keepin' her legs crossed. Everyone knows Perry Meacham – randy old sod! Always got his fingers in some

434

honey-pot. Me, I'd sooner go to bed with a young man meself. And this one's all mine.' So saying, she reached under the table to squeeze Tully's thigh. It was a possessive gesture, calculated to set Maggi's teeth on edge and it did. She was certain Jinks was putting on a show to provoke her but she was at a loss to understand why. They had never been close but she had always thought of the girl as a friend. It was a shock to find out she wasn't.

'So what happened to Ginny? Where is she now?' She glanced around the room, half-expecting her to appear. 'What became of her after your father died?'

'I kicked her out, of course.' Jinks shrugged. 'What do you think?'

'But she was having a child.'

'Everyone knows we hated each other – we never made any secret of that. How that woman crowed over me while Pa was alive. One night when she was drunk she came right out and said it – her baby had been sired by somebody else. I thought as much all along but you should've seen Pa's face.'

'So where is she now?' Maggi whispered. She knew Ginny of old; her own worst enemy, hiding her insecurities behind rash words and an abrasive manner.

'Oh, she's doin' all right.' Jinks was sulky, not entirely willing to talk about it. 'Pa left her a bit of money – she made jolly sure of that. Just as I made sure she wasn't gettin' her claws on the Silver Star. Bought herself a little love-nest in some alley off Lonsdale Street and hung out the red light.' She gave a short laugh. 'Lucky's Place, she calls it. At least she's a bit more honest about her profession these days.'

'But she can't raise a baby in a – in a –' Maggi almost choked on the word. 'I'll have to see her, make sure she's all right.'

'What for? You don't owe her nothin'. 'Cept maybe an extra kick now she's down.'

'We used to be friends.' Maggi frowned.

'Well, don't expect any thanks for it.' Jinks wriggled her shoulders, tossing her dark curls. 'No one likes a Lady Bountiful who comes around showin' off an' crowin' about her good fortune, shovin' it down everyone's throat.'

Maggi stared at her, wondering how the happy-go-lucky

Jinks she remembered could have changed to become such an embittered young woman. She was like a spider, feeding on Tully's youth and enthusiasm, draining the happiness out of him and pulling him down into her own dark web of despair. Maggi shivered, realising that a lot of Jinks's resentment was directed not so much against Ginny as herself.

'Why Jinks? What did I ever do to make you resent me so? You can't be jealous, surely, because I've had a little success?'

'Jealous? Me? Don't you flatter yourself.' Jinks gave a short bark of laughter. 'You really don't know, do you, Maggi? You haven't the slightest idea.'

'Then maybe it's time you told me,' she said gently, pushing away her tea. Suddenly, she wanted nothing in this woman's house. 'And make the most of it because I shan't come here again.'

'Mags, you don't mean it?' Tully looked at her, stricken.

'I don't visit where I'm not welcome, Tully. If you want to see me you can always come to the theatre or Mrs Hennessy's. She'll know where I am.'

'But –'

'Not now. I want to hear what your wife has to say.'

Jinks began pacing the room, unable to be still as her voice rose higher and higher in hysteria as she let the resentment flood out.

'It's all your fault. You and your precious Peg Riley. If you hadn't come here dragging that Ginny behind you, Pa might never have seen her, never wanted her. He might still be alive today.'

'You can't blame Maggi for that.' Tully came at once to his sister's defence. 'You're being unfair.'

'Unfair, am I? You think your sister's so clever, so wonderful, don't you? An' you want everyone else to think the same. Well, I don't. I know what she's really like. I saw what she was doing because I was watchin' you. She picked the pockets of our customers like a practised thief. An' I saw how you hated it, too. How you tried to stop her.'

'So why didn't you say something before? Why wait until now?'

'Because Pa would have sent her away and you'd have

436

gone with her. As it happened, I didn't have to do anything – Ginny beat me to it. And you had to sacrifice yourself, didn't you? I'll never forgive her for that. To avoid giving evidence against your criminal sister, you had to run off to sea.'

'Hold it right there, Jinks, you've got it all wrong! I always wanted to go to sea – I was desperate to go. I only went because I thought Maggi was safe here with Peg. How could I know what Ginny was going to do? Anyway, what about it? It's all water under the bridge now.'

'Maybe. An' then maybe it isn't. I daresay there's a few people who'd like to know that Mary Gold, the famous Southern Songbird, started life as a pickpocket and a thief.'

'No!' He spoke with such vehemence, both girls stared at him in surprise. 'You are both dear to me and I won't have these old troubles dug up again. I didn't come back here for that. I want you to forget these quarrels, both of you. Let us wipe the slate clean and make a new start.'

'Willingly,' said Maggi and held out her hand. Jinks took it with a sigh.

'That's more like it.' Tully nodded his approval, letting go a long sigh of relief.

'But you still haven't told me,' Maggi changed the subject, hoping to relieve the tension 'How did you make your way back to Melbourne? Not aboard the *Sally Lee*?'

'No.' He met her gaze, pressing his hands to his head. 'Oh God! You don't know about that, do you? It was dreadful – worse than anything I could have imagined. Unbelievably cold and nobody was dressed for it. Only the older, more experienced sailors had the sense to carry warm clothes. I'd never have signed on – never – not if I'd known we were going halfway to the Antarctic and with that incompetent devil in charge of the ship.'

'You don't mean Captain Carpenter?'

'No. The ship's mate who took over when Carpenter died.'

'Oh, Tully.'

'We avoided the icebergs and got round the Horn but I don't know which was worse – the cold or the heat – and I don't think the so-called Captain had any idea where we were. Somewhere off the South American coast. The last tropical storm was too much for the *Sally*. We lost the ship, the cargo and most of the crew – all drowned.' Tully's eyes widened, becoming unfocussed as he relived the horror of watching that sharp grey fin streaking through the water towards Hobley and his friend's screams, cut off when he disappeared beneath the surface forever. 'Jem died in the lifeboat – only hours before an American clipper picked us up. Far as I know we were the only survivors of the wreck – me an' Pieface.'

'Pieface? Don't tell me you've still got that awful dog?' Maggi laughed uncertainly, wanting to lighten the mood and draw him away from such painful memories.

'No.' Tully smiled, picking up her cue. 'I had to leave him with the Captain of the clipper. He said if Pieface had been that lucky for me, he'd be lucky for him, too. He liked the way the dog could catch seagulls. A good trick when you're out on the open ocean and don't know where the next meal's coming from. So that's it,' he sighed. 'Most of it, anyway.' Maggi knew he had skated over the worst of it. There had to be much more to the shipwreck than he was saying. But she asked him about the rest of the journey instead.

'So where did you go with this American ship? Liverpool? London?'

'No. Only as far as San Francisco. I stayed there for a month or two and a black man taught me to play the piano. Then I worked my way back to Melbourne aboard another clipper. They weren't too happy when I left but I've turned my back on the sea forever. If I never set foot on the deck of a ship again, it'll be soon enough.'

This had been a long speech for Tully and as she listened, Maggi realised he had picked up an American twang on top of his Irish brogue.

'Bravo!' she applauded him softly.

Anxious to draw her husband's attention back to herself, Jinks wound her arms about his neck and gave him a moist kiss on the cheek. 'You're never going to sea again, never. I need you here.'

'See how she loves me?' Tully's face softened with pride and he returned his wife's embrace with a kiss on the lips, showing Maggi that in spite of the jealousy and her other faults, he was still very much in love.

438

She rose and made her excuses soon after that, pleading tiredness. With bad grace Jinks allowed Tully to walk his sister back to her lodgings. There was life on the streets even at this early hour of the morning and, lost in their thoughts, they walked in silence. Somehow, Jinks managed to come between them even when she wasn't there. Tully didn't speak until they reached Mrs Hennessy's door, pushing his bowler hat to the back of his head.

'You didn't mean it, Mags? That you weren't coming to my place again?'

'Strictly, it isn't your place, is it? It belongs to Jinks.'

'No. We're equal partners in the venture. The Silver Star is as much mine as hers – bought and paid for.'

'Come on, Tully. You can't buy a place like the Silver Star. Not on a seaman's wages.'

'I know. But I had Jem's gold nuggets as well.' Tully looked somewhat abashed. 'He didn't trust the gold escort or the Treasury – said he'd get a better price in England himself. Smuggled them out in a money belt and in the heels of his boots. We talked about it a lot, while we drifted at sea. He knew he was going to die. Said he'd no family, no one he cared about and – and if he didn't make it, the nuggets were mine.'

'I think, Tully,' she said slowly, 'there's a lot more to this than you're saying.'

'Please, sis. Don't ask. I still have nightmares. I can't talk about it. Not yet.'

'All right. So you're the half-owner of the Silver Star – paid for with Jem's nuggets. I wouldn't have thought even Jinks was as graspin' as that. You're her husband and ought to share it by right, yet she makes you pay?'

'Oh, it wasn't as simple as that. Harry had a sleeping partner – he needed to be bought out.'

'Tully, look what you've done.' Maggi felt bound to speak out. 'You're a young fool. You've tied yourself to this woman in marriage and business as well. You'll never be free of her now – never get out.'

'I don't want to be free of her, Mags.' He spoke gently, realising this news was hard for her to accept. 'Jinks is all right. She doesn't mean what she says, not the half of it. Her tongue runs away and she gets a bit jealous, that's all.'

'And that's your excuse for her, is it? You think jealousy and a shrewish tongue are normal and healthy in a woman?'

'I love her, Mags,' he said simply. 'She's all the woman I'll ever want.'

Maggi hesitated, realising her brother was still in the throes of infatuation. She would only create a rift between them if she continued to criticise his wife. 'If you're happy then there's no more to be said. She forced a smile. 'You know I want only the best for you, Tully. I wish you well.'

'Thank you, sis.' His expression cleared and he kissed her briefly on the cheek. 'Be seein' you.'

'Yes,' she said, observing he had been careful not to say when. 'Thank you for walking me home.'

Tully saluted and broke into a jog, anxious to get back to his wife. Maggi sighed, watching the tall figure loping along until he was out of sight. He wasn't her baby brother any more, he was somebody's husband. She had come to Melbourne to find him only to lose him to Jinks. Thankful as she was to see him home and safe from the sea, she was sorry to see him bound so closely to that woman. He was so young, so sure of the future and what it contained. She could only hope the disillusionment wouldn't be too painful when it came.

She received odd looks from her friends at the theatre when she asked directions to a certain side street where she had been told Ginny Luckett lived. She made the visit early one afternoon when there was no matinee at the theatre, dressing with care, relying once more on the navy suit which made her look like a governess or a charity worker. She wanted to be quite sure no one would mistake her for a lady of the night. The street was easy to find. Very conscious of herself, Maggi walked along it, keeping her head down and hiding her face under a broad-brimmed hat. In spite of this precaution, she was accosted by a coarse-featured girl in cheap clothes and with a mess of paint on her face.

'Get out of 'ere, you. T'ain't your patch.'

'I'm not here to take business from you. I'm looking for Ginny Luckett. Do you know her?'

'Lucky Luckett, you mean? Who wants her? We don't like charity women pokin' their noses round 'ere.'

'I'm not a charity lady. I'm a friend of hers.'

'Friend? Nobody 'as friends. Not 'ere.' The girl pointed to a house on the other side of the street. 'Over there. Red door. But don't you tell 'er I sent you.'

Maggi saw it was the only house in the street with clean curtains and the red door had a shiny brass door knocker in the shape of a horse shoe. There could be no doubt as to the owner's profession. A red light shone in the window as well as another outside.

Maggi's knock was answered by a diminutive Chinese girl in black cotton pyjamas. She looked as young as fifteen but was probably older.

'Ginny Luckett?' Maggi asked. 'Does she live here?'

'Missy Rucky busy right now,' the girl said in a sing-song voice. 'You wait?'

'Yes, I'll wait.' Maggi sat down in the tiny hall where there was very little light and room for no more than a hall stand and a couple of high-backed chairs. The girl retreated, supposedly to a kitchen at the rear of the house.

Moments later, Maggi discovered the reason she had been asked to wait. Even with the door closed, she could hear the rhythmic creaking of a bed and the unmistakable sounds of a couple joined in the act of love. The man achieved his climax with a shuddering groan, making no attempt to smother the sounds of his pleasure. This was followed by a throaty giggle which Maggi identified as coming from Ginny. The bed creaked again as the man rose from it and she heard laughter and raised voices as he prepared to leave. Maggi glanced around the hall looking for a coat cupboard – anywhere she could hide, so that the man wouldn't have to pass her on the way out.

While she was standing there, undecided and poised for flight, the door swung open and he came out, slamming his hat on the back of his head. She recognised him. It was Doctor Parker. The same man who had been the ship's doctor aboard the *Sally Lee*. The man who had taken Ginny from Bullivant House and so callously returned her. The father of her child. To Maggi's relief, he gave no flicker of

441

recognition although he raised his hat and leered at her in passing, calling over his shoulder to Ginny as he went out of the front door.

'There's a lady to see you, Lucky. Better not keep her waiting.'

'A lady? Oh Gawd, what is it now?' There was a disgruntled sigh from inside. 'Orright, let's know the worst of it. You better come in.'

'Hello, Ginny,' Maggi stood in the doorway and paused.

She had meant to do the surprising and instead she was taken by surprise. Why had she assumed Ginny would be living in squalor, in need of rescue and help? While the parlour wasn't large, the carpets and curtains were expensive and of a rich cherry red, the room dominated by a curtained four-poster bed, presided over by gold cupids and continuing the theme of dark green and cherry red. The wallpaper reflected the same scheme, a tangle of bright red peonies and dark leaves, the ceiling draped with swathes of fabric in rich shades of dark green and red. The curtains had been drawn to shut out the daylight and the oil lamps burned low, their red glass shades casting a rosy glow in the room. A room fit for a courtesan, opulent and very exotic.

In the hope of shocking her visitor whom she expected to be some straitlaced lady on a mission of social reform, Ginny had deliberately posed herself against a pile of fat pillows, wearing nothing but an expensive pleated silk robe. Open to the waist, the robe was a rich dark green, chosen to match her colour scheme as well as to emphasise the marble white perfection of her flesh. The breasts were still high and firm, the nipples daringly rouged with the same dark red salve as she used on her lips. Unable to help herself, Maggi stared, fascinated and shocked. She had never heard of anyone rouging their nipples before. Even the girls at the theatre did no more than brush a little powder across their breasts and shoulders to enhance their sheen. Ginny looked exactly what she was: a pampered, expensive whore. Her hair, which had once hung lifeless and lank, very much the badge of her poverty, was now a shining halo of chestnut brown curls. Far from being dragged down and degraded by her chosen

442

lifestyle, she seemed to be thriving on it. The strained, haggard look had gone from her eyes, her hands were soft and elegant as if she had never carried water or washed a dish in her life. Recognising her visitor, she relaxed and laughed.

'Well, I'll be buggered! If it isn't Mags! What brings you here?'

The sight of that familiar monkey grin was enough to assure Maggi that this was Ginny indeed, for all her newly acquired luxury and outrageous taste.

'Come in or stay out but don't stand in the doorway, you'll let in a draught.' Ginny shivered, pulling the robe together to cover herself. 'Welcome. Welcome to Lucky Luckett's den of iniquity.' Raising her voice, she yelled to the girl in the kitchen 'Rosie! Bring us a pot o' fresh coffee an' some of those buns.'

There was an answering sound of assent from the kitchen as Maggi came in and closed the door.

'Well, well, let's have a look at you. Quite the lady now, aren't we, Mags? The Southern Songbird, isn't it? I always said you'd land on your feet.'

'No thanks to you if I did.'

'Oh, come on. You can't hold that against me forever. I did what I had to do at the time. Couldn't have you runnin' to Harry with tales now, could I? Poor old Harry. I did love him, you know. Everyone kep' sayin' I was after his money, but I wasn't – well, only a little bit. He treated me like I was special. No one else did. I tried to be a good wife to him.'

'Too good, if Jinks is to be believed.' Maggi wasn't quite ready to let Ginny off the hook.

'Seen her then, have you? Little Miss Acid Drop?'

'Mrs Acid Drop now. She married my Tully.'

'Go on?' Ginny screwed up her face in disbelief. 'Bit sudden, wasn't it? Last I heard of Tully, he was off to sea?'

Maggi recounted as much as she knew of her brother's adventures, not forgetting Jem's gold nuggets which had given him enough money to buy a half share in the Silver Star.

'So. He's not done so bad either?' Ginny narrowed her eyes in thought. 'Wish somebody'd slip off the plate an' leave me a bag o' gold nuggets.'

443

'According to Jinks, they did.'

'You don't want to believe all you hear.' Ginny grinned. 'Wasn't as much as she thinks. Came at the right time, though. I'd still be shakin' me tits for a penny if it wasn't for Harry. So tell me, how long has your brother been married to the charmin' Miss Napier?'

'Only two weeks. He's besotted with sex – thinks he invented it. Oh, Ginny, he's still such a child, for all he plays at being a man.'

'Man enough for Jinks Napier anyway.' Ginny's smile was sly. 'Half her luck! I'd like to have started him off meself.' She saw Maggi's frown. 'Aw, let him go, Maggi. You're like a mother hen over the lad. Always were.'

'But I wanted – I had such hopes for him.'

'I know. But you can't live the lad's life for him. Not any more. A man who survives a shipwreck an' comes back with gold in his pants don't need no older sister to hold his hand while he crosses the road.'

'I don't think he needs me for anything,' Maggi sighed.

'He probably doesn't – not right now.' Ginny looked up and smiled at her little maid who had knocked at the door and was coming into the room wheeling a tea trolley. 'Here's our Rosie with coffee an' cakes. Come on, Mags. Eat up an' cheer up.'

'Where did you get –' Maggi glanced significantly at the door after Rosie had gone. 'You haven't – she isn't –?'

'An apprentice? No,' Ginny laughed. 'That was her idea when she came here but I talked her out of it. I said she could answer the door an' look after the housework instead. Poor little devil ran away from her gran'pa – owns the Chinese laundry. Her hands were red raw when she came to me – a mess of blisters and sores. They used to make her scrub the sheets with carbolic in near boilin' water.'

'Like Kitty.'

'God, yes, poor Kitty. I forgot all about her.'

'I haven't. People should know about Bullivant House. It should be closed down.'

'I'm workin' on it.' Once again Ginny's smile was sly. 'Puttin' a word about here an there in the right ear. But I was tellin' you about Rosie. Her gran'pa came round wavin'

444

his arms an' shoutin' at me in Chinese. I told him to sod off. He did, too – so he must've understood that all right.' And Ginny laughed until it turned into a paroxysm of coughing.

'You still have that cough.'

'Yes. But it's not so bad as it was. Not now I spend half the day in bed an' don't have to work so hard.'

'Some people might disagree with you about that.' Maggi was thinking of her own turbulent sex life with Hamish and his irritation when she had been unable to please him.

'Doctor Parker's a friend – one of my regulars. He gives me some physic to help it.'

'I saw him going out. Ginny, how can you bear to deal with him after all that . . .'

'After all what? I'm not proud. Parker's a man of influence in this town an' I've never been one to let sentiment get in the way of business.' She shrugged. 'The sex was always good an' we get on famously now we have it on a proper business footing.'

Maggi frowned, unable to think of sex as a business arrangement.

'Ginny, I was wondering. That's really why I'm here. Whatever happened about the –'

'The baby? A bouncing boy. Parker thinks the world of our little Harry. Pays for someone to mind him, too.'

'You named the baby for Harry? Ginny, you're impossible.'

'I know.' She smiled wickedly. 'I only did it to get Jinks hopping. Nobody ever calls him Harry, anyway. Goes by the name of Stinker most of the time. A loud noise at one end and a bad smell at the other.'

Maggi smiled but really she was thinking it was no bad thing that Ginny's baby was being raised by somebody else. She seemed neither interested in nor affectionate towards her baby son. She appeared to read Maggi's thoughts.

'I'd be a terrible mother anyway. I've no patience and I can't have a baby here, can I? Not in this line of work. More coffee?' She held out her hand for Maggi's cup. 'But what about you, Mags? Oh, I know you're the Southern Songbird an' your face is on the billboards all over Melbourne an' the whole town at your feet. But if you don't mind my sayin' so, you look a bit pinched on it to me. What happened? Where did you go when you left the Silver Star?'

While Maggi told her about her meeting with Callum MacGregor at the wharf and of her work at Lachlan's Holt, Ginny munched her way through three cherry-encrusted buns filled with cream. Apart from nodding occasionally to show she was paying attention, she didn't say anything until Maggi paused, faltering as she came to describe Hamish's death.

'So tell me again, sweetie, because I'm not quite clear.' Ginny frowned, licking the cream from her fingers. 'Which one of the brothers was it you loved?'

'Have you heard a word I've been saying?' Maggi was exasperated by her apparent indifference. 'I loved Hamish, of course. I'd have thought it was obvious.'

'Not to me,' Ginny murmured. 'Not to me. An' now tell me this. Which one of them loved you the most?'

'I don't know.' Maggi was growing impatient. It was sympathy she was looking for not an inquisition. 'Does it matter now Hamish is dead?'

'I'll let you into a secret.' Ginny pushed the tea trolley aside and lay back on her pillows, grinning her monkey grin. 'An' pay attention 'cos it took me a long time to find this out. I know your Hamish – the type, anyway – all flash an' dash, white teeth an' hard thighs. Jus' the sort to steal a girl's heart. An' he'll be twice as romantic an attractive now that he's dead. He won't have to get crabby an' old an' grow hairs in his nose.'

'Ginny!'

'Well, he won't. He'll always be there in your heart, your first love; fresh as the day you met him. But the man you should be lookin' out for is the man who loves *you*.'

'No thanks! I see quite enough of those – fawning over me with flowers every night at the stage door.'

'I don't mean stage door johnnies. They just want to show off – to be seen at some fancy place, havin' supper with the Southern Songbird. You go home, Maggi. Go home for Christmas. Then maybe you'll understand what I'm tryin' to tell you.'

446

Chapter Thirty-Three

'What do you mean, you want to go home for Christmas?' Perry Meacham thumped his desk with his fist, making Maggi blink. 'And where's home, for heaven's sake? The theatre – is this not your home?' He made an expansive gesture with his hands. 'And what am I to do now? I have you booked for a special appearance, New Year's Eve at the Cremorne Gardens, and I've been considering an offer for an extended European tour.'

'Then don't. Not without discussing it with me first. Perry, if you were making these plans, you ought to have said so before. You can't just take it for granted I shall be here to do whatever you want; go wherever you want. Harley's been waiting for you to draw up a proper contract for next year and so far you haven't. Far as I'm concerned, that leaves me free. Free to go and come as I please.'

'You an' your Harley ruddy Maitland!' Meacham's face fell even further. 'He won't agree on a fair price.'

'Fair to you or to me?'

Perry snorted. 'Fair to both of us. All this publicity costs, you know. He's getting to be a right pain is young Maitland – more trouble than a proper theatrical agent. Come on, Maggi, I thought we were friends. We have an agreement. We don't need contracts, do we? Not between you an' me.'

'Of course not, Perry,' she said sweetly. 'I shall welcome the break. It will give me some time to consider other offers.'

'Offers? What other offers?' he growled.

'Nothing firm as yet. But until we agree on a new contract, I'm free. As you are free to hire or fire me, as you please.'

'And don't think I won't, young lady!' He leaned across the desk, wagging a finger at her. 'You girls are always the same.' He put on a mocking falsetto. 'I'll do anything, Mister Meacham! Just give me a chance, Mister Meacham – all I want is to do my best for you, Mister Meacham. Hah!' He returned to his normal voice. 'Bit of success an' it goes straight to your head. You're not indispensable, you know. There's plenty of young hopefuls, anxious to please, burstin' out o' their breeches to take your place.'

'How nice for you. Then maybe I'd better quit while I'm ahead. Isn't that what they say? Leave while the audience is still applaudin' you, shoutin' for more?'

'What do you mean, leave? You're not going anywhere. I've a lot of money invested in you. It cost me, you know, to make you into a star.'

'So you keep saying. But you've had it all back, Perry Meacham. Every penny and more. I made a lot of money for you, so we're even on that score. An' you can forget the European tour because I'm not going. Nothin' on earth will persuade me to take ship an' cross over the ocean. Not again.'

'Why can't you do New Year's Eve?'

'I told you, I'm going home. I'll do a whole week at Cremorne Gardens, if you like, but not until after Christmas – at the end of the month.'

'And what makes you so sure you'll be here at the end of the month?' Sulky and suspicious, Meacham wriggled in his seat.

'Because the MacGregors' wool will be packed and ready for shipping by them. I'll come back on the dray when they bring it down to the wharf.'

'So that's it. You're a country girl at heart all along – goin' back to the farm!' He stabbed an accusing finger at her. 'That ruddy farm, hundreds of miles away at the back of beyond, in the middle o' nowhere!'

'Don't work yourself into a rage, Perry. It isn't good for you. I'll be back before the end of January, I give you my word.'

'Good. I'll draw up the contract and send it around to Maitland right away.'

'Never mind the contract. Let's shake on it this time.'

'But you will come? Promise you won't let me down?' Cautiously, he stretched out his hand to seal the bargain and she took it, leaning across the desk to kiss him on the cheek. 'I dunno. 'S always the same. Soon as you find a good 'un an' get her properly trained, she's off gettin' wed.'

'I'm not getting wed, Perry. Marriage is the last thing on my mind.'

'Yeah, yeah. That's what they all say.'

The journey, this time with the Cobb and Co. mail coach, was speedy enough but many of the passengers suffered from travel sickness and while Maggi herself was unaffected, she had to sit opposite two elderly ladies who were less fortunate. They spent most of the journey exchanging smelling salts and dry-retching into inadequate handkerchiefs. Maggi was relieved when the coach pulled up outside the Post Office at Beechworth. There she left her bag to be collected later and went to borrow a horse.

The ostler at the stables looked at her smart riding habit and raised his eyebrows, scratching his head.

'I can give you a horse but I don't know how you'll manage, miss. We've no side saddles here.'

'An' what would I be wantin' with that?' She grinned, making him blink as she tucked up her skirts, amazing him with her colourful red-striped stockings and booted feet. 'Give us a leg up.'

Too astonished to do anything but obey, it occurred to him only as she was riding away that he had no idea where she might be going with his horse.

'Miss! Miss, where are you takin' him?' he ran after her, yelling.

She turned, giving him a smile that reflected all the joy of her homecoming. 'I'm going home, of course. Home to spend Christmas with the MacGregors at Lachlan's Holt.'

She paused to look at the homestead before riding in, the familiar expanse of sloping roof and shady verandah sharply outlined against the distant hills and clear, limitless blue of an Australian sky. She passed the family graves near the

449

original settler's hut, fenced to keep the sheep away from them, and felt a fresh pang of sorrow, seeing Hamish's headstone for the first time, so bright and new beside the weathered stone which had been raised for his father. She passed the stone ha-ha that Patrick had built last winter, almost breaking his back as he dug out the one-sided ditch and built up the stones to keep the sheep away from Elizabeth's rose garden.

Approaching the house she had a sense of déjà vu as she recalled her misgivings the first time she had arrived here with Callum; a grubby urchin, truculent and unsure of her welcome, daunted by the neatness of the MacGregor women and very much afraid she wasn't going to fit in. Today she rode up sure of her place in their hearts and with a thrill of pleasure at the thought of seeing them all again.

She dismounted from the borrowed horse and tied him to the hitching rail outside the house, before opening the front door to call out: 'Anyone home?'

Moments later Lilias was hugging her, almost knocking her off her feet. 'Maggi! Oh, Maggi, this is wonderful. What a surprise!'

Elizabeth came from her room to see what the exclaiming was about. She had grown thinner and more frail in the months Maggi had been away and was now walking with a stick. 'Twisted my ankle,' she said in response to Maggi's querying look. 'Silly thing to do. Kiss me, Maggi,' she ordered, offering her cheek. 'This is the best Christmas present we could have had. Now the shearing's finished and the wool is packed, Callum was talking of going to Melbourne to fetch you. You've beaten him to it, it seems.'

'He was?' Maggi felt suddenly breathless at this news.

'I talked him out of it, I'm afraid. Said you might not be ready to come back to us. And he's been so busy himself, supervising the sorting and packing of the wool – kept him on the run day and night.'

'It's just so lovely to be back.' Maggi placed an arm around each of them.

'Harley writes to me every week,' Lilias put in. 'And in nearly every letter there's news of you. He says you're the toast of Melbourne already, singing to packed houses every night.'

'I suppose that's true.' Maggi smiled. 'I have had some success.'

'This isn't like you, Maggi.' Elizabeth put her head on one side to consider her. 'You never used to be so modest?'

Maggi sighed. 'Well, I like to sing an' it's nice to be popular but I find it doesn't mean so much to me as I thought. An' they make such a fuss all the time, as if I'm a princess or somethin' when underneath it all, I'm still just Maggi. The same Maggi who looked after your horses an' used to go buskin' for pennies in the street.'

'And Harley tells me you found your brother again, safe from his travels?' Lilias put in.

'Yes. Yes, he's well,' Maggi said but with such meagre enthusiasm that Lilias and Elizabeth exchanged meaningful glances as she bent her head.

'You must be tired after your journey,' Elizabeth said. 'Cassie shall make up a bed in –'

'I'd rather have my old room over the stables,' Maggi said quickly, afraid Elizabeth was going to offer her Hamish's old room. 'I'm too excited to be tired and I'm longing to see all the horses. How are they?'

'How do you think? Pining for you.' Lilias rolled her eyes. 'Most of all, Nero. No one else can get near the brute. Only Callum.'

'And how's Callum?'

'Much the same as the horses, I suppose.' Lilias gave her a pointed look, leaving Maggi to interpret the remark as she would.

'I must change.' Maggi smiled, giving nothing away. 'I'm dying to get out of these corsets and city clothes.'

The stables were just as she'd left them but not quite so clean and well-kept as she liked them to be. Her attic bedroom was dusty and somehow much shabbier than she remembered it. It took her a moment to realise that she was the one who had changed and grown soft, away from the daily routines of caring for animals and tack. A way of life which firmed up the muscles and calloused the hands. She looked at her

451

hands now, pampered and soft as a lady's, with the mani-
cured, oval nails she had once sighed for. In riding breeches
again and one of her work shirts she felt more like her old
self and it was Nero she visited first. Nero, who heard her
arrival and began stamping and kicking the walls of his stall
to get her attention, earning himself a shout from Patrick
Hegarty.

'Will ye stop that, you brute!' He looked out of the stall he
was cleaning to see who was there. 'Oh, so it's you. Back
again, are ye?' This was the only greeting he gave to Maggi.
He had heard nothing of her fame and fortune in Melbourne
and wouldn't have cared about it if he had. 'Well, the good
Lord be thanked for that. You can take over here any time
you're ready. You might've chosen a more convenient time
to leave us. The shearin' and sortin' to be done an' the
stables to care for as well. But that's womenfolk for you. No
consideration for anyone else.'

Maggi smiled, cutting across his tirade. 'Is Nero perfectly
healed? Is it all right for me to ride him?'

'That's a matter of opinion, any time. But he's back to his
old self again if that's what you mean. I wouldn't touch the
bad-tempered divil meself.'

'Oh, Nero, have you missed me?' Maggi patted the big
grey, laying her head on his neck. Unused to such demonstra-
tions of affection, he tried to nibble her hair.

'See?' Patrick nodded. 'Horrible creature – perverse as
always.'

Mounted and clear of the stables she set off in search of
Callum. Until she did, she couldn't tell if there was unfinished
business between them or not. This time she wanted to meet
him alone, away from the well-meaning but inhibiting influences of other people; Lilias in particular whose matchmaking
instincts were in full cry.

If Callum had made up his mind that he didn't want her,
she had already decided what to do. She would stay a few
days until after Christmas to please Elizabeth and then go
back to Melbourne to take up her singing career, no harm
done. She might even tell Perry Meacham she'd changed her
mind about the European tour.

But he wasn't so easy to find. The men in the wool shed told her he went out riding Bothwell but nobody knew for sure where he'd gone. She rode out to MacGregor's creek and he wasn't there. Hot and beginning to feel the effects of her journey at last, she was about to give up and go home when she thought of the pool at the falls. Quite a journey but the only other place he was likely to be at the close of a hot afternoon. Digging her heels into Nero, she encouraged him into a brisk canter until the hills slowed them to a walk. At least it was cooler as they climbed, trees affording more shade, the spicy smells of wattle and eucalypt scenting the air.

On approaching the falls she saw Bothwell and knew she had guessed aright. Nero pricked his ears and snickered, attracting the attention of the big black horse who was tethered nearby. Naked to the waist, Callum was standing on the stones in the middle of the creek which led to the falls and the pool, catching water in his hat and sluicing himself. He was also singing at the top of his lungs, tunelessly and without inhibition, certain he was alone.

All round my hat I will wear the green willow,
All round my hat for a year and a day
And if anyone asks me the reason I wear it
I'll tell them my true love is two hundred miles away – yy!

Maggi dismounted and tethered Nero before she came to the water's edge to show herself, hands on hips. He reached the end of the song for the second time, sustaining a last note so off key that it made her squeeze her eyes shut and wince. As soon as he saw her, he stopped singing, squinting at her as if he wasn't sure she was really there; that she might be a figment of his imagination.

'Well, Callum MacGregor. Who gave you permission to murder my song?' she called, relieving the tension by making a joke of it. 'An' besides, you have it all wrong. It's ten thousand miles, not two hundred.'

A smile spread slowly across his face. 'We're both wrong. You're here. Merry Christmas to you, Maggi, and welcome home.' Purposefully, he strode from the water, splashing and

453

shaking droplets from his hair like a dog. He kept coming toward her and before she realised what he would do, he pulled her into his arms, making her give a little shriek of surprise. He was cold, half-naked and soaking wet. He stifled her token protests with a thorough and extended kiss which left her breathless and robbed of the ability to think.

'What? What's that for?' she whispered when she recovered herself enough to speak.

'Because I felt like it.' He grinned. 'And I had to be sure I wasn't imagining things. That you're really here.'

'You wanted me here?'

'Here or in Melbourne. Anywhere. And on whatever terms you like.' He swept her into his arms again.

'Callum – wait a minute – Oh, Callum, wait!'

'No. I've waited long enough.' He kissed her again, longer and more slowly this time, pulling the pins from her hair and unravelling it from its city tidiness until it fell in gypsy profusion about her shoulders. His hands, calloused from hard work, were surprisingly gentle and the awkwardness and inhibition she had so feared just wasn't there. Only his lips and her own, exploring each other's bodies as he helped her out of her clothes and the need for the ultimate closeness became more urgent, taking up all their attention. Too anxious to pause or discover some way to be more comfortable on the ground, he supported her, sitting astride him in his lap, as they came together for the first time, mating naturally as two wild creatures of the bush. Afterwards, shaken by the power of the feelings which had so suddenly overwhelmed them, they sat staring into each other's faces as if they would keep the moment, committing it to memory for life.

Maggi was first to break the mood, turning away to retrieve her breeches and her blouse, a little shamed by the force of her own emotions and in need of the security of her clothes. He seemed to read her thoughts.

'Don't feel any shame or regret, Maggi. I don't. We should have done this a long time ago; the first time we were here. Things could have turned out very differently, then.'

Dressed, she sat down on a rock to look at the water, shaken by what had happened between them. They had made love but she was suddenly shy, not knowing him well

454

enough to ask if it meant as much to him. Their bodies recognised, loved, yet there was so much between them which remained unsaid.

He sat down beside her, gathering her into his arms as she began to talk, unable to stop herself. Of Perry Meacham and her success which still surprised her, of Tully and Jinks, Mrs Hennessy, even Ginny – anything and everything but themselves, until he stopped her stream of nervous chatter with a kiss.

'I saw Hamish's headstone,' she blurted, knowing they would have to talk of what still lay between them. He looked away and squinted into the distance, his jaw set. 'It's no good, Callum. We have to be able to talk about him – say his name. Otherwise Hamish will always be here, like a spectre, lookin' over our shoulders an' comin' between us the rest of our lives.'

'I know.' He sighed, taking her hand. 'I know how much he meant to you, Maggi, and I know I can't take his place – I'm resigned to that. I know I can never be more than second best.'

'Oh, but you're so wrong.' She placed his hand against her cheek, reassuring him. 'I'm not saying I didn't love Hamish – oh, I did. But we were never comfortable together, never in accord. Hamish never wanted to build anything – to think of the future or father a child. And when I spoke of marriage, he shied away. All he wanted was excitement – pleasure from his body and mine. And while I'm being this honest I must tell you, there wasn't all that much pleasure in it for me.'

'Maggi, I don't need to hear this. You don't have to say any more.'

'But I must. Then we need never speak of it again. I'll be able to let Hamish go; lay him to rest. Before we became lovers, it was good between us. We played like children together because that's what we were. Happy, irresponsible children. I didn't realise it at the time but I was trying to force him into another mould. I wanted him to be more like you.' By now, she was crying softly, the tears pouring down her cheeks. He held her close, letting her weep, while he told her his side of the story.

'We never understood one another, Hamish and I. He was

455

fun-loving and I called him frivolous. He saw me only as a figure of authority, the oppressive elder brother, taking the place of the father he'd lost. The father he ought to have had. But for all his lack of responsibility and devil-may-care ways, it was Hamish who came up with the means to save Lachlan's Holt from our greedy neighbour. I shall always owe him that and be grateful for it. But if I'd known he would bring you into our feud and use you as his pawn against me, I would never, never have brought you to Lachlan's Holt.'

'Callum, I don't think he planned it that way. It just happened.' She shivered. It was getting late; the heat had gone from the sun which no longer blazed but had turned into a bright red orb, floating in the orange lake of the sky.

They finished putting their clothes in order and retrieved their hats. Then they brought the horses down to the water to drink, taking care to keep them apart. Just as the two brothers had been rivals, their horses were rivals too.

Maggi held her breath, waiting for him to speak, wanting to hear that he hadn't acted on the spur of the moment; that his feelings were powerful as her own. She had to be certain, even now, she wasn't mistaken in him. The warmth of his smile reassured her.

'I want to marry you,' he said. 'And I don't want to wait.'

'Oh, Callum, the banns have to be read and we'll need a licence or somethin' won't we? Before –'

He grinned, patting the pocket of his shirt. 'I've been carrying round a licence for weeks. I planned on coming to Melbourne to get you, if you didn't come home yourself.'

She stared at him, taken aback. 'But how did you know? How could you know I'd accept?'

He laughed, imitating her brogue. 'Could it be I've the second sight? I had plenty of time to think of you while you were gone. I decided I wouldn't take no for an answer. I was going to stand outside your window singing *Wear the Green Willow* until you said yes.'

'Oh, Callum.' She smiled, her heart overflowing with love for him. This time she had no illusions. They would have to work hard to keep Lachlan's Holt, she accepted that. And sometimes, if he could spare her, she would go back to the city and sing. She would have the best of both worlds. He was a good man, a quiet man, and she should have seen it, recognising his worth before. She would be his help-meet, his friend, and their life together would be satisfying and full.

She followed him home in the failing light, weaving their way down through the granite outcrops, winding their way to the plain where the races had taken place, Nero forever competing, straining to overtake Bothwell. Because they were ridiculously happy, they sang as they went, mostly the Irish songs which were already becoming a part of the folklore of this new land. But there was one song they sang more than once; the song they had made particularly their own.

> *All round my hat I will wear the green willow*
> *All round my hat for a year and a day . . .*

You have been reading a novel published by Piatkus Books. We hope you have enjoyed it and that you would like to read more of our titles. Please ask for them in your local library or bookshop.

If you would like to be put on our mailing list to receive details of new publications, please send a large stamped addressed envelope (UK only) to:

Piatkus Books: 5 Windmill Street
London W1P 1HF

PIATKUS
The sign of a good book